BORDER MONKEYS

BORDER MONKEYS

THARUN CHELLEY

The Book Guild Ltd

First published in Great Britain in 2018 by
The Book Guild Ltd
9 Priory Business Park
Wistow Road, Kibworth
Leicestershire, LE8 0RX
Freephone: 0800 999 2982
www.bookguild.co.uk
Email: info@bookguild.co.uk
Twitter: @bookguild

Typeset in Minion Pro

Printed and bound in Great Britain by 4edge Limited

ISBN 978 1912362 196

British Library Cataloguing in Publication Data.
A catalogue record for this book is available from the British Library.

Printed on FSC accredited paper

I would like to dedicate this book to the person who always believed in me and showed me the real meaning of care and wonder.

Mary Houghton

1

Water everywhere, surrounded. It's all I taste, feel, and see. I keep moving my arms, feeling the water seep over them and into my clothes. I look up and can see nothing but the blue water around me. I swim upwards, knowing I am miles away from the surface. I keep trying to move up; yet, I seem to get nowhere.

My eyes begin to blur as the salty water stings them. I blink repeatedly, trying to see, but all I can do is struggle. The more my eyes sting, the harder it is to open them. I pivot for a while, panicking as I struggle to get out of this pit. I can see the surface; yet somehow I do not seem to have the strength to get out. I keep trying, but my legs are trapped, motionless, in this aquatic prison. I begin to panic even more, darting my head back and forth.

Suddenly, I wake to find myself outside a garage. I look around, and can see I am still where I was when I fell asleep last night. I rub my eyes to wake up, stretching my arms. I run my hands through my hair; it seems to be getting longer every day. I look down at my skin, and sleeping out in the sun is making me darker every day. I already have brown skin, but it seems to be getting darker every day. I think it's time for me to go get something to eat; to get out of here and get me some strength for the day.

Bloody sun, never seems to want to go away. Always there, beating down on me, making me sweat like a pig's arse. I remember when England used to be cold, when it used to rain all the time. What happened to the rain in England, where did it go? Now the sun is everywhere, shining down with its heat. We have to make do with all this rubbish everywhere, junk on the streets and watching every street corner to make sure nobody tries to kill you; plus, to top it all off, it's bloody boiling here. The smell of the rubbish is not helped by the heat from the sun, which just makes it staler.

My name's Layton, in case you're wondering. I am what they would call a 'survivor', from the catastrophes which happened. I am a product of the world which we now call home.

About twenty years ago, I'm not entirely sure, there was a financial breakdown or something. I'm not a hundred per cent on all the details. I really should know how it all happened, disappointingly, I just don't. I suppose it would help with the explanation if I did have a specialist's understanding of how the world went to shit, but I don't, and this is the only world I have ever known. I'm not too sure what the world was like before all of this, because this is the only world I know.

Basically, what happened was there was global inflation. The banks shut down and everybody lost their hard-earned cash. Then there were strikes and countries declaring war on each other due to them not having anything. The United States no longer exists; now it's just a bunch of warring states, trying to take control of the territory. It's much the same in Europe. Africa is now a desert wasteland, especially after a load of other countries pulled their money out and left the continent in a state of civil war, run by warlords and thieves. The Asian nations are still at war with one another. As the breakdown was happening, India saw it as an opportunity to nuke Pakistan into oblivion and China decided to take on its old rival Japan. Now Asia is split into two parts, with the western, central and southern parts being under Indian control and the eastern and northern parts under Chinese control. This includes Russia, by the way, the part that is in Asia; the west belongs to India and the east belongs to China. Both countries have been fighting over Australia, which is now a nuclear disaster. Asia and Australia are more or less no-go zones.

As for places like England, we only have to take care of ourselves. We don't have to care about being involved with political decisions and national war zones. We just look out for our own interests and what helps us to survive.

A major problem which occurred throughout Europe, and wasn't so much of an issue anywhere else, was disease. Just like in Asia, all the European countries went to war with one another, so as a result everything was lost in the result. Now the military is gone and we are all just scavenging, looking for food, shelter and to make our way in the world. Many of the people who were once seen as rich or the most powerful in the world relocated themselves; nobody really knows where they are. Rumour has it that they all have a lifetime's supply of food and fortifications to keep any intruders out.

As for the rest of us, we have to fend for ourselves. We just try to get by with what we know and what works best for us. I personally find the best way to get through the day-to-day life is to just be by yourself. The key to survival is being an individual and not relying on or helping others. You will either get them killed, or they will end up getting you killed.

Money has no value now; however, if you have the correct items then you can get a lot of what you need. If you want to get yourself some nice tables or food, even chairs; if you have, say, a radio which works or even a television, then they can be of some real value. That really depends on whether your area has electricity or not. I try to keep it going on my own. I was born in what used to be a very nice commune. Unfortunately I lost it all after it was ravaged by raiders and they killed the people

I once lived with, so now I am on my own. I prefer it that way, having nobody there to tell me what to do, and the only person I really have to care about is myself. All I have to think about is where I am going to sleep for the day. It's good to keep moving; if people know you're staying in one place, you'll probably end up dead. Always be on the move, always go from place to place, not committing to anywhere you could call a home. A group will just hold you back as they will want to create a society, which we know now does not work. If you are by yourself you can constantly be on the move and not have to wait for anybody, and you will never be hindered.

The world, on the face of it, is pretty bad. Moreover, this has brought many opportunities for business-savvy people like yours truly here. As money means nothing now and people just barter with what they have to get food, water and so on, I thought of a way to get what I wanted. Are you ready for the secret? Well, here it is. It's stones. Stones, you may ask? Yes, stones. Now I'm not talking diamonds, as pretty as they are to look at. I mean stones that can be thrown at people. I'm surprised nobody has thought of this. People all want to protect their families, and what better way to protect them than with a rock in your pocket? Some things are still of high value, like coffee, sugar and branded alcohol. Annoyingly, those things are impossible to get hold of these days. So I decided to make my own wealth selling what I call 'action stones'. An action stone will protect your family when danger arises. Want to get rid of that mugger while keeping your distance? Just use an action stone and your family is safe. Also, you don't have to get your hands dirty.

If that doesn't work, I have decided to copy whisky labels onto bottles containing coloured water. I have my own way of talking people into the sale; For some reason once I started doing it, everybody did it. Nobody has an individual thought these days; they all just want to steal their ideas from somebody else.

Funnily enough, though, the one institution that seems to have survived is the pub. They have to make their own alcohol these days and food is not of the quality it once was; yet they have been able to keep going. I guess in times of need all people really want to do is get off their faces. Saying that, I could do with a drink right about now.

The Old Bar – what an unoriginal name for a pub. I wonder what ale they got today at this wonderful joint? Probably has the aftertaste of mud; that is usually the flavour. Sometimes, if you're lucky, you even get a little bit of grit in the ale. Once I actually found a pebble in my beer, and almost choked on the thing as it was covered by the murky sewage looking concoction that was inside my glass. Well, only one way to find out.

I make my way to the bar, and can see behind the barman barrels and jars of what I assume to be his own distillations of whisky. I suppose we could argue that it's a form of hooch; yet it still hits the spot. You have to be careful, though – the number of people I have known who've become ill from alcohol poisoning is ridiculous. Many go blind, even die.

"Barkeep," I call out in my usual sophisticated tone, smiling as I do so, "I will have a pale ale, old boy."

"Don't talk to me like that, Layton," the barman demands. I know him, his name's Alf, and he doesn't like being condescended to very much.

"Thanks, Alf," I reply.

He walks over and pours ale into a pint glass, then walks back to me. I look at it, foaming with a whitish-yellow colour on top of the brown ale, which looks more like syrup than beer.

"So how will you be paying for this, may I ask?" Alf asks me.

I turn and pull out a nice shiny rock for him. "With one of these." I display it to him, confidently looking down at the rock in my hand, then back up at him.

"I already have one of those," he tells me. "I have fifteen of them; I don't need any more of those stupid stones," he states, a hint of anger in his voice.

"You can never be too careful," I reply in my best sales pitch.

"Fucking hell, just take the beer, I can't be arsed with your shit," Alf says, turning away, frustrated.

"Well, thank you, sir." I respond, and turn to make my way over to take a seat.

I sit down, sipping away. I almost gag on the first sip; the beer is harsh and strong, nearly burns my throat out. I look down into the glass and see the gloopy, syrup-like sludge. I try to swirl it around, for some reason it has no real motion to it, just a muddy water. I put it down to be safe.

I look up from the horrible syrup and can see a good friend of mine. I think that's him; I know that brown guy with the bald head, who always has a goatee on his chin.

"Oi, Amrit," I call out.

Amrit looks over, sees me and makes his way to me.

"What you doing here?" he asks me, sounding concerned as he makes his way to me.

"I'm having a drink," I reply innocently.

"You know Bal and his crew are looking for you. If they see you they're going to kick your head in," Amrit tries to warn me.

"No they're not," I respond, feeling a little hesitant.

"What actually happened?" Amrit asks, confused.

"All I did was sell him some stones, I don't know what he's so arsey about." I take another sip of my beer and look up. "Oh shit." I squirm as I look over and see Bal and two of his henchmen walking in my direction.

"If you need anything just give me a shout and I will…" Amrit starts to say, but then Bal and his goons are standing around the two of us. Without hesitation, Amrit just gets up and leaves. He nods at me as he walks off into the distance.

"Cheers, mate," I call out as Amrit departs, not even bothering to turn around to make sure I am OK.

"Layton," Bal says to me.

I look at him, and he is wearing his usual black trench coat. His hair is slicked back and his face bearded, the look he always has.

"Bal," I respond, "how you doing? I was just leaving; we'll have to catch up soon," I add, trying to get to my feet.

The large man with his bandana and beard just puts his hand on my shoulder and pushed me back into my chair.

"You're not leaving so soon," Bal announces. "You haven't even finished your drink yet," he points out, making sure I stay put.

"Oh, so I haven't," I agree as I look down at my beer.

"It's not very good to waste things, now is it?" Bal says to me. I start gulping down my ale. "Now, I think you know the reason why we are here to speak to you today."

I think to myself that it's probably not to discuss the local ale on offer and maybe try one of Alf's famous meat pies.

"What's that?" I ask stupidly.

"You sold me what I thought was a ruby," he explains. "However, it wasn't a ruby now, was it?"

"Well, I sold it to your little friend Damien," I state. I look around, confused. "Where is Damien anyway?"

"He's dead," one of Bal's large men says.

"Oh, I see," I respond. "Well, you can't blame me then, can you? I don't even know what you wanted with a ruby."

"I gave you two bags of sugar for that stone," Bal shouts. "How did you manage to sell Damien that bloody stone anyway?"

I think back to how I managed to get away with selling Damien that stone. I picture in my head when I last spoke to him, a flashback, I suppose you could call it.

"How much do you want for it?" Damien asked me.

"Just two bags will do," I replied. I handed him a box with the stone inside it.

Damien was just about to open the box.

"Oi, mate, don't you trust me? There's a ruby in there," I told him.

He looked up at me and I could tell he was feeling guilty for peering into it. The truth of the matter is, Damien was always a little slow, and it wasn't too hard to get him to fall for things.

"Yeah, I trust you," he replied, and passed me the sugar.

"Trust is a valuable thing," I remember saying.

"You're a good guy, Layton," Damien said to me. "I trust you wouldn't do something to get me in trouble." He sounded very trusting.

"I would never do such a thing to you," I said to him.

I bring myself out of my flashback and back into the room, with the familiar faces surrounding me.

"I don't know," I say to Bal. "I just sold it to him," I tell him, trying to be persuasive.

"Instead of a ruby," Bal shouts, "you sold him this!" He then pulls out of his pocket a large, fat grey stone and slams it on the table. Written on the front of it is the word Ruby.

"Well, it's a stone which I named Ruby, so technically it is a Ruby," I explain, trying to cheer him up. No smile appears on his face.

"You think you're funny?" he barks. "Well, you're not going to find it funny when I shove this up your arse," he tells me, sounding very violent, even in his voice alone.

"That's a little bit weird," I reply, feeling a little uncomfortable.

"Look here, you mongrel..." he begins. He's only saying that because I happen to be half English and half Indian. I don't understand why he is saying this, there is no reason for him to speak to me like that.

"Bit racist," I point out.

"You're going to come outside with us," Bal orders as he rises up and snarls. "We're going to have a little chat."

We all know what it means when Bal says he wants you to come out to have a little chat with him.

"Oh, come on," I moan as his henchmen lift me up off my seat. "We can talk about this," I call out as they lead me outside.

They drag me into an old, rubble-strewn car park with broken-down cars and bricks everywhere. Two of Bal's henchmen hold me up high so my feet are barely touching the ground.

"We can talk about this like adults…"

I try to reason with them, but before I know it I feel a huge punch across my face; then another in my stomach, and once again in my face. Then it's the turn of Bal's third henchman. He decides to hit me in the face twice, then twice in the stomach. They let go of me and I collapse to the ground, spitting blood.

"Let this be a warning to you, Layton," Bal says, kneeling down to my eye level. "Nobody rips me off."

I feel my guts begin to swell up. "Can't throw your own punches, Bal?" I taunt him.

I quickly realise that this was a bad idea, because he stands up, pulls back his leg and kicks me right in the face, knocking me out cold. That bastard almost knocks my teeth out. They walk off, feeling proud of themselves.

I'm passed out for a moment before I come round, feeling as if I have just been put through the ground. The sky is spinning and I can't keep focused on one thing. OK, maybe if I did pass out for a moment, I will feel better. They're lucky the fight wasn't one-on-one, because then things would have been a lot different. Yeah, they're lucky they got away.

Shit, that really hurt – who kicks a man in the stomach? My eyes are blurring. My head is spinning in circles. Maybe if I just take a little nap – yeah, that's right, a little nap. Oh wait, my pint is still in there. I'll go get it once I take a little nap, then I will go and finish my beer.

2

I wake in the car park with my head banging three ways to Friday. Fuck me, those guys hit hard. My eyes blur when I try to open them, making my head hurt slightly. I stagger to my feet, looking around, dizzy and confused. I turn around and can see an exit not too far away. I slowly make my way out of the car park, back to the dump that is the street ahead. I walk along, blood trickling from my nose and my eye beginning to swell up. I slowly walk down the street and start to feel hungry and dizzy all at once. I think I need to have a sit down.

"Fuck me," I say as I sit on an old barrel surrounded by piles upon piles of rubble. I look down at my stomach as it pulsates with the pain of hunger. I feel like I am shedding pounds with every second that passes.

I rummage around to see if there's anything to eat. A tin, a box of preserves, anything; I just need something so I can have the strength to keep going. I look over and see a random can of tuna just sitting on the ground. It's been an hour since I last ate something; I guess now is a better time than any.

I quickly look around to make sure that nobody is waiting to steal the food from me, and start to make my way to the tuna when I hear footsteps. I stop and look up, but do not see anything. I continue to make my way towards the tuna, and once more I hear footsteps. I look up again and still don't see anything. I pick up the tuna and pull out a knife I have in my pocket. I start cutting the can open. When I manage to get my way halfway there, I start to hear someone breathing beside me.

I look up and see a dog standing in front of me. I look at it again before realising that it is just one of those small Yorkshire terriers, one of those really gentle dogs. The kind of dogs I have seen in old magazines, usually taken care of by old people.

"OK, boy," I say, "I will leave you now." I try to edge away, making sure not to make any sudden movements that could startle the creature.

"Woof!" The dog barks at me. I look at it and can see that it is staring at the can of tuna I have in my hand. It has its tongue out, dribbling, wagging its tail with its eyes wide open.

I look back at the dog and can see he does look hungry. Sadly for this poor little fellow, I'm hungrier and I'm sure somebody will give him some scraps around here. It can't be that hard for a dog to find food around here, surely.

"Sorry, buddy," I say, "this tuna is for me, you won't like it."

He starts to walk towards me, wagging his tail, looking very excited and a little playful.

I am just not in the mood right now. "Oi, go away, dog!" I shout, this time trying to be a lot firmer. "I would give you this, but I am a man, you are a dog, and I need this more than you."

He walks towards me again, a little closer this time. I look at him and he stares up at me with his eyes wide open. Guilt starts to seep its way into me.

"You poor guy," I say, "you must be starving." He just sits there, staring at the can in my hand.

"Woof!" He barks at me one more time. I look down at him and back at the can. I start to think to myself, Should I give him the can? Should I open it so he can eat as well? I pull out my knife again and place it on the can.

"It's OK, boy," I reason with him. "We can share the tuna, we can share a meal together. You've probably been out here for days, just looking for food with nobody here to feed you."

Then suddenly I hear a snarl. I look down at the dog, and his snarls become growls.

"Whoa, boy, take it easy now," I say as he starts to dribble and snarl at me. "No need to get pissy."

He gets up on all fours and stares at me.

"OK, boy," I murmur, "easy now, easy."

Then, with no hesitation, he just pounces and attacks me. I drop the can and can feel him wigging on top of me as I almost lose my footing.

"Ah!" I call out. "Ah, you little shit, what the fuck are you doing?" I eventually throw him on the ground and he makes a run for the tuna.

"Woof!" He barks again as he starts to make his way to the can.

"Oh no you don't!" I shout as he thunders his way to the food. I leap on top of him and grab him, pulling him away. "Now go away," I demand.

I am about to pick the tuna up from the floor when the little shit bites me on the back of the leg.

"Ah, fuck, fuck, fuck!" I cry out as I try to shake him off me. His jaw is locked onto my leg and he won't let go of me.

I decide to drop to the ground and roll, thinking that might work. Well, it doesn't; he just keeps his grip. I run around with him bouncing behind me, but he still just grips on to me. I manage to shake him off by doing a large kicking motion, flinging him a few yards away. He walks off, then turns and faces me.

"Garr," the dog growls at me, like he is laying down a challenge.

"Roar!" I shout at the dog as we face each other.

"Garr!" he snarls at me.

"Roar!" I shout at him.

"Garr!" he snarls at me once again.

"Roar!" I shout at him.

Then we charge at each other. There's no way this dog is taking my lunch from me. He leaps up in the air and I pull back my right hand. I swing and punch the dog right in the face, knocking him out. I turn and look at him motionless on the ground.

"Yes!" I shout. "How you like me now? I am the greatest, you little shit, all will bow to me."

I then turn and see him getting up.

"It's all right, mate," I say to him. "It's OK that you lost." I continue to celebrate with many great dance moves, raving to myself.

Then he gets up and runs at the tuna next to my feet, grabs it, and before I notice, he runs off.

"No, wait!" I shout, but he is gone. That little shit stole my tuna from me. He got lucky this time, next time he's mine, and next time it's personal.

I stagger through the street, past the rubble of what I can tell was once a thriving town. All I can see now is a load of people thrifting one another.

The name of this town is Oadby. I heard once that it was a very promising town with schools, shops and a lot of houses. Now, looking at it, all I can see are the deserted houses, the closed schools and the abandoned shops. There are a lot of people wearing handmade body armour, just to keep themselves safe from thieves and bandits. I look over and see a man in a big grey coat with what looks like rubber padding underneath, selling what looks like a car battery to another large gentleman. The other man hands him some motor parts – screws, bolts, those kinds of things. You can get a lot of stuff if you have enough bolts and screws on you; batteries as well. People all want to keep their motors working, so if you got enough of them, you can stay safe for a while. I'll put it like this: they go for a lot more than my stones do. The fun part is, just how do you get hold of the screws and bolts?

It's so hot today. Well, it is June after all. I guess it's good barbecue weather. I look at all the food sellers with their kebabs and burgers. You know what, I could do with a burger. Actually, let me just have a look at what this guy has to offer. He does sweat a lot, and look at the size of that belly! Also, why is he wearing a vest? Why is it that when it's really hot, the fattest guys in the world decide to take their tops off or wear vests so the whole world can see them? Nobody wants to see it, mate, just put it away.

"How can I help you, mate?" he asks me as I stagger over to his stall.

"What meat is that?" I ask, pointing to the burger that is grilling right in front of me. I look down and a load of steam wafts up into my face, and the smell of the meat juices penetrates my senses. The guy looks down and I can already tell his bullshit meter is about to go up a notch.

"It's venison, pal," he answers, as confident as ever.

I look at him, look at the burger, look at him again, then back to the burger.

"Venison?" I respond in a questioning manner.

"Yes, venison," he repeats.

I look at him once again, then at the burger, then at him, then once more at the burger.

"Seriously, venison?" I ask him once again.

"Yes, it is venison," he repeats.

I look at him once again, then at the burger – oh, you get the idea.

"Freshly caught this morning," he says.

I look around at the lack of a forest, or any trees, really. All I see is row after row of broken-down buildings and cars, smoke coming from their engines creating a fragrance of diesel throughout the town. I don't know where he caught this venison. I haven't seen a deer for years, especially around these parts. The Midlands has lost all of its wildlife; the only thing we see now is the odd pigeon knocking about. Other than that, nothing. Besides the stray dogs and cats that roam the streets, there's nothing close to wildlife that I can think of.

"So where did you catch this venison?" I ask him.

He looks at me, and his face goes from salesman to serious within a moment.

"Look, pal," he starts, "do you want to buy a burger or not? I got plenty of customers who want to buy and you're holding them up."

I turn around and can see nobody standing behind me or waiting at his stall. Either he is delusional, or he is bullshitting me again.

"I do," I reply. "I was just surprised you said venison, not beef or lamb or something." Something realistic, I mean; he would have had an easier sale if he just said rat, which it probably is.

"Are you calling me a liar?" He grunts.

I decide to sound shocked and offended at the question. "What?" I say, sounding surprised "Nobody is accusing anyone of being a liar," I explain, quite convincingly if I say so myself. "You said that, not me."

I look at him staring at me with a snarling expression.

"You know what, sir? I will have a venison burger, and how much will that be?" I ask, trying to sound as excited as I can at the thought of this burger. The impression I am trying to give is that this is the first burger I have had in years, and hopefully he will give me a good price for it.

"Five bolts," he responds.

A little expensive, I feel. Maybe I can get a cheaper price.

"I will give you two bolts for it," I reply in my best haggling voice.

"Five bolts."

"OK, OK, you're a tough man," I say, flattering him. "Let's make it three bolts, then."

"Five bolts," he responds.

"OK, what about four bolts, and I throw in this magic stone that can make you very rich?" I offer, with every ounce of passion. I then pull out a stone that is a little bit shiny and looks very nice. "Look at it – this one will make any woman you speak to fall in love with you and want you in her bed as soon as you speak a word to her." I try to convince him, to sell him the dream of the magical stone.

"Five bolts," he says to me.

"Oh, come on!" I shout.

I look at him and see no emotion on his face, just a blank painting looking back at me. I come to realise that there is no chance of him budging.

"Fine then, five bolts, here," I say as I pass him five bolts for a supposedly venison burger.

He takes the burger off the grill and puts it in a very stale-looking bun.

"Any sauce?" he asks me. I look over and can see what looks like a tub of what could be some kind of reddish sauce, covered in flies and half of it is hanging off the counter.

"Um, no, I'm fine thanks," I answer. I take the burger and he gives me a smile as I walk away.

I take a few steps away from his stall until he is out of sight. I look down at my purchase, gazing through its different layers. I take a bite out of the burger. For some reason, I want it to be a nice thick, juicy piece of venison. After I have bitten into it, I chew it for a moment.

"It's fucking rat," I mutter to myself through my mouthful of burger. Well, food is food I guess. I better eat this, then find myself some shelter for the night.

I finish my burger, which is far from a symphony of flavours, and head down the street towards what looks like a row of warehouses, each looking a little more abandoned than the one before it. The sun doesn't help with how I am feeling. It just hits me, burning my face. My leg really stings from that little arsehole of a dog. My trousers are starting to stick to the blood, making my leg sting that much more.

The one thing I will need to do, which I have to do every day, is look for a safe place to stay for the night. I need somewhere that I can be comfortable and secure to crash for the evening to come. I really need to think of somewhere comfortable. The other night I slept in a cardboard box, which was nice, I guess. Last night was not quite the same experience; my back is still hurting. I look at the different buildings I walk past and I really don't have a clue of anywhere I can stay.

"Hold on," I suddenly say to myself out loud, feeling this brainwave just strike me.

There is a girl I had a little, let's say, meeting with the other day. She had a nice little house she was squatting in. I remember it was a nice little bed she had. I mean, I didn't stay overnight, but if I woo her enough, maybe I can spend the night tonight. I turn around and begin to walk the other way, back into the town centre.

So here I am in this melting pot of traders, robbers and disaster-struck people. I don't mind it, for some reason I do know some people who think it's a complete shithole. I don't know really; I don't know anything different. This is the only kind of life I know.

I continue to walk down the street, feeling the strength returning to my legs. My face is still hurting from the beating I took earlier, I feel as if I'm just becoming accustomed to the pain. I look around as I walk through the street and see a group of drifters standing on the corner. Drifters are very rare. To be fair I do envy them in many ways. They are people who you can live quite happily without seeing. They tend to go out of their way to short-change you at any opportunity they get. The best thing to do if you ever do come across them is to just try and avoid eye contact with them. I have come across them many times, and I have learned that I do not want to lose any more of my possessions. Last time I bumped into a drifter, I ended up losing my underpants.

I see them all looking around, trying to find their next mark. I suppose some people would call me a drifter, with my precious stones I tend to try and get rid of. Everybody has to do something to get by, I guess.

"Oi, mate," a voice calls out to me.

Don't make eye contact, I say to myself as I carry on moving, trying to get away from him as quick as I can. I then see, out of the corner of my eye, that this man is coming closer and closer, moving much faster than me.

"Mate, oi, mate," the voice calls out again.

I look over and see a man in dungarees with very badly kept dreadlocks storming towards me. He has a very large jacket on, which I know he is probably keeping all of his shit inside. I look over at him and I notice; he's caught my eye.

"Shit," I blurt out as he walks straight towards me. His dreadlocks flap behind him as he continues to storm towards me with a purpose in mind.

"All right, mate?" he calls out, introducing himself to me in a very fast-paced, loud voice. "I got a deal for you, a good deal, good deal. Let me show you my goods, because I got a good deal, good deal," he rattles off while opening his coat. "I got watches, loads of cutlery, some pens, and loads of stuff for loads of people," he states as I look at all of the items in his jacket.

"Um…" I mutter as I look at the array of different items on show inside his jacket.

"Mate, I got a good deal. Not going to keep you too long, mate – watch for shoes, watch for shoes, watch for shoes, how about it, watch for shoes?" he says, trying to put the pressure on, making me feel very uncomfortable.

"Um… uh…" I mutter once again, about to lean down, feeling the need to take my shoes off.

"How about spoons, mate?" he tries. "Spoons for shirt, mate, spoons for shirt."

I look around, trying to find an exit, an escape route so I can be rid of this weird man.

"Spoons for shirt, spoons for shirt," he keeps repeating to me. I can't think of anything to say that could be remotely clever. I just decide to do the first thing that pops into my head.

"Ah!" I scream, right in his face. He is taken aback by my reaction and I pause for a moment before deciding to make another noise. "Ah!" I shout once again, and he moves back as I scream as loud as I can.

I then quickly turn and start running away. I can see him out of the corner of my eye, still standing there confused as I run as fast as I can. I feel the ground under my feet as I keep going as fast as I can, moving as far away from him as I can. I run down through all of the broken houses, my feet beginning to fly through the air, I am running that fast.

I suddenly come to an immediate stop, halting right in the middle of the street, looking up at the house I was running towards. I struggle to catch my breath as I realise how out of shape I am. I even begin to cough with the exhaustion, which leads me to holding my stomach, repeatedly coughing.

"Fuck me, I'm unfit," I say to myself as I try to speak through my sporadic breaths.

I look up at the house I was running towards, feeling slightly relieved as I look at its broken-down and moulded exterior. I wonder what her name is? I must know – was it Jane? Kelly? No, not that. Sam… Sam… Samantha, yeah, that was her name. I walk towards the front door and raise my hand to knock. I knock several times before I finally start to hear some movement. The door flies open and I see someone standing there, glaring right at me. I forgot she was a redhead.

"Hey, you," I call out to her, trying to sound as smooth as I can.

She comes walking towards me. I don't know why, but she looks very angry; her face has gone very red all of a sudden. She then slaps me right across the face, almost causing me to fall over.

"Ouch!" I say, grabbing my cheek and in a lot of pain.

"Wanker!" she shouts as she slaps me over and over again.

"OK, OK," I say, backing away. "My face already hurts," I state, rubbing my face and looking at her. "What was that for?"

"You come here for a shag," she shouts at me, sounding angrier by the second, "then you just leave without saying anything!"

"Yeah," I say, thinking about it. "I didn't want to wake you," I offer, trying to calm her down.

"Then to top it off, you took my food and wrote on my wall Layton is a sex god!" she shouts.

"No, I didn't," I say.

She points to this little patch of wall under the front window, and I see in black writing Layton is a sex god across the wall.

"Oh, shit." I remember writing it. I was very drunk the day I did all of that. "Well, I was so proud. Also, you have nice food," I tell her, trying to joke around.

"Prick," she says, walking towards me aggressively. "You fucking wanker!" She hits me repeatedly, and I'm starting to bruise now with how hard I'm being struck.

"I'm joking, I'm joking," I tell her. Then I see somebody coming from behind her, a large, looming figure. This large man stands behind her, bald-headed, angry-faced, and stares at me. "Who's he?" I ask, looking at him.

"Who am I?" he shouts. "Who are you?" Samantha grabs him and points at the wall, pointing right at the graffiti, then at me. "Oh, you're him," he says.

"Look, mate." I try to reason with him. "I am just here to stay the night with Samantha and then be on my way."

They both stand there, looking at each other, then at me, confused.

"Samantha?" the man says to me. "This woman is my girl, and her name is not Samantha!" He clenches his fist.

"Oh," I say, a little confused, "is it not?" I look at her, thinking I must be at the wrong place.

"My name's Charlotte!" she snaps, and her face has become very red with all the anger she is feeling.

"Oh," I repeat. "Oh yeah, Samantha was another girl I slept with, yeah," I add, realising my mistake.

"Look, mate," the man says, "you sleep with my girl, get her name wrong, and then try to come here for afters?" He storms towards me as Samantha – well, I guess Charlotte – stands there behind him.

"OK, mate," I say, holding my hands out, "I didn't know about you and her. It's all a mistake."

He pulls his hand back and clenches his fist. He throws his fist and punches me square in the face, knocking me out cold. I land square on my back, blacking out. I look up at the sky for a moment as it begins to spin, making me feel quite sick and a little dizzy. I look at the light as it begins to hurt my eyes. I try to keep them open for as long as I can, but they just grow heavier by the second. I decide to submit to the heaviness and allow my eyes to close, causing everything around me to go black. All I see is a blank sheet of darkness surrounding me and a nasty, sharp pain at the side of my face from where I have been struck.

Well, two chapters in and I've been knocked out twice already. Great start, I guess.

3

I wake what feels like a few hours later, looking at a dark, blank
nothingness. My back is creased up and my legs are raised. I feel
around and brush my hands on lots of tins and other objects. I
feel a little more and find something soft and motionless. I look
up and I see a little light peering through, giving me a little view
of where I am. I then feel the soft, motionless thing again. I lift
it up and stroke it, and come across what feels like a small head
and some feet.

"Oh my God, gross!" I shout out as I realise it is a rat I am
holding in my hands. I throw it to the side and realise where I
am. I look around and see that I have been knocked out and
thrown in a bin. "Fucking seriously," I say as I look around.

I lift myself up and raise the lid of the bin, feeling the sun
pierce its way through. I push it wide open and look outside to
see that I am back in the middle of the street. I am far away from
the house I tried to get into; I guess there's no chance I can get
back in there again. I better get going, no point staying here in a
bin. It really does stink in here.

I walk down the street, trying to make my way through the
different cars and beaten-up buildings. I decide to walk down
an alley, to get anywhere. I actually have no clue as to where I

want to go, I just want to get somewhere as soon as I can. I keep looking at the boarded-up buildings, and I hear some laughter in the background. I think it's children I am hearing; I think they're playing around the corner. I walk around and see them running around. There are about three of them kicking a ball. I turn around to get away from them, still limping from the dog bite.

"Oi, mister!" one of the kids shouts out. I turn around and look at him, feeling tired, in pain and not happy that I am about to interact with a child.

"Hello," I say to him as he runs right at me. I look at him as he stands in front of me; he looks about seven. He then walks up to me and kicks me right in the knee. "Ouch, you little bastard!" I shout, and he starts to laugh as his little friends, one fat, one small, come walking towards me.

"Ha, you're gay," the one who kicked me shouts at me, laughing.

"How does you kicking me make me gay?" I ask. His friends just laugh at me.

"You're well old," the fat one says.

"How am I old?" I ask as he continues to laugh at me.

"You're gay and old," the one that kicked me shouts, pointing and laughing as I look at him, thinking They are just a bunch of little idiots.

"You're a twat," the little one behind them yells at me. How does he know such language at his young age?

"You know what?" I retort. "You," I say, pointing at the kid that kicked me, "your parents don't love you and never will, and regret ever having you."

He looks back at me, his face going white from shock. I turn to the small one and point at him.

"You, young man, will never grow past the height you are now. You will end up as someone's bitch when you get older." I turn my anger on the fat one. "You, bitch-tits, I'm surprised you can even walk. Also, you kind of look like me in a way. Yeah, you do a bit. It's probably because I fucked your mum senseless and out popped you."

They all stop laughing, and I can see them getting very emotional.

"Oh, are you all going to cry now?" I ask them as they look at me. Then all of them, out of nowhere, just burst out crying. They scream and cry at the top of their voices.

I quickly turn around and just walk away, and I keep walking and walking to make sure they are out of sight. I keep walking towards another street, making sure I avoid them completely and do not have any more interactions with any more children.

As I make my way down the street, I suddenly begin to feel hungry. I'm not in the mood for a burger again; I would rather have something with a bit more sustenance. The problem is, I am beginning to notice the sun is going down; this could be a problem. When the moon comes out the streets are pretty dangerous.

I remember this girl I used to know a few years ago; she was waiting outside the pub for her boyfriend. He promised he would come and meet her, and she stood there for a while until the sun started to go down. She decided to wait a little longer; problem was, it was now getting dark. Then out of nowhere, this bandit or border monkey or someone, he just came up to her and grabbed her by her hair. She tried to struggle, to get him away from her, but he just dragged her by the hair. She kept trying to get away, but she had no chance. The man dragged her away, and by the time her boyfriend showed up, she was long gone. It's not that I'm afraid somebody will try to have their way with me; it's just I don't want to, you know, die.

I walk down the street until I see a group of people on the corner. This seems to be how my life is: I just walk around and I either bump into people on the street or I see people on street corners. I look over at this group and I immediately know it is not a good idea for me to be here. I can see two people, dressed in leather, with bald heads. I believe they are border monkeys – yeah, that's who they are. They are joined, yet, there is somebody with them, who doesn't seem to look like your usual border monkey. This man is very slim, tall and quite smoothly dressed. He has a very large jacket on, and he is wearing a wig, with a strange-looking mask. They are dragging some man and woman into what looks like a van. One of them is dragging the woman by her feet and another is dragging the man, who looks like he is passed out with blood running down his face. They throw them into the van and I can see them walking around.

"Who's that there?" I hear a voice call out from their direction. I look over and see another man standing across the road from them, looking right at me. The others look up at me as I stand there for a moment, stunned.

"Shit," I mutter, backing away.

The one with the mask starts to walk towards me slowly. So as a result of this, I'm not staying for a chat. I just turn and run away. I don't look back, but I can feel them looking at me as I run as fast as I can away from them and into the distance.

I really have run a lot today. I run away, towards a group of warehouses I am familiar with in the distance. I make my way there, making sure not to lose my footing. I stop for a moment and look around. Then I notice somebody I know quite well. I walk forward for my own sense of reassurance. I am pleased when I realise it is my good buddy Amrit lurking about near some rubbish bins. I go to see what he is doing.

"Amrit," I call out, trying to get his attention. He quickly turns and looks back at me as I wave my hand at him. He beckons me over and I rush across to him without a moment's hesitation.

"All right, Layton? Heard you took a bit of a beating earlier," he says, looking at the bruise on my face. "Looks like they did a number on you," he tells me, looking at my eye, which is now starting to bulge out a little.

"Yeah, I'm fine," I say. "Cheers for the help, by the way," I add sarcastically.

"Mate, I can't take a beating," he tries to explain to me. "You OK though, I mean for real?" he asks, sounding like he has some genuine concern in his voice.

"Yeah, I'm fine. Do you have a bandage or anything? I was attacked by a dog earlier," I say, feeling my leg beginning to sting.

"A dog?" Amrit asks.

"Yes, a dog," I respond. "Now do you have a bandage? It is starting to sting," I repeat, starting to feel the heat from the wounds.

"Oh yeah," Amrit says. "Just let me have a quick look." He takes out his rucksack and starts looking through it. "So what kind of dog was it?" he asks me curiously.

"Um... it was a big dog, um, a Great Dane mixed with a Rottweiler or something," I tell him, trying to sound convincing.

"Wow," Amrit responds. "You were lucky to get away – what startled it?" he asks, sounding a little sarcastic.

"I don't know," I admit, trying to not say much about the fight. "Now, those bandages."

"Oh, of course." He rummages around and brings out this first-aid kit. I try not to question where Amrit gets these things from; whenever you're hurt, he is the best man to come to.

"All right, get your leg out."

I sit down on a tatty old bench and roll up my trouser leg. Amrit gets out a bottle.

"OK, I need to clean it first so you don't get an infection," he tells me as he pours the contents of the bottle onto a cloth.

"Ah, ah, the pain, ah!" I shout as I feel the burning sensation running through me. My forehead starts to sweat from the agony I am in.

"I haven't put it on yet," Amrit says. I look down at him and see him kneeling near me with the cloth in his hand.

"Oh, OK, um, I'm ready," I tell him.

"OK." He raises the cloth.

"OK," I repeat.

He then gets a cloth out, pours what is in the bottle onto it and whacks it on my leg. It burns like crazy and feels like he has just poured hot lava on my leg.

"Ah, you cunt, that hurts!" I scream as I feel the burning sensation devouring my leg.

"Stop being a girl," he responds. "OK, now I got to bandage it – sorry I don't have any stitches." He then proceeds to wrap my leg in a bandage. "So what you doing out here?" he asks me as he continues to wrap my leg.

"Oh, I'm just looking for a place to crash," I say as he continues to bandage me up like a mummy.

"Well, if you want," Amrit says, "I found this disused warehouse if you fancy it. It's not much, but it's warm and nobody bothers you there."

I think to myself, Do I want to go there?

"I'm not sure," I answer.

"Oh, come on," he says. "There are other people, there's food and everyone gets along."

"I don't know, I'm not a massive fan of people."

"Look, you need a place to stay, you're hungry and you're wounded. There's no way you are going to survive the night in the state you're in. It's not up for discussion: you're coming with me," he demands.

"I'll find a place," I tell him.

"No you won't, like I said, it's not up for discussion," he repeats, sounding a lot harsher than before.

"Fine," I say, to make him feel better. "But you know I don't like staying in one place for too long."

Amrit finishes my bandage and sticks it together so it won't come loose.

"I know, that's why it's only one night," he responds.

I look down and see that he has done a very good job of getting me up and running again.

"Not too bad," I admit. I stand and move around to try and get the blood flowing.

"It should be fine," he explains. "The bite wounds weren't that deep."

I look at him and feel that he is on to me and my story about the dog.

"Yeah," I say, just agreeing with him.

"Right then, let's go. It's this way," Amrit explains, leading the way.

We begin walking down the street. It's getting dark, so most people try to get indoors as quickly as possible. This is because the PTB patients will be coming out in their numbers; they seem to mostly come out at night, although I have seen a lot of them out during the day.

Now what are the PTB patients, you may ask? Well, they are people who were infected by the main disease that hit Europe after the crash. Most the people I know generally just refer to them as 'infected'. Don't ask me what PTB stands for. What it does is it infects the skin, making it turn grey. You get a lot of spots and throw up. You lose the ability to talk, but you can still think. Now, if somebody with PTB touches you, spits at you, bites you and so on, you have a high risk of being infected. Some people caught the disease just from having an infected person sneeze on them. They usually stick together, knowing that nobody is going to help them.

They come out, and then there are the border monkeys. Why they call themselves that I have no idea. They like to hunt the PTB patients for sport, and anybody else who happens to be around when they're out. You can tell who they are because they come in on their motorbikes, swinging their chains and just attacking people. Basically, they're a bunch of pricks. All they do is drift from place to place, killing and raping as they go.

Keeping your distance from them is always a very good way to survive.

Amrit leads me to an abandoned warehouse, which looks huge. It is larger than any place I've stayed. We walk forward to the front door. Amrit pulls out a gun, just to make sure we're both safe. I pull out my knife to do the same.

"What is that?" Amrit asks me, bemused.

"It's a knife," I answer in a serious tone, making sure he isn't thinking it's a good idea to make fun of me.

"Looks more like a toothpick. What are you looking to do – poke the bad guys to death?" he asks, chucking to himself.

"Hey, fuck you," I bark at him. "It may be small but it works just fine."

"Is that what you tell all the girls?" he responds.

"Look here, you…" I begin, trying to make a point as I look down, feeling my face flush with heat at his insults. However, before I can say anything else he stops me in my tracks.

"Stop, stop!"

We both look up and we can see this grey figure, barely clothed, just walking in front of the warehouse.

"Infected," Amrit explains to me, pointing. I don't say anything; I just nod at him and we both look at the PTB patient, gazing at it with curiosity.

"What is it doing?" I ask.

"I think it's looking for food," Amrit responds.

It then turns and looks at us. I can see that all of its teeth have gone, and its eyes have no pupils in them any more. It has the features of what probably used to be a woman, although it's a bit hard to tell. It keeps groaning and drooling. It drags its feet and makes its way past the door and out of our sight. We both stare for a while in the direction of the infected as it drags itself away into the distance.

"Well, that was scary," I say to Amrit.

"Yeah," he agrees.

We make our way to the front of the warehouse. Amrit gets out a key and opens the front door, and we walk inside.

"Who's there?" a voice calls out. It is dark inside, with a little bit of light, not too much.

"It's me," Amrit replies. "I brought my friend Layton." We both walk further into the building right after Amrit locks the door.

"Great, another mouth to feed," a woman shouts as she turns to go back to sleep.

I'm about to say something when Amrit grabs me and we make our way to the other side of the room.

"Right, you can sleep there and I will sleep over here. If you need blankets and pillows, they're in that corner," he says, pointing to a corner where there are stacks of pillows, blankets and other things that look very comfortable.

"Thank you," I say.

"Well, I would love to stay up and chat," he says, "but I am shattered and would just like to get some sleep."

"Yeah, that's fine," I say. I then lie down and stare at the ceiling. "Amrit?" I whisper to him.

"Yeah?" he responds.

"You do know this is just for one night? I don't want any of your games to get me to stay for longer than I want to," I tell him.

"Of course I do," he says. "Now go to sleep so I can get rid of you sooner." He turns over and goes to sleep.

I have no idea why I said that to him. Maybe it's because I feel a genuine sense of friendship towards Amrit that I feel I have to leave him. I know that friendships can be dangerous things to have; they can get in your way.

Tomorrow I will head off and away from here. I don't know when I will see him again – it might be days, weeks, months, even years. It's really hard to say right now. All I know is that I will be off in the distance, probably looking for another place to crash for the night.

4

I wake the following morning with a bad back and a sore neck. I manage to sit myself up and look over to see the rest of the people in the warehouse. I never got a proper look at them last night as it was so dark. I can n ow see Amrit being joined by four other people standing around a fire.

What is that I smell? Is that… breakfast? The smell of sausages is wafting through the air and into my nose. Oh, that does smell really good. OK, I'm up; nobody will take breakfast away from me, especially on such a lovely morning. Well, I can't really tell if it is a lovely morning. I'm in a warehouse that has no windows; I mean, it looks like there used to be windows, thought now they are now boarded up with graffiti-ridden planks of wood. It could be raining outside for all I know.

I make my way towards the group and can see them with a big pot in the centre of the room. Amrit and two others are standing at the pot, whereas the other two are sitting on the floor near a group of used beds.

"Oh, you're awake," Amrit says.

"Morning," I reply as I make my way forward. "So, what's for breakfast?" I ask, hovering around, staring at the food, tasting it through my nose before my mouth gets a chance.

"Well, Annie here has rustled up some sausages with baked beans. It's delicious," he states, and I can see his mouth beginning to water as he speaks.

"Smells it," I respond.

"It sure is," Annie announces as she turns to face me while stirring the pot.

"Oh, where are my manners?" Amrit says. "Layton, this is Annie."

Annie nods at me with the big, powerful jaw she has on her. She is quite a big lady, with a massive pair of—

"This guy here is Rodney," Amrit explains, pointing at a large African-looking man.

"All right, mate?" he says. I guess he's from Birmingham, listening to that accent. I shake his hand as Amrit continues the formalities.

"These two sitting down are Michelle and Dillon."

"Hi, how are you?" Michelle asks me.

"I'm fine, thanks," I answer.

"And Rhea should be back soon," Amrit finishes.

I look around at the group and can see them trying to keep some attention on me; somehow a lot of it is being taken up by the sausages sizzling in front of us.

"So how do you know Amrit?" Annie asks me.

"Just from around," I reply.

"Layton and I met a few years ago," Amrit explains to the group.

"Oh, I see. Well, take a seat – looks like breakfast is ready," she announces.

We all sit down in a circle while Annie and Rodney pour the sausages and beans into bowls. I get handed a bowl and dig right in. I crunch down on the succulent sausage, burning my fingertips as I do so, digging through the mushy beans. I've missed beans for so long, and now I get to eat them with these amazing sausages. So tender, so succulent.

"How about you use a spoon?" Amrit says, holding out a spoon in front of me. I take the spoon, and before I even think about thanking him, I just go straight back to my breakfast.

"So what brings you here?" Michelle asks me as I dig into the bowl, scraping the edges with my spoon.

"Well, I just needed a place to stay," I say, chewing on a piece of sausage, "and Amrit said that I could crash here for the night. Don't worry, I'll be heading off soon enough," I inform them, making it clear I'm not trying to be too much of a burden. I don't want them to think I would just stay here to take them for a ride.

"You don't have to rush off so soon," Dillon says to me as I tuck into another piece of sausage.

"I don't want to be any trouble," I admit.

"No, it's fine," Rodney says. "The only person to worry about would be Rhea, she isn't too keen on sharing," he tells me, causing me to become a little fearful.

"She'll be fine," Amrit says.

"We'll see," I say. I want them to think I'm contemplating staying. This is just so they get the scent that they don't know I have already made my mind up about leaving. We continue digging into our breakfast and in one quick sweep we go silent with the enjoyment of what we are devouring. This type of food is difficult to get hold of, especially tasting so good, so I take full advantage of enjoying and savouring every mouthful.

The front door swings wide open and a woman is standing on the other side. I look over and she walks into the room. She struts forward, swinging a rucksack on her back, a shotgun strapped in front of her, every now and then bobbing by her side. She has dark brown hair, tied back and with a headband around the front. Probably for safety reasons; it's not much of a fashion statement.

"Oh, he's awake," the woman says.

"Ah, Rhea, you're back!" Amrit welcomes her as she walks

in, swinging her rucksack that looks like it weighs a ton and slowly throwing her shotgun over her shoulder.

"I'm not too keen on having another mouth to feed," she says.

"Oh, so it was you who said that last night?" I ask as she comes and throws her rucksack on the ground in front of us.

"Yes, it was. I know you probably mean well, but we can't afford to take care of ourselves as it is. The last thing we need is some other guy coming in and eating everything," she says stubbornly.

"I'm not going to do that," I tell her. "I'm not even going to be here long."

"How do we know? For all we know you might be a psycho killer; you might slit our throats in the middle of the night."

I am really beginning to dislike her and I have known her for a matter of seconds; not long enough really to form an opinion, sometimes in situations like this one can't help but do so.

"Woah now," Rodney calls out as I stand up.

"Look here, you slag," I shout at her. "You have no idea who I am. Besides, I'm leaving soon anyway," I repeat.

"Don't you call me a slag," she says as she storms toward me.

"What you going to do about it?" I bark. "Look at you, I bet you were just out there opening your legs just so you can have a packet of biscuits."

"Fuck you!" she shouts, and punches me right in the face.

"Ouch!" I cry, clutching my face as I fall to the ground. "What is with people hitting me lately?"

"Rhea," Dillon shouts, "go to your bunk."

"What?" she moans. "But Dad, he started it."

"No he didn't, you did," Dillon shouts even louder. "Now go to your bunk immediately."

Rhea turns and storms off to the other side of the warehouse.

"I apologise for my daughter," Dillon tries to explain as he turns to me. "She is very headstrong, she reminds me of her mother. She means well; she just has a funny way of going about it."

"It's fine," I say, rubbing my jaw to try and soothe it better in the hope that another bruise doesn't occur.

Dillon then turns to look at the rucksack Rhea brought in.

"Now, let's see what she got for us." He looks inside and pulls out a load of tins. Corned beef, Spam, beans, sweetcorn and tuna. She managed to get eight cans of each. "That's my girl," Dillon says with pride in his voice. He takes the tins out of the rucksack and places them gently on the floor.

"What time is it?" Amrit asks Rodney. He gets out his watch.

"Looks like it's coming up to 11.30," he states, staring at the hands as they tick around.

"Well, Rhea did the morning shift so I guess Layton and I can do the afternoon shift," Amrit says. I look at him strangely, a little hurt that he just put me forward for a job.

"Shift to do what now?" I ask him.

"Scavenge," Amrit explains. "Try and get food, weapons, supplies and so on for the group."

"Oh," I respond.

"You'll help, right?" he asks.

"Amrit, I told you, I'm going to go soon."

"OK," Amrit says, "well, we have to get you a better weapon then. Can't send you out there with that toothpick." Once again, he points while looking at my knife. I know he is trying every way to get me to stay; he does try. Well, I guess I could find myself a nice sword or even a gun to stop me getting in trouble.

"Well, I guess we better suit up then," I say, trying to ignore the comment he just made about my knife. I walk over to where Amrit and I were sleeping to get all my belongings before we get moving. I get my gear together, throw on my large brown coat and begin to make my way to the front of the warehouse. I turn, and can see Dillon speaking to Rhea.

"You're going with them," he explains to her.

"No I'm not, I've just been out scavenging," she tells him, sounding frustrated.

"Look, I know you have and I know you want to be big, brave and strong, but you don't have to be. This new man may be a great asset to us; we need him probably as much as we need you. So you're going."

Rhea just grunts and heads towards Amrit and me.

"Here, take this," Dillon says, pulling out a necklace from his pocket. "This used to be your mother's."

"Dad," Rhea says, "you always give me that when I go out to scavenge."

"Well, I didn't this morning," he says, "and I was worried sick. I want you to take it. It's like your mother is watching you when I can't."

"Fine," Rhea agrees, taking the necklace from him and putting it around her neck so her dad can see her wearing it.

"That's my girl," Dillion responds with pride.

Rhea gets up and walks off, grabbing her rucksack. She is about to leave when he looks over at her again.

"Hold on, madam," he declares.

"What now?" she asks.

"Aren't you forgetting something?" he asks. She tuts; then walks over to him and kisses him on the cheek. He does the same to her. Rhea then turns around and heads off.

"Come on, then," she says to us as she walks past, stomping her boots and rustling her leather jacket, slinging her rucksack over her shoulder.

Amrit gives me a quick look and we both head out, following her to the front door. I look behind and can see everyone around the fire. Dillon comes forward slightly, then stands still in the distance away from us, watching as we leave. Rhea swings the door wide open, as if she does not want Amrit and me to come with her.

"So, where to?" I probe as we walk outside. We look around

and can feel the sun beaming down on us. The street looks empty with only a few broken-down cars to keep it company. We start walking, making sure not to step on the broken glass which is scattered like sprinkles on a cake.

"OK," Amrit says, "well, we need to get a generator so we can get enough heat for the winter."

"Why?" I ask. "It's boiling out here."

"Well," Amrit says, "it's better to be prepared now so we don't have to suffer when it comes to it."

"Yeah, idiot," Rhea taunts.

"Oi!" I respond abruptly.

"Will you two shut up?" Amrit barks as he pulls out his gun and makes his way into a building. He holds it up and keeps it aimed.

Rhea lifts her shotgun and I take out my knife. Rhea looks at my knife and chuckles to herself.

"You won't be laughing if I shove this up your nose," I say to her. She turns to square up to me.

"Come on, you two, let's go," Amrit says.

We stop looking at one another, turn and start to make our way through the building. We go through what looks like some broken scaffolding. Amrit seems to know exactly where to look, and I haven't got a clue. To me it all just looks like a metal-and-brick maze. Amrit just seems to know his way around; good thing we have him here or else we probably would end up getting lost.

"So," I say to Rhea, "have you always been this bitchy?"

She ignores me, acting as if no words had left my mouth.

"That's cool, you don't have to speak," I say as we start to make our way through the room. "It's probably because you can't think of the words to say to me," I taunt, trying to be brash.

"What?" Rhea shouts at me.

"You can't get enough of me," I explain. "I understand completely."

"Yeah," she utters sarcastically.

"Yeah, I know," I say, also including sarcasm in my tone. "You're only human."

"OK," she mumbles.

"Besides, you'll probably take anything," I continue.

"Look—" she says firmly, turning and facing me head on.

"You two get over here quickly!" Amrit interrupts.

Rhea looks at me, frustrated, then turns and heads towards Amrit. I quickly follow and see him hunched behind a bollard, looking over the top of it. We both quickly crouch down next to him. Amrit looks over and holds his hand out to signal that there are some men on the other side.

"Right, there's three men over there and they seem to be waiting on something."

I quickly pop my head over and look at the men.

"Oh shit," I whisper. I know straight away who it is.

"What is it?" Amrit asks me.

"It's fucking Bal and his crew," I say.

Amrit pokes his head up and back down again. "It's fucking Bal!" he cries.

"Who's Bal?" Rhea asks us.

"Just some guy," I reply.

"The guy who did that to Layton's eye," Amrit states, pointing at my face.

"Oh, I see," Rhea says.

"Yes, that guy," I agree abruptly. "So what do we do?"

"I'm not sure," Amrit says. "He's standing next to what looks like a very good generator, I don't think he is going to just give it away."

"Why don't we just pick them off?" Rhea asks.

"No, it's too risky," Amrit states. "They might catch a whiff of it and start shooting at us."

"I got an idea," I say, with a sudden heroic brainwave.

"What?" Amrit asks.

"I will create a distraction. You guys slip in behind them and nab the generator," I tell them, feeling the fierceness beginning to grow within me.

"It's a generator, Layton, it's not like it's a fucking radio that we can just pick up," Amrit makes very clear to me, sounding confused at my plan.

"OK," I say again. "Right, well I'll distract them, then you two swing behind and shoot them."

"What if we shoot you?" Amrit asks, a bit concerned. "It's a big risk."

I think about it and realise that it isn't the best idea. I probably will get shot, and I don't know if this will work. I think it's time to think of another plan.

"Ah, yeah, that's true," I say. "Actually, yeah, forget that idea."

"We should take the risk." Rhea smirks.

"Ha ha, very funny," I say.

"Actually, yeah, let's risk it," Amrit declares. What a traitor, I think to myself.

"What?" I say.

"It was your idea," Amrit points out. "You wanted to be the distraction."

"Yeah, but you don't have to make out you're agreeing with her," I say, a little hurt by his wanting to endanger me.

"Poor baby," Rhea laughs.

"What is your problem?" I snap.

"Look." Amrit interrupts us. "What is your plan, Layton? You're going to shoot them while we move around, throw something at them?" he asks, frustrated.

"Um, no," I say.

"Well, what then?" Rhea asks, sounding confused.

"This," I say.

I then stand up, and I can feel Rhea tugging at me, saying, "What are you doing?" Amrit is telling me to get down. For some reason I am feeling thus sudden sense of heroism, so I choose not to acknowledge what they are saying and begin to make my way forward.

"Yo, Bal, me old matey!" I shout out.

"Oh, not this idiot," Bal moans as I approach.

"Fancy seeing you here," I say to him. "Not your kind of scene, this, is it?"

"You want me to knock him out?" one of his henchmen calls out.

"No, it's fine," Bal says. "What are you doing here, Layton? Didn't you learn your lesson last time we bumped into each other, or do I have to show you again?" he asks me intimidatingly.

"No, because this is going to end here," I say. "This is it, this is where I make my stand against you. No more will you try to pick on me. No more will you try to rip people like me off."

"You ripped me off," Bal interrupts me.

"Nonetheless," I continue, "I will end your reign of terror now." I put my hand in my back pocket, pull out my knife and hold it in front of them in the most aggressive way I can. I look at them, hoping to see fear and loathing, somehow all I seem to see is them bursting out into laughter

"Oh, Layton," Bal shouts as he begins to chuckle.

"Look at the iddy-biddy knife," one of his henchmen snorts.

"I do shits bigger than that," the other henchman says.

Then I get really angry. I'm sick of everybody thinking that they can just laugh at my knife. It is dangerous in the right hands, it really is. I hold the knife over my head and pull my arm back like a propeller about to launch.

"Fuck you!" I shout out, and throw the knife at them.

I aim for Bal, trying to hit him right in the skull to split it wide open. I was never very good at hitting a target. So instead of achieving my heroic plan of striking him, miss slightly and it goes straight for the henchman to the right of him. It flies through the air like a dart, and hits him right in the eye. Now, you would expect at this point for an eye to be gouged out and for there to be lots of blood. Well, no – I forgot that this knife is pretty blunt and yes, it is quite small. So all it really does is hit him in the eye and bounce off.

"Ow!" the henchman calls out. "That fucking hurt, you dick!"

"Be quiet," Bal shouts at him.

"No, it really stings – ow!" the henchman continues. "Is it bleeding?" he asks the other henchman.

The other one has a look at it. "Nah. It may leave a bit of a bruise, though," he tells him.

"A bruise?" I say to myself, disappointed.

"Yeah, it really hurts," says the henchman I hit. "You're a dick, you know."

"Who, me?" I reply, confused.

"Yeah, you. You can't just go around throwing things at people."

"Um, sorry," I mutter reluctantly, still confused.

"Well, you better be," he shouts.

While he is rubbing his eye, I can see Amrit and Rhea making their way behind them. I see them slowly coming towards Bal and his men as they are focused on me.

"You could've had my eye out," the guy moans.

"OK, Layton," Bal says to me, "I think we've had enough fun today. I just don't want to see you any more." He pulls out a gun and points it at me.

"Wait, Bal – you can't do this!" I say to him.

"Um, yes I can," he replies.

I can't argue with him; he can do this. yet, I'm still distracting him.

"No, you can't," I demand again.

"Why can't I?" he asks.

"Because I love you," I say. I can see Amrit pulling a funny face as soon as the words leave my mouth.

"Don't be stupid," Bal shouts as he clicks the safety off his gun and points it even more fiercely in my direction.

"I do because… I'm your son," I say, to distract him even more.

"How?" Bal says. "I'm only five years older than you, you bloody fool."

I realise he is right as soon as he announces that, and feel a bit foolish for saying something like that out loud.

"Well, um, well…" I begin. "I'm your brother," I state.

"No you're not," he replies.

"I'm your lover!" I shout out.

"Nope," Bal states.

"Um, well, um…" I say to myself.

"This guy'll try anything to live," I hear one of the henchmen chuckle to the other.

"Layton, you're boring me now," Bal says. I can see his finger is on the trigger, about to pull.

"Oh shit!" I say out loud.

Then, to my relief, Amrit and Rhea come out swinging and knock the two henchmen out cold. They both collapse to the ground like two collapsing statues. Bal turns and sees both his henchmen knocked out cold.

"Oh, what is this?" he exclaims, frustrated.

"We did you in, Bal!" I shout.

"We're taking the generator," Amrit states. "Just be cool, OK?"

"I always liked you, Amrit," Bal starts saying to him. "You always had promise, now you're going to have to watch your back around me." Amrit just shrugs at the comment as if he is just brushing away a piece of dust from his shoulder.

Amrit and Rhea take the generator and begin to make their way back through the building.

"Look, mate, you best watch yourself," I say to Bal.

"Oh please," he responds, trying not to sound bothered.

"Yeah, watch your back, Bal," I repeat as he stands there, staring back at me. "You got lucky this time."

"Did I now?" he replies.

"Yeah, take this as a warning," I say.

"Or what?" he demands, raising his gun and pointing it right at me.

"Oh," I say as I walk behind him, pick up my trusty knife, get back up, turn and run after Rhea and Amrit. I can sense Bal shaking his head as I run off and lose sight of him.

They're just making their way out of the front door when I catch up with them.

"Layton, can you help us with this?" Amrit calls out to me.

I get under the generator with Amrit and Rhea, holding it up as all three of us grab an end and carry it.

"Well done on the distraction," Rhea says to me.

"Well, thank you, Rhea," I say to her in a welcoming manner.

"Yeah, I'm surprised he didn't kill you," Rhea admits sarcastically. I know she is trying to get under my skin. I will try and be the mature one and not allow it to bother me.

"Well, you got to remember," I say, "all you got to do is be the eye of the distraction."

Amrit chuckles to himself as I say this.

"Being the eye of the distraction means that you can take whatever your enemy wants and move it from his gaze, which means that you can ultimately achieve your goal," I state, trying to sound profound.

"Is that a saying, or is it just you saying a load of words?" Rhea laughs.

I turn and give her a dirty look, and realise that we are almost at the warehouse. There is some smoke coming from it. In addition, we can see that there are bikes outside. All three of us put down the generator and look at what is occurring at the warehouse.

"What's happening?" I say.

"Shit, Dad!" Rhea exclaims as she starts to walk forward.

We stop and stand like a group of trees for a moment. We gaze over and see what look like a group of Border Monkeys just strutting about and making themselves known.

"What are border monkeys doing out this early?" Amrit asks.

We look at them, and I can see one that I know I will always remember. He is a slim man, dressed very differently to the rest of them. He is wearing a long coat, and for some reason he has a red mask on and a purple wig.

"Who's that guy?" I ask Amrit.

"I have no idea," he replies, just as confused as I am.

"Let's go, troops," the man calls out to his gang of border monkeys, and they all get on their bikes and ride off.

We watch their bikes get further into the distance, until they are more or less out of sight. At that point, the three of us get straight to our feet and rush over to the warehouse, leaving the generator behind. We quickly throw the door wide open and hurry inside, making sure we're not seen.

Once we enter, we are shocked by what we see. There is blood all over the room and Rodney, Michelle and Annie are laid flat out in front of us, riddled with bullet wounds.

"Where's my dad?" Rhea calls out as she runs off to find him. "Dad, Dad, where are you?"

"Why would they do this?" Amrit cries as he kneels down next to Annie.

I walk towards him, and I'm about to say something when I hear Rhea burst into yells of screaming and tears.

"No! Why? No, Dad, no!" she calls out.

Amrit and I run over to her and see her collapsed to her knees, tears running down from her eyes and over her face, which has become as pale as the clouds. We look up, and we can see Dillon in front of us. He is hung from the ceiling by his hands, his body stretched out and his eyes gouged out. I can see something carved into his chest.

"Shaq, the last king," I read as I look up at Dillon's hanging corpse. "Who's Shaq?" I ask the other two.

"I have no idea, mate," Amrit says to me. "I haven't got a clue."

All three of us look up at Dillon once more, hanging just in front of us. We stand there, frozen. I can't even move a muscle. It is as if we are glued in the positions we are in, stationary, our bodies not allowing us to move. We all just remain standing there, staring at Dillion displayed in front of us, hanging, looking so uncompromised.

This is another reality of living in this world, I guess: you can never be too safe. I guess to survive, you have to make sure you're not killed by the same guy as Dillon was. Nobody deserves to have this done to them.

5

We decide to leave the warehouse. We brought Dillon down from where he was hanging. It was very difficult to detach him, he just felt so delicate. We lay him down on his bunk, just so he could be at some peace.

Rhea placed a sheet over him, covering his face as a sign of respect. I look at her and can't help but feel some sympathy. It must be difficult for her to go through what she is going through right now. It is difficult enough losing somebody, let alone having to see your parent strung up like that. Rhea was in a complete state – to be fair, she still is. She is absolutely devastated; she can't even look at us. Once we decided to leave, she was the first of us to want to get out of there as soon as possible. Amrit decided to place some sheets over the rest of the group, again as a sign of respect. He left them all looking calm and peaceful, as if they are just sleeping.

We decided that we had to leave, just in case any more border monkeys decide to come back to finish the job. We travel through a park which has swings and slides that haven't been used for many years now. You can see the rust and cobwebs starting to engulf them like blankets. We continue on, trying not to stop in case anybody comes after us. I can't help but think that this is why I always say we must keep moving. It is never a good idea to stay in one place for too long, because other people get a whiff of it and will come and raid you. Therefore, keeping on the move is the best way to go.

We eventually make our way through the park and into what looks like an abandoned neighbourhood. There are lots of boarded-up semi-detached houses, hundreds of them. I can imagine that they all had families living in them once, going in and out, not worrying about how the day was going to end. I can only imagine this kind of life, though. I have never lived in a house. I have only crashed in the odd one every now and then, just for a temporary stay. I can't say whether living in a house is something to be desired, or something that is overrated.

I remember this girl when I was growing up, who used to tell me about how she dreamed of how her life would be if she lived in a house, with a garden, a family and so on. Some people just think like that; all they do is dream about what life would've been like if it was still the past.

We make our way through into what looks like it used to be a normal neighbourhood. There are cars outside on the driveways, and the houses look pretty much intact, apart from the boarding on the windows. Amrit decides to go up to one of the cars to flip open the bonnet and see what is inside. He pulls out a screwdriver, jams it right in and flings it wide open.

"Shit – just what I thought," he says as he looks inside.

"What is it?" I ask.

"Somebody's taken the engine; they've probably done the same for all the cars on this street," Amrit explains, looking at the cars lined up across the road.

"Shit. Well, what should we do?"

"We should try and find a place to hold up for the night," Amrit replies.

"Are you sure that's a good idea?" I ask.

"Yeah. We need to find a place where we can regroup and

work out what we are going to do next," he says, sounding very determined.

"I suppose. What does Rhea want to do?" I ask him.

We both turn around and see Rhea sitting on the kerb, hunched over as if she embodies loneliness. She does not look as if she wants to talk to anybody, and just remains there. Her long brown hair is coming loose and the ponytail she usually wears is beginning to flow into separate strands. I decide to see if she is OK.

"Rhea, are you all right?" I ask her in the gentlest way I can.

"I'm fine," she says, trying to wipe away a tear trickling from her eye. "Just give me a second."

I get up and leave her to it. It can't be easy seeing what she just saw. I can't imagine that kind of pain. I decide to make my way back towards Amrit.

"How is she?" he asks, looking concerned.

"She's still a bit… you know," I say.

He nods at me and looks at a nearby house.

"We'll make camp here," he declares.

I turn around and see Rhea up and walking towards the house. Together we walk forward. Amrit breaks open the door and we all walk inside. Amrit then gets what looks like a cabinet and moves it in the way of the door, blocking us all in.

I begin to walk through the house, looking at all of the different pictures on the walls, ornaments and so on. Take away the rot on the walls and it looks as if people could still be living here. I feel as if we are intruding in a family home, acting like trespassers.

"I'll check upstairs," Amrit says.

I keep looking around downstairs and make my way into the living room. There is a giant board where the window should be looking out onto the street. While facing the garden, I manage to notice a window still intact. I decide to walk through, looking at an arrangement of sofas around what looks like a television.

I guess this is how people used to arrange their living rooms back then. At the end, there is a large table that leads through to another room which I can only imagine is a kitchen. I walk through and can see a stove, a fridge, a microwave – I wonder if any of this still works? If it does, then we could have a hot meal.

I look at the fridge, a white box-shaped thing, and decide to open it; I just want to see if there is any food inside. I really could do with something to eat right about now. I place my hand on the handle, pull it open and look inside. Suddenly I see a rat just sitting there eating something; I can't make out what it is. It looks up at me and pounces.

"Ah!" I scream, stamping as it falls on the floor. "Oh, go away – ah!" He eventually turns and runs away from me. I keep stamping, for no real reason, and watching the rat until it eventually turns and runs away out of sight. I then turn and look in the fridge. The smell that comes from it is awful, like rotten eggs mixed with shit. It's disgusting. I quickly close the door before I make myself throw up.

"Found anything?" Rhea asks me as she walks into the room.

"No, not really," I say, trying to hold back the puke that is building up in my mouth.

"Oh, OK," Rhea replies as she walks into the kitchen. She seems lost and very distant, not herself. She walks to the sink and gazes through the window into the garden ahead.

"Is everything OK?" I ask her, already knowing the answer and having an idea of the strong politeness she is going to answer me with. She turns to me for a moment, then turns back to gaze out the window again.

I slowly make my way towards her to offer a gentle ear. I know that she and I have not seen eye to eye as of yet; though, she, Amrit and I are on our own in this situation so I need her to know that I will be here for her. Even if she does not believe it, even if I don't believe it, in a strange way I need to convince her to convince herself that everything will be OK with me around.

"Hey," I say gently, once more trying to get her attention. I move closer and see her fighting back the tears. "Is everything OK?" I ask her once more. I quickly poke my head around the imaginary wall that she is creating for herself and catch a momentary glimpse of her eye. She turns and looks at me for a split second. I can see her eyes beginning to water and her top lip starting to tremble.

"Excuse me," she says, and leaves the room without a moment's hesitation. It looks disrespectful, I know that this is a moment of reconciling with her loss and coming to terms with the savagery of the event we witnessed. I do not wish to pry any further and I know that she is travelling to hell and back right now, so I decide that the most caring thing to do is give her space and let her decide, in her own time, when she is ready to feel human again.

I make my way outside and into the garden. I stroll through the kitchen door and onto what looks like the remnants of a footpath, although it is hard to tell now. There are weeds, grass and other forms of plant life which have grown all over what used to be pieces of cement blocks, and now it all looks like an extended piece of turf. I remember finding a magazine all about gardens a while ago. How people used to keep them and take real pride in how great their roses and fuchsias looked next to their freshly cut grass. People used to have ornaments – I think they called them gnomes – that just sat there, I guess. Seems like the older people got, the less they cared about the outside world, instead caring only for what was going on in their lives. Now the outside world has come tumbling down on them and years of hardship and turmoil have made their gardens a complete mess. Because of all the chaos and a lack of money to maintain it, this garden is now a hideous sight.

I read a book about a garden in India once. I found it when I was roaming through a house and saw that it was about a wonderful Indian garden, with peacocks and flowers. The book also mentioned all the mystical wonder of India, and its history of yoga and meditation. Hard to imagine now, especially with the war with China. I have no idea how those two governments kept going with nothing to finance them. Now they've made Asia a no-go zone; you only go there if you want a sniper to shoot you down.

The book mentioned the British Parliament too. That's long gone now. I mean, there is still some form of government action going on here. Well, barely, it's all in remote parts of the country, from what I've heard. It's usually people trying to create their own forms of government; their own rules and civilisations. Also, like I mentioned before, the armed forces are only taking care of people who were recognised as rich before the crash. The more important people. When I was younger – well, sometimes even now – I would just sit there and wish that I had been born into one of those families. They seem to have it made before they leave the womb.

I see something I have never seen before. It's this pointy-eared creature just poking its head up through the grass. Is that what I think it is? Is that, a, rabbit? I never in all my life thought I would see one. I am so hungry, I don't want to harm it as it has its own wonder. Look at it, how free it is, how it can just run through the grass. He just hops around, not once stopping to care about what he is doing. He has no idea that the world around him has gone to shit over the past fifty years, or that he is walking through what used to be someone's home. He pokes his little brown head up and looks at me. I stare back at him. I feel, for the first time in years, slightly peaceful. He then turns and hops away, as if he is off on his own mission.

"Layton!" Amrit calls out. I turn and can see him poking his head out the kitchen door to get my attention. "Look what I found."

I follow him inside and he takes me to a cabinet. He opens it, and it takes my breath away when I see a bounty of protection in one place. Inside is a whole range of weapons: guns, AK-47s, shotguns, machetes – you name it, and it's there in the cabinet.

"We need to take full advantage of this," Amrit proclaims.

"I second that." I quickly go for the machete, which comes with its own satchel. I think it's called a satchel, I have no idea. Nevertheless, I do look pretty solid with this machete on me.

"That is definitely an improvement from your last deadly weapon," Amrit says, chuckling to himself.

"I didn't know you thought of my penis as a deadly weapon."

He quietly smirks to himself, and when I turn I can even see Rhea chuckle slightly. Amrit turns too, and seems happy that she is chucking as well.

"Grab yourself a weapon," he says to her. "Who knows when we'll have to move on next?"

"Yeah, you're right," she responds, and she quickly bends down to get the gear she needs. She grabs an axe, a handgun and an assault rifle. Amrit gets himself a handgun as well, a knife, a cricket bat and a shotgun, and I take my machete, a knife, an assault rifle, a pistol and a metal baseball bat. We get our gear together and quickly turn to the living room.

"OK," Amrit says, "we all have to get some sleep, so we will be crashing here tonight. Make sure you have your weapons near you during the night, keep them close. We leave at daybreak."

"'We leave at daybreak?'" I repeat sarcastically.

"Yeah?"

"Just say we're leaving in the morning like a normal person," I say. "Don't be a knob about it."

"Fuck you, Layton. Fine, I will dumb it down for you. We have to wake up when Mr Sun comes up and skip on out."

"Maybe if you had hand puppets," Rhea calls out of nowhere.

"Oh, look who's perked up," I point out.

"Yeah, well, I got to have some fun," she says, as if that is meant to create some kind of sympathy within me. I just find it annoying; I mean, she has been quiet all this time and the only time she talks is to insult me. Well, I guess if it cheered her up, I can't really be a dick about it now, can I?

A few hours pass and all three of us are camped out in the living room under some sheets we found upstairs. We all have our own pillows and are the perfect mix of comfortable and ready for action. We know we have to sleep lightly tonight, because we will be moving on in the morning. I'm glad Amrit is taking my advice about not staying in one place for too long.

"I don't see why we couldn't sleep in the beds," I say to him in a quiet, harsh tone as I look over and see Rhea about to doze off.

"Sorry, princess," Amrit replies, "but I thought we would be safer here. At least here we can be vigilant," he adds, making me out to be stupid for bringing up the idea.

"Yeah, but we would have been better rested upstairs," I say.

"And if someone was to break in, what would you do?" Amrit asks me.

I look at him as if he is an idiot. "I would get my gun out and shoot them," I reply.

"And what if you're sound asleep? Then what?"

"Well,"

"Exactly," he interrupts.

"Well, there is only one way to find out," I huff, pretending to gather my things.

"Don't you dare," Amrit says.

"What?"

"Don't you dare go upstairs and sleep in one of those beds."

"What you going to do if I do?" I ask him in a threatening manner.

"If you do, I will come up to the bedroom and stick this gun up your arse."

I look at him for a moment, and then I know exactly what to say.

"You often think about sticking things up my arse," I say. "You know you do, Amrit."

"Fuck you, man," he snaps, turning around.

"What, mate, what?" I ask.

"Why you got to make it weird?" he says.

"Because you were winning," I reply.

We look at each other and just burst out laughing. We continue through the night, reminiscing about old times as if we are two old war veterans. We talk for another hour until both of us doze off, knowing that in four hours' time, all three of us will be getting up and out of here. What will tomorrow bring? What adventures will we have? All I know is, it's going to be a shit ride to hell.

Also, there is not a chance that I can just leave them now. If none of this had happened, I would be out of here, running around looking for a place for myself. I guess I have to stay with these two a little longer than I had originally planned. Oh well, could be for the best, I guess.

6

We wake the following morning to complete silence. It feels as if nothing has changed from the night before that could have an impact on our upcoming day. I sit on a sofa and look in my bag for something to eat before we head off.

I rummage through and find a tin of peaches. I wonder how long this has been sitting in my bag for? It looks edible; like it might give us some energy for our journey ahead. I pull out my knife and open the tin, revealing the tinned peaches in all their juicy glory.

"Anybody want one?" I ask Amrit and Rhea as they are getting ready, looking over at me, still shaking off their tiredness.

"Yeah, go on then," Amrit says as he walks over to me. He dips his fingers into the tin, pulls out a slice of peach and wolfs it right down.

"How about you, Rhea?" I ask. She is sitting up tying her hair back. She turns and looks at me as soon as I offer.

"Yeah, sure," she says as she stretches out and walks over. As she puts her fingers in the can to take a slice of peach, I look at her and can see that she has a strange look in her eyes. It is the kind of look somebody has when they have been crying all night. I decide not to ask her if she is OK. The last thing people need when they have been upset all night is for somebody to pester them with sympathy.

I lift the tin of peaches and tip them all into my mouth. They are soft and mushy, and retain just enough sweetness to make them remotely edible. I eat them in one go and afterwards feel a limited sense of strength. As soon as I am done I throw the tin on the floor. I give a long sigh, trying to take in as much air as I can. I quickly rub my hands over my face and through my hair. I then look down at my bag and begin to play with the strap. I know that we will soon need to get our stuff together to move out.

Amrit pulls the barricade he made in front of the door out of the way so we can leave the house. We gather the weapons we found, even carrying spares in our bags just in case we run into trouble, and make our way out onto the street. The first thing we do is pull out our guns, look around and make sure that nobody is creeping up on us. We then turn to our left and start walking.

I look up and can see the sun tearing through the clouds, making them disappear until the sky is all blue. It feels like a ton of supplies I am carrying on my back, with the weapons and so on, and sweat is already starting to seep through my clothes. It doesn't help that the sun is burning holes into my face, roasting my skin.

As we finally make it to the end of the street, it feels like a relief. I look over to the right and can see a dead border monkey lying on the side of the road. He has all the attributes of your average border monkey son of a bitch: green hair, leather padding, a tank top, a bandana and tattoos. I remember reading a magazine article about punks, and that is more or less what the border monkeys looks like. For some reason though, the punks I read about seemed to be cool, and to have their reasons for being punks. These border monkeys are just a bunch of pricks who like to cause trouble.

We stop to investigate this dead guy and see if we can find any supplies on him. See if this border monkey can do something that all other border monkeys fail to do, which is be useful. Amrit moves towards him and looks over. Rhea and I stand back to keep watch so that nobody tries to attack us while Amrit essentially robs this guy.

"He doesn't have anything useful," he says. "Just a knife and – oh." Amrit pauses.

"What is it?" I ask.

"What do we have here?" he says, his tone starting to become more excited by the second. He reaches into the man's pocket and pulls out a knuckleduster.

"Fuck me," I say. "That can be of some help."

"Let's see if any of those monkeys try to fight me now," Amrit says as he puts the knuckleduster on his knuckles and begins to move his fist around like he's going to fight.

"OK, let's keep moving," Rhea says. Amrit quickly puts the knuckleduster in his pocket and we get moving down to the next street.

We walk past the houses, the used-up cars, the trees and the parks; in all honesty it is very difficult to keep my eyes open. I am so bored right now I can barely see.

"Let's play a game," I say to try and keep my morale up.

They both look at me with disgust. I think they were enjoying the silence, whereas I was just finding it annoyingly monotonous.

"I spy with my little eye," I begin.

"Please stop," Rhea interrupts before I can finish my sentence.

"Just trying to get a dialect going."

"Well, nobody cares," she responds.

"I care. I care about both of your well-being," I finish sarcastically.

"You're a prick," she retorts. "I bet no girl finds you even remotely attractive."

"The fact you have to say that means you find me a little attractive," I explain, trying to needle her.

"Oh please, I wouldn't even touch you if you were the last man alive!"

"Yeah, sure. I bet all you think about is me in your pants." I do a little hand action to put my point across even more.

Rhea looks at me in disgust and moves to the other side of Amrit, putting him in the middle of the two of us.

"Moving away because I'm making you too hot, hey?" I say to her.

"No, it's because you disgust me," she replies.

"You won't be saying that when I'm done with you."

"Oh, will you two just shut the fuck up?!" Amrit shouts. "All I have had for the past three days is you two bickering. Either fuck and get it over with, or shut the fuck up and let's keep moving."

We continue to make our way down the street. Amrit looks at us and we both nod at him, and continue to walk on.

I see even more boarded-up houses as we carry on. Now we have come to a bunch of tall flats which tower over us. Each window is boarded up, trying to keep whatever was out from getting in, and whatever was in from getting out. We walk forward and can see a group of people huddling at the corner of the street. We go to have a better look at them. One of them turns around and we quickly back off.

"Shit, infected!" I shout. Amrit pulls his gun out, and so do I.

"All right, be ready," he says.

"Will do."

We both manoeuvre around, looking at the infected, making sure we are ready just in case anything happens.

"I feel sorry for them," Rhea says as we stare at them. "They look scared."

They turn and we can see one of them eating what looks like a rat, with blood gushing down his chin from his mouth. It looks like there are two men and two women. All of them have missing teeth, and one of the women seems to have a missing eye.

"They look hungry if anything," I say, lacking the sympathy that Rhea is showing.

"We should go," Amrit urges.

"We should help them," Rhea says.

"I think Amrit's right. We should leave," I state, trying to look around for a pathway to lead us away from here.

"Of course you would want to leave," Rhea shouts. "You're just allergic to helping people." She turns and faces the infected. "Put your guns away at least."

"Um, no," I say, being stubborn.

"Just do it," she tells us, "or you're going to scare them."

"Just do it, Layton," Amrit says.

"What?" I say, stunned.

"Just do it," he demands.

"Fine," I say.

We both take our guns and put them in our bags. In addition, we take out our melee weapons; Amrit his machete and me my baseball bat.

"See, was that so hard?" Rhea asks sarcastically.

"Yeah, whatever," I grunt.

She turns and looks once more at the infected group in the corner.

"They look scared and hungry. Nobody cares about them and nobody looks after them," she says, sounding sympathetic as she looks over at the infected gathered in front of us.

"That's because they are freaky, sick people. You know, if they touch you, then you will be infected. They probably want to eat you," I say.

"How do you know that?" Rhea argues. "For all you know they might be really friendly and want to find shelter and food – just like us."

As soon as Rhea stops talking, one of the male infected

makes what sounds like an animal groan. A female one groans too, and slaps her face. All three of us stare at them as they have this unusual interaction. The male one rubs his face and picks up the rat he was eating, then rubs it on his face. The female one who was talking to him lets out a groan which sounds more like a cat than a human and then slaps him in the face, causing him to fall on his side.

"Right," I say out loud. "OK, well, now you see: they are perfectly happy by themselves. Look at them, they're having a great time – look, that one can't get enough of his rat, and I bet she's the main heart-throb of the bunch. Also, she can't get enough of slapping the others, she's loving it," I say, pointing at the one with the missing eye. "They've got their own thing going on and so do we, so let's go."

"I can't believe I'm saying this," Amrit admits, "but Layton is right."

I give him a snarl for his sarcasm.

"We have to keep moving; there's only four of them here now, but they always seem to attract more. There'll probably be about fifty here in an hour. By nightfall this place will be swarming with infected, and then we will have no chance."

"He's right," I say.

Rhea just looks at us, and I can see disgust in her eyes. She turns and starts to walk away from us, towards the infected.

"Rhea, what are you doing?" I shout.

She is about three or four metres away from them when one of the infected comes towards her. It is the blonde woman with the missing eye. She slowly approaches Rhea, crouched down. Rhea kneels down to her level.

"Hey there. Are you OK?" she asks, as if she is talking to a child.

Amrit and I stand there looking at her, trying to make sure she is OK, just in case anything crazy happens.

"Here," she says, reaching into her back pocket to pull out

what looks like a dried piece of meat. She holds it out to the infected woman. "Here. It's meat, food. You can eat it and you will be strong," she explains, as if she's talking to a baby.

"Why is she talking to her like that?" I ask Amrit.

"I have no idea," he replies.

"I know they are infected but there's no need to talk to them like they're retarded. I mean, they are kind of retarded, but you know, there's no need to make it so clear to their faces," I state.

"I can hear you," Rhea shouts out to us. She then turns back to the infected woman slowly crawling towards us. "I know you're scared, but I won't hurt you," she says softly as the infected woman crawls closer and closer.

"Laaaamnaaa," the infected woman says to Rhea.

"What did she say?" I ask.

"I have no idea," Rhea answers, still kneeling.

"Laaaamnaaa," the infected woman cries again. The other three infected turn and face Rhea. "Ooo, ooo, laaaammmnnaaa!" she shouts.

"What the fuck?" Rhea says. Then suddenly the infected woman finds the strength to lunge at her. Rhea falls onto her back and starts to crawl away as the infected woman bears down on her like an angry dog. The other three infected turn and start staggering towards Rhea.

"Fuck!" Amrit cries as they begin to close in on her. Before we can get to her, the infected woman pounces on top of Rhea and starts trying to take a bite out of her.

"Get off me!" Rhea yells. She struggles to get the woman off her. I quickly run over, pulling out my bat, and smash the infected woman in the head, causing her to fall off Rhea and onto the ground. I turn and see Amrit using his machete to attack the other infected; then charge at one of them coming towards me. I take a huge swing at it and hit it on the shoulder. The infected still comes at me.

"Die, you cock!" I shout as he comes at me once again, and I swing my bat again and hit him right across his head. It explodes – well, with the amount of blood that comes out of it, it might as well have exploded – covering me.

"Ew," I say to myself as the infected brain splatters over my top.

"You OK?" Amrit asks me as I wipe my face.

"Yeah. I didn't ingest anything," I tell him as I make sure not one speck enters my body. I know that one drop can infect you.

I turn and see Amrit take out the remaining infected with his machete, stabbing it in the back of its head. It collapses to the ground like a ton of bricks. All four of the infected are now dead, and none of them are going to be attacking us again any time soon. I see Rhea sitting on the ground, a little shaken by what just happened. Amrit runs towards her, with me following closely behind.

"Are you OK?" Amrit asks as he helps her to her feet.

"I'm fine, thanks."

We look at one another until we hear a noise. Sounds of cats groaning, and "Laamnaa" again and again.

"I think we need to go," I insist. I turn see more infected coming out of the buildings nearby, and they are starting to gather more numbers.

"Laammnnaaa," they chant as they walk slowly yet steadily towards us. We begin to panic the closer they get, each of us looking for an exit.

"Come on, let's go!" Amrit shouts, and we all turn and start making our way out of here.

We run down the street, managing to avoid every one of the infected that come towards us, just about getting away from them. We continue running through the streets until we come to what looks like a load of storage units; rows and rows of them positioned right in front of us.

"Quick, in there!" I say as I see an abandoned storage unit

ahead. We sprint to the door, which for some reason is slightly open. Amrit flings it wide, Rhea and I run straight in without looking backwards, and once we are in, Amrit quickly closes the door.

"Everybody OK?" he asks.

"I'm fine, thanks," Rhea replies.

"What the fuck were you thinking?" I shout as she stands there. "You could have got us all killed."

"You weren't bitten, were you?" Amrit asks Rhea, in a calmer tone than mine.

"No, I'm fine," Rhea whimpers.

"That doesn't answer my question though, does it?" I say.

"I thought I was being nice."

"Oh, being nice? Look where that just got us!" I shout at her in disgust. I then start to walk to the other side of the storage unit we are now trapped in.

"I'm sorry, OK?" she cries. "I thought I could help them – I couldn't help my Dad so I thought I could try and help someone in all of this."

I turn back. Now I can't help but feel bad for being such an arse to her.

"So what now?" Amrit asks us.

"I have no idea," I respond, crashing my back into a wall and slowly sliding down to sit on the floor.

"Well, there's no way we can leave here right now," Rhea says.

We all look at the door and come to the same realisation. All three of us look at each other, knowing that we will have to camp here for the night. We may have to go hungry tonight, but at least we will be safe. I take on board what Rhea just said, realising that she hasn't yet had a chance to mourn the death of her father. This world we live in just can't help but be unfair.

7

After spending so many hours in the storage unit trying to keep away from the infected, I'm bored. We sit around and look at one another, pondering our next course of action.

We need to do something to pass the time; however it is very difficult to work out what that something is. I decide to stare at my hands for a while as I sit next to this large grey wall. I look at the lines I've had since childhood, seeing how nothing had quite changed as I've grown into adulthood.

"Oh my God, I'm so bored," I moan. Amrit looks at me, and I know that he feels exactly the same way.

"So am I, actually," Rhea says.

"Oh, are you?" I say to her sarcastically. "Well, that's a shame, as you're the reason we're in this fucking place."

"I already said sorry," she snaps.

"Well, all's well that ends well, then."

"What does that even mean?" she asks, sounding very disgruntled.

"Shut up, you two," Amrit demands. "Look, I have an idea how we can get through this."

"How's that?" I ask, frustrated.

"Well, I got something that I've been saving. I was holding

on to it, just in case of a time like this," he explains, rummaging around in his pocket.

"What do you mean, 'a time like this'?" Rhea asks.

"You know, a time when I don't have any way out and I'm trapped somewhere for a long time."

"So what is it?" I ask, confused.

"Well," Amrit says, "when I was travelling through Sheffield – you know, when I was with that biker crew?"

"Yeah," I say, following what he is saying.

"Well, we decided we needed to find a way to get our heads out of the gutter; get our minds free from this place. So my friend Rocco, he made this pill which takes the initial buzz you get from weed, and compressed it so you get the excitement you get from ecstasy or even heroin. He said it gives you a trip that you will never have again. It will take you to the stars and back; out of this world and to another planet." Amrit pulls out a blue pill and shows it to us. "This is a very rare commodity. It is flooding into Leicester, which is where we are, from Sheffield, and has now taken over the East Midlands. Those who know about this pill, they're the ones who're using it, really. They're the people who are really taking advantage of it; it hasn't quite gone mainstream."

"What do they call it?" I ask.

"Rabbit," Amrit replies.

As soon as he says that, Rhea and I start laughing.

"Rabbit? What kind of stupid name is that?" I ask, wondering why somebody would name anything that.

"Well, they call it that," Amrit explains, "because it makes you as free as a rabbit in a meadow. You hop from reality to reality and your feet don't wish to touch the ground."

"Wow," I say.

"How many do you have?" Rhea asks him.

"I have about ten. I don't know the effects, though, because I've never taken it," he admits.

"You've never taken one?" I ask, feeling a little shocked.

"No, I just have them on me," he explains.

"So how do you know they won't just blow our brains out?" I ask, trying to get across the sense of danger I feel.

"Shall we all take one together," Rhea asks, "or should one of us take it and explain what it's like?"

"I would say we should all take it together, but what if we all just start killing each other?" I say.

"Yeah, that's true," Rhea agrees. "Then we should nominate one person to take it first, just to make sure it's safe."

"Yeah, I second that," Amrit says.

"I think Layton should take the first one," Rhea states.

"Fuck you," I reply.

"Well, you got nothing else to offer," Rhea says. "You might as well do something useful."

"Look, we can all draw straws for it," Amrit says. He reaches into his pocket and pulls out three straws.

"You just keep straws in your pocket?" I ask him, confused.

"Yeah, why?"

"Just asking."

Amrit holds the three straws in front of us as Rhea and I gather round.

"OK," Rhea says, "I'll go first." She reaches out and pulls out a bright pink straw from Amrit's hand. She looks at it and smiles hesitantly.

"OK, I guess it's me now," I say. I reach for the white straw, get hold of it and pull it free.

After I pull mine out, Amrit displays the remaining blue straw in his hand. All three of us look at our straws and of course I am pissed off with the result.

"Oh, shit," I huff, as I can see that I have literally drawn the short straw. I knew this would happen. I just knew that I would be the one who had to, as they say, take one for the team. It's been ages since I did something like this, and I'm not sure how my body is going to react to it.

"Well, I guess it's up to you," Rhea says to me. I give her a dirty look, and out of the corner of my eye I can see Amrit reaching out to me.

"OK." Amrit sighs as we all sit down in a circle. "You take this – just wash it down with a little water and you should be fine. Remember, though, you don't have to do this," he states very clearly.

"Yeah, I know," I say. "I just can't be arsed listening to those freaks outside."

"OK then, mate." Amrit hands me the pill. I look at the small blue pill, about the size of a small coin as I roll it around in my fingers.

"Good luck," Rhea encourages me.

"Thanks," I say. I look at the pill and take a deep breath. I pull out a bottle of water that I have been carrying with me and open it. I then take the pill and place it in my mouth, followed by a chug of water, getting the pill down my throat and into my bloodstream. As soon as I finish gulping, I look up at them.

"Well?" Rhea asks. "Do you feel any different?"

"No. Do I look any different?" I ask, touching my face to make sure no parts are out of place.

"No," she states.

"Can you stand?" Amrit asks me.

I stand up for a few seconds, then sit down again.

"Yeah," I say, "I'm fine."

"OK," Amrit says. "Probably gone off or something."

I sit there looking at him as he is talking. I look at Rhea as she starts to say something, until suddenly my body goes stiff. I look forward and I feel my pupils go in and out.

"Layton?" I hear Amrit say to me.

"Layton, are you OK?" Rhea asks.

But I can't respond; I just can't speak to them.

I keep looking forward and feel myself floating up into the air. I blink, and everything begins to look blurred. I blink again and everything looks even more blurred. I blink once more and I am in a completely different place. I am no longer in the storage unit; I look forward and see that I am now in a forest. All the trees have purple leaves with red branches, and I can see just a long, distant pathway between the trees.

As I walk I see a lot of unusual animals running around. They all have these incredible wide smiles on them, and keep farting bubbles for some bizarre reason. Then out of nowhere this giant rabbit pops out. I look away and it vanishes. I turn and there it is on the other side of me. I turn again and it is standing right in front of me. At first I think it is a giant rabbit moreover, after a while it just looks like a guy in a rabbit costume.

"Hi, Layton, welcome to Paradise." The rabbit welcomes me with a goofy voice and very floppy ears

"Hi," I say, a little scared.

"My name is Muffin," he tells me. "Take my hand, we're going on a little trip."

"OK." I take his hand.

We then start flying through the sky. I can hear what sounds like jolly children's music. I start to feel very happy with this cheery keyboard playing in the background. The birds smile as they fly by. The sky is bright blue and even the sun has a face.

"Morning, Layton," the sun says to me. "I hope you have a nice day." He gives me a little wink, just to make me feel that bit better.

We fly to the top of a mountain and Muffin takes me to this table. We sit down and are joined by a talking lollipop called Steve, a snooty kangaroo called Bacon, a talking snowman called Blob and a talking burger called Glue. I don't know how I know all of their names; they just pop into my head straight away as if they are my closest friends.

"Marvellous weather we are having," Steve says.

"So wonderful," Bacon replies.

"I hear the footsy is in," Glue states.

"Oh, is that so?" Blob responds in a strong, gloopy voice.

"Oh, Layton, you must try the tea," Bacon tells me.

I hold up a white teacup in front of me, and it has a face.

"Please drink from me," the teacup says. "Go on, make my day, pretty boy."

"Um, OK." I start sipping.

"Yes, oh yes," the teacup shouts. "Yes, you dirty bitch, drink, drink me good. Thanks, baby, you're a star," the cup says to me at the end. I put it down and look up.

"Wonderful, isn't it?" Bacon says.

Then suddenly a siren goes off in the background, which disturbs our little tea party.

"Oh, you know what time that is?" Steve asks us all.

"Let's dance, gang!" Muffin shouts, and everybody starts dancing. I can't help it, I start to dance as well. I begin moving my arms around, moving my hips and shoulders. I am having a very good time right now. The birds even sweep down to have a dance.

I look forward and see this figure standing at the end of the table. I look away for a moment, then look again – suddenly it is gone. Nah, it's probably nothing. Let's just get back to dancing.

"This is amazing," I cry as I continue to dance.

"Come, Layton," Muffin says to me. "We're now going to roll around in Marshmallow Land."

"That sounds amazing!"

Suddenly I am rolling on a load of fluffy marshmallows. I am bouncing up and down on them, high-fiving the clouds, looking at the colourful background. I then land on this giant waffle that is covered with syrup. I can't help but start licking it. I lick it all over and feel so sweet and warm inside.

"Hi, Layton," a little talking turtle that just comes up to me says. "Do you need the toilet?" It's strange; as soon as he asks, I feel the urge to go to the toilet, and it is a strange sensation.

"Well, yes I do, Mr Turtle."

"Here," it says, "pee in my mouth." It opens its mouth and I pull down my zip and go to town in the turtle's mouth. I pee in it and it feels damn good.

I then look up and see that figure again, just staring at me in the distance. I look up at it and it walks off into the party that is happening. I decide to follow. I walk past the giant waffle, the marshmallows, and come to what looks like a sea of curry. I get into the curry and swim my way across. I suddenly feel this hunger come over me, so I decide to chew on a piece of chicken. To add to my enjoyment, I find a piece of candy lace instead, sitting on a piece of chicken. I pick it up and start nibbling on it. It tastes so sweet; also, it does not seem to want to break away.

As soon as I finish with the laces, I make my way to the other side. Looking ahead of myself, I see that figure once more glaring back at me. I then bump into what looks like a group of women in cowboy outfits. One of them glances at me and takes her bra off, showing off her giant, round boobs.

"You want to feel my goodies, Layton?" she asks me. Well, I think the answer to this one is pretty obvious.

"Yes please," I say. I walk forward, holding my hands out and squeezing them in and out.

I then look in the distance and can see the figure again. I move away from the cowgirl and begin to run after the figure I have been seeing. I see it go through a cloud of dancing crisp packets. I run through them and make my way to the other side of the cloud. Suddenly I realise the cloud has stopped moving. I stand there and look at the figure standing a few yards ahead of me. I decide to walk towards it, closer and closer. I am about to put my hand on the figure's shoulder when a voice comes out of it.

"Why did you leave me?" the figure asks me.

"Excuse me?" I reply.

"Why did you leave me?" the figure says once more. It slowly turns around, and I can see it is a male. But this is not any old male that I am looking at here. I suddenly feel cold and scared; my heart starts racing and I want to run away, but I can't. I can't take my eyes off this person in front of me, I just can't stop looking at his face. It is a face I have not seen in a very long time, a face I thought I would never see again.

"It can't be," I utter in shock.

"Why did you leave me?" the figure asks again.

"No, it wasn't my fault," I try to convince it. "I'm sorry, it wasn't my fault!" I plead.

"Why did you leave me?" the figure asks. "Why did you leave me?" he shouts.

"Adam," I say to him, "Adam, I'm sorry, I didn't know what to do."

Suddenly everything around us goes pitch-black, and there is nothing but fire surrounding us. I look up, and it is only me and Adam standing there.

"Why did you leave me?" he keeps on repeating. "Why did you leave me?"

"I'm sorry," I say to him again.

"Why did you leave me?" he asks one last time. He then just stares at me blankly, not saying a word to me.

"No, please, Adam, no!" I plead.

Suddenly I look up and I am back at the party. Adam is nowhere to be seen and I am standing with Muffin, Bacon and Steve in the middle of the party.

"Come on, Layton," Muffin shouts out to me, and we all start dancing again.

We bust out some major grooves and Bacon decides to do some backflips. I decide to try to forget seeing Adam and instead try to feel free like a bird, flapping my arms back and forth, not once wanting to leave this magical place, until suddenly I begin to feel sick. Then I can hear somebody calling out my name.

"Layton?" a voice calls out to me.

I feel sick still; I think I'm going to puke.

"Layton!" the voice calls again.

I look around, still feeling sick. I can't hold it in any more… here it comes. I lean over and puke out a whole load of vomit.

"Layton," Amrit says. I look around and see that I am back in the storage unit.

"Oh, I'm back," I say. I look down and see that I am wearing nothing but my pants, with my trousers around my ankles. "Why am I like this? Where are my clothes?" I ask Amrit and Rhea, who are staring at me, looking shocked.

"Oh yeah," Rhea says. She gets up, walks over to me and slaps me across the face.

"Ouch!" I cry. "What the fuck was that for?"

"What was it like?" Amrit asks me as I rub my eyes to clear them. I sit up and look up, already beginning to miss my experience.

"It was amazing," I begin. "There was a talking rabbit, a kangaroo, talking turtles, giant waffles… I take it I was just lying here the whole time?" I look at them, and in unison, they look at each other with concerned expressions on their faces.

"Not quite," Amrit tells me.

"Oh. What, then?" I ask, looking at their awkward faces glaring back at me.

"Well," Amrit says, "let me walk you through what you did."

"OK."

"You started by dancing and taking your clothes off," Amrit explains.

I recall dancing with Muffin, Bacon and Steve. "Oh," I say out loud, and can see myself dancing both in Paradise and in the storage unit. I see myself taking my clothes off and busting a groove in my pants.

"Then you jumped up and down," Amrit continues. "Then you started to lick me."

"Oh," I respond. I see myself jumping up and down the walls in the storage unit, thinking I was on the marshmallows. I then see myself licking what I thought was syrup on a waffle, but was actually Amrit's face.

"Then you started pissing all over," Amrit explains to me.

"Oh," I say to myself. I think back to when I thought I was peeing in the turtle's mouth, and what must've really happened.

"Oh my God, why won't he stop?" Rhea was shouting out, as I had my dick out, spraying piss everywhere.

"We can't stop him or he will freak out," Amrit tried to explain to her.

"Oh dear," I say as I recollect it.

"Then for some reason you started chewing Rhea's hair," Amrit says. I think back to when I thought I was chewing on candy laces, thinking they were a bit tough.

"Oh dear," I say, as I see myself chewing on Rhea's hair.

"Oh my God, it is so gross," she shouted as I stood there, rubbing my nipples for some reason and chewing on her hair. I was creating a pool of saliva everywhere as well, really making a mess.

"Then you started to head towards Rhea with your hands out," Amrit explains. "You tried to grab her."

"Shit," I say, looking at Rhea. She gives me a filthy look. I think back to when I thought I was walking towards the sexy cowgirl, when in reality it was Rhea.

"I'm going to fucking kill him," she told Amrit.

"It'll be over soon, trust me," Amrit tried to convince her.

"I swear I'm going to fucking kill him," she said again as I walked towards her, holding my hands out, squeezing them in and out, drooling and making a weird perky noise. I even remember some saliva coming out of my mouth like a dog as I was heading towards her.

"Then you just did some dancing," Amrit finishes off by telling me. "Then you threw up, and here you are."

"Bloody hell," I say to them. "Well, um, sorry."

"Now we have to sleep in your piss and puke!" Rhea shouts.

"Sorry, I was nominated," I say.

"It's true, we did nominate him," Amrit states very clearly to Rhea.

"Fucking hell, how did I end up here?" Rhea asks herself. "If you need me I will be trying to sleep," she adds, turning away.

"Yeah, you better rest as well, Layton," Amrit says. "We got to get going in the morning, and that must have taken a lot out of you."

"Yeah, it did."

"Oh yeah, before I go to sleep, mate," Amrit asks me, "who's Adam?"

I look up at him, wanting to tell him the truth, but can't bring myself to. Maybe it's better he doesn't know the truth; ignorance is bliss, as they say.

"Oh, nobody," I reply, protecting myself. "Probably just some random druggy ramblings, I guess."

"OK," Amrit says. "Well, you get some sleep. See you in the morning." He then lies down and turns onto his side. I remain sitting with my back to the wall. I look at the wall ahead of me and I can't think of anything else.

"Adam," I say to myself. "Why did I have to see Adam?"

I ask myself once more, in a quiet tone so the others can't hear me. I remain staring at the wall, feeling myself growing tired and drifting off. I turn onto my side, face the wall I was leaning on and close my eyes. Before I know it, I am asleep. Another day has gone; now it's time to make my way into a new morning, another day to try and make something good out of this shit-storm.

8

The following morning, we wake to silence. I listen closely and hear nothing, which must mean there are no infected outside the storage unit. This probably means we are free to go. I can't believe I pissed myself last night; that pill, the rabbit, was way too much for me. I stink of puke as well. I wonder if there is somewhere I can wash up?

Well, I guess there is only one way to find out: I have to go out into the world and see if there is a pond or a stream or something where I can get this stench off me. I'm bloody starving as well; all that puking up last night really emptied my stomach.

I look over and see Rhea getting her stuff together. I think I better apologise for what happened last night. I mean, I did stick her hair in my mouth. I don't really think that is something that she would take to kindly to, especially considering how snobby she can be. I walk over to her as she is putting things in her bag. I look down and can see her trying not to make eye contact with me.

"Hey, Rhea," I say in a calm voice.

"Yeah," she responds in a very abrupt tone.

"I just want to say that... Um..." I pause for a moment to

gather the correct words. "I just wanted to say sorry for last night."

She pauses for a moment, then just carries on putting her stuff in her bag.

"I mean, I had no control over what I was doing. If I had the chance to go back I would not take that pill again. I just want to say I'm sorry," I tell her.

"Look," Rhea responds abruptly, pushing her bag to one side. "Let's just get one thing straight. I'm sure you're a nice guy deep down."

"But…" I suggest

"Well" She begins. "Your just a bit, um, goofy. And a little bit, odd"

"Goofy, odd" I repeat to her, feeling nothing but concerned in my mind.

"I know it was the luck of the draw that you took that pill," she explains, "but it was really gross. I'm not mad, it's just… it weirded me out."

I look at her and pause for a moment.

"So we're cool, yeah?" I try to reason with her.

"Yes, I guess so," she says reluctantly.

"Well, isn't that a relief?" Amrit pipes up in the background. "Shall we get moving then, seeing as we're all friends?"

We look at each other and gather our belongings. I swing my bag over my shoulder and almost go flying to the ground because of how heavy it is.

"First thing we need to do," Amrit starts to say, "is find some food."

"Righto, Captain," I reply in a jokey manner. Rhea tuts to herself and walks right past me. I give her a dirty look; I mean, why is she finding it appropriate to judge me right now? She needs to sort her attitude out, especially now that we are all in this together.

Amrit walks over to the shutter holding us in. He leans over, grabs the hatch at the bottom of the door and flings the shutter wide open. He then walks outside, all the while looking left and right to make sure that there is nothing there. Rhea and I quickly follow him. I look up and see that the sun has gone in. The clouds have joined together to form a sea of white in the sky, making it not exactly warm and not exactly cold. I wonder if it is going to rain. Well, it is England that we are living in, so it is bound to rain at some point. Many of my memories of living here involves rain and the lack of joy it gives us all.

We make our way to the end of the row of storage units. We decide to peep around the corner just to make sure that there is nothing there that could be of any danger to us. We quickly look back, then make our way through.

We walk down what looks like another derelict street filled with wrecked cars and boarded-up houses. It feels like the same repetitive action every day, going from street to street, looking at similar houses and cars; boredom, that is all I know these days, just being bored.

We keep going until we come to the end of the street, and there is nothing there, just a giant field which leads to some trees and a forest up ahead. I don't think I have ever spent too long in a forest. I have been to some in the past, though as time has gone on, I have learnt to not really trust them. Nobody does. Most of the border monkeys hang around there; they usually form their base in the woodland. You can always tell where they are, usually by the sight of a group of trees and a giant plume of smoke coming from the centre. Also, you see all of their bikes parked outside.

I know somebody who went to one of their bases once. He said that they have their own little concrete homes there within the trees, and they don't exactly take care of them. They are usually covered in litter, cans all over the place, and blood seems to be a theme that they like to have. Well, that's what many people say. I'm only going on what I've been told, I don't actually have anything to base this on. Really, I just don't like the look of forests.

"What should we do?" I ask the others as we stand staring at the field.

"I'm not sure," Amrit says as we continue to stare into the distance.

"Let's go this way," Rhea says out of nowhere. She then turns and starts to walk along the fence separating the town from the field.

"Where are we going?" I ask her.

"I got a feeling that our best shot will be in a town centre or something," she says.

"What gives you that idea?" I ask, confused by what she is saying.

"Because there will be all those buildings – not a lot of room to get lost. Also, all three of us have lived here all of our lives, so we should know where everything is."

"So, to Leicester town centre?" Amrit says.

"Yeah, I guess so," I reply. "Maybe I can pick up some new jeans," I say as a joke, and the others chuckle slightly. "Surely there will be others there."

"Probably," Rhea states.

"Could be dangerous," Amrit says.

"Well, it's worth a try," I tell them.

"Let's go for it," Rhea says.

"Yeah, let's." Amrit follows.

We make our way along the side of the fence and towards our destination. The walk is long and boring, not really the most interesting of journeys I have ever been on. I look over and can see that we are about to pass by a park; I can tell by the swings. The slide is smashed in half and the benches are broken, but it still looks like a park to me.

We decide to walk a little further, looking at the flowers and grass that have grown much more than I believe they should have. We continue on until we come to a bridge. It's an old, broken-down ruin, engulfed with moss covering every inch. We have a quick glance underneath and can see a stream flowing through. I decide to walk towards it, with Amrit and Rhea following close behind.

"What are we doing here?" Amrit asks me.

"I feel I need to get clean," I tell him, looking at the water. "I think we all should," I add as I see them both looking down at me and the stream.

"Yeah," Rhea says.

As I walk towards the stream I begin to take my clothes off. I start with my shirt, then my shoes, closely followed by my trousers. I take off my socks, which I have not done for a while. I've been wearing them longer than I should have and they have come to feel as if they are sticking to me. I manage to scrape them off and find myself stripped down to my pants. I dip my toes in the water and take them out straight away. The water feels so cold it is closer to ice than liquid. I decide to brave it and clamber in, feeling the cold cover my legs. I scoop water in my hand and brush it through my hair. I wash my face over and over until I begin to feel the dirt peeling from my skin. I cover my body with the water continuously until it too feels like my face.

Afterwards, I kneel at the edge of the stream and look over at Rhea bathing, covering herself in the water. I catch a glimpse of her half-naked skin as the water trickles over it. I quickly look away, not wanting to embarrass her, or myself for that matter. Amrit is washing the top of his head, somehow managing to make it shinier than before. I turn around and end up looking back at Rhea. I try to catch a quick glimpse. She catches me, I stop for a second, looking away, then slowly peer at her again. I look at her, and instead of getting embarrassed, she just smiles slightly, then looks away to wash her hair. It isn't tied up as it usually is; instead it floats down by her shoulders. I don't want to look for too long, and have to look away again.

I get up and dry myself with an old shirt, scraping myself under my arms and around my waist. I lean over and brush my hair, feeling the water begin to seep away from me, making me feel dry. I look up and see Amrit walking towards me, fully clothed just like me.

"Let's go," he says, walking past. Rhea follows close behind him. I decide follow too, making sure I don't stay in the same spot for too long.

"Layton?" Rhea says to me while we walk.

"Yeah?"

"Sorry if I've been a bit mean to you."

"Oh," I respond, surprised. "Um, it's alright"

"I've just had a lot to deal with," she adds. If she's talking about her dad, then yeah, OK, I feel sorry for her. I can't forget that she was a bitch to me before he even died, so cut the crap, sweet cheeks.

"That's fine," I say. I have to keep up appearances; I can't exactly be a bitch to her. A part of me does feel sympathetic towards her.

"Cool," she responds.

We continue to walk on past all the homes, passing through barricaded fences until we come to what look like old, abandoned shops. We make our way past them and know that we have to be cautious, just in case anything surprising happens. We finally get past the shops and through to the main road. I see a sign which says Uppingham Road. I know this place, it leads to the town centre. We must be close. We walk a little further and come to what looks like an old doctor's surgery. It looks abandoned, nonetheless, there might be supplies inside.

"I think we should go in," Amrit says as all three of us stand there looking at the surgery.

"I agree," I say.

"Should one of us keep watch?" Rhea asks.

"I don't think so," Amrit says to her. "I don't think anybody will be coming around here for a long time. We can just go in."

A part of me does not feel great about going in. Not for any ethical reasons, no; it's more because this place has probably been rinsed dry. I would be surprised if we even find a plaster in there.

"Come on, let's go," Rhea urges, and we walk through the car park to front door of the surgery.

Amrit snaps the door open and we head inside to see what we can find. I follow, making sure not to step on anything that could arouse too much attention. The place is well and truly abandoned: there are cobwebs on the ceiling, covering the decoration that was once there. The part of the room which looks like the reception seems as if a bomb's hit it, judging by how much of a mess it is in. There are pieces of paper covering the floor, and broken chairs strewn across the room.

"Well, this looks messy," I say silently as we make our way forward. All of us raise our guns, keeping them aimed to make sure that nothing is coming our way. We walk forward, aiming all over, looking out for any danger that might creep its way in front of us, and find more chairs that have been abandoned on the floor.

"Let's go behind there," Amrit says as we move through to the other side of what looks like a waiting room. I look up and see a sign which says, Wait here and your doctor will call you. There is a poster bearing the letters NHS. I remember hearing about this NHS. Apparently, everybody got free healthcare, paid for through their taxes. Then the government got rid of it for some reason and people had to pay for their own healthcare. I heard that for a dislocated finger you would have to pay up to £1,500, which was a lot of money, especially when it used to be free on the NHS. I remember somebody telling me it was because Parliament decided to privatise the health service, or something like that; I think they did the same with schools as well, I'm not entirely sure. It seems this was one of the things that led to the 'Great Fall', as they all call it.

Amrit goes up to a door which reads STAFF ONLY. He pulls down the handle and finds that it opens straight away. We all look at each other, surprised.

"Well, that was easy," I say.

"Yes, it was," Amrit replies, as perplexed as I am.

We decide to walk in, Amrit leading the way, followed by myself and Rhea close behind. We make our way inside and look around to see if we can find any supplies. I can't really find anything, just a few used needles and that's about it. Nothing that can really help us if we need treatment; no bandages, no pills, nothing. We walk a bit further, making sure we don't break rank. Looking around, all I see is empty shelves.

"There's nothing here," Rhea says. "I think we should go, it just looks empty throughout."

"Yeah, I agree. Amrit, there's nothing here," I say, looking around.

"There must be something," Amrit declares. "This whole place can't be empty."

"Looks like it is," I say. I kick an empty box. "Look, mate, there is nothing in this place."

"I'm not giving up so easy," Amrit says.

"It's not giving up, there's just nothing here," I say, trying to show some concern, though really I'm just bored and want to go. "Let's go find some food, mate." I try to reason with him because I know we are all starving.

"I'm not just leaving," Amrit states abruptly. "You might want to go feed yourself, but I want to make sure we're healthy."

"All right, princess, don't get all pissy with me. Look, all I'm saying is that we need to go because it's not worth wasting time here."

"Help!" Rhea yells out of nowhere.

Amrit and I turn around and aim our guns towards her. A man with long, greasy hair and what looks like a tattered old brown jacket is standing right behind her. He looks angry and I can tell that he has some teeth missing, with his mouth covered in as many wrinkles as a prune. He has his arm around Rhea's neck, holding what looks like a piece of broken glass to it. He is holding the glass so tightly that it is starting to cut through his hand.

"OK, let's not do anything stupid." Amrit tries to reason with the man.

"What are you doing here? Why are you here? Who are you?" the man shouts at us, shaking as he does so.

"Is he infected, do you think?" I ask Amrit.

"No," Amrit says, "he doesn't look infected, just a bit thick is all."

"Oh, I see."

"Who are you and why are you here?" the man shouts at us once again.

"My name is Amrit. This guy here is called Layton," Amrit tells him, pointing at me.

"Who are you?" I ask the man. He stares at us.

"My name, my name…" he repeats. "I can't remember." He looks at us, staggers slightly, and his eyes begin to roll around.

"He's pissed," I exclaim.

"Yeah, he's off his face," Amrit agrees.

"Can you get him off me?" Rhea calls.

"Get out of here!" the man shouts at us.

"OK," Amrit says as we keep our guns aimed at him. "Let go of our friend and we will leave you alone." He edges forward, gently lowering his gun to show that he means no trouble.

"You go, she stays with me," the man says. Rhea looks at us in terror.

"I'm not sure it works like that," I say, trying to see if I can reason with the guy.

"She stay with me," the man shouts once again. "She stay with me, you go. She going to be my wife." Rhea gives him a look of disgust.

"OK, crazy person," I say, "how about you leave her alone and I give you a magic stone?"

"What?!" Rhea says.

"Oh, for fuck's sake," Amrit mutters to himself.

"Yeah, look." I pull out a round black stone, quite shiny as well. "This here is magic stone – you have three wishes and they can be anything you want."

"Layton, that's not going to work," Amrit whispers to me.

As soon as he says that, the man drops the piece of glass, letting go of Rhea as well, and walks right up to me.

"Is it really magic?" he asks me, amazed.

"Seriously?" Amrit asks.

"Yes, it is," I say. "You have to be alone, rub it and make a wish," I tell him, waving my hand around to look mystical.

"Oh yeah," the man says. He grabs the stone and runs off, laughing to himself. As suddenly as he was here, he is gone.

"OK, what just happened?" Rhea asks.

"I can't believe that worked," Amrit remarks.

"I knew it was going to," I gloat.

"How?" Rhea asks me as I make my way to the door.

"Simple: just perfect salesmanship," I say, feeling quite proud of myself.

"Oh, come on," Amrit retorts, "you gave away a stone to a drunk."

"You've always got to know your market." I smile. Amrit and Rhea just look at each other.

We head back past all of the deserted chairs, papers and posters that litter the place and stride over to the front door, smashing it open and making our way outside.

"Well, I guess we got to head in that direction," Amrit says, looking forward.

"I guess so," Rhea agrees. "I'm sure we will find some food somewhere."

"What's the plan?" I ask Amrit.

"Well, first we need to find food," Amrit announces, "then we need to find shelter."

"I wish we were still at the warehouse," Rhea says.

"I know," Amrit replies reassuringly.

"Come on then," I say with urgency. "We need to get going, get ourselves out of here. Let's head for the town centre and make camp there."

The two of them look at me and we begin our journey to the town centre, through the remains of shops, streets of abandoned cars and so on, until we come to a road leading to what looks like a very tall building in the distance. There is a lot of smoke everywhere and we know that there might be some trouble. So, this is where the journey will become more interesting; in a good way, I hope.

9

We make our way to Leicester city centre, which looks like a war zone. There is a giant building in front of us which looks like it has gang signs graphited all over it. In fact, every building that we come across seems to have spray paint coating it.

There are a lot of signs showing a hand print. I'm not entirely sure what it means. It's not like any other symbol I have seen before; nothing like any of the religious symbols that I have come across in my time. It's sort of a hand design with a bit of an Indian look to it. Behind the hand is a hammer, and both symbols are enclosed in a circle.

"What's that symbol mean?" I ask Amrit as we make our way through the town centre.

"I have no idea," he replies.

We come to what looks like a giant barricade. We stand there and gaze upon its intimidating presence. It is incredibly large and covered with wood and metal. All three of us slowly creep up on it. I can't help but feel excited by the majesty of the barricade, and yet it is a daunting spectacle. We walk further to see a door in the front of it, with that symbol imprinted on it: the hand and hammer.

"Do we knock?" I ask Amrit and Rhea, hoping they have some sort of answer.

"I'm not sure," Amrit disappointingly responds.

"Hello," Rhea shouts out unexpectedly. Amrit and I turn and look at her with concern. "What?" she asks as we glare at her.

Suddenly we hear a creaking noise, and we all turn and face the door. The door begins to open slightly and then comes to a stop, leaving a gap just large enough for one person.

"What now?" I ask Amrit and Rhea as we all stand there staring at the door.

A moment later, a figure appears from behind it. As it comes closer, it becomes apparent that this is quite a large person. Looks like a man from how he is shaped, with a large trench coat, a balaclava and a hood over his head, accompanied by some very heavy-looking boots. He is swinging a machete by his side as he walks purposefully towards us. We look at him as he comes closer and closer, standing our ground, making sure not to flinch at any point. He halts right in front of us and stands there, glaring at the three of us. We stare back, trying to see his eyes through the slit in his balaclava.

"State your business," he demands. We look at one another, waiting for somebody to speak. "I said state your business," he demands once more.

"We seek shelter," Amrit announces.

"Yes," I follow, "shelter and maybe some food."

"Is that so?" the man says, turning towards Rhea.

"Yes," Rhea replies. "We will not be any trouble; we are just hungry and cold, looking for rest and food."

He looks at us one by one. We just stand there staring back at him. He then turns and looks at Rhea, and she glares right back at him for what feels like minutes.

"Very well. Come this way," he instructs. He turns and walks back towards the door. He waves his hand and the door opens wider, giving room for all of us to get through. As soon as we walk through, it slams behind us with a giant crash. I quickly look behind at the door, then forward to where the man has led us, and my breath is taken away by what I see.

There are crowds of people gathering in the middle of the town centre at what looks like a marketplace. They are all dressed in raggedy clothes. We walk past them and see some people standing at the side. They look rather like border monkeys, yet they don't seem to be acting like them. They are wearing bandanas with hoods on their heads, and are standing with machetes and baseball bats. They look like underdressed security guards.

"I guess they're the people in charge," Rhea whispers to us as we pass. To be fair, it has probably been two years since I last set foot in the city centre. They are known for being dangerous places, so most of us stay on the outskirts. I know Amrit hasn't been near the city centre, and I can only assume Rhea is the same.

Making our way through the street, we can see people selling all sorts of items. "Get your tinned fruit!" they shout out to all. "Get your meat!" cry others. I look over and see the meat on offer. Looks kind of fresh. Still, I can't really trust it.

"Wait here," the man who led us in demands. He then turns and walks away from us as we stand looking at him, until he is engulfed in the crowd. We stand there waiting until suddenly, a large man charges up to us. He pushes his way through the people to get to us, making his presence very well known.

"Well, this looks interesting," I mutter to Rhea and Amrit as the man comes stomping towards us. He is dressed in what looks like camouflage trousers, big boots and a leather trench coat, with a bandana over his mouth and on the top of his head; looks like the standard clothing for this place. He stops us in our path.

"State your business," the man says to us in a deep, booming voice. We glance at each other, then back at him.

"We're here for refuge," Amrit says.

The man stares down at us. The crowd which was surrounding us suddenly moves away, like this man is a monster or something.

"You are here in the city of Leicester, under the governing of the Union," the man says. "You will have to state your reason for being here to General Singh." He looks at us all one at a time. "If you have any questions, now is the time to ask."

"No, I have nothing to ask," I make clear to him.

"No, not a word," Amrit states, and Rhea just shakes her head.

"Very well," he says. "Now follow me."

He turns, and we all start to follow him. As we move through the town centre he nods at the other people who are dressed like him. They are all standing with weapons. I look at the man leading us away and he has a machete on his back and a gun swinging from his side, as if he is some kind of soldier or something. We follow close behind, making our way through the crowd, past the clock tower, past the shops and different market stalls that make the place look like a medieval urban paradise, until we come to what looks like a town square. There is a giant fountain in the centre with benches, and it looks pretty well kept. The man leads us to a building I recognise as Leicester Town Hall, now bearing the symbol with the hand, hammer and circle. He leads us up the stairs and into the building.

As we enter, I can't help but feel as if we have entered a Victorian oil painting. There are all these pieces of art on the walls looking completely untouched; chairs that look as if they are from another era, an older era beyond my knowledge. I can sense nothing but silence. The hustle and bustle that was outside is muffled by the walls of the building.

He takes us through the building, up even more stairs until we come to a room. There is a giant door in front of us, again with that symbol. The man opens the door and walks inside.

"In here," he instructs us.

We step inside and see a man sitting at the end of the room behind a desk. The man looks middle-aged with long hair and a beard, which looks pretty well kept. He is wearing a pitch-black leather jacket. I gaze around the room and it looks huge, with a large red carpet and a large wooden desk. There are some huge windows at the side of the room, with the sun shooting through, blinding us, and there are two other men who look like guards standing either side of the man in the leather jacket.

"This way," the man who led us here says to us. We obey.

"Yes?" the man behind the desk bellows to the man who led us here.

"These three seek refuge here, General," he explains. "I brought them to you to state their business."

"Very well, leave them with me. Thank you, Canine," the general says, nodding.

"Very good, sir," Canine says as he leaves us and walks away. He goes and stands at the other side of the room, positioning himself right next to the door, and shapes himself like a statue. He glares over at us, piercing us with his eyes. Well, I think he is piercing us with his eyes; I am actually struggling to see them.

"Please excuse Canine," the general says to us. "He can be a bit official." He rises from his seat. "Personally, I just want people to feel comfortable in our presence."

He makes his way towards a plant on a desk nearby and pours some water on it. "Please sit," he says to us. We turn, grabs some chairs nearby and sit in front of the desk. "Now, state your business," he says as he walks over and sits down.

We look at each other, a little hesitant.

"Don't worry, I don't bite," the general laughs reassuringly. We look at each other once more.

"We seek refuge here," Amrit says, finally breaking our silence. I look at the wall with its posters bearing the symbol of the hand, the hammer and the circle.

"You wish to seek refuge in our humble little town?" the

man remarks. "Well, my name is General Singh, and we can use all the help we can get."

We look at each other, all feeling a little better about ourselves, yet wondering what he might have planned for us.

"We can't just allow anybody into this city. We need people who can contribute to our society. Now, who are we? I'm sure you have seen our symbol all over the place." He points to the symbol on the poster, then stands to step beside it. "I take it you don't know what this means? Well, the hand is the unity of all us in society together, the hammer is the hard work we put in to build our society, and the circle also represents the unity of one society, one community moving forward."

"How do you keep people working for you?" I ask him. Amrit and Rhea give me the dirtiest looks in the world. General Singh just laughs to himself and looks at me.

"Well, it's simple," he begins. "People love structure, they love order. So when we tell people to work for a better tomorrow within the structure, they jump at the opportunity. That is how the Union survives: human nature plays its part."

We look at each other, then at him once again.

"Now, who are you, may I ask?"

Again we look at each other, seeing who will answer first.

"Well, let's start with you." He points at Rhea. "What is your name and how old are you?"

"Um," Rhea reluctantly replies, "my name is Rhea Brigs and I'm twenty-two years old."

"Very good. Now you," he says, looking at me sitting in the middle.

"My name is Layton Rai and I'm twenty-four years old," I say. To be fair, we are only guessing our ages. Nobody really knows how old they are. It's hard to say because we're only working it out based on the last time we were told. I could be years older for all I know, or even years younger. Nobody celebrates birthdays, probably because there is no reason to do so.

"OK, very good. Now you." He points to Amrit.

"My name is Amrit Johal and I'm twenty-six years old."

"Very good. Well, my name is Avatar Singh and I am fifty years old," he says to us, and smiles. "This is my, well, what you could call my base of operations." He rises to his feet and begins to pace around the room. "Now, you want to be a part of our little community here?" he asks, looking at us individually.

"Yes, we do," Amrit replies without hesitation.

"Well, if you wish to be a part of our community, then you will have to prove your worth," General Singh informs us.

"OK," I say, "what do you want us to do?"

He looks at us and I know that he has already made up his mind. He makes a show of contemplating it, but I can tell that he knew what he wanted to do with us the second we walked in.

"Well," he turns to us, "if you wish to be a part of this community, then you will have to prove your worth. I cannot admit you to the general population until you have done so. We have a housing unit in Oadby, not far from here. We already have a group stationed there, so I would like you to go there and just keep an eye on it. There have been a lot of border monkeys around the area and we need more people there to defend our outward branch."

We look at each other, confused.

"Why can't you just let us in?" Rhea asks him, quite forthright. "You have no reason to distrust us."

"I also have no reason to trust you," General Singh interrupts her. He then paces back over to his seat and sits down. He opens a drawer and pulls out a cigar, puts it between his lips, lights it and begins to puff away. "You know, it is actually against my religion to smoke," he says before taking another drag of his cigar. "Well, I guess that's no use now, considering how things have come to be. What's the point in holding on to old charms?"

He reaches into his pocket and pulls out a gun. He places it gently on the table and turns it to face us.

"Now, you see, in this world the only religion is power. What is the definition of power, we might ask? Is it somebody who controls another human being, or somebody who gains respect from another human being?"

I can feel his tone beginning to change, and become a lot more rapid and firm. He raises the gun on the table and points it at Rhea.

"Now see, if I was to shoot you between the eyes, would I gain power from the fear your little buddies would have of me, or would I be respected? That is power; power is uncontrollable and unpredictable." He clicks the safety catch. "Should I shoot you, or should I shoot him?" he says, pointing the gun at Amrit. "Or him?" he adds, pointing at me. "No," he says, and points the gun once more at Rhea. "You are far more valuable here. Do you know what we do with our valuable people?" he asks, as she sits there frozen. She shakes her head, and I can see her go to cover her hands, as if they are beginning to sweat from being nervous in this man's presence.

"Well, we help them," he says, and his tone suddenly becomes a lot brighter. "We help them help us be incorporated into our family."

We look at each other, clueless.

"First things first, you will have to stay in one of the dorms. Then in two days' time you three and some others will be shipped off to our outpost. There you will stay for as long as we need you to stay, then we will call you back. Simple." He is about to get up, but sits down once again. "Or perhaps you will be of more use staying right here; I haven't quite decided."

"What about food and provisions?" Amrit asks him. General Singh takes a puff of his cigar, then looks at Amrit.

"Those are the things you will have to find for yourselves," he says as he puffs once again on his cigar. "We have limited supplies and can't just hand them out to new recruits," he tells us, a false note of sympathy in his voice.

"Then why take us in?" Rhea asks him.

"Because you're here," he replies. "Also, we could do with the extra soldiers. If you work hard enough you may even get to Canine's level – who knows?"

He makes a fist and bangs on the table. Suddenly two of his soldiers come marching into the room. They are dressed top to bottom in Union clothing, with the symbols on their chests.

"OK, men, take these three to the dorms. Make sure they are clothed and fed."

They come and stand directly behind us.

"First of all," the general says, "we can't have you going around with all those weapons on yourselves; we have to confiscate them."

We all sit there, stunned, looking at one another, perplexed at his demand.

"No, we need them," Rhea says, standing up.

"You can't take these off us," Amrit says, also standing up.

"Yeah," I agree.

"Oh," General Singh says, "but I must."

Two other men come closer to us and stand just a few metres away. The men standing right behind us take our bags and start searching us for more weapons.

"Hey," I say begrudgingly. Amrit reluctantly hands over his knife and tries not to look at them as he does so. Rhea has other plans.

"Go away," she shouts, pushing one of the guards away. "You can't do that."

"Now, there is no need for that," General Singh says. "If you keep your weapons," he adds, still puffing on his cigar, "then we can't have you staying here. If we have people who aren't resident here just entering our community with weapons, you will be seen as invaders. Therefore, we will have no choice but to defend ourselves, so we will have to kill you."

We hear the guards behind us pull out their guns and take off the safety. We turn and see several guns pointing at us.

"So, the choice is all yours."

We stop for a moment, looking at one another. I look at Amrit and he murmurs his lips. I can tell he is trying to think of something to say, but can't think of the words. We both look over at Rhea and she just shakes her head at us, showing us her answer. Amrit looks down for a moment; then up at General Singh, and takes a deep breath.

"OK," Amrit says, and hands the weapons over. He looks at Rhea, suggesting that she just doesn't argue and gets in line.

"Fine," Rhea states, and takes her weapons out and thrusts them at the guard behind her. I decide to follow suit, handing over my machete and knife. We all sit down, feeling naked without our weapons to protect us.

"Very good," General Singh says. He then gestures with his hand and Canine comes and stands right behind us.

"Yes, sir."

"Escort these people to their dorms," General Singh instructs.

"Yes, sir," Canine says. "On your feet," he shouts at us.

All three of us get up and are escorted out of the room.

"Good luck," General Singh says to us as we leave.

We are taken through the giant door and can hear the thud as it closes behind us. The next stop for us is the dorms, which I have no idea about. Personally, I have a feeling that it is going to be like a prison. I think we have made a major mistake in coming here.

I daren't tell Amrit and Rhea that I feel this way, just in case it worries them; in case they want it to be a great life for us and me feeling this way throws it all out of whack. I suppose the main reason I don't want them to know how I feel is because I am afraid they will feel the same way I do. That would be worrying.

10

We are guided through the streets to a giant building. We look up and down, gazing at the magnitude of it. It has its own unique look, resembling an old student's residence. There are a lot of windows and the building actually looks quite nice, not as boarded up like most of the places I have become accustomed to.

We are taken to the door, where there is a guard keeping watch. He looks us up and down, then opens the door. Canine takes us through the door and up the stairs. Of course, the lifts aren't working. Rhea, Amrit and I are pushed by Canine behind us up the stairs, which just keep going and going.

"Keep going, you scoundrels," Canine barks at us.

We are not told where we are going or who we are going to see. All I know is that this place could really do with a paint job. The walls look like they used to be white, now they seem to have more of a grey colour.

"Wait there," Canine says when we get to the fourth floor.

"Where to now?" I mutter to myself, hoping nobody hears me.

"Say something, did you?" Canine snaps. He storms towards me and gets right in my face, right in there so that I can smell his breath. He stares at me, and his eyes feel like laser beams.

"Is that a question?" I ask, confused.

"Yes, did you say something?" he asks me.

"No," I reply, shitting myself slightly.

"That's a lie. I heard you," he says. Then why ask? I think to myself. If you already know the answer, or if you are not going to care about what I say, then why even ask me the question? What a dick!

"OK," I say.

"That's enough out of you until you get to your dorm," he demands. "Is that understood?"

I don't say anything this time, I just give him a courteous nod. He takes a step back, turns and begins to thump his way ahead of us. Amrit, Rhea and I follow as we are guided through a corridor which looks to have many rooms branching off it. There are doors with numbers on them. Yet for some reason, they don't look like flats. They all look like bedrooms. We walk past and peer into the ones which are open. I can see a person fast asleep in a bed, and they do look reasonably comfortable. We are led through the corridor towards another door. Canine opens it, and I am surprised by what I see. We are taken inside and I can see a kitchen and what looks like a living room. There are three people sitting in the room, and they stand as soon as Canine takes us inside.

"You three stand there," he commands us as soon as we walk into the room.

We stand there gazing over at the other three facing us. Two girls and a guy, they look around the same age as us, which is handy.

"These are your new housemates," Canine says to the three standing on the other side of the room. "They will be having rooms 5, 9 and 12. Make sure they settle in, and tomorrow they will be reporting for work duty."

He then turns for the door and makes his way out of the building. Us six, I guess I should say, are left staring at each

97

other with that perfect mix of awkwardness and discomfort. I look at one of the girls and she stares back at me; I quickly turn away like a pathetic child, as if I have just learned how to use the toilet.

"Hi," this girl with black hair says, walking towards us and smiling. "My name's Becky."

"Hi, I'm Amrit," Amrit says, shaking her hand. "This is Layton and Rhea." Rhea and I wave.

"Hi, my name's Mark," a guy in the middle with cornrows says to us. He is much taller than Amrit and me, and has much more of a booming voice. "How do you do?" he asks, holding his hand out to me.

"I'm fine, thanks," I respond, shaking his hand.

"I'm Jane." The blonde girl on the end smiles. She comes up to hold her hand out in front of Rhea. Rhea shakes it and nods back at her. "Ryan's still asleep at the moment. He does the late shift. He'll probably be up in a couple of hours," she tells us, looking at the door.

"Cool," I reply awkwardly. "So," I say, pacing around the room, "what do you guys do for fun around here?"

They all look blankly at me.

"Well," Mark says, "there is nothing really fun to do around here." He walks over to a chair to take a seat. "I mean, we work, then when we are done working, we just come back here and eat, shit, then sleep," he tells us while sitting down and stretching his legs.

"Lovely," Rhea says.

"Not the way I would put it," Becky says to Mark. "Besides, you lot must be starving, let me get you guys something to eat."

"We are pretty hungry," Amrit says as Becky pulls out some tinned noodles and pours them into a pan.

"I take it that we have to tell you all of the rules, then?" Becky says. "We get our work duty, which will be allocated to you tomorrow. Work starts at eight so you have to be up and ready by 7.30, no later. Canine is head of this block, so he will send his guards to take us to the right places. Work finishes at five, then the late shift starts at six. Lunch is at your work duty; though for breakfast and dinner, you're on your own. Also, nobody out after curfew."

"Curfew?" Amrit asks, confused.

"Yes, curfew. After curfew, which is ten by the way, unless you are on a late shift, you are not allowed out. Your will be given your badges tomorrow," she tells us.

"Oh, fun," I respond sarcastically.

"Oh, sarcasm, I love sarcasm," Becky retorts.

"Yeah, well—" I say, smiling.

"They don't," she interrupts. "You are not to be rude or cheeky, or else we could all get punished."

"OK," Rhea says.

"Well, as you guys are here," Mark says, "how's about we have a little welcoming party?" He walks out of the living room and heads to his room. We all look at each other, baffled. He then returns with a plastic bottle with an orange liquid inside. "My own recipe," he tells us, looking at the bottle.

"Is that what I think it is?" I ask him.

"Yup, my very own hooch," Mark says with an element of pride in his voice. "They don't allow alcohol on the premises, so we have to be a little more inventive," he tells us, admiring what he has made.

"How did you make it?" Rhea asks.

"Ah, now that is a secret," he answers, winking at her. Rhea gives him a little smile as Mark makes his way to the cupboard and takes out a few glasses.

"This stuff is lethal," Jane states as Mark starts pouring.

"Well, I guess one couldn't hurt," I say.

"Is this a good idea, considering we have to be up early tomorrow?" Amrit says.

"Oh, come on, you tool," I say. "Have a drink – when was the last time we had a chance to have one?"

"I suppose," Amrit says.

"Just one drink, bud," Mark says, handing him a glass. "We're not looking to get shit-faced here."

"Oh, fuck it," Amrit says as we all take a glass each. "Here's to us."

"To new roommates and hopefully new friends," Mark says, raising his glass to us.

We all take a sip and the hooch is nothing to be desired. It is sour and bitter, and burns the tongue. We all just about take one sip, then pull away. Even Mark can only handle one little sip and he's the guy who created this drink. Then we turn and see Rhea downing the drink. She tilts the glass and drinks until the glass is completely empty. She then turns and looks at us, as we all stand there, confused.

"What?" she asks as we all stare at her, amazed.

"Nothing," I say. She smiles and sticks her middle finger up at me. We all laugh and continue to finish our glasses, and Mark pours more hooch into Rhea's glass.

An hour later and the bottle is now empty. We are all gathered around in a circle with the empty bottle in front of us. The noodles we were supposed to eat are in a bowl in front of us, but nobody seems to want to have at it. I feel euphoria, a sense of freedom, and also a sickly sensation. I believe I may be in a vortex of drunkenness. I sit there leaning my back against the wall, trying to stop myself collapsing on the floor.

"I like you," I hear a voice say to me. I turn, and it is Jane right next to me with her blonde hair covering one of her eyes.

"Well, I think you're OK yourself," I respond, feeling a little awkward.

"Come to my room," she says. "I've got something to show you." She forces her hand into mine and holds it very tight.

"Um, OK," I say. We get up and start walking.

"Uh-oh, Jane's at it again," Becky says, chuckling to herself.

"Is she usually like this?" Rhea asks, smirking.

"Yes, she is," Becky replies. "Whenever she has a drink she just wants to get into the pants of the first guy she sees."

"No, I don't!" Jane shouts at her. "I just want to show him something." She leads me away from the group and I can hear them chuckling to themselves. She takes me down the corridor to a bedroom, swings open the door and drags me inside.

"OK," I say, turning to her, "so what did you want to show me?"

"I wanted to show you something underneath my..." she begins, then gulps. I look at her and she blinks a lot, then tries again. "I wanted to show you the..." She gulps again.

"Are you OK?" I ask her, concerned.

"I'm fine," she says. "I just think you're a really good-looking guy, and that's not the hooch talking," she gulps.

"I think you might need some water," I suggest, feeling awkward.

"No, I don't need... oh shit." She bends down and throws up right in front of me.

"Ah!" I gasp, moving out the way as she spews vomit all over the floor in front of me. I quickly step away as the yellowy goo trickles towards me like lava. The smell is as bad as it looks, like stale alcohol and food.

"I'm fine," she says, wiping her mouth. "We can still get off with each other," she suggests, breathing quite heavily.

"No, I'm OK, thanks," I reply. "I'll let you clean up."

"Fine then, you frigid twat," she shouts.

"A little unnecessary," I say as I turn and walk out of her room and head back towards the living room.

"Wanker," she calls out.

"OK," I say.

I make my way back to the living room to find everybody

still sitting in a circle. A new person is standing there too; a man with dark hair and glasses.

"Hi, my name's Ryan," he says to me.

"Hello," I respond awkwardly.

"I take it you had a bit of Jane then?" Ryan says.

"Yeah, he did," Mark responds in a jolly tone.

"Yeah," I say. "Well, if by 'had a bit of her', you mean she threw up all over the place, then yeah, that just happened."

They all look at me, smiling.

"Typical. Come take a seat, Casanova," Mark says to me.

"Thank you," I say.

"Did you notice her breath?" he asks me as soon as I sit down.

"Yeah," I say, confused. "It's really bad."

"In case you're wondering," Ryan says, "Mark and I have both had a go on Jane. We noticed her bad breath."

"Yeah, even Becky's had a go," Mark says to us. We all turn and look at Becky.

"What? I was lonely and she was easy," Becky says. "Well, I thought she would be good, but she just threw up all over the place, I think the hooch is not good for getting it on, especially for Jane."

"Same with us," Mark says, looking at Ryan.

"So she just throws up?" I ask them.

"Or passes out," Mark tells us.

We look up and can see Jane come staggering back into the room, laughing to herself. She comes over and sits next to Rhea.

"Hi," she says her, croaking as she speaks.

"Hi," Rhea replies jokingly, looking at the rest of us awkwardly as Jane gets closer and closer to her.

"I love your hair," Jane says.

"Thanks," Rhea responds awkwardly.

"You have really nice skin," Jane says. "I wonder how it tastes?" she asks, licking her lips.

"Oh my God, is this happening?" Rhea says.

Jane puts her arm around Rhea's shoulders and begins to kiss her on the neck.

"Wow, this is awkward," Rhea says. "Feel free to stop her, anyone."

"Hey, I did it, now you have to," I say.

"Oi, I'm not," Jane responds, trying to hold in more puke. "I'm a woman," she says as she puts her legs over Rhea and starts kissing her. Rhea squeals slightly as Jane forces her to the ground. Jane continues to kiss her, then suddenly stops. We look over, wondering why she stopped.

"Is she OK?" Amrit asks.

"Jane?" Becky says. She is completely still.

"She's fine, listen," Ryan says. Suddenly, we hear it: a giant snore from Jane as she lies there motionless on top of Rhea.

"OK, can somebody get her off me?" Rhea calls out to us.

"Oh, but you look adorable," Amrit says sarcastically.

"Fuck you," Rhea says. "Her breath really stinks."

Mark pulls Jane off Rhea and throws her over his shoulder.

"I think it's time for bed anyway," Becky says to us.

"Yup, and it's time I went to work," Ryan explains. "See you all later."

I walk into the corridor and up to the door of my room. I open it and walk inside. There is nothing special about it: just a room, a desk and a bed. I know the bathroom is down the hall because I saw it. Saying that it does look comfortable. Yeah, I think I could get used to this place. I guess I am ready to call somewhere home. I think I was exaggerating before, but now, on reflection, I think we're in the right place. I think everything is going to be OK from now on.

11

I wake the following morning and my stomach is twisting around, feeling like it is doing somersaults. I try to sit up, but the heaviness is too much for me to handle. I just about manage to open my eyes. As soon as I do, my head begins to sting as soon as I get the first glimmer of light, so I shut them immediately.

I lie there, in pain. The pain is then followed swiftly by a sickly feeling. This is followed very closely by regret. I am having what they would call a hangover. The only saving grace is that I suspect everybody is feeling this way. It was a very good night, a pleasant way to get everybody in the mood.

Shit, I've got work today as well. I hope that I get a bit of time to recover. I wonder what would happen if I just decided to call in sick? I'm guessing there are no sick days here. Why am I even here? I've managed just fine on my own for so long. I always had the philosophy that staying by myself, watching out only for myself, would be the key to survival. How have I managed to end up in a community? Why am I now working for somebody? Well, I guess it's not all bad. I did get a bit of action last night – if you call seeing a girl puke up in front of you a bit of action. Her breath really did stink, though.

I finally sit up, feeling bloated from all the booze the night before. I lean forward to try and get the air out of my stomach, but it doesn't come to anything. I slowly look up and see a clock in front of me: 6.45. Fuck me, I guess I better get up and get ready for work duty. Why do I have to work? Why can't they just feed me and bathe me? I won't complain.

I finally rise from my bed and stagger over to the door. I open it and look outside to see Amrit leaning against a wall near the bathroom door. I go over to him to see if he is all right. He is rolling his head on the wall, pushing it as if to try and get his head to go through.

"All right, mate?" I croak.

"Err," he replies. I think that is his drunken way of saying good morning.

"Who we waiting for?" I ask him.

"Rhea," he says abruptly.

"Oh." I stare at the door, as if I could just open it and have Rhea get out so that I can puke my guts out. This is probably the longest Amrit and I have gone without speaking. It's amazing. The more I think about that, the more my head hurts. I stand there and lean my head against the wall. Before I know it, my eyes close once again. I try to open them, but they feel better closed. I feel better not having to strain my eyes too much. I look down the corridor and see Mark in full work attire. He walks past us and nods.

"Morning," he belts out in an unnaturally chirpy tone.

"Hey," I respond, and Amrit nods.

"Oh yeah," Mark says to us, "your work clothes are in the wardrobes in your bedrooms. I suggest you get changed into them once you're washed up."

Our heads continue to spin in circles, playing havoc with our stomachs. Mark turns and starts walking towards the living room.

"The fucking wardrobes creek too much" I say to Amrit.

"Why is he so chipper?" Amrit asks me, groaning.

105

"I have no idea," I reply. Amrit shrugs at me and continues to watch the door.

Suddenly the bathroom door swings wide open and I can see Rhea standing there. She has nothing on but a towel around her torso. I don't know why but I can't stop looking at her. I think it's probably because this is the first time I have seen her like this.

"Hey," she says to Amrit and me. Amrit slouches his way into the bathroom. For some reason I can't help but just gaze at her. "How are you?" she asks me.

"I'm fine," I say, still taken aback by what I am seeing.

"Cool." She smiles and turns to head towards her room. I can't take my eyes off her. Why do I keep staring at her? Those piercing blue eyes, like drops of water. Stop it, you're going to make a scene. Just look away, look elsewhere.

I can't; I have to look at her once more. She turns to me and smiles; a smile I know I will remember and won't be able to forget. Finally, she closes the door. I feel relieved that I can stop looking at her, but sad too.

I stand there for a few moments, just staring at the cream wall in front of me. I gaze at it, noticing the different cracks that have appeared there. I wonder how many people have walked past that wall, brushed their hands on it? When this place was a halls of residence, how many students walked back and forth, not even noticing this wall? I wish I could jump into the memories this wall must have; see the sights it has seen. I wish that I could go back to that time. I wish I was a student at that time – from the sounds of it, student life in England was pretty fun. Unfortunately, that is all in the past now; this is the new reality.

Suddenly the bathroom door opens and Amrit comes staggering out. He doesn't even notice me, and heads straight to his room. I quickly turn and walk inside.

The bathroom is very bright; too bright for mornings. The light shines down, covering the room in a cloud of yellow.

I stagger to the bright white toilet and undo my flies. It feels like forever since I've had a piss. Finally I unload into the toilet. Fuck me, that feels good. That feels fucking good. Fuck me, this fucking piss feels fucking amazing, fuck. I finish, flush the toilet and make my way to the sink. I quickly wash my hands, then my face. I look down, and I have an allocated toothbrush just sitting there. It is white with bristles, nothing fancy. I squeeze toothpaste onto my brush and begin to brush. I'm not going to lie, it has been a while since I brushed my teeth, so I just keep brushing and it feels good. It feels like months of dirt and muck are being washed away and my teeth will finally be spotless. I rinse and spit, feeling a sensation I haven't felt for a while. For the first time in ages, a part of me feels clean.

I leave the bathroom and head back to my bedroom. Now, where is that wardrobe? I look and see it straight away: a brown box in the corner of the room. Hardly what I would call a wardrobe. Saying that, it's hardly what I would call a box. I sift through and find fresh pants, socks, boots and what looks like a blue boiler suit. I take my old, manky clothes off and put the suit on. The pants feel so good and fresh. The socks are tickling my toes as I put them on, so cosy and warm. After I put the boiler suit on I put the boots on. How did they know my size? Doesn't matter – all that matters is that it all fits. I turn around and head for the door; I need to get some food in me if I'm going to start the working day.

I enter the living room and see everybody in their blue boiler suits gathered around the counter. I head towards them and see what it is we are eating for breakfast. Porridge, yum, I think to myself. Well, I guess it's better than nothing. I look over and see Amrit slowly shovelling porridge into his mouth, chewing very slowly. Rhea is eating too; I notice her hair is tied back, with her headband around her head, keeping it all in place; this isn't anything new. I look at her face. Her eyes; I cant help but somehow get a little caught up in them – she has such deep-set eyes. Her skin is so fair, yet rosy. Her hair is dark and enchanting. Wow, I am sounding like a flowery idiot right now. Let's have some of that porridge.

"Here, mate," Mark says to me, pouring me a bowl.

"What time is it?" I ask him.

"It's 7:20am, so eat up quick," he says. "Roll call is at 7:45am" I can't help but think to myself that an hour ago I was fast asleep. I quickly wolf down the porridge and feel it burning my tongue. I know that I have to eat it, but can't get past the burning sensation. I look over and see Jane standing in the corner of the room.

"Morning, Jane," I say, trying to be a dick and make her feel as awkward as possible for some reason.

"Hi," she responds, not really bothered.

"We already had our awkward moment," Rhea says, pointing to Jane. "I guess it's only fair that the two of you have yours." I look at Jane and chuckle to myself.

"Sorry about last night," Jane says to me, sounding embarrassed. "I don't know what came over me."

"It's fine. It was kind of fun really," I say, trying to not make her feel as bad. "I guess it will be Amrit's turn tonight?"

Amrit gives me a very dodgy look.

"If he plays his cards right," Jane suggests. She gives him a wink and heads out of the door.

"Unbelievable," Amrit remarks.

"I know," Mark says, "she's a proper slag, isn't she?"

"Charming," Becky says in the background

"I felt violated," Rhea says, causing us to chuckle slightly to ourselves.

"I would say that, but we didn't get a chance to get to that stage, unfortunately," I respond. Rhea rolls her eyes at me and chuckles to herself.

"Oh well, her loss, mate," Mark says, and we high-five like a couple of bros. "On that note, it's time for roll call."

We all put down our bowls and make our way out of the dorm. We head straight down the stairs and outside. In front of us is Canine in his usual intimidation gear, and there are five vans behind him. There is a guard stationed at every one of them. The rest of the halls empties out onto the street as we form a queue near the vans.

"Quickly now," Canine calls out to us. We all assemble in front of him, not one of us out of place. I look around and it looks like there are about forty of us lining up. Everybody is silent. Canine paces up and down, looking at us as if we are a regiment about to go into battle.

"OK. Cell Block A will go in this van," he says, pointing at the van on the end. As soon as he says it, everybody from Cell Block A runs straight into the van and it heads off. "Cell Block G will go in this van," he continues, pointing at the next van. As before, Cell Block G get in the van. "Cell Block H in this van."

"That's us," Mark mutters. We all scurry together and rush into the back of the van. As soon as the last one of us gets our foot inside, the doors shut behind us as we are on our way. We can't actually see where we are going, however it feels like there are a lot of turns involved. I look up and see a sign on the ceiling which states, Silence in the van, which I'm guessing means I got to shut my mouth. No problem – I will make my own entertainment in my mind; let my imagination take me away. I got nothing.

"We're here," the driver calls out, stopping abruptly. The doors fly wide open and we are escorted out of the van. A guard is standing there waiting for us.

"Get in line," he says.

We queue up before the doors of what looks like a factory. There is a slow-moving queue in front of us, with a guard stationed at regular intervals. Another guard walks up and down the queue, barking out orders.

"Jewellery is fine; any sharp objects which could be seen as a weapon will be confiscated and you will be punished," he says. "I repeat, jewellery is fine, any sharp objects which could be seen as a weapon will be confiscated and you will be punished."

We are patted down and then sent inside. Another guard takes our block and escorts us to a work station. The noise is incredible. There is a real hustle and bustle, with rows of people talking to one another, darting back and forth and working hard. Guards walk up and down the rows, keeping their eyes on all of the workers. I guess it's only travelling to and from work when they don't like chatter. Maybe the guards aren't morning people, but while you're working they don't care if you talk shit as long as the work is done. Fair enough.

"OK, you lot," a man shouts, gathering our block together. He calls us to the corner of the room. He has slicked-back brown hair and wears glasses. "This is for the newbies. I know some of you have met me before; my name is Rob. Do as I say and the job will be done and nobody gets in trouble. Decide not to do so, and I will make your life difficult and you will be punished, understand?"

We all nod to show that we do.

"Good, come with me." We follow him to another work station. "We have a lot of litter here," he says as we look at the piles of rubbish in front of us. "Now, what we need is for you to sort the metals and the plastics. Anything else goes in the bins. Simple, not easy to fuck up. Get it done." He then walks off and leaves us to it.

"Well, he's charming," Amrit remarks sarcastically.

"Yeah, a real inspiration," she states sarcastically.

We all chuckle and get on with the work. Opposite me, I can see Rhea working away.

"You OK?" I ask her

"Yeah, I'm good," she responds. "How about you?"

"I'm good."

We continue separating the metal and plastic.

"So, Layton," Mark calls out to me, "what would you rather?"

"What?" I ask him.

"Bit tits or big ass?"

"Um…"

"Seriously?" Becky says.

"Probably tits," I respond.

"What about you?" he asks Amrit.

Amrit looks up, then awkwardly looks down. "Um… I'm not sure."

"Come on, mate," Mark says, "everyone has a preference."

Amrit looks at me as if to drag out an answer he can latch on to. He looks down at his plastic, then back at Mark again.

"OK," Amrit says, "probably ass."

"An ass man?" Mark says.

I chuckle and get back to the can in my hands, which is stuck to a piece of plastic that has meshed with the paper label.

"I can't believe we have to do this with our bare hands," I say out loud.

"I know, it's rank," Jane states from across the work station.

"This is just unsanitary conditions," I say. "The Union must know this; they must know it's unhealthy."

"Does it matter?" Becky asks. I look at her, then up at the giant symbol of the Union on the wall.

"No, not really." I decide to get on with my work instead of causing trouble.

We continue working for another few hours, doing the same thing over and over again. The time flies because we spend the morning talking about random bullshit. Then suddenly a buzzer goes.

"Lunch," calls a man over a tannoy.

"This way," Becky says to us.

We turn and head down the factory, past all of the different work stations. We enter a giant hall which has a sign on the top saying CAFETERIA. There are rows of workers sitting together eating lunch; old workers, young workers – a real mishmash of people everywhere. We get in the queue and a group of other workers in grey boiler suits serve us all food. It's strange, though; the people serving don't look very well fed. They're all so skinny. I try not to think too much about it.

We all pick up a tray and are served two sandwiches, an apple and a drink. The drink is water, by the way; nothing too crazy. I collect my food and make my way through the hordes of people, and manage to find a spare table for us to sit at. I quickly sit down with Mark, Becky, Jane and Amrit, with Rhea following closely behind.

"Wow, the queue's huge," she says as she plants her tray on the table. Suddenly a large, round, red-headed girl bumps into the back of her. "Sorry," Rhea says, even though she wasn't the one who did the bumping.

"Fucking watch where you're going!" the girl shouts, her face turning red.

"Excuse me?" Rhea replies, confused.

"Yeah, you dopey bitch, watch where you're going."

"Fuck you," Rhea spits, walking forward to confront her.

"What did you say, toothpick?" the girl shouts, glaring at her.

"Enough," a voice calls out. We turn and see a guard standing there, staring at the girl.

"Yeah, watch your back," the girl says as she is pulled away by her friends who are standing right behind her.

"Come on, sit down," I say to Rhea, gently grabbing her by the arm and drawing her towards her seat. She continues to stare in the direction of the girl as she takes her seat.

"Who the fuck is she?" she asks.

"That's Scarlett; best to stay out of her way," Becky responds as she takes a sip of water.

"Why, what's she like?" I ask. She is about to respond when Jane interrupts her.

"She knocked me out once. I was minding my own business

just walking through the yard and she just punched me out of nowhere. Then her little friends started kicking me. They ran off when a guard came round the corner," she tells us.

"Shit, I'm so sorry, Jane," Rhea says.

"It's fine."

"So she's just a bully," Rhea remarks.

We sit there eating our lunch. I look in my sandwich and it is corned beef. Not the greatest taste, but not the worst. We finish our lunch, then head out into the yard. We are allocated forty-five minutes for lunch. We finished eating in fifteen, which means we have thirty minutes to doss about.

"Yo, Amrit," Mark calls out as he throws him a football.

"Nice," Amrit says. We all start to kick it around, passing the ball to one another. I try to perform some skills. Unfortunately due to my lack of skills, I fail in my attempt.

"Over here," Rhea calls out. I pass the ball to her and she starts to do some kick-ups.

"Check you out," I say.

"Try and tackle me," she challenges. I run towards her and she manages to bypass me, with the ball still at her feet. "You aren't good enough for these skills," she says. Rhea then runs past Mark and Amrit and manages to pass the ball through their legs, while still keeping control of it. She even throws in a few spins before facing them.

"OK, I'll get in goal. That bin and that bench is the goal." Mark points, standing in between them.

"OK," I say, "get past Amrit and me."

Rhea looks at us, passing the ball back and forth between her feet.

"Yeah, go on," Amrit says.

"Come on, Rhea!" Becky calls out from the bench on the other side where she and Jane are sitting like Rhea's cheerleading squad.

"OK," Rhea says. She then starts running with the ball and

I decide to try and get it off her. I run at her, but she crosses the ball over, causing me to fall flat on my face.

"Shit," I mutter to myself. Rhea then goes up against Amrit, who comes storming out at her. He tries to take the ball off her, and she spins around, causing him to fall flat on his face as well.

"Ah!" he shouts as Rhea whizzes past him.

"All right, come on then," Mark says as Rhea comes storming towards him with the ball. He runs towards her, and Rhea stops, flicks the ball up and kicks it up a few times. Mark gets a little bit closer to her, leaving a gap between him and the goal.

"Watch out," Rhea calls out, flicking the ball over Mark. He turns and sees the ball go over him and bounce its way into the goal.

"Woo – go Rhea!" Becky cheers from the sidelines.

"Go Rhea, go Rhea," Jane cheers.

"Well, that was good," I say to her.

"Next time I'll give you guys a chance," she patronisingly declares. I chuckle with her as Mark runs off to try and get the ball, Amrit following. Then I see somebody coming up behind Rhea.

"Oh, watch out," I say as Scarlett walks up and nudges Rhea in the back.

"Watch where you're walking, bitch," Scarlett calls out as she walks past. Rhea just gives her a dirty look as Scarlett walks away with her friends.

"You OK?" I ask, as she looks a little shaken up.

"You know what?" she says. "I'm just going to ignore her. All she wants is a response out of me, but I don't care."

"Good on you," I say.

Before we know it, we are back to work. Back sorting the shit out to find the clean shit compared to the shit shit. It is a long, boring job, but Mark keeps us entertained by telling us about how he once got a mouse into Rob's office and scared the shit out of him. It entertains us until the final buzzer goes, ending our working day.

We all get back into queues and into the vans once more. The vans take us back to the dorms, the only time when we are silent throughout the day. We are dropped off outside our halls and all of a sudden with no hesitation, the vans are gone. We stagger our way up the stairs to our cell block and into the cell.

"Hey," I say to Ryan as he is getting ready for work. He nods, and I mosey my way back to my room.

With a giant thud, I collapse onto my bed. The room is spinning from how tired I am. I look at my hands and they are blistered and bruised. I think I have officially done a hard day's work. Same thing tomorrow, I guess. Roll on tomorrow, I suppose. Now I think about it, I actually did enjoy today. This is something I could get very used to.

12

Water everywhere. I look around and can see nothing but the blue ocean surrounding me. I try to swim out. My arms don't seem to have the ability to do so. All I do is pivot, not getting anywhere. I look up at the surface, trying to head in that direction.

Why can't I move? I can't see anything around me but the deep blue darkness engulfing me. I feel an urge to just let go; let myself sink down to the depths, letting go of everything. I should let myself go. I begin to sing, feeling the water flow over me, pushing me further down. My eyes are beginning to sting from the salt; maybe if I close them, I will begin to soothe myself.

As soon as I do, I feel as if I can't breathe. Every breath I try to take feels as if it is the last I am ever going to take. I feel faint, and begin to panic. All I can do is drift into a deep sleep and away from it all.

I wake shaking my head, trying to see clearly. I feel far more refreshed than I did yesterday. I quickly skip to the bathroom and do my morning routine of brushing my teeth and washing my face, not forgetting my morning piss; then head straight back to my room to get my boiler suit on. As soon as that is all done, I head straight to the living room for breakfast where I see everybody congregated eating porridge once again.

"So how did you find your first day?" Becky asks me as I sit down with my breakfast. "You crashed out as soon as we got home last night."

"Yeah, it was good; I was just so tired from actually working for once," I state as I feel my legs about to relax once again into slumber.

"Welcome to the working world," she responds jovially.

I sit and dig into the bowl of oats in front of me, slushing them into my mouth and feeling the warmth go down my throat. I look over and see Rhea sitting at the other end of the room.

"Morning, Rhea," I say as she scrapes the bottom of her bowl for the remaining crumbs.

"Morning," she replies.

"Are you ready for another day in paradise?" I ask sarcastically.

"Yeah, I can't wait," she responds, equally sarcastically.

Suddenly Jane gets up and runs off to the toilet, slamming the door behind her.

"What's up with her?" I ask Becky.

"I don't know, she's been like that for the past few months. She's been eating more than usual. Not sure what it is."

"Huh," I say, confused. I look over and see Jane come out of the bathroom, wiping her face.

"You OK?" I ask her. She looks up at me and hesitates for a moment.

"I'm fine, thanks," she replies. I decide not to ask any more about it and allow her to go about her day.

We all finish our breakfast and head down the stairs for roll call. I find myself standing with the others in the regular formation, waiting for Canine to bark his orders at us.

"Is everybody here?" he shouts out.

We all look around; looks like everyone is here. I can't see anybody missing. Saying that, I don't really know everybody in the building so I can't exactly say for certain if they are here or not.

"Right then," Canine says. He turns, looming over us. He is about to speak when suddenly somebody comes running out of the building.

"Sorry, sir," the man says as he rushes to stand with Cell Block A. He looks half-dressed, as if he's just woken up.

"You're late," Canine says.

"Sorry, sir, I overslept," the man replies nervously.

Canine points to the guard standing by one of the vans, and he comes marching towards the man who was late. The guard pulls out a gun, points it at the man's back and tells him to walk. He nudges him forward and they walk around the back of the nearest building and out of our sight.

"Cell Block A," Canine continues, "you will be making your own way to work duty. I suggest you hurry up, you don't want to be late."

They stand there, confused, looking at each other and unable to make a decision as to what their next move should be.

"Now!" Canine shouts, and suddenly everybody in Cell Block A starts running aimlessly.

"Where do we go?" a woman cries out as they all rush forward, trying to get to work. Before we know it, they are scattered in front of us, running in circles until they are all eventually out of sight.

Canine then does the usual roll call and we are sent to the van that we were put in yesterday. We all sit there silently, this time feeling awkward.

Even when we get to work and are patted down, then go to our work station, it's a full ten minutes of silence until somebody finally speaks.

"Anybody got any plans for the weekend?" Jane calls out.

The weekend? I don't even know what day it is, let alone when it's the weekend.

"What day is it?" I ask hesitantly. They all laugh at me, then finally tell me.

"It's Thursday today, mate," Mark says. "We get a half-day some weekends; sometimes we even get the day off. Depends on how much work we do throughout the week."

"Fair enough."

We continue doing our work, splitting the plastic and metal from the paper. There is so much crap here; people really do waste a lot.

Before I know it, it's lunchtime and we are all sitting together at a table in the cafeteria. On today's menu is Spam sandwiches, not my ideal lunch, but I guess it will do. Then I see Rhea storming across the cafeteria.

"That bitch!" she yells as she slams down her tray.

"What happened?" Mark asks, concerned.

"That bitch Scarlett," Rhea says, "she keeps trying to piss me off. She tried to pull my hair, then when I moved out the way her and her little friends started laughing. Stupid bitch, I just want to kill her."

"I thought you said you're not going to let her bother you?" I ask.

"I know, but she is getting on my last nerve."

"If you want my advice," Jane says to Rhea, "I suggest you smack her one." This results in surprised looks from the rest of us.

"Jane," Becky says abruptly.

"It's true," Jane says, "she's just a bully, and she will keep being a bully until somebody fights back."

"I guess," Rhea says to herself. We all sit there eating, in awkward silence.

"Hey," Amrit says, suddenly perking up, "does anybody know what happened to Cell Block A?"

Mark and Becky look at one another, concerned.

"What?" Amrit asks.

"Well," Mark explains, "I heard from the work station behind us that the guy who was late was taken behind the residence, and after we left he was shot. The rest of Cell Block A, because none of us know how to get here, were lost and then they were picked up by other guards. Because they were late for work they were seen as skiving, so they were all beaten and now they are in punishment."

"What's punishment?" I ask.

Mark sighs slightly before answering.

"Punishment is when they send you to a giant room. They torture you, starve you and beat you; if you are woman they can sometimes take advantage of you down there." His hand begins to shake as he sips his water. "They will keep you there for as long as they want. They will keep you there for a day, maybe a week or a month – I know one person who has been there for about a year now. These are the rules the Union has brought in: you have to pull your own weight, and slackers will be punished. Some people have even died in there." He takes another sip of his water, then looks back at us. "When your punishment is done, they brand you. They get a hot metal rod and brand you with the symbol of the Union, so that you remember that the Union will always punish you if you cross them."

"That can't be true," I say, not wanting to believe it.

"It is," he replies, and undoes his boiler suit to show the symbol of the Union burned into his chest. We all gasp, looking at that symbol we have come to recognise, engraved on his flesh. It has left a reddish-pink outline on his chest, resulting in a very deep burn scar.

"What happened?" Rhea asks him. "If you don't mind me asking?"

"Well…" Mark begins. He hesitates for a moment, taking a deep breath, then another large gulp of water.

"Mark, you don't have to," Becky gently interrupts. Mark raises his hand to show that he is OK with telling us.

"Not too long after I came here from Nottingham, I was working very hard, trying to make a name for myself here. Everything was going well until I got in a tussle with some guy."

"What happened?" I ask.

"Well, I didn't agree with what the guy was doing, so I told him. He attacked me, so I attacked him back. I don't know what came over me; I just beat him into the ground. I just kept beating him and beating him. The guards just watched me beat the living shit out of this guy. Only after I was done did they jump in. They grabbed me and said that I had assaulted a fellow worker. The guy who took my sandwich was told he was being done for theft."

He takes a giant gulp of water this time. "They stripped me down to my underpants, tied my hands and feet together, and then tied my hands to the ceiling. They whipped me, beat me; they basically used me as a punchbag. I was there for three days, no food and no water. Right opposite me was the guy I beat up. He was hanging in front of me, being given the same torture I was. I had to watch him being beaten and he had to watch me. The only difference was, his body couldn't take it any more, so then I had to watch him die.

"At the end of my time in punishment, they got a big metal rod with a circle on the end. It was bright red and I could see steam coming off it. They pushed it on my chest and fuck me, it burned. I can still feel the burning today. I was then dumped outside my dorm and Becky came out and got me," he says, stuttering slightly and breathing heavily.

"Fucking hell," I say, not know what else to say.

"Yeah," Mark says, "fucking hell." He finishes his water and slams his cup on the table. "I hate the Union. You come here thinking you're getting a better life, when really you end up in prison."

"Not too loud," Becky says to him. She looks over at one of the guards patrolling the lunch hall and signals to Mark and the rest of us to keep our voices down, to make sure we do not get into any trouble.

"That could happen to any of us," Amrit states as we all look at one another. "We should get out of here."

"It's not that easy," Becky says. "A branded man like Mark will be watched over and over again. Also, it is very easy to get into Leicester nowadays; but, getting out is a completely different story."

"It can't be that difficult," I say.

"They have guards on every corner here," Becky says. "There is no way of getting out."

We continue to eat our lunch, all feeling concern and sympathy for what Mark went through. It can't be as bad as he says, though. The Union give people shelter, food and warmth, and all they ask is for us to play our part. It can't be all that bad, can it?

After we've done eating we go out into the yard. I walk around, just looking at the different people wandering about. A lot of them are really nice and nod at me as I walk past. Then I see Amrit sitting in the corner smoking a cigarette. Where did he get tobacco from? I walk over to him to say hello.

"All right, mate?" I say.

"All right," he responds.

"Where did you get tobacco from?" I ask him, confused.

"Well, after we got back yesterday and you passed out like the lazy twat you are, I went out to the market and there was a man selling roll-ups, so I bought a few. Would you like one?" he asks me condescendingly.

"Yeah, sure."

He passes me a cigarette, then walks over to take a lighter from a guard, lights it, then walks back to the guard to give him back his lighter. I breathe in, and it feels harsh but warm. Hurts a little; it's been a while since I smoked. It starts to taste ok after a few puffs

"Thanks," I say as I take another drag.

"Don't worry about it," Amrit says. We sit there for a while, smoking away and staring into the distance.

"Crazy shit, that story Mark told us," I say.

"Yeah," Amrit replies. "That's why we need to start making plans to get out of here, before something like that happens to me, you or Rhea."

I look over and see Rhea talking to Becky and Jane, laughing and joking.

"She seems happier since we have been here," I say, "besides that bitch Scarlett. Rhea seems different; there's something about her I didn't notice before. Something I refused to notice before."

"You like her," Amrit states as he takes another drag on his cigarette. I turn to him, stunned by his statement.

"No, I don't," I state abruptly.

"Yeah, you do."

I look at him for a moment, stunned at how he can be so confident in what he thinks he knows.

"How did you... what?" I say, confused.

"Mate, I have known you for years. I know when there's a girl you want to fuck and a girl you want to be with. She's somebody you clearly want to be with," he says, still puffing away at his cigarette. "I can't blame you; she is a very pretty girl."

"Yeah," I reluctantly admit. "I didn't want to do anything because, you know..."

"Know what?" he asks.

"I didn't know whether you liked her," I say. "I didn't know whether you thought she was a bit of all right."

"You're an idiot," he says, sighing to himself.

"Mate, the last thing I want is a girl coming between us."

"That is not going to happen."

"How do you know?" I ask.

He sits up and looks at me, confused.

"You really don't know, do you?"

"Know what?" I ask.

"Layton," says, "I'm gay."

I look at him for a moment. I didn't know.

"Gay?" I reply, baffled. I look at him, trying to think of something else to say besides the word 'gay'. I am trying to give him my best reaction, but it's a shock that he didn't tell me, and that I didn't work it out.

"Yes, gay," he replies.

"You mean, like, gay gay?" I say.

"Yes, I'm gay," Amrit tells me once again, as he knows I'm finding it a bit of a shock.

"You mean gay, like, 'you love cock' gay?" I ask.

"Brilliantly put," he responds sarcastically, "but yes, like that, you fool."

"Oh," I say. "How about that?" I look at him once more, and have another question. "Amrit?"

"No, I have never found you attractive," he interrupts.

"I wasn't going to ask you that," I say straight away. I then look back at him for a moment and decide to ask him. "Why, what's wrong with me?"

"I don't know," Amrit says. "I'm more into manly men; you're not really that."

"What you mean?" I ask bluntly, rather high-pitched and quite hurt by that statement.

"You're not really butch or like a guy," he replies, trying not to be offensive and failing. "You're like a little sister," he suggests.

"Wow, the gay guy just called me a girl," I blurt out, still feeling hurt.

"Yeah, I guess I did," he chuckles to himself. We both burst out laughing and turn to face the rest of the people in front of us.

"So you think I got a chance with her, then?" I ask, pointing at Rhea. We both take another drag from our cigarettes.

"No chance, mate," Amrit responds.

"Yeah, thought as much."

We sit there, pondering. I guess we learn something new every day. I never knew that Amrit was gay, but now I know it doesn't make any difference. I still think he's twat whether he's gay or straight, but he will always be like a brother to me.

After we finish our work duty, Amrit, Rhea and I decide to explore the city and get a proper feel for our new home. We walk around, looking at all of the different stalls selling their products from food to clothes, all across the centre of the town square. We walk a little further and see a man, a rather skinny man who seems to be selling something hot. We go over to see what it is. He is serving what looks like a hot, bubbling tomato soup, its piercing orange colour just shining through at the top of the barrel.

"Looks like tomato," I say to Rhea and Amrit. We can taste the soup through the smell which wafts over to us.

"You want some?" Rhea asks. I look again to see what the soup actually contains.

"Not for me," Amrit says. The man behind the counter then comes walking towards us.

"Fresh cup of soup?" he asks as I look down at it. I'd feel impolite if I was to turn around and say no to him. I look at him and can see he looks as if he has lived beyond his years. He is old, with skin so thin that his bones are beginning to show through it.

"Um, yeah, go on then," I say.

"Very good," he replies. He turns around and walks over to the big barrel of soup. He lifts a cup and pours the soup into it using a ladle, with some of the soup managing to overflow the cup. He hands it to me and I can see Rhea staring at it, pulling a face.

"Thank you," I say, looking down at the thick, lumpy soup.

"What would you like for it?" I ask, feeling around in my pockets.

"Nothing for this," he replies while stirring the soup with the large metal ladle.

"Really?" I say, confused. "Why is that?" There must surely be a price, I think to myself; this seems too good to be true.

"Union rules," he tells me. "Simple foods as soup and bread are equal and available for all within the Union," he remarks, sounding as if he is quoting a handbook, and stuttering slightly as he speaks.

"OK," I say, surprised. I raise the soup and take a look at it. It appears to have a lot of lumps in it, white bits sticking out through the orange liquid. I take a sip and gag slightly. It's sour, hot, and the white bits make it taste very sharp.

"How is it?" Rhea asks as I bring it from my lips. I hand it over to her. She sniffs it first, then takes a sip herself. As soon as she does, she coughs a few times and hands it right back to me.

"That good, huh?" I say, chuckling. I then look over and see a guard come walking towards us.

"Soup," the guard demands. The old man behind the counter quickly turns, grabs the ladle and tries to pour some soup into a cup. I can see his hands shaking as he does so. I quickly look at Rhea and Amrit and they look just as disheartened as I am.

"Is everything OK?" Amrit asks the man as his hands continue to shake.

"I'm fine," he says, finally filling the cup of soup and turning around. He holds the cup and walks over to the guard, holding it out to him.

"Quickly now," the guard snaps.

The old man keeps walking, his hand shaking even more. Then he suddenly trips and spills the soup all over the guard's trench coat. The guard steps back for a moment, arms out, looking down at his jacket, then back up at the old man. The old

126

man just stands there with his mouth wide open, shocked and looking quite fearful.

"Oh my God," the old man says, "I'm so sorry… uh, please…"

"Right," the guard shouts, shaking off the soup. He grabs the man by the arm.

"No, please, no," he cries. The guard then turns to the man and slaps him across the face, causing a little spittle to come out of the old man's mouth.

"Oh, come on," Rhea says, "it's only a bit of soup!"

The guard stops, turns and stares right at her, glaring right into her face.

"Another word and I will take you as well," he shouts.

Rhea is about to speak when Amrit places his hand on her shoulder to stop her. She looks at him and he shakes his head, then turns and looks back at the guard.

"I thought as much," the guard says. He then grabs the man and drags him away, not bothered that the man's feet are scraping across the ground, causing him a lot of pain. We all just stand there staring at them, bewildered by what we have just seen. I hope this isn't an example of things to come.

13

After about an hour, I find myself sitting in the middle of the living room in our dorm. I look outside the large window at the end of the room, gazing into the distance. I can see a lot of people going about their business, a few couples walking down the street, groups of friends strolling through, and the odd guard here and there, patrolling the street as the sun is about to come down. It's strange; being out in the dark is usually a dangerous thing to do. Now I know we have to stay inside once the sun goes down. Some would argue it, yet, I feel oddly safe.

"All right, Layton?" a voice calls out as I stand staring aimlessly into the distance. "Layton!"

"Sorry," I say, breaking out of my daydream. I turn around and see Becky entering the room. "Hi," I say as she walks in, smiling at me.

"Daydreaming, were you?" she asks as she struts to the kitchen.

"Yeah, just in my own little world," I tell her as she starts to clatter about with the pots and pans. "What you doing?" I ask as she looks inside the fridge.

"I thought I'd make a start on dinner," she tells me as she rummages through the contents of the fridge.

"Oh," I say, "what are we having?"

"Well, I thought I would make my famous tuna casserole," she announces as she brings out tins upon tins of tuna.

"Nice," I reply as I go to sit down. I take a seat and look up at her. "Where does all of this tinned food come from?"

"What do you mean?" she asks.

"I mean, we come across all of this tinned food and preserved things, but we don't know where any of it comes from."

"Well, a lot of it, the Union makes. They make a lot of the food we eat here. Also, before the end of the world, as you might call it, they had stacks of tinned preserves stored away. They were taken, recycled and people just made them themselves. Then I guess as the population went down, there was enough left for the rest of us," she states, juggling a can of tuna in her hand.

"That makes sense, I guess," I say, still a little confused.

"It's confusing, I know," she admits as she grabs a tin opener and begins to open the can. "But, that's just the way it is." She opens the tuna and puts it into a bowl.

"Yeah," I say. "I find a lot of things confusing, to be fair."

I look over and see Ryan enter the room, looking very fresh.

"All right?" he calls out as he strolls in and takes a seat.

"How come you're not at work?" I ask him as he sits there staring at me.

"They told us that the late shift is off today, so I get to come home and see all of you fine people," he says, crossing his legs.

"Well, that was nice of them," I say, smiling as I see him looking very frustrated for some reason.

"Yeah, you'd think that," he says as his head turns and faces Becky. "Tuna casserole?" he asks as she empties something else into the bowl and starts to mix it.

"Yup," she replies as she continues to mix. I look at the

mixture and see it is turning a weird pinky-yellow colour. It will probably taste better than it looks right now.

"So how long have you been here?" I ask Ryan, realising I haven't really had a chance to talk to him yet.

"Long enough," he comments in a very closed-off way. "Seen some real shit in the time I've been here."

"Well, Amrit, Rhea and I were in town earlier," I say. "We were at the soup stand and the strangest thing happened. The soup seller accidently spilt some on a guard, and the guard took him away."

Ryan just looks at me and chuckles slightly to himself.

"That's the guards for you: they're all nice when you're doing what they want, then you make one little slip and they kill you," he tells me.

I look at him, a little confused by what he is saying.

"They didn't kill him," I say, feeling a little frustrated with what he is saying.

"How do you know?" he asks, looking at me with a hint of despair written across his face.

"How do you know they killed him?" I ask, trying to outsmart him.

"Because I know this place a little better than you," he says abruptly, more or less ending the discussion.

I look at him, a little bemused, until I see Rhea walk into the room.

"Hello," I say as she walks in and looks at us all.

"Hi," she responds, smiling. She then turns and looks at Becky. "Do you need any help?" she asks as Becky transfers the casserole into what looks like a baking dish.

"No, I'm fine, thanks," Becky replies. Rhea shrugs her shoulders, then comes and sits with Ryan and me.

Becky puts the tray into the oven, closes it and turns a few knobs. "OK, that'll be about twenty minutes," she says, coming over to join us all.

"Sounds good," I say as she takes a seat.

"Where's Jane?" Becky asks, and we look around at one another.

"She said she doesn't feel well, she's been throwing up a lot," Rhea announces as Mark and Amrit come and join us.

"Oh," Becky says. She looks a little concerned, "I'll go check on her," she says, getting up and walking off into the corridor.

"OK," Mark says as she walks past him. "Something smells good."

We look over at the casserole cooking in the oven.

"Yeah, it does," Ryan says, walking over to the sink. He gets himself a glass of water and walks back, sipping.

"I was telling Ryan about what Amrit, Rhea and I saw today," I explain to Mark. He looks at me, smiles a little, then sighs.

"You come to expect that," he says. "Amrit told me about it. You will get used to seeing people just disappear for no apparent reason."

"Well, he did spill it," I say.

"A little soup," Mark replies. "Being a guard means you get a free pass on anything that the citizens may do."

I look at him and can't help but feel he's rather bitter when it comes to the guards. I know he's had his issues with them, but the guards do what the Union expects, and the Union expects brilliance.

Becky comes rushing back into the room, over to the oven and swings the door wide open. A gust of smoke comes floating out and wafts into the living room. The smell of tuna seeps into my nose, with the tang of a crisp topping. Becky brings it out, and the smoke coming from the top shows it is piping hot. She places it in front of us and brings one plate and several spoons.

"OK," she announces as we all lean in to grab a spoon each. "Let me just do a plate for Jane." She spoons some of the tuna onto the plate, then turns away. "OK, you can all dig in."

Without hesitation, we jump straight in. I dig spoonfuls

131

of the tuna and shovel it into my mouth. It's hot, but the tuna chunks seem to melt in my mouth as soon as they enter.

"This is good," I say through my mouthful of food, swishing the tuna around my teeth.

"Yeah," Amrit says, "Becky sure can cook."

"She's always been a good cook," Ryan states as we continue to eat, devouring the lot.

Following dinner, I'm suddenly overcome with tiredness. I wander off to my bed and slip into a deep sleep. My stomach is all warm and fuzzy from the food, and my feet begin to relax in the warmth of the bed. I feel my body just relax; my hands go numb and my face feels calm. My eyes are heavy, yet they are massaging my eyes as I sleep through the night.

I wake the following morning feeling very refreshed and still subtly full from the night before. I lumber out of bed, throwing the sheets off me as if to keep something from pressing me down. The cold strikes my feet, making me quickly pop them back under the sheets. I feel warm and snug, not wanting to move. I cocoon myself in the sheets, wrapping myself up to experience the soothing feel of comfort.

"Layton." I hear Rhea banging at the door.

"What?" I ask, trying to get her to leave so I can catch a few more moments of sleep.

"I'm going town with Becky," she says. "Is there anything you want?"

"Town? Don't we have work duty in a bit?" I ask, suddenly worried we might be late.

"It's Saturday, you twat. We have the day off."

"Oh," I say. "I'm fine, thanks."

"All right, see you later," she says as I hear her walk away.

"The day off," I mutter to myself as I begin to relax again. I know I could just rest and sleep for a little longer, but to be honest I don't really want to. I always like finding stuff out for myself, so I think I might just find out about Leicester. I get up, finally awake. I might skip breakfast and just go see what I can find out there.

I get dressed as soon as I leave the building and walk through the street to see where I am living. I look at the different buildings and sights the city has to offer. I can see a row of pubs on one side of the road, full of people all talking and cheering. I decide to go and investigate, and look up at one of them.

"The Queen of Bradgate," I read out loud. I peep inside and see groups of people sitting around drinking. I then notice somebody sitting on a sofa reading a book. Amrit!

I walk inside and feel the warmth of the room cover me, making me feel all safe and homely. I look over at Amrit sitting there flicking through the pages, engrossed in his book.

"Morning," I say as I walk over.

"Oh, hello," he replies as I sit opposite him.

"What you reading?" I ask.

"Oh, this. A Tainted Secret," he says, closing the book. He shows me the front cover and I gaze at a woman hunched up with not much clothing on. She looks as if she is hiding her face for some reason.

"Oh," I say, "what's it about?"

"Nothing really, just murder and that," he explains. "Do you want a drink?"

"It's a bit early, but yeah, I wouldn't say no to a cheeky ale."

"Oh, please, it's the Union, remember," he raises up and strolls to what looks like a bar. I see him talking to the barman. The barman is pouring something that I cant quite make out.

"Hope you enjoy this" Amrit says as he walks over towards me with two brown transparent drinks in his hands.

"What is it?" I ask him

"Well, they call it tea" Amrit tells me

"Tea" I respond surprised

"Try it, let me know what you think" he encourages as I look at the drink.

"You're the boss" I say to him. I raise the glass and place it to my mouth. The drink is not what I would call a sensation of wonder. It is sour and full of gravelly bits. My tongue is already feeling unusual from drinking this stuff.

"Good?" Amrit asks as I take the glass away from my mouth.

"Yeah," I say, trying to be polite.

"Tastes like piss, doesn't it?" He smirks.

"Yeah, a little bit," I reply, slamming the glass down on the table. We both laugh as we look at each other and feel a little contempt at the whole situation.

"Do you remember those comics we used to read?" he asks me.

"Which ones?"

"Superman, you remember those?"

"Yeah," I say, "they were great."

"I always wanted to be like him," he says, "and just be able to fly away into the distance."

"Yeah," I say, feeling the same euphoria at the thought.

"I wonder what Superman's kid would be like?" Amrit muses.

"Well, if he had it with another Kryptonian—"

"Why not a human?" he asks.

"Oh, come on," I say. "As much as I love Superman, him having a kid with Lois Lane is just impossible."

"How's that?" he asks.

"Well, if Superman was to have sex with Lois, he would probably kill her. His thrusting alone would be like a bulldozer smashing into her. Then when he reached orgasm and ejaculated, the sheer strength of it would tear her human body apart. Wonder Woman would probably be able to handle it, but Lois would probably die," I explain.

134

"OK," Amrit says.

"It's like if Batman shagged Wonder Woman," I continue, and he looks at me, a little bemused. "The force she created would rupture him and he would die if she got too excited."

"Or," Amrit says, "given she is an Amazon, she probably wouldn't be able to feel anything from Batman. Or any human for that matter."

"How's that?" I ask.

"You know Wonder Woman?" he begins. "She was always supposed to have had that love interest with Steve Trevor."

"Yeah," I say.

"Well, a human wouldn't have the power to thrust hard enough, or have a dick powerful enough to arouse someone like Wonder Woman. Only person who could pleasure her is Superman, and the only person who could handle Superman is Wonder Woman."

"Well, this is the stupidest conversation I have ever heard," a voice says as we look at each other. We look up and see Becky and Rhea standing over us, looking down.

"Oh, hello," I say.

"So what brings you two here?" Amrit asks.

"We went to shop for some supplies," Rhea says.

"Yeah, we got some good things," Becky adds.

"Great, why don't you two pull up a seat?" I ask.

"Sure," Rhea says, sitting next to us. We then look up at Becky, who is still standing looking at us.

"Sit down, Becky," Amrit says.

"Oh no," she politely refuses, "I'm going to head back to the dorm. Besides, I hear there is going to be a large speech at the clock tower in the next ten minutes."

"Oh yeah?" I say, a little excited. "Where you hear that?"

"There's a poster outside."

I look up and notice a large poster being put up.

"You guys better head down there now if you want to get

a good spot," she says. We look at each other and without hesitating, jump to our feet, rushing straight out.

We head for the clock tower in the centre of town. Crowds of people line the street in front of us. I can see the tower poking out above the crowd as we push our way through and look for a good spot. Amrit points at a large wooden stage planted in the centre with a group of guards around it. Groups of people surround the stage, all looking as eager as we are. There are many still trying to find a good place to watch, some of them barging past us as we try to stand still. I feel one of them barge into my back, but just ignore it. I look over at Rhea and Amrit, and notice that they are frowning at the stage.

"Did I mention," Rhea says, "I don't like crowds?" Amrit and I chuckle as we look forward, and I see Canine come forward and glare at everybody.

"Ladies and gentlemen," he calls out, and the crowd goes deathly silent. "General Singh."

General Singh comes forward and presents himself to the crowd. A group of around eight guards I believe are standing nearby, I can't tell how many for certain. They begin to play trumpets as if presenting a great leader to the people.

"This should be interesting," Amrit says. I look at him and feel that the sarcasm is not needed.

"My friends," General Singh calls out to us all, "a new dawn is coming. We, the Union, are here to take care of all our children!" The crowd begin to clap.

"Children?" Rhea asks, bemused.

"We come to you all to bring you a world of peace. The Union looks to help others and show them the luxury and peace you have all become accustomed to. We will look to help other communities out and show them the way to live," he says, presenting his arms as the crowd cheers again. "I raise my left hand to push away our enemies, and bring in my right hand to welcome our friends." The crowd continues to cheer as they look up at him, gleaming.

"Are they really eating this shit up?" Amrit asks.

"Everybody has a purpose," General Singh states. "We come together as one people. For we find those among us who do not belong; who must be disposed of, yet we send them off as friends."

I can't help it but feel he is beginning to sound like a true leader to me. I believe every word he is saying.

"The Union comes to you all as one. The Union stands for liberty, freedom and human achievement. We have no choice but to bring you all love. It is through our love that you can be a part of our Union." He looks around at us all. "Now, I have a task for one of you fine people here today." He holds his hand out and points, moving his hand around like a compass needle. "I choose you!" he shouts, pointing at a man. The man jumps up in joy as two guards approach him.

"Yes, it's me," the man calls out as the people around him pat him on the back.

"You, my friend," General Singh says, "have a very important task ahead of you."

I can't help but feel a little jealous, wishing it was me who was chosen. The guards bring the man to the stage where General Singh is standing and present him to the crowd. He raises his hands and cheers, and we applaud him as he is escorted away.

"Very well done," General Singh congratulates him. "As for the rest of you…" He waves his hand and Canine comes forward with a basket. He and two other guards then begin to throw something out of the baskets.

"What's that?" I ask.

"Is that bread?" Amrit says as hundreds of loaves are thrown to the cheering crowd.

General Singh then turns and walks off as Canine and the

other guards throw as much bread as they can into the crowd. I feel very proud to be amongst these people. The crowd comes rushing forward, jumping as high as they can to catch a piece of bread. I see some people clambering over others, jumping on each other's shoulders just to try and grab a piece.

"So the bribery of human trust begins," Amrit says.

I look at General Singh and can't help but feel that he is doing something special here. He is building a civilisation that can thrive in a time of need, and the Union are the peacekeepers in all of this. I feel that we can all learn from him, and that we can all be one. General Singh, followed by Canine, is led away and the trumpets begin to play again as he leaves the stage. I look at him in awe as he walks away and feel that he is the most important man on the planet.

In the moments after the speech, I see many people walking away, a lot of them with wide smiles. They seem cheerful, and in some cases euphoric. I feel a smile spread across my face as I think back on his words. I know General Singh means to build a better future for us all. He is here to build a better world for us all. He will punish the bad and take care of the good. Isn't that what a good leader does? The Union will spread its message of hope to all the different cities. I wonder if the whole of England will become part of the Union?

As Rhea, Amrit and I make our way down the street, we see a little park hidden amongst the buildings. We walk towards it, looking at all of the trees that surround it and the lush grass in the centre. I see that some people walking past us don't look as happy with the speech as I am. They are disgruntled, and look as if they feel worse for being there.

"Here's a good spot," Amrit says as we make our way to the patch of grass in the centre of the park. He sits down and looks up at Rhea and me. Rhea soon follows him, and I decide to take a seat as well. We all sit there in a triangle, looking at one another, all contemplating the majesty we have just witnessed.

"What an amazing speech," I say.

Rhea picks a piece of grass and starts to play with it, and Amrit sits there with his arms resting on his knees, listening.

"He spoke with such conviction, such pride about bringing about a society that can really work for us all here," I continue. "I feel he is somebody who really gets us all; who really understands how civilisation can be fixed. The Union will bring about its changes and will make us all stronger for it."

Amrit frowns. "You didn't believe all that shit, did you?" he asks, looking frustrated.

"What?" I say, shocked.

"You really believe him?" he says, sounding disappointed. "You believe that he can control as many people as that? He said that the Union will be expanding to other parts of the country to spread their message. What does he mean by that? How will he be doing it? Will the Union attack people, kill them and string them up under his orders?"

"You've been a complete dick since we got here," I say, a little annoyed. "All you do is moan about this place. If you don't like it here, why don't you just leave?"

"I can't leave," Amrit says.

"Why?" I ask.

"Because I have to make sure you don't get yourself killed," he explains. "Also, Dillon was a good man, so I have to make sure you're safe," he adds, looking at Rhea.

"I don't need protecting." She frowns.

"I know," he says, "I just feel obliged to make sure you're alive."

She looks at him, and her frown begins to fade.

"OK," she says, still not convinced. "I think this place is OK, though."

I see a group of guards go walking past, not bothered with their presence.

"It would be nice if there weren't so many of those guards

around the place. It would be nice to have enough people who could just make peace," Rhea adds.

"We can't live under governors," Amrit explains. "We can have a people who can come together as one. We need to join forces, as many do. When I say join forces, I don't mean use aggression. We can't all be as one if we are killing each other. We should all be taking care of each other."

"I used to know a place like that," I say.

"Oh yeah?" Rhea says. "Where?"

"It's gone now, it doesn't matter," I say as I spot Mark in the distance. He looks over and catches sight of us, then turns and heads toward us. On the way, a guard confronts him directly.

"Excuse me," Mark says politely.

"Hello, Mark," the guard says. "Fancy a duel?"

"No," Mark replies, "because you will lose. Now move." He barges past the guard and walks over to us.

"All right, mate?" I ask as he approaches, recovering the smile he dropped when the guard stopped him.

"Yeah, I'm all good," he says.

"We saw a speech by the 'great' general," Amrit says to him.

"I would hold back on the sarcasm," Mark explains, "just in case somebody is listening."

"Fair enough," Amrit says, smirking.

"Amrit is being a hater," I tell Mark, feeling like a snitch.

"Oh, how so?" Mark asks, looking at him and chuckling to himself.

"Layton is upset that Amrit doesn't believe in General Singh," Rhea explains, sounding just as sarcastic as Amrit did a moment ago.

"Oh, I see," Mark says. "Well, as much as I would love to talk about him, I have come to tell you that Becky is going to be making a large dinner today, so make sure you don't eat too much. Ryan has had to go into work for the next few hours, but he'll soon be back."

"Why has he had to go into work?" I ask.

"Orders," Mark explains.

"Very well," I say, looking off into the distance. We all sit there, feeling as if we have a long day ahead of us. The truth of the matter is, I know we have a long, fruitful life ahead of us.

Days become weeks as time goes on. I go to work and back, not caring about the next day. I feel very inclined to display my full loyalty to the Union, not wanting to display any form of hatred towards them. I am beginning to love my work, starting to feel as if this is the place for me.

I feel that I can really be myself here. I feel that I can really be somebody special as a part of this world. Only time will tell how great I can be while I am here. I am motivated; I really want to make my way to the top. I know I can make something of myself within the Union.

14

Back at work, we never see anything more of Cell Block A. There are rumours as to what happened to them, but we don't really know. It's one of those slow days, just aimlessly looking into the air, then staring at the wall. Very rarely do I have a day like this, but they do come every now and then.

I stand there looking through the different metals and rearranging them, trying to make sense of it all. I keep thinking about what Mark said about being branded, having to carry that symbol on his chest for the rest of his life. Amrit keeps talking about leaving. He suspects that this place is not what it seems to be, and says that at any point we could be subject to the horrors we have been told of. I don't know, though; I think this place is pretty good. I mean, we get three square meals a day, a bed, running water and a job. What more can people ask for? If you step out of line then being sent to punishment is probably the best course of action.

I am standing here aimlessly working away at my desk when a looming figure comes up to me. I am assuming he is one of the guards. I mean, he has the big trench coat, the covered face, the machete; all the attributes of a stereotypical guard of the Union. He comes toward me and places his hand on my shoulder.

"Rob wants to see you," he says.

"OK," I reply. I turn and look at everybody else, and they look just as bemused as I am. I am then escorted away from my work station, the others fading away in the distance behind me.

I am taken to an office in the corner of the room. The guard opens the door and I am led inside, where Rob is sitting behind a desk.

"Layton," Rob says, "take a seat."

I walk over and sit down.

"How are you, man, would you like a drink?"

I'm not entirely sure why he is being so nice to me. When we first met him, he kind of came across as a bit of a dick.

"No, I'm fine, thanks," I say. He nods at me and sits back in his chair, putting his feet up.

"So how are you finding it here?" Rob asks me confidently.

"It's good," I reply hesitantly.

"Yeah, if you work hard enough, you never know – you may become a guard. Or you may even end up in my seat," he chuckles to himself. "I guess you're wondering why I brought you here."

I nod, trying not to put a foot out of place.

"Well," he says, rising to his feet, "I am here to tell you that we have been observing you over the past couple of days you have been here, and we like what we see."

"Thank you," I say, surprised as I have not really done anything special; nothing that could make me stand out.

"I mean," he continues, "you work hard, you seem passionate about what you do. What I would like to know is, do you think we are doing a good job here at the Union?"

I look at him for a while before answering in earnest. "Yes, I do."

"Good," he says. "So if we were to ask you to perform a task for us, would you do so?"

I look at him and feel hesitant. Knowing what I know, it

doesn't take me long to realise that I should just go along with what he says.

"Yes," I say. "What do you want me to do?"

"OK," he replies. "It's good that you will, but I haven't quite thought of what I want you to do yet."

"OK," I say, sounding a little surprised.

"I will keep you posted," he says. "In the meantime," he gestures with his hand for me to get up, so I do, "I want you, my little brown friend," (Bit racist, I think to myself) "to just crack on with your work and I will inform you about what it is I want you to do."

"OK," I say.

"And one more thing," he adds. "I would like you to accompany me tonight. Feel free to tell your friends; they may be interested in knowing what responsibilities we give those whom we deem to be hard workers."

I feel uncomfortable, but don't feel strong enough to tell him that I don't want to do whatever it is he wants me to do this evening.

"OK," I say, not really wanting to say anything that could be used against me.

"Very good. Now, off you go, back to work," he orders patronisingly, waving his hand.

"OK," I say, and walk straight out the door.

I head back to my work station without saying a word and just get right back to my work.

"What was all that about?" Rhea asks me as soon as I get back.

"He wants me to do something for him," I say without hesitating.

"What?" Jane says.

"I'm not sure yet," I reply. "He said he hasn't decided yet."

They all look at one another, just as baffled as I was when I was in the office.

"Probably wants you to be his little rent boy," Amrit jokes.

"Seriously?" I say. "You're going to say that to me?" I feel that making this kind of joke is unnecessary.

"What," Mark blurts out, "just because he's gay he can't make a gay joke?"

"Wait," I say abruptly, "you know he's gay?"

"Yes, Layton," Mark replies, "we all know. We could tell when we first met," he adds, as if I am an idiot.

"So everybody knew you were gay except for me?" I shout at Amrit. I then realise I spoke too loud as people around turn to look at us. I smile, as awkward as they look, then slowly turn back to my work station.

"How long have you known Amrit now?" Rhea asks me.

"Clearly not as long as you lot," I announce, getting on with my work.

"Oh, look at him get mad," Amrit teases.

"I'm not mad, I'm just hurt," I say in my most matter-of-fact tone.

They all chuckle at my expense until I see, out of the corner of my eye, Scarlett walking down the way. She barges into Rhea and keeps on walking.

"Oi, watch it!" Rhea shouts.

"What, bitch?" Scarlett shouts back. "Shut up, yeah? You haven't got shit." Then she and her friends walk off.

"She is getting on my last nerve," Rhea says to us.

"Don't worry about it," I say, trying to reassure her. She doesn't look like she feels that reassurance, though, to be fair. I think she looks more like she is going to snap at any second.

During lunch, we are sitting at a table in the cafeteria, eating. I can see Scarlett and her friends at a nearby table, just staring at Rhea. Rhea tries not to make eye contact with them because she doesn't want to provoke anything. Neither do I really; they look like all they want is for Rhea to get wound up. Rhea then picks up her tray and walks around to sit opposite me so that her back is to them.

"I'm not going to give them the satisfaction," she makes clear to me.

"Best way to do it," Becky agrees. We continue to eat our corned beef sandwiches in peace.

"You look nice today," I announce to Rhea, trying to make small talk.

"Why?" she asks, looking confused.

"I don't know," I reply, embarrassed.

"Um, OK." She shakes her head awkwardly. "You're an idiot," she chuckles to herself.

I look over at Amrit and see him rolling his eyes at me.

Suddenly, Scarlett is standing right behind Rhea. She punches her right in the back of the head, causing Rhea to jolt forwards.

"Whoa, now!" I call out, rising to my feet. Scarlett jumps on top of Rhea, and Rhea tries to cover her face as Scarlett pummels her. Becky and Jane jump at Scarlett's two little friends to keep them away. The whole cafeteria erupts as the commotion continues.

"Leave her alone," Amrit shouts.

"Get off me," Rhea cries out as Scarlett continues to manhandle her.

"Stupid bitch, think you're all that?" Scarlett shouts as she claws at Rhea and grabs her hair.

I look over at the guards and they are just standing there, chuckling to themselves. I quickly move over to try to get Scarlet off Rhea, but I'm met with a giant left hand to the face, causing me to fall flat on the ground.

"Scarlett, that's enough," Mark shouts, but she keeps on going, hitting Rhea in the face and kicking her in the stomach. Rhea then manages to twist around and punch Scarlett in the stomach, causing her to fall backwards and recoil from her.

"Yeah, bitch, watch yourself," Scarlett says as she turns and walks away.

"Rhea, are you OK?" I ask.

"I'm fine," she replies hesitantly. She feels around her neck, then suddenly I can tell something is up. "No," she mutters. "That bitch – no!" she cries.

"What is it?" Mark asks.

"She took my necklace. That stupid bitch took my necklace," she shouts, and turns and chases after Scarlett.

"Shit," Amrit says, and we all run after Rhea.

Out in the courtyard, we can see Scarlett walking away.

"Oi!" Rhea shouts. "Oi, slut, where you going?"

"You want more?" Scarlett shouts back.

"Give me back my necklace now," Rhea yells.

"What, this?" Scarlett asks, pulling out the necklace and dangling it in front of her.

"Yeah, give it back."

"Make me," Scarlett spits.

Suddenly see three guards come rushing towards us.

"Oh, thank God," I say to myself in relief.

"OK, what is going on here?" one of the guards shouts as he looks at us gathered around the two women. We all look nervously at each other, none of us wanting to say anything that could be out of place.

"She took my necklace," Rhea tells the guard. The guard looks at her for a moment, and I know he is contemplating what to do. He then turns around, walks towards Scarlett and stares right at her.

"Did you take her necklace?" the guard asks Scarlett.

"Yeah," Scarlett replies nervously.

"Do you want it back?" the guard asks Rhea.

"Yes, I do," Rhea says confidently.

The guard looks at us all. He then walks over to Scarlett and glares right at her. She pulls the necklace out and holds it in front of him. He takes the necklace off her and waves it in front of the crowd.

"Well then, you two have to fight for it," the guard says.

Amrit and I look at each other, stunned.

"Listen, everybody, these two are going to fight for this necklace. If anybody jumps in to help either one, they will be sent to punishment. The winner will be rewarded the necklace." He walks up to Scarlett, places the necklace in her pocket and winks at her, before walking away.

Scarlett looks over at her friends as they edge away, knowing that they can't help her. I'm getting a feeling that Scarlett is nervous all of a sudden. Everyone in the courtyard gathers around to form a circle around the two women as they are about to fight. I look over at the building and can see Rob looking out of the window; then back at Rhea and Scarlett.

"Give it back," Rhea shouts at Scarlett as she walks up to her. Scarlett suddenly starts to edge away, not looking completely up for it. Rhea then walks towards Scarlett and punches her in the face, causing Scarlett to stagger backwards. Scarlett tries to throw a punch back, but it's slow and lazy, meaning Rhea can see it from a mile away. Rhea throws a combination of punches, causing Scarlett's nose to bleed.

"Come on, fight back," the guard shouts at Scarlett as she keeps taking Rhea's punches. Rhea then punches Scarlett in the stomach and again in the face, causing Scarlett to collapse to the ground. Rhea gets on top of her and goes to town on her, punching her several times in the face, causing her to bleed more. I can even see her eyes start to swell up. Then Rhea throws a massive right hand, hitting Scarlett right in the jaw, causing a couple of her teeth to come flying out, knocking her out cold in the process. Rhea then sits back to take a breather.

"Well, I guess Scarlett can only fight when the other person doesn't see it coming," Mark says. We all cheer and celebrate Rhea's win. Rhea then goes to Scarlett's pocket and pulls out the necklace.

"I'll take that," she snarls. She looks down at Scarlett's motionless body and spits in her face.

As we start to walk towards her to congratulate her, out of nowhere, the guards jump in front of us.

"OK, you're coming with me," one of them shouts, and grabs Rhea by the arm. Another lifts Scarlett to her feet to carry her away.

"Wait, what're you doing?" I cry.

"Fighting in the workplace is not allowed," the guard says.

"But you told them to fight," I retort.

"What did you say?" the guard asks, squaring off in my face.

I look over and see Mark watching me. He quickly shakes his head to tell me not to say anything.

"Nothing," I mutter, trying not to piss the guard off any more than he already is.

"That's what I thought," the guard says, and turns and grabs Rhea by the arm and drags her away.

"Wait, please, no!" Rhea cries as the guards take her away.

All of us stand there staring. We want to run over and grab her; to tear her away from them. But before we know it, they are out of sight.

After work, we get back to the dorm and I am pissed off. I rush in and the first thing I do is kick a chair, which kind of hurts, still, I made myself clear which was hitting a chair, to prove a point. I turn and see that Amrit is just as pissed off as I am.

"What the fuck?" he says. "They can't just take her away."

"They can," Mark begrudgingly admits.

"They told her to fight, though," I shout, furious.

"They told me to fight as well," Mark says. "That's how they get you. Rhea was going to be taken away regardless. She had already scuffled in the cafeteria. Scarlett is too fat and stupid to realise when she is doing something wrong. Now they're both in punishment."

"Does this mean they're going to… that Rhea is going to be…?" I stammer.

"Yes," Mark says, "exactly that."

"Dear God," Amrit says.

"You knew about this?" I shout, storming towards Mark and staring him right in the eyes.

"Yes, I'm sorry," he says guiltily.

"Why didn't you stop this?" I demand. "You could've stopped Rhea from fighting and being taken away."

"There's nothing more we can do," Becky tells us. "We just have to wait."

"That could take days or months," I cry, not meaning to raise my voice but hearing it get louder.

"I know," she says. "But there's nothing we can do but wait."

We all stand there in silence. None of us can make eye contact. We feel angry, upset and disappointed all at the same time. For the first time, I am starting to have second thoughts about this place.

I am fast asleep, absolutely shattered after the day I have had. I am dreaming about a number of pointless things, nothing that can really grip me with a great story. I actually found it quite difficult to fall asleep after what happened to Rhea; I can't help but feel worried for her.

I am all snug, sleeping away, until I suddenly hear banging at the front door to our dorm. I try to ignore it, turning away, but then I hear the banging again, this time stronger than before.

"Layton Rai?" a voice calls out. "Layton Rai, come to the door at once."

I get up, rubbing my eyes to wake myself up. I stand up and walk towards my bedroom door, then stop in my tracks.

Shit, I realise, this is exactly what Rob was saying: he wants me to see him tonight. This is going to be annoying. I open the bedroom door, and walk into the corridor to see the front door shaking from being pounded so much. I am about to open the door when I quickly glance over and see Becky standing outside her bedroom. I am about to speak to her, but she steps back inside and shuts the door. Stunned, I turn and open the front door. I am standing in front of a giant guard, glaring down at me.

"Layton Rai?" the guard says.

"Yes, that's me," I yawn.

"Come with me," he demands.

"Can't I put some clothes on?" I ask, as I am standing there in nothing but shorts and a T-shirt.

"It won't be long," he says.

I reluctantly go with him and am taken down the stairs. I am really struggling to keep my eyes open as I am led outside. It is freezing cold, and of course it is raining. I am then pushed into a van, which drives off.

The ride is bumpy and not something I would recommend to anybody. Just like when we go to work, I have no clue what direction we are travelling in. I am beginning to feel as if I am not in full control of what I am doing. Other people are dictating my actions, not giving me a chance to make my own decisions. This is something that I will have to endure for the time being, but maybe if I work harder, I can have more of a say in what I do.

The van suddenly comes to a stop. The doors open and I look out at a group of guards who are looking back at me.

"Come with me," one of them says.

I shrug and step out of the van, walking along the path with the guard towards what looks like our work placement. I see Rob standing in the distance. He marches up to me and glares right at me.

"Evening," he says, and a horrible cold wafts through my clothes and into my skin.

"Hi," I reply. "What is it you wanted?"

"Good, straight to business," he says. "Well, I have brought you here because we have a predicament that I want you to help me with," he explains as we walk through the factory towards some guards standing with their backs to us.

"OK," I say as we come up right behind the guards.

The guards move out the way and we see a family in front of us. There are two adults, a man and woman, and three children: one girl, who looks about ten; a boy, who looks about seven; and a baby being held by the woman.

"You see this family?" Rob points them out to me.

"Yeah?" I say as I look at them, frightened and shivering.

"Well, we suspect they were going to attack our great Union here," he tells me, looking at this family standing in front of us, not looking like there's much violence in them.

"OK. How were they a threat?" I ask, feeling a little confused.

"Well, we thought they had weapons and planned to attack us. We decided to go into their little town, not far from here, and took out all the residents there. That just leaves this lot," he explains, pointing at them as if they are not people.

"Please," the woman cries out, "we've done nothing wrong." I look at her and her family, noticing that they all have dirt on their faces, on top of what could be very pasty skin.

"Shut up!" Rob shouts. "We suspected them of having weapons, so we decided to investigate."

I look at him, then at the family.

"Well?" I ask, thinking, There better be a very good answer.

"Well what?" he replies.

"Did they have the weapons?" I ask.

He looks at me for a moment, gulps, then looks at the family and back at me.

"Well, no," he says reluctantly. "But, they could still be a threat."

"How? They didn't have weapons, they're no threat; let them go," I say, trying to sound reasonable.

"Ah, it's not that easy."

"Why?" I ask.

He then walks back towards me and stands right in my face.

"Well, if word gets out that we made a mistake, people may not have trust in us."

"What, so you just punish innocent people?" I shout.

"True," he says. "That is why you're not going to tell anyone about tonight," he tells me in a very conniving voice.

"Then why bring me here?" I ask.

"I brought you here," he says, "to test what kind of person you are. Will you sacrifice these innocents for the well-being of the people?"

I look at him, then back at the family. I can't help but feel sympathy for them.

"Let them go," I demand.

"Very well," Rob says. He waves to one of the guards and they grab the family to take them away. "Let's go," he suggests. We all walk forward with the family, heading out of the factory grounds.

"Please, sir, let us go," the little girl says to me. I try not to look at her, try not to make her feel as if I can give her some kind of hope. We are then led towards a border next to what looks like the remnants of a park.

"Stand here," one of the guards says to the family.

"OK," Rob says to them as I stand there looking on. "This young man has said you should be set free."

"Thank you," the mother says, sounding very grateful.

"Yes, thank you," the father adds.

"It's OK." I nod to him.

"Right," Rob says, pointing to the guards. They move out of the way, and there is an open field behind them. "All you have to do is run to the other side. OK, now go."

The family hesitate for a moment, looking at the guards and me.

"Go, go," Rob urges, waving his arms.

"Mum?" The daughter tugs the hand of her mother standing next to her.

"Let's just go, honey," the mum calmly says, edging the children around.

The family then turn and start running away, sprinting through the field. I feel a little relieved to see them go, until I hear a noise – a click; like the safety off a gun. I turn and see a van nearby, with a man on top, sitting behind what looks like a giant Gatling gun.

"No!" I shout as I see his finger moving over the trigger. The guard begins to fire, shooting at the family as they try to run away. "Stop, just stop!" I scream as the bullets fly through the field. The dad is hit right in the back, causing him to crash to the ground.

"No!" I cry as I see him crumple. I try to run at the man with the gun, but before I can get close, I am held back by one of the guards standing nearby. I look back and see the mum, still carrying the baby, fall to the ground. The bullets keep flying and I am watching the little boy and girl running and running. Come on, keep going, come on, keep going. The bullets keep firing, but the boy and girl manage to dodge them and run off into the distance.

"Thank God," I say to myself.

"Well, that was fun," Rob remarks.

I turn and grab him by the shirt, holding him close to me.

"Why did you do that?" I shout, feeling my face burn with anger.

"It wasn't my idea," Rob tries to explain. "It was his," he says, pointing in the distance. I look over and can see General Singh standing in the background, just looking at us. I let go of Rob and look straight at him.

"This way," one of the guards says to me, and escorts me away.

He throws me into the back of a van. I look back at the group of guards standing outside; they have an attitude like they have conquered a nation. I glare at them and can see they don't think anything wrong has happened here. They don't seem to care that an innocent family has just been killed; they just care about doing their jobs. They have no idea what they have done. Even if they do have an idea, do they even care? Who do they think they are? What kind of people think they can kill innocent people? If the family didn't have any weapons then they should've just let them go. There is no reason to keep people as prisoners if they haven't done anything wrong.

This replays over and over in my head, and I feel a hard pain in my chest. I look out at Rob in front of the van, and he looks at me with that stupid smile on his face.

"See you in the morning, Layton," he says patronisingly as the van doors close.

I am then driven through the city – well, I assume I am as I am back in moving darkness once more. As quickly as it arrived, the van pulls up once more outside the dorm. The doors open and I am led outside and into the dorm. I stand there, knowing that I am going to have to climb these stairs, try not to explain any of this to my friends. Why did they do this? Why did they think this was a good idea? This Union is straining my loyalty – maybe the others are right.

15

Today is slow. After Rhea was taken yesterday, today is just a slow fucking day. I really cannot be fucked with work today. I really just could not give a shit. I want to believe in this system, I really do, but my belief is being tested now.

Well, I say I believe in the system, but after what I saw last night, I can't help but feel a sense of doubt about it all. Not just a sense; I can't help but be overwhelmed by doubt. I want to think we have joined something worthwhile, yet all I seem to be at the moment is troubled. That family were innocent people, they'd never done any harm to the Union. I don't want my belief to be tested; I just want it to be easy for us all. I wonder if Rhea is OK; I wonder if she is suffering, I wonder if those kids managed to get away.

I stand here staring at these parts and I just don't know what to do with them. I put the metal in the metal box, the plastic in the plastic box, the excess in the waste box, over and over again, and for what? I don't exactly get much for it. I was wondering how to buy stuff around here. Apparently, it depends on the hours you work. The longer you work, the more you get. Doesn't matter about shift patterns, it all depends on how long you work. If you ask for more shifts, the more stuff you can get. I suppose that's how they get people to work as hard as they do. Personally, I'm working the bare minimum, eight till six.

"I wonder if she's OK." Jane says as we work in silence. "I hope she is, I always liked her."

"I'm sure she's fine," Becky adds, trying to sound optimistic.

"Yeah, let's hope so," I say. I really want to tell them about last night, but I know I just can't. We just continue to work as normal until I see a guard heading straight towards us.

"Here we go," Amrit says.

"Layton, with me," the guard demands. I look at him and can barely see his eyes through the gap in his balaclava. I then turn and look at the group. They smile and nod.

"All right, see you guys soon," I say as I leave the work station and head off with the guard.

I wonder what Rob wants from me today? I am really not in the mood for his bullshit. I would usually crack a joke about how this guard is walking. I mean, look at him, he looks like he has a horse's rod stuck up his arse. Maybe he really needs a shit; that's probably it, he really needs a shit. The toilets are down there – go have a shit, then come get me. Don't come get me while you're in mid-shit. What an idiot, I think he should be fired.

He opens the door for me to go in and I see Rob sitting there with a drink in his hand. Looks like whisky, though I can't really tell.

"Layton," Rob calls out to me as I walk over to take a seat. He is wearing a weird yellow flowery top with skin-tight chinos and sunglasses for some reason. This is not a good look for him; I can see his gut hanging out. "How are you today?"

"Fine," I reply. I do not want him to think I am comfortable with having a full-on conversation with him right now.

"Good, good," he says with very little feeling. "Nasty business, that, yesterday."

"Yeah," I say.

157

"Some people have to be shown order," he explains. As soon as the words leave his mouth, I just want to get up and punch him square in the face.

"OK," I say, making sure I don't cause any disruption.

"You understand why it happened that way?" Rob asks me. I look at him for a while and have no idea what to say to him, I just want to leave the room right now.

"No," I say, stuck for words.

"You will," he tells me.

"OK," I again reluctantly respond, restricting my words. He then swills his drink around, dipping his fingers in and licking them.

"That Rhea, my God, can she throw a punch," he says, throwing a punch into the air. Well, I think it's a punch; it looks more like one of those middle-aged guy things when they try to be cool but it just comes off as weird. "She doesn't look like a bad piece of treacle either; I think she'll be a nice little squeeze for me one day."

OK, this guy has officially entered Twatville now. Scratch that, he's the Mayor of Twatville. My fist tightens and I clench it hard, really wanting to punch him. I want to kill him, I really do. I don't say anything because he still looks a bit, you know, crazy, so I remain stationary listening to his bullshit.

"You know what I mean, brother?" he says, trying to get a response from me. "I might have her sent up here so I can get a taste of her pudding. Oh yeah, high-five me, brother."

Do I high-five him? He just said he wants a piece of Rhea's pudding. I have an idea of what he means. Fuck it, I'll high-five him. Fuck me, his hands are small. As soon as he high-fives me, I recoil. I feel terrible for giving him the satisfaction of humouring him.

"Sorry," I say as he does a little dance back to his seat, "is there a reason why you called me in?"

"Yes, before I forget. We're just a couple of lads having too much fun, aren't we?" he chuckles to himself. "Come with me," he orders, hopping to his feet, and does a little dance before opening the door.

"OK," I say as I rise to follow him outside.

"Now you see," he begins as we start walking through the different work stations, "we work here as the Union; we work in an oiled machine." I think he means to say that the Union works as a well-oiled machine, but whatever. "So, we can't have people making mistakes. I mean, the centipede can't live if his leg's broken, yeah?" What is with this guy fumbling through his metaphors?

"Yeah," I say.

"Now follow me," he orders as he minces towards a door and gingerly opens it. "After you, my good sir. Now you look like a good man," he begins as we enter another room full of workers. "Even the big man General Singh has noticed," he adds, looking at me like a proud parent.

"Yeah?" I say out of curiosity.

"He needs people who are strong and seem to like it here, and he just asks that you do a few simple things for the Union. He likes you to work and provide for the Union, help us help you help you, you know, that philosophy. But, he doesn't like to admit there is just one problem."

I look at him glumly, trying to think of a response, but unable to.

"The way you acted last night. You really need to toughen up," he says, clenching his fists.

"Yeah, OK," I reply hesitantly.

"So," he says as he leads me to another door, this time opening onto what looks like a car park, "we have to get rid of the scroungers; you know, trim the flesh kind of thing."

I don't say anything.

"So we have the guards. Now I ask you: would you like to be a guard one day?" he asks me, getting very close to me for some bizarre reason. "I mean, would you like to be stood there, giving orders and being given the best treatment?"

"I suppose," I say.

"Well, that's great," he says as he walks a little further towards what looks like some scaffolding. "Because if you're going to be a guard, that means you will have to fight for the Union, maybe even kill for the Union. You think you could do that?" he asks, looking me up and down as if it is some form of challenge that has been laid out to me.

"I don't know," I say.

Rob looks at me with a serious expression on his face. He takes his sunglasses off and walks toward me.

"Doubt," he says, "is a powerful thing. Once you rid yourself of it, you will be much stronger for it."

He then turns and waves his hands in the air. Suddenly two guards come towards us. They are dragging what looks like a woman. I can't tell who it is because she has a pillowcase over her head. Shit, it's not Rhea, is it? I stand there staring at the two guards bringing her towards us.

"Now this will be fun," Rob says to me enthusiastically. The guards halt in front of us and throw the girl to her knees. "OK, let's see your mettle," Rob says in my ear. He then turns and waves to the guards. One of them pulls the pillowcase off the girl's head and I can see who it is.

"Recognise the girl?" Rob asks me. I look down and I can see exactly who it is he has presented in front of me.

"Yeah," I say.

"You know her name?" he asks me.

"Yes."

"Well, who is it?"

"Her name's Scarlett," I reply hesitantly.

"Yes, it is," Rob says, "and she is the one who got your friend thrown into punishment."

I look down at her and I can see that she has been through

160

a hard time. Her face is pale and bruised, with what looks like scratch marks all over her body.

"You see, this one has been causing trouble for a lot of people; she even stole from your friend. I mean, she got the shit kicked out of her after, no offence, honey," he says, holding his hand up to Scarlett. "How can I put this? Our system is like a delicate ecosystem, a rainforest if anything. So, scum like this here, is a fungus, a tragedy, a pollution to our system."

I look down and I can see Scarlett panicking. I can tell that she is so scared she can barely speak, struggling to breathe, with tears trickling down her face.

"What do you want me to do?" I ask Rob as directly as I can.

"What do I want you to do? Well, there are a number of things you could do. What do you think you should do?"

"I don't know," I say.

"No, you don't," he replies. "That's why the great general himself sent me here to teach you. I mean, this girl here is scum, she is just a disgusting, immature loudmouth who needs to be erased." He then walks toward Scarlett and spits in her face. She gasps as it strikes her cheek. I can't help but watch on, unable to find the words to speak out.

"OK," I manage eventually.

"I mean, she would probably do anything for me now," he suggests. "Won't you, honey?" he adds in a baby voice to Scarlett. "Go on, make a pig noise, snort like the little piggy you are. Snort for me," he demands.

She hesitates at first, then starts to snort like a pig. It's very uncomfortable to watch, I can't help but feel a little sorry for her.

"That's a good girl. Now lick my hand," he commands, holding his hand out. Scarlett starts to lick his hand, like she is a dog or something. "Good girl, good girl," he patronises her, patting her on the head. "She'd probably suck my dick if I told her to; I mean, she is weak. She is of no use to this world right now, so she needs to be eliminated."

He pulls a gun out from his back pocket and hands it to me. "Do the honours, boy scout."

I don't know why, but instinctively I take the gun from him.

"Point it at her, then," he demands as I keep staring at the gun. I turn and point it at Scarlett.

She looks up at me and mouths, "Please. Please don't." I just look down at her, unable to look her in the eye.

"I can't," I say to Rob.

"Sure you can," Rob says. "Just clear your head and shoot."

I've never killed anyone. This is the first time I've held a weapon in days, and I have never actually had to pull the trigger. I stand there for what feels like an eternity, I don't know what to do with myself. Should I pull the trigger or not? I just don't know.

"Come on," he encourages, "be one of us, be one of the Union, and be a guard for us."

I keep my eyes focused on Scarlett as she stays there on her knees looking at me, pleading for her life. A good couple of minutes pass before Rob gets frustrated.

"Come on now," he says.

Without noticing it, I lower the gun.

"No, this is not the way," I stutter, just about managing to get my words out.

"Oh, for fuck's sake," Rob snaps, and grabs the gun off me. "You need a job doing, just do it yourself." He then turns and points the gun at Scarlett. He doesn't even hesitate. "I mean, it's one less mouth to feed," he tells me in a matter-of-fact way.

"No, please!" Scarlett cries, but as soon as she speaks, Rob pulls the trigger. The noise shatters my eardrums, making my ears feel as if they are going to bleed. I look down and see Scarlett on her back, with blood all over the place. There is a giant hole in her forehead where the bullet entered.

Rob stares at her motionless corpse for a good while, as do I. I mean, she was bad but I did not want this to happen to her. I don't really know what to feel. Is this redemption, is this vengeance, revenge, or even justice?

Rob then turns and raises the gun. He points it directly in my face.

"Right, why should you live now? You're clearly not made of the strong stuff. Give me one good reason why I shouldn't kill you right now. Why should I let you live?" he asks me as I stare down the barrel of the gun.

"If you were going to kill me," I say, "you would've done it already."

We stare at each other for a while and I can see Rob's finger hovering over the trigger. Then suddenly he begins to laugh. He raises the gun and moves it out of my face.

"I guess there's some strength in you after all," he says as he puts the gun back in his back pocket. "General Singh would like to see you tomorrow. I don't know what it's about, probably something to do with you being a guard or something. You will come here for work duty, then somebody will get you and take you to the headquarters, OK?"

"OK," I say.

"Right. Now I guess it's time you got back to work; we've had enough fun for one day."

We begin to walk away, and I turn and see the two guards dragging Scarlett's body away. Rob takes me back through the rooms, and the guard who took me to see him is waiting outside his office.

"OK, this is where we part ways. Remember, you can be more than your friends," he says to me. He then signals to the guard and I am taken back to my work station.

"Are you OK?" Becky asks me.

"Yeah, I'm fine," I respond abruptly.

"What happened?" Mark asks.

I hesitate for a moment before answering. I look down at my work, then back up at the rest of them.

"Scarlett is dead," I say, feeling my throat begin to tighten.

"Shit," Jane says.

"How do you know?" Becky asks me.

"Because Rob wanted me to kill her," I mutter.

"Did you?" Amrit asks.

I look up at him, and he looks back at me. We stare at each other for a good while. For some reason, I can feel my eyes begin to well up; I don't know why.

"No," I say. He looks at me for a moment, gathering his thoughts before speaking.

"I know," he says to reassure me.

We both then look down at our work and just get back to what we were doing, separating the plastic and the metal and all that bullshit. Even when it comes to lunch, I just feel drained and motionless. I feel sick all of a sudden; I mean, it's the first time I have seen somebody killed in front of me. The thing I keep worrying about is what they are going to do with her body. Are they going to bury her or cremate her? Will they just dump her on the street; will they feed her to a bunch of infected? I really don't know.

I then start to think about those kids. What if they were found and didn't make it? What if they were harmed, or even killed? Then I start to think about Rhea; I hope she's OK, I really do. I hope she manages to survive what they are putting her through.

Before I know it, I am lying in my bed just staring at the ceiling. I can't look anywhere else, and I don't really want to. Then out of nowhere, Becky comes and opens my door.

"Hi," she says to me.

"Hi," I say back to her.

"Dinner's ready if you want some," she offers.

"Thanks," I say, "I will be there in a second."

She nods and smiles at me before beginning to back away.

"Cool," she says, and walks off.

I turn and sit on the edge of my bed, pondering. I keep asking myself: Why am I here? What does General Singh want with me? Where is Rhea? Am I safe? I don't know. I really don't know anything right now.

16

Before work the following morning I decide to get up early and sit outside the halls of residence. I remember seeing a bench outside; it looks very well kept, with not a lot of dirt and decay.

I have a quick breakfast and sit there, just looking at the cold sky. It's peaceful. No guards to order me around. No vans to drag me to work. Nothing, just pure silence. I close my eyes for a moment and feel a gentle breeze across my face. It feels cold, yet soothing. I have a cigarette in my hand. I look down and I can see I have barely smoked any of it. It is there burning away in my fingers, yet I have no interest in raising my hand to my mouth. I close my eyes once more and try to forget everything. I take myself away from everything that I know and enter my own little safe place, where only I am welcome. I feel as if I have forgotten everything now; that I am away from it all.

Then I see him. He is standing there, right in front of me.

"Adam," I call out to him. He says nothing, just remains staring at me. "Adam, I'm sorry."

He still stands there, pale and motionless. He looks at me with his large brown eyes, a cut over the right one.

"I didn't know what to do," I explain. "I wish I could take it back." A tear begins to trickle out of my eye and down my cheek.

"Please, Adam, I didn't mean for any of this to happen," I try to tell him.

He then turns and begins to walk away.

"Adam!" I cry out. "Adam, please, don't go!"

He does not turn back to face me. He just keeps walking away, until he is gone. I look up. My hands are cold and my feet are numb. I can't stop looking in that direction. Then I see it hopping around, its pointy ears waving; a little brown rabbit just dancing around in the distance. I don't know why it is here; if it is the one I saw before. I just can't take my eyes off it.

Then I hear the noise of an engine. The rabbit hops off into the distance. I feel sad watching it leave, as if I will never see it again. I look up and see the vans making their way to the halls. I guess it's time to get to work.

Like everybody else, I get in line. The rest of my cell come walking out, with one person noticeably missing: Rhea. We get into our line and the usual protocol is carried out, with Canine coming out and calling for each cell one at a time. This time, however, Cell Block A are there, ready to be called. They get into their van, all looking the worse for wear, bruised and very unwell. Our cell block is called and we get into our van as promptly as ever. The journey is quiet as always.

We arrive at work and leave our van. We queue to be let in, the long line in front of us waiting to be searched, and I notice a couple of guards heading towards me. They look like the standard guards that I have seen all over the place, although these two, I know, are coming for me. I know who sent them. They come up to me and without a word, turn me around and escort me to another van. I quickly look back and see Amrit, Becky and Mark looking worried. Inside the van and the door closes, plunging me into what feels like eternal darkness as the van sets off to take me to its destination.

The van comes to an immediate halt and the door opens.

I look forward and can see a bright light shining down on me. Outside, I can just about make out a guard standing right in front of me. He leans in and grabs me by the arm, forcing me out of the van. I am led through a building I do not recognise; it looks to be an abandoned warehouse. The smell is the first thing that hits me: a damp, soggy, muddy kind of smell. I can see two more guards standing ahead of me, with a man sitting in a chair between them. There is another chair in front of him; I assume that one is for me. I am dragged forward and forced to sit on this crooked chair. I look straight ahead and see a figure in front of me. I search around and can see nothing else; the room is pitch-black. The only sound I can hear is dripping in the background. Then the figure in front of me speaks.

"Well, you're here," he says. He looks up and I can see that it is General Singh sitting right opposite me. I knew that I would be speaking with him today, but I still feel nervous around him. "Welcome. I thought we could meet in more humble surroundings," he tells me, holding his hands out and presenting the room.

"This is certainly that," I say. He chuckles to himself at my response.

"Well," General Singh says, "I believe you are happy with your accommodation?" He sounds very peaceful.

"Yes," I reluctantly reply.

"Good," he says. "There is no point in taking people in if they are going to be unhappy with what we provide for them. The Union only seeks to help those who need to be helped."

"Thank you," I say in response to his patronising grandeur.

"No," he says, "there is no need to thank me. Words are meaningless; I believe that your actions can speak louder, don't you?"

I look forward, and I can't help but gulp.

"Yeah," I respond hesitantly.

"What wisdom can you find that is greater than kindness?" he says, leaning back and crossing his legs, looking smug.

"Man is born free and everywhere he is in chains," I remark.

General Singh uncrosses his legs and looks surprised. "I did not know you knew of Rousseau," he says, perplexed and surprised.

"I came across him a while ago, while I was on my travels. I found many books written by him, and I would read them to pass the time. He had some interesting views," I tell him, thinking back to a library I once stayed in to keep out the cold.

"Good," he says. "Fetch us a drink," he asks a guard standing nearby. The guard then turns and walks off. "I have been saving this for a while now," he explains to me. "Very good stuff."

The guard returns with what looks like a bottle of alcohol and two glasses.

"Here," General Singh offers, holding a glass out to me. I take it as he begins to open the bottle. "This is a fine whisky, Black Label, I believe. My father kept a lot of his drinks when the world went to ruin." He pours the whisky into my glass, then pours one for himself. "A fine whisky for a fine occasion," he says, holding his glass out to me. I move mine towards his and he clinks them in a friendly gesture.

We both sip the whisky and it does taste good. It is smooth and warm, a drink that does feel like it was worth holding on to.

"Thank you," I say to him again. He nods in response, then takes another gulp of his drink. I just gently sip mine.

"Rousseau often spoke of liberty," he tells me. "He influenced so many. Much of his voice I have brought to our community, living through his vision," he adds, raising his hands as if to present the city to me. I look around and can't help but feel that this is not a civilisation that Jean-Jacques Rousseau would've imagined.

"OK," I say.

"Rousseau spoke so much of equality, too," he continues.

"It is my belief that what he is saying is that those who have knowledge should teach those who are lacking that intelligence."

"OK," I counter, "but didn't he also say, People who know little are usually great talkers, while men who know much say little?"

He pauses for a moment and looks right at me. He then chuckles and nods.

"Very true," he cheerfully replies. He takes another sip and swirls the whisky around in his glass for a moment. "Now, I guess you're wondering why I brought you here."

I nod, not wanting to say anything out of turn.

"Well, you, Layton, have really stood out compared to your peers. I mean, you haven't been here long, but I know you have done very well," he tells me, looking me up and down.

"Thank you," I say.

He smirks a little. "I believe that you will go far here. All you need to do is keep working hard and you will be fine," he states, leaning over as if he is some kind of mentor.

"OK."

"Now, before we move on, do you have anything you wish to ask me?"

I look at him, and there is only one thing I want to ask him. I know I shouldn't, but I must.

"What has happened to my friend Rhea?" I ask.

He pauses for a moment. Shit, I hope I haven't said anything stupid. I was trying not to speak out of turn, but now I think I'm going to be killed.

"Loyalty. Loyalty is a gift," he says, raising his voice to a loud whisper.

"Sorry?" I say, confused. He leans in towards me.

"Loyalty," General Singh says again. "Do you know the story of the rat in the box?"

"No," I say.

"Well, there once was a rat that played with all of the other

170

rats. That rat was playful and enjoyed life. Until one day, the rat got in a fight. The rat killed another rat. The rat was then put into a box and left there for many days, hours and seconds, in complete darkness with no food or water. His owner wanted the rat to know that it was being punished. After this, the rat was released from the box and entered the general population once more. For a while the rat looked as if it had learned its lesson; then it attacked again, killing another of its own. To prevent another incident, the owner killed the rat."

I look at him, confused. "I don't understand."

"You can never tame nature," General Singh says to me. "Your friend Rhea, she is a spirited one, a compelling person. However, she has a violent streak in her."

I can't help but feel he is looking for more excuses to punish her.

"She was provoked," I say.

"I know," General Singh replies. "Her nature is to defend. She is having the appropriate punishment; you will see her soon. As for the person she fought, her nature was to bully. A bully will always be a bully; therefore they cannot be changed. To have a harmonious society, bullies need to be exterminated, and you did the honours."

"I didn't kill her," I try to explain.

"I know," he says, sounding a little enthusiastic for some reason. "That is because it is in your nature to be resistant. You do not wish to do certain things because you are afraid of consequences. That is your nature."

I can't help but feel the more he says this, the more he is making me out to be weak.

"What is your nature?" I ask him.

He leans back and tilts his head forward to glare at me.

"To lead," he responds. I think he actually believes this. He thinks he is a great leader. "Let me show you something," he says.

We get up from our seats and begin walking towards a table which has a sheet over it. It looks like there is something underneath it.

"What is this?" I ask him.

He looks at me and pulls the sheet off. A body lies on the table; I can recognise that it is Scarlett. I back away, repulsed.

"Why are you showing me this?" I ask him.

"My plan was for you to be the one to be rid of this girl" he explains to me "I wanted you to be the one to be rid of this disease. But, you were unable to do so. No need to matter, there will be time for you to get thicker skin."

I'm getting frustrated as he keeps speaking as if I was the one who pulled the trigger.

"I didn't kill her," I repeat sternly. "It was Rob who killed her, not me."

He does nothing more than shrug off what I say.

"You had a choice," he explains. "You could have disobeyed, yet like an intelligent person, you thought of the consequences and realised that it would be better to kill this worthless shit than keep it."

I begin to get frustrated that he isn't accepting what I am saying. I didn't do anything, but he keeps talking to me as if I was the one who pulled the trigger.

"OK," I say to him. "You know it was Rob who did it. It wasn't me, it was him who shot Scarlett."

General Singh glares at me.

"Why was it you came here, Layton?" he asks. He glares at me once more, his eyes piercing mine, feeling as if they are striking the back of my skull.

I look up at him, lost for words. "I don't know," I say.

"I mean, why did you come to our society, our community?" he asks me. "Why here of all places; what was the reason you wanted to come here?"

I think for a while before giving my answer.

"Well, I came because – I mean, we came because we wanted shelter. We thought things would be better closer to the city than they are on the outskirts," I admit, remembering what we went through before we came here.

"Yes," he says, "much better than dealing with those damn border monkeys; I mean, they are nothing but a waste of space. You don't see any here, that's for sure."

He begins to walk in another direction, beckoning for me to follow him.

"Why is that?" I ask. He stops.

"Security," he says. "Now follow me."

My frustration grows with every word he says to me. I feel them scraping against my spine every time he says another word that just doesn't fit with what I am saying. He is not giving me a straight answer to anything.

We walk to a room that is hidden behind a curtain. General Singh takes me inside to have a look.

"Now," he says, "like many others, I am fascinated with the infected. I look around and I see these pour souls and how they are suffering so much."

I can hear a man calling out for help.

"What's that?" I ask General Singh. I dart my head around, trying to hear the sound again so I can work out what it is.

"Ah," he says, "this is the real reason why I brought you here."

We walk forward towards the man screaming.

"You're probably much too young to remember how this all started, with the financial crash and people being infected. Well, it is all intertwined," he explains to me as we continue to walk. "I was quite young when it started, just finishing off at university, with the whole world ahead of me. Then we found that the value of the currency had dropped. The privatisation boom collapsed, which was a major cause of inflation. Then came the wars and the different countries fighting for territories," he adds as we walk through another sheet to a different room.

"Then came the infected. Not a lot of people know that many European countries used a form of toxin on certain towns, which infected the people living there. It caused their skin to become pale and made their minds go a little loopy." We stop outside a door. "The military abandoned the people, allowing them to roam and infect others. As a result of this, many lives were lost."

He opens the door and we walk into what looks like a doctor's surgery. I can see the man who was screaming out for help. Next to him is an infected person who appears to be dead.

"Help me, please help me!" the man calls out to us.

"So what is it we are doing here?" General Singh asks. "We want to look for a cure for the infected. We want to help them. Now, there is no point in finding somebody who is already infected – no, we must find a healthy vessel and infect them so that we can figure out how to cure them."

"How will you do that?" I ask.

"Let me show you," he says.

We walk towards the infected body. I look over at the man who was calling out for help, and I begin to recognise him. This is the same man who was picked out of the crowd during General Singh's great speech as a volunteer to help with a great task. He is tied to a chair with bruises all over his body, sweating and with tears running down his face.

General Singh pulls out a syringe, inserts it into the dead body and draws out a red-black liquid. "OK, so this is infected blood, now what we need to do is infect somebody who is not infected. Let's take this subject here," he says as he walks over to the man in the chair. "He is a perfectly healthy human being, not any health issues that I know of," he states, presenting the man like a piece of prized meat, as if he has brought him in fresh from a hunt.

"What are you going to do?" I ask, looking around to see if I can find some implement to free the man. I keep looking back and forth, but my eyes begin to hurt from all the looking around, and I resume looking at General Singh, who glares at me with a haunting grin on his face.

"Simple," he says. He then pushes the syringe into the man's shoulder, pressing hard to make sure the needle digs right into him.

"No, don't!" I yell, and try to lunge at him. Before I know it, I am being pulled back by two guards. "This is madness, why are you doing this?" I shout.

The man screams as the syringe is stuck into his arm. "Ah, please, no, ah!" He begins to panic. "No, why did you? Oh my God, ah!" he calls out, sweat pouring from his forehead, tears running from his eyes, looking as if he is going to faint from the shock.

"I am trying to save those who cannot save themselves," General Singh says. He then presses the plunger and I can see the infected liquid go into the man in the chair. General Singh pulls the syringe out and throws it on the floor. "You see, this man has been infected with the blood of an infected victim. Slowly it will seep into his bloodstream, causing him to feel tired and nauseous; then he will have a fever. Then he will become one of them," he explains, pointing to the infected on the table.

Suddenly two men in lab coats come rushing in to take the man into another room.

"No, please, no," he calls, struggling to breathe. "Please, help me," he cries, looking right at me. I do nothing more than look back at him as his eyes beg me to help; I know I can do nothing to save him. The guards just drag him, not supporting him in any way. Then he is gone, out of sight, away from this place.

"You're a monster," I say to General Singh, collapsing into myself, struggling to breathe myself as I try to come to terms with what I just witnessed, rubbing my eyes in disbelief. I keep rubbing my hair as if I am trying to clean myself, feeling sweat begin to form on my forehead. I look down at my hands and see they too have begun to sweat, so that whenever I touch something it leaves a mark, showing that I have been there, like my hand's own signature.

"You're in shock," General Singh says to me. "We are only trying to keep people alive. If anything has value these days, surely human life does," he adds, so sure of himself. "Since the crash, so many scientific records have been destroyed, such as what temperature the human body boils at, what temperature it freezes at, how to cure certain diseases. We now have to work from scratch. We are trying to bring back human biology, so we can keep our civilisation alive."

I start to feel light-headed. I stagger and land on the table where the infected body lies. I look at the body, startled, and stagger away.

"I can't believe what I'm hearing," I gasp, finding it hard to breathe.

"I want you to be a part of this, Layton. I want you and your friends to become a major part of the Union. Be a part of our future by reconnecting with civilisation's medical past," he says, standing there with his hands behind his back, very composed.

"You're insane!" I shout at him. "There are textbooks, thousands of them." All he has to do is look, and he will find those books that he so desperately wants. He does not have to punish people just for his own curiosity.

"Where?" he asks. "Where are all of these textbooks you speak of? No, we need to bring order back to the world; we need to bring value back. We can help people."

I stagger away and quickly turn to run out through the way we came in. I can see some guards standing there. Shit, I guess I'll have to find another way out, I think to myself, and quickly turn and run the way the men in lab coats came from.

I can sense the guards about to chase after me, but as I make a run for it I hear General Singh say, "Let him go" as I run through the door. I run through and try to keep going, until I suddenly stop.

"What the fuck?" I mutter to myself. I can see people all around me. To the left of me there is a man with electric cables attached to him, shocking him every five seconds. I stagger forward and see what looks like a man's body with a dog sewn to where the head is supposed to be.

"Oh my God," I gasp. Turning, I see a young boy crying, with blades where his hands should be; a woman dragging herself on the floor, her legs shredded. As well as all of this, I can see a lot of dead bodies around. Then it hits me; the smell is incredible. All I smell is flesh and rotting.

"We are answering humanity's every question," General Singh says behind me. I turn and see him walking towards me. "We are trying to educate everybody. We will teach this to the children and they will thank us."

"You can't do this. You can't, it's wrong," I plead, trying to find a shred of humanity within him.

"Is it?" General Singh asks. "You will learn about this work one day. One day, the world will look back on what I am doing here and see that I am helping them all," he says, holding his hands out in an angelic pose. "They will look back on what I have done, remember who I am, and thank me for what I have done and honour me for what I am. They will know my name and all will desire to be a part of the Union, as I and the Union have saved the world. I have saved the world," he says, his voice beginning to grow louder. "I will be the one they look to for help. General Singh, the one who saved the world."

I crumple to the ground.

"People will know what you are doing," I say to him, "and they will know it is wrong. This has to stop."

He just looks at me, stares at me right in the face, once again piercing right into me.

"Well, who's going to stop me?" he asks.

I just want to be away from him; I just want to be anywhere except this place. I can't bear to look at the person I have just come to understand, the person for whom I now feel nothing but hate, disgust and fear. Rather than look at him any more, I turn, try to move away, to get away from him. Until I see a guard and he hits me straight in the face with the butt of his gun.

Through the daze, I feel somebody come up behind me and pinch my shoulder.

"No," I say as I feel it press into me, like a claw digging in.

"Sleep now," a voice gently remarks behind me. "Tomorrow is a new day."

I begin to drift away into the distance. My eyelids grow heavy, and even the sweat can't seem to open my eyes open. I feel my greasy skin drift away from me, losing feeling in my hands, then my feet, and then I just collapse and lie on the ground. My eyes close and I drift into the distance. Frankly, I am glad I am out cold now. I am glad I do not have to see any more of this. I just want my eyes to be shut and for me to be away from all of this.

17

I like to think of myself as a happy-go-lucky kind of person; the perfect blend of sarcasm and reality. I like to think I bring a bright light into a dark existence. I like to think that people are all bright lights that shine through the sky at night. I like to believe that all people can join together in one happy circle of unity and aim to make life better for all.

When I was a child I saw a butterfly. It was so graceful, so pure. I thought it was a little angel that had come to show me that Heaven existed. The innocence of youth, I guess. My friends and I would play football with any random ball we found, just making the best of what we had. When I went to the schools that were dotted around the place while I was growing up, I always spoke to girls. It is harmless now, but at the time it seemed that the world was at our feet; that we could change the world, bring it back to its former glory, and make it the thriving global community it once was. We would read old textbooks, look at the globe and believe that we could change everything.

The truth of the world was thrown in my face just three hours ago. I wake with a pounding headache, rolling back and forth in my own bed. I look down and see one foot on the bed and one hovering above the floor. Did I really see what I think

I saw? Am I now a citizen of a society that does what it wants? Well, I guess this is the harsh reality of it all; I think I better just go with it, end of story.

Fuck that. Is this what the world has come to, when a sadistic twat thinks that he can rule over a city and use its citizens as lab rats? When an innocent family are gunned down just for living in the wrong place? No, I will not stand for this; I mean, some of the people I saw in there couldn't even stand. Now is not a time to make jokes; I need to do something about this, something to make this all right again. But when was it ever right? It has been two years (that is only an estimation) since I arrived in Leicester; how long has it been like this? Is every city in England like this? Is every city in the world just like this one?

I have so many questions, yet no answers, which is probably why I have so many questions. I need to get up, I need to see if I can bring about this profound change that has popped into my head. I sit up and turn to the end of my bed. I am about to get up when I feel a surging pain go through my head. I guess that is what happens when the butt of a gun hits you square in the face.

I fall back down onto the bed and stare up at the ceiling once more. It's amazing how when light shines on a blank surface, you can make some form of pattern out of it. Strange, how the eyes work. OK, take two, time to get up once again and get out of here. I try to sit up, feeling the pain in my head. I am going to fight it this time, I'm not going to fail. I push up and rise to my feet. For some bizarre reason, this feels like some sort of accomplishment to me. I make my way to the door, staggering as I go, however I make it in the end. Almost fall back on the bed twice, though. I open the door and head out through the bright light which is cast across the corridor.

Eventually I arrive the living room to find Becky, Mark and Ryan sitting there. I take a seat. They all look at me, perplexed, each of us waiting for someone else to break the silence.

"All right?" I say in order to start some sort of conversation.

"How are you feeling?" Becky asks in her usual concerned voice.

"My head hurts," I say. "Other than that, I'm fine. Ryan, what are you doing here?"

Ryan just smiles at me and does not answer.

"You've been asleep for a while," Mark says to me.

"What do you mean?" I ask. "It's only been about three hours."

"No," Ryan replies sternly, "it's been about a day. It's Saturday today, which is why I am here."

I sit there looking at him, confused.

"What? No, it's not been a day," I say, beginning to feel worried.

"Yes, it has," Ryan responds. "You have been out a very long time."

"Wait," I say, "they only hit me in the head; that couldn't have knocked me out for a whole day."

They look at each other, then turn to me as soon as their silent conversation is over.

"Layton," Becky says to me, "they don't just knock you out."

I look at her, waiting for an explanation.

"They give you an injection to knock you out for a prolonged period of time. The aim is to get you to forget certain things," she tells me, making me far more worried than I was before.

"How do you know this?" I ask.

Becky looks at Mark, then down at the ground.

"Tell him," Mark says to her. Becky takes a deep breath before finally answering.

"Well," she begins, "I used to work for General Singh's science division."

I look at Mark and he nods; then at Ryan and he does the same.

"Go on," I encourage.

"I used to work for him in his science division," Becky

repeats. "First I was working in medicine, helping to make medical supplies for everybody in the city. 'The Union expects…' he would keep telling me. Always with that same bullshit. I didn't mind the work; before I came here I worked on a number of medical supply wagons, and my Dad was a doctor before all of this, so he taught me a thing or two about medicine, just so I could take care of myself."

She takes another breath before speaking again. The rest of us remain silent.

"So when I came here and General Singh found out about that, he wanted me to work within that department."

"OK," I say, "then how did you end up here?"

Becky pauses for a moment and starts to fumble her hands. She does this for a good thirty seconds before she finally looks up at me.

"Well, General Singh started a programme which he called the Lost Science programme. He wanted to rediscover medical information we have lost," she explains.

I know exactly what she is talking about, as I have witnessed those very practices.

"Yeah," I interrupt her, "that's what I saw yesterday; I saw loads of people being experimented on."

"Yeah," Becky says to me. "Well, I was one of the first to work on the project. First it was fine; we were only experimenting on dead bodies. Then he wanted us to experiment on living people. What happens when the human body is electrocuted; what temperature does the body burn at, boil at, freeze at; how long does it take for a human to drown – these were the things he wanted us to find out," she tells us, breathing very quickly and stuttering ever so slightly.

"He told me it was because we lost the records," I say to her.

"Bullshit," she responds. "He knows we can find the records, he just wants to make out that he rediscovered everything so he can be seen as a great leader."

I can't help but agree with her.

"So," I say, "how did you end up here?"

She pauses once more, this time looking up as she fumbles her hands.

"Well," she says, "I was working on the experiments. I mean, I didn't like it, but I didn't want to cross General Singh. Then one day, he told Canine to bring in a child, only seven years old. General Singh wanted to know what temperature a child will boil at.

"It was at that point that I said, 'No, I won't do it. There is no need to know what temperature a child will boil at.' The guards stated that I had to do the experiment, but I put my foot down saying, 'No, I will not. I will not boil an innocent child just for his curiosity.'

"I was taken to punishment. I was whipped and beaten for three days straight. Then I was sent here. When you work in the science division you get your own house with a bedroom, a toilet, a kitchen, everything. One step down from a guard. Now I am here, picking through rubbish, because I did not want to boil a child."

We look at one another, contemplating what the other is going to say next.

"Do you regret it?" I ask her in a sincere manner.

She looks at me and pauses once more before finally speaking.

"Yes and no," Becky hesitantly responds.

"How do you mean?" I ask.

"Well, no because I know that I could never harm a child, and I can live with that." She pauses for a moment. "Then again, yes because I found out later that they boiled the child anyway. They were going to do it whether I wanted to or not; they just needed somebody to do it. I stood up for what I believed in and lost everything, while that child was killed and the people who worked on the experiment are still living in luxury."

We all gaze at one another, unable to make a sound. I look down at the ground to avoid looking anybody in the eye.

"We need to leave," Ryan says all of a sudden.

"What?" Mark says, bemused.

"Yeah," Ryan says, "I'm sick of this place. They make out that they are rebuilding civilisation and that everybody can make their way to the top, yet there is no manoeuvrability. All they have done is sold us a dream."

"He's right," Becky adds. "We can't just sit around wondering what we are going to do. We have to take action."

"Do you mean take on the Union?" I ask her.

"No," she replies. "We have to leave and try to rally together. Who knows what other cities they might infect? They could be working on invading London as we speak, or for all we know they might have already done so. They might have stretched up north to Manchester or Leeds, we don't know. I say we tell Amrit and Jane that we are all joining together and leaving." I can't help but feel slightly motivated by every word she is saying.

"There's just one problem," Mark interrupts. He stands to confront her. "How are we to get past the Union? They control the whole city, there is no way we can get past them."

Suddenly we hear the door shut; Amrit and Jane have come back with food.

"Hey, what's going on?" Amrit asks as he and Jane walk into the living room to put away their shopping.

"We are planning on leaving," I say to them. "We have just been saying that we are all sick of this place, and that we have to get out of here."

He looks at us and smiles for a fleeting moment.

"I agree," Amrit says. "What do you guys think we should do?"

"Hold on," Mark suddenly says. "I want to leave as much as the next person, but there is no point in just saying we should leave. There is no mode of transportation that will get us out of here. We don't know the route in and out because we are always in the back of those fucking vans when we go to and from work." He sits down, defeated. "Let's face it, we're trapped here."

One by one, we nod in agreement.

"I know a way," Jane suddenly says. We all turn and look at her.

"You do?" I ask.

"Yeah," she says. "There is an abandoned yard around the corner from here. The guards don't go there because they don't see the point. They usually go to other places to get things that they need, sexual stuff mostly, or food or, other things," she explains to us.

"How do you know this?" I ask her. She looks at me and raises her eyebrow. "Oh, I get you," I say. Of course she knows.

"After work duty, there is one guard on patrol," she begins to tell us. "His name is Finch, not the brightest spark in the world, but he tries. Doesn't know whether he owes people stuff or not. I can distract him while one of you gets one of the vans and we can use it to get out of here. It's an abandoned garage that nobody else wants to guard, so Canine made sure Finch was the one to do it."

We look at her and Becky smiles. I think she is feeling some pride that it was Jane who came up with a plan for finally leaving this place.

"So if this Finch is guarding it," Mark says, "it's not exactly abandoned, is it?"

"Oh yeah." Jane giggles to herself. "Anyway, I know that I can distract him," she tells us, and we can all think of a few ways she will do that.

"I'm sure you do." Mark smirks. "OK, so that's that part of the plan sorted. However, what happens after that? We have no idea what the route is. The roads look the same and we have no idea how to get out of here. The guards have created their own crossings and their own lines to get things in and out of here."

"I have an idea," Becky says. "It's a long shot, but it might work. If we go down the Braunstone Gate sector and straight up past the Hinckley Road zone, we can make our way out of there. General Singh usually uses that area to get goods in and out. I remember when I worked in the science sector, we would sometimes travel up there. Or even better, we can go up Narborough Road."

"That's insane," Ryan says. "That area is crawling with guards."

"I know," she says, "but if we make out that we are transporting waste, they will let us through. It's bound to work."

"I don't know," I say.

"It's the best shot we have," she encourages us, trying not to lose any of the motivation that fills the room.

"Right then," Mark says, "so the plan is tomorrow morning, before work duty. We need to be out of here at 5.30 in the morning. The guards will not be ready at that time. We then get the van, get to Narborough Road and get out of here," he informs us, as if he is planning a military expedition.

"That could work," Amrit agrees.

"Yeah, I think it could," I add.

"So we all need an early night tonight," Amrit says. "Everybody needs to travel with essentials alone, and get plenty of rest, because tomorrow we leave for freedom."

"Yes," we say in unison. We all smile, but then I suddenly stop.

"Wait, what about Rhea?" I ask them. "We can't just leave her here."

"We have no idea when they will release her," Becky says to me.

"Well, we didn't come here together, but we should all leave together." I try to hammer the point home.

"Layton's right," Amrit says. "I don't like to admit it, however, on this very rare occasion, he is right. Layton, Rhea and I came here together; we can't leave her behind."

The others look at us one by one.

"Very well," Ryan says, "change of plan."

Before he gets a chance to say anything else, there is a thud at the door. We look at one another, stunned and perplexed.

"What was that?" Amrit says. We turn and look at the door, then all go rushing towards it. Mark is the first to approach. He opens it and Rhea is outside, lying on the ground in front of us.

"Rhea!" I cry, and we all go rushing to her. Amrit and I lift her and bring her inside.

"Oh my God!" Jane exclaims.

"Is she OK?" Becky asks as we carry her through and into her room. We put her down on the bed, all of us gazing at her. She is sweating a lot, has bruises all over her arms, and struggles to open her eyes.

"Rhea?" I say to her gently.

"Somebody go get some water," Mark demands.

"I'm on it," Ryan says, rushing off to the kitchen. Slowly, Rhea begins to open her eyes.

"Rhea? Rhea?" I say.

"She's waking up," Becky says.

Finally, Rhea's eyes open. She looks at us, then slowly sits up. Becky and I put our hands on her shoulders to help her up.

"Are you OK?" Amrit asks.

"I got it," Ryan says as he rushes back in the room, almost knocking his glasses off from how fast he is running.

"Rhea, what happened?" I ask her. She looks at us, takes a big gulp, then speaks.

"They beat me," she hesitantly explains. "They just kept beating me, and they whipped me over and over again." She pants after every word, breathing very heavily.

"Shit," Mark says.

"They hung me up by my hands and kept hitting me," she says, breaking down. I put my arm around her to comfort her.

"All for a necklace," Becky says.

Rhea then sits back, pulls out the necklace and rolls it around in her hands.

"It's not just a necklace," she says. "My Dad gave it to me. It's the last thing I have that reminds me of him. It means more to me than anything the Union can give me. I will fight to keep that memory of my Dad; I don't want somebody to take it away from me and I won't allow them to do so." She coughs a little. "Now I am left with this," she adds, pulling up her top and showing us her lower back. I am taken aback by what I see: a round red mark burned into her back.

"Oh my God," I whisper. The mark of the Union, imprinted on Rhea's back.

"They branded her." Amrit raises his voice. "They fucking branded her!"

Rhea lies down and I immediately stand. I look over at Mark and Amrit. All three of us walk outside into the hallway.

"It has to happen tomorrow morning," Mark says.

"But she can barely walk," Amrit tries to explain.

"I suppose if we devise a plan where she doesn't have to do anything…" I say, trying to find a middle ground.

"I don't care," Mark says. "I know she is in pain, I know she is hurting, but it's now or never. Tomorrow morning and not an hour later," he says, walking back into Rhea's room. Amrit follows.

"Shit," I say to myself. I know that tomorrow is the time that everything has to change. I guess it's an early start to get out of here. Personally, I can't wait to put this place behind us, so we can have a future that actually involves living.

18

Today is the day. I know that we haven't really planned anything properly; indeed, it could be argued that we are just winging it. However, we have to get out of here, by any means necessary. It's five in the morning. I don't think I have ever got up this early. Why would somebody want to get up at this time? It just doesn't seem natural.

"Layton," I hear Mark calling, "get your arse out here."

"OK." I quickly get my clothes on and head out to see everyone. Shit, I'm the last one to get ready; everyone else is already in the living room.

The first person I see is Rhea. She is sitting there, tired and bruised. I can't believe what they did to her. She breaks into a slight smile as I walk into the room, but I can tell she's in pain. I smile back in acknowledgement.

"OK, good," Mark says, "looks like we are all here. So, it is five o'clock at the moment, and the guards change over at exactly six o'clock. That gives us an hour to get the hell out of here and over to the edge of Narborough Road."

"How does he know this?" I whisper to Amrit.

"Hush," Amrit responds harshly. What a dick; I was only asking a question.

"So, the plan," Mark continues. "Layton and Jane, you two head towards the garage, where Jane can distract Finch."

"On it," Jane says with enthusiasm.

"Oh, I'm stuck with her?" I say, not so enthusiastically.

"As for the rest of us," Mark says, "we will hold off until you bring the van back. Remember, this is the only hour in the day when nobody will be patrolling except for a few minor guards. It's now or never. I wish you all the best of luck, now let's go." Again, how does he know this? He must have no life whatsoever if he's studied the guards' timetable.

Without any arguments, Jane and I head straight outside. We make our way down towards the garage, which Jane knows oh so well. As soon as the door opens, I am struck by the frosty air, sticking to my face like pieces of iced glue. It is bitterly cold outside, and my face feels like an ice cube. There is an unusual fog over the city, probably because it's the early morning.

"It's just down here," Jane says as we make our way towards the garage. We walk on and come across what looks like a storage unit. "One second," Jane says. She bangs on the door a few times and we see it begin to open. "OK, you go around there," she whispers to me, pointing. I quickly hide behind a bench and two bins, so that I can't be seen, yet can see everything in front of me.

A man opens the door. This must be the famous Finch.

"Hello?" he calls out, leaning to the side, his stomach sticking out under his top.

"It's me," Jane says, walking up to him.

"Well," he says, smiling, "I was wondering when you would come back."

I take another look at him and he looks very greasy. He has a pot belly, greasy black hair and what looks like an attempt at a goatee. it just does not look good. There is basically nothing about him that could come across as appealing in any way.

"I was wondering if I could have something from you." Jane asks him seductively.

He smiles and begins to stroke her arm in a very creepy manner.

"Well, you know how it is. If you want something from me, you know what to give me, sweetness," he says, licking his lips.

Jane turns to walk inside the garage, and as she does so Finch slaps her rear end. The guy couldn't come across as more of a creep. I can hear him chuckling to himself as they both disappear inside. Then Jane comes running to the front of the garage and signals for me to follow her.

"Where you go?" Finch calls out.

"Coming," she says reluctantly.

I look around to make sure the coast is clear before moving off. I look left, then right, and nobody is around to stop me. I pace towards the garage and try to use stealth, but it just seems as if I am walking very slowly, so I decide to pick up the pace a bit.

"I'm going to wreck you today, Jane," Finch snorts to her.

"Yeah, baby," Jane responds as if she is being paid to do so, "give it to me, how do you want me?"

I walk a little further and see Finch pull down Jane's trousers as she is bent over a table. I can see a van sticking out, pointing to the entrance of the garage. I walk a little closer to get a better look – not at Jane's arse, before you sex freaks ask; just to have a look at what Finch is planning.

"Yeah," Finch says. "I promise I will be gentle," he remarks creepily as he pulls down his trousers. I can see his hairy behind sticking out like a gorilla's. Looking around, I see a frying pan in the room for some bizarre reason.

"Are you ready for me?" he asks in a weird seductive voice, bending over to kiss Jane on the behind before standing up straight. OK, that's enough. I move towards him, raise the frying pan and smack him across the back of the head. He collapses like a sack of shit on the ground.

"Finally," I say to Jane. "That shut him up."

"What you do that for?" Jane asks me.

"Shit, is there another guard?" I ask, concerned.

"No, I was going to distract him," she tries to explain.

"You were distracting him," I say. "And now he is knocked out cold." Why is she complaining?

"Yeah, but you were meant to wait," she protests.

"Wait for what?" I look down at him and back up at her. "Oh, you've got to be kidding me. You wanted some sex?" I ask her, feeling confused and slightly disgusted.

"Not exactly," she says.

"Yes, you did."

"OK, fine," she confesses. "I just didn't want it to be over so soon."

"Well, I'm sorry to disappoint," I say.

I then look down at Finch lying on the ground, and something catches my eye. I can't take my eyes off his private region; I just can't look away.

"My God."

"What?" she asks me.

"That there," I say, "is the smallest, hairiest penis I have ever seen in my life."

Jane looks down at him briefly, before looking back up at the numerous shelving units positioned all around us.

"We need to find something to tie him up with," she says, occupying herself. Meanwhile, I am stuck in a trance, staring at Finch's privates.

"Amazing," I announce. "You can't tell where the dick starts and the balls finish."

I can hear Jane fumbling around in the background.

"Here," she says, holding a piece of rope. "Tie him up with this, and I will gag him with this." She holds out a handkerchief, then looks at me and sees me still in my trance, looking down at the passed-out Finch. "OK, let's get to it and stop checking out his dick."

"I'm not checking out his dick," I say defensively.

"You kind of are."

"How am I?"

"You have been staring at it for the last thirty seconds; that counts as checking it out," she says.

I think for a moment and realise she is kind of right.

"Shit," I say. I then decide to just get on with the job at hand. I wrap the rope around Finch's feet and hands so he has no escape. Jane ties the handkerchief around his mouth so he can't scream for help.

"Well, that looks interesting," Jane says as we look at him in what looks like a fish pose.

"I bet when he woke up this morning, he did not expect his day to end up like this," I state.

"Right, the keys." Jane rummages around for them. "He always keeps them on the desk," she explains, finding them straight away.

"Nice," I say.

We rush over to the van and jump in; me in the driver's seat and Jane in the passenger's. I start the engine and off we go to fetch everyone else.

We pull up outside the dorms. The rest of the group run straight to the van and jump in the back. As soon as they are in, I head straight off, putting my foot down, zipping through the roads, trying to get to the border as fast as I can.

"OK, take a left up here," Mark directs, "then we should be able to get out of here." How does he know that? I ask myself.

"Sure," I say without question and turn left. The sign says Narborough Road. This is it, just got to get to the end of this road and we're home. Come on, you piece of shit, pick up some speed.

"Come on, Layton," Amrit calls out to me as we see a gate open before us, "nearly there now." We speed up, and I fumble my way through the gears. Then all of a sudden, the gate closes. I push down on the brake.

"No, no," Mark shouts, "this shouldn't be happening!"

"What is it?" Becky asks.

"I'm not sure," Ryan answers.

"Why have we stopped?" I hear Rhea murmur in the background.

"The crossing is closed," I say. Everyone falls silent, unsure what to do next.

"Shit," Amrit says.

"What do we do now?" I ask them.

"They knew we were coming," Mark says all of a sudden.

"How?" I ask him.

"I don't know, they just did."

Suddenly two guards appear in front of the van. One points for me to get out, while the other indicates for Jane, sitting next to me, to stay inside. I get out without resistance and see Canine standing right in front of me.

"All right, Canine?" I ask politely. Then out of nowhere, the bastard backhands me in the face. "Ouch, bitch!" I cry, holding my face.

"You scum," he says.

I glare at him. "One day, Canine, one day," I quickly glance at his hand and once more at his face, "I'm going to take your hand away from you."

He chuckles to himself, in a weird, Canine sort of way.

"I'd love to see you try," he challenges me as he leans over into my personal space.

"OK, that's enough," I hear Rob call out in the background. I look over and see him walking towards us. He is surrounded by four guards, all watching over him. "You, come with me," he says to me.

I follow and feel Canine staring at me as I walk past him. Rob and I walk towards a little outpost. He takes me inside and I see a man sitting there: General Singh.

"Hello again, Layton," he says as I walk inside. Rob closes the door, leaving us alone. "We have to stop meeting like this." That doesn't really make that much sense as this is the first time the two of us have actually met under these circumstances.

"We're leaving," I say with force as he sits there behind that desk, stirring a cup of what smells like stale tea.

"Please," General Singh says, "take a seat. No need to be so… daunting," he states in his usual patronising manner.

"Very well," I say, sitting down opposite him.

"Now," General Singh asks me, "why on earth do you want to leave? You can have a very good life here: success, a good home, food, warmth – you will be very comfortable."

"What about the day you experimented on me?" I ask him.

He sits back for a moment, and I can tell he is thinking of his answer.

"I know it seems bad. But we have created a world, a world that I saw being destroyed—" he calmly remarks, looking back at me as if hoping for me to display some form of agreement.

"What world?" I interrupt. "This is no world to live in. You have turned people into slaves—"

"Yes, I know." He forcefully interrupts me, slamming his fist on the table. I sit there, stunned, and he takes a deep breath before speaking once again.

"Years ago, I had a family – a wife and children. We were very happy, we lived right here, in this city. Oh, she was beautiful – Sierra, her name was. She was wonderful. My one true love," he states.

"OK?" I say.

"One day, bandits came to our home. They murdered my children, and then they tied me and my wife up. They took her and raped her repeatedly, right in front of me," he recalls, snarling. "They beat me and raped her. Then they killed her. I watched as the light disappeared from her eyes. They then took me and, thinking that a quick death was too much of a luxury for me, they decided to bury me alive.

"They tied me up and buried me, leaving me for dead. I wasn't ready to die, though, and I fought my way out of that grave. It was raining as well, which made the soil turn to sludge. I crawled out of the dirt, and I roared for my family. I remembered there were three bandits, and I remembered their faces. You see, Layton, I never forget a face.

"I found where they were living. They all had families of their own, so I went in at night when they were all asleep, tied up the three bandits and woke them up. I had also tied up their wives and children; some were just babies. I made them watch as I burned their families alive in front of them. Then I cut out their eyes, so the last thing they ever saw was their families being killed."

He takes a sip of his tea to take a breather. "It was then that I realised that civilisation had ceased to exist. Before all of this, you couldn't just kill somebody and get away with it. There was order, rules and regulations. So I found a man, twenty at the time. He had been trained by his military father. He knew how to use a gun, but had never had a home. He had no family; nobody. I took him and taught him about law and order. We managed to get more people interested in our plan, so we gave it a name – the Union, we called ourselves. That young man, though, he was ferocious with his punishments. Jerome was his real name, but after several years, and seeing what he could do and how ferocious he was, Canine seemed more suitable for him. He has been with me ever since."

"Like a loyal lapdog," I say in disgust.

General Singh smirks. "Or a good friend."

"You're so full of shit," I say. "You say you want to create law and order – does that mean harming children, killing people, making them terrified?"

"Change will come by any means," General Singh tries to explain to me.

"You take in refugees looking for a new life, then you work

them to death, torture them, or experiment on them," I state angrily.

"We are all refugees," he says. "We are all looking for somewhere to go, all trying to find a new beginning."

"Mine is not here," I say to him. He nods and looks at me once more.

"I know," he says, "and I can't stop you. You and your friends are free to go."

He stands up and walks towards the door. I get up and follow, just to make sure he doesn't try anything. He opens the door and I turn to walk out.

"One last thing," he adds, stopping me in my tracks.

"What?"

"You do know that once you and your friends leave, we will hunt you down, we will pursue you and find you?"

I turn to face him.

"You can do that," I suggest. "But I will be waiting for you to find me, and when you do, I will kill you."

He smiles, looking almost proud. This is followed by a sigh, and I know he is about to speak once more.

"I always liked you," General Singh says to me as I try to turn away.

I quickly look back at him, bemused. "What?"

"I always liked you," he says, pacing towards me with his hands behind his back. "I know what will happen to our two paths. You see, I was thrown into this world, tossed and turned, hit by every wall, crashed into every cliff, and I ended up, well, like this." He then raises his hand and points his finger at me. "However, you, Layton, you will leave this world a king," he states. He lowers his hand and looks at me with a misguided form of admiration.

I turn and storm off, straight towards the van. I walk past the guards all standing there with their guns and other weapons and get into the van without saying a word. I take one more look towards the outpost, and General Singh looks back at me. He nods at me once more, and I straight away turn to face the gate. Suddenly the gate opens, and as soon as it does, I am off. I put my foot right down and speed straight out of there, trying to get as much distance between us and the Union as possible.

This is the next stage of the journey. What adventures will we have now? Shit.

19

"Keep driving, Layton," Amrit calls behind me as I push my foot down on the pedal, practically touching the floor. "Keep going before they decide to come after us."

We keep going, not looking back. Well, there is no way I can look back; I think that's part of the reason why the back of the van has no windows. Also, I don't want to look back.

There are momentary silences in the van, broken by the odd cough or sniff. I don't know why, but it's comforting when somebody makes a sound; it just calms me in some way, I don't know how to explain it. I guess it feels as if I am driving a coffin of corpses otherwise.

We keep driving away from Leicester, looking at all of the abandoned cars covered in a thick, smoky residue. I can just about make out what were once houses and trees; I don't know really, it all just looks black and destroyed now. Suddenly it gets very smoky outside, and it's hard to see where I am going. We keep going, just driving along, and then the van comes to a stop. It just halts, jolting forward slightly, then crashing back down.

"Shit," I shout out, "is everybody OK?" I look back, and everyone is groaning with frustration.

"Why have we stopped?" Jane asks.

"Shit, what happened?" Rhea says.

"Where are we?" Ryan asks.

"Hold on, let me get out and check," I say, opening the door slightly.

"Are you sure that's a good idea?" Amrit asks. I immediately close the door and look right at him.

"How can it not be?"

"What?"

"How can it not be a good idea to see why we have stopped?" I ask him, noticing how much I am beginning to fumble through my own words.

"Because, retard," he retorts, "we have more or less an army coming after us, so when I ask if it's a good idea for you to go stick your dumb, bog-eyed face out the van, I mean it."

"I'm not bog-eyed." Arsehole.

"OK, this is getting us nowhere," Mark says. "Amrit, I think you should go with Layton to see why we have stopped."

"What?!" Amrit shouts.

"So it is a good idea," I remark smugly.

"No, it's not."

"Oh, for fuck's sake," Becky shouts. "One of you go or I am going to force you out."

"Right," I say, "I'll be right back."

I then unlock the door. I try to look outside first, but it's all smoky and hard to see where we are. I open the door wider and step outside. There is a horrible smell in the air, like… burning, yeah, that's it, burning and rotting. I decide to walk around for a bit so I can see what we have stumbled upon. I walk too far, though, because I lose track of the van.

Suddenly I stumble on something and fall over. I sit up and notice the smoke is beginning to clear. I look down and realise that my hands landed on something to break my fall, and now they feel slimy and sticky.

The smoke clears and I can finally begin to make out what

is around me. Then I wish the smoke would come back. I can see nothing but bodies; just bodies littered around the place. In the background are piles of what looks like grey ash. I look back down at my hands and realise I have landed on one of the bodies and my hands are covered in blood. Suddenly I feel the urge to throw up. Then the urge becomes a reality and I do throw up.

"Layton!" I hear a voice calling behind me. "Layton!"

I remain there on my knees.

"I'm OK," I say dishonestly. I look around and see more faces just looking back at me. The charred faces of people who were once alive are looking back at me, facing me with what feels like their souls.

"Layton!" the voice calls. Then someone grabs me by the shoulder. I look behind me and Amrit is standing there.

"Amrit!" I call out. He kneels down next to me.

"What happened here?" he asks, looking around at the ashes and bits of bone. I gaze around as well, seeing the smoke trying to clear, but unable to, like a blanket that has been sewn to a bed.

"I don't know," I say. I place my hand on the ground, lifting what feels like dust. For all I know this could be bits of mashed-up bone, ground into a dusty paste. "Amrit?" I ask.

"What?" he says, still amazed by what we are seeing.

"Why are we here?" I ask him. "What have we done to come here?"

He looks at me, looks around, and then looks back at me again.

"We were going to come here regardless," he says.

"What?"

"Whatever we do in our lives, it leads us to where we are going to go. We have many different moments in our lives, and they are what we have gone through to lead us to this moment right here. So what we do in this moment will determine what we go through in the future."

"OK," I say, not quite understanding.

"Come on," he says, "everybody is waiting for us. Let's go back to them."

I nod as we rise to our feet. We take one last look at the grey cloud we have found ourselves in, then turn and walk away as fast as we can. I feel my lungs beginning to clog up with the smoke which is surrounding me. Since throwing up, I can't help but keep coughing all the way to the van. It comes to a point where Amrit has to hold me up in order for me to keep moving forward. As we make our way through the mist, I can see Mark pacing up and down. He looks anxious, nervous, maybe even frustrated. I can just about see my feet now, as all of the smoke slowly starts to clear.

"Are you guys OK?" Mark asks us as Amrit slowly lands me back on the floor so I can catch my breath and learn how to breathe once again.

"Yeah, we're fine," he says, wiping some of the dust away from his forehead and eyes. "We were just a little startled by what we saw."

"A little?" I gasp.

"It's not good, is it?" Mark says, looking around.

Becky and Ryan come from behind the van, making their way to us.

"Well, I've just managed to clear a way through so we can get moving," he tells us, making me feel slightly relieved.

"What're we going to do now?" Becky asks Mark. I don't know why we are turning to him for the answers, I just don't have the strength in me right now.

"I don't know," Mark says.

"We have to keep moving, surely," Ryan states.

"This wasn't supposed to happen," Mark says. It seems out of character.

"What do you mean?" Amrit asks him.

"Yeah, what do you mean?" I repeat.

Mark then moves around to the front of the van and sits down. I look over and see Rhea and Jane coming out towards us.

"I guess it's time you all knew," Mark says.

"You don't have to," Becky tells him, sounding sympathetic.

"No," he says, "I do." He then looks down at the floor and back up again, slowly rubbing his eyes as he does so.

"What is it?" Rhea asks, eager for answers.

"Well," he begins, "this area here is called the dumping ground."

We all look at him, confused.

"What do you mean?" Amrit asks.

"This is where people who are not good for the system are dumped," Mark begins to explain. "The Union finds people who they deem unfit for the society that they have built. They burn them and throw them in piles like that. Sometimes they don't even bother to burn them, they just kill them and dump them out here. They are people who have caused trouble, or people that the Union just believes we should be rid of. Sometimes, it is just killing somebody for the sake of killing them. Rather than have bodies just lying around the place, or a building to keep all of the dead in, we just dumped them all out here."

"What do you mean, 'we'?" Rhea asks.

"Well, I know all of this because I was once one of the guards."

We all look at him, stunned by what he has said. The realisation is too much for us to come to terms with.

"What do you mean, you were one of the guards?" I ask.

"I mean I was one of those fuckers walking around with guns and balaclavas," he states. "I would lead the killing of somebody, which a lot of the time meant escorting them out here. Sometimes they weren't even killed; the people in charge would just tell us to leave them here. They would die in pain. I can't imagine the hell I put some of those poor people through."

"What happened?" I ask.

"What do you mean?"

"Why are you no longer a guard?"

"Well, I was patrolling one day and I got into an argument with one of the other guards. One thing led to another and I beat the shit out of him. It was only later that I found out he was the son of General Singh's friend," he admits.

"So what happened?" I ask him. I suddenly feel a nudge from Amrit, and he gives me a look that tells me to stop talking.

"I was tortured and beaten. I have the scars all over me," Mark tells us. "I came to realise that the Union does not fight for the rights of the people. They make out that they are for the people and work just so we can all live together in harmony, when in reality they only work so that they can have their arses clean. They are only in it for themselves. I'm glad I was kicked out. I was told I had to be a bottom feeder and pose as somebody who had only just come here," he explains, sounding very disappointed.

"Oh, Mark," Rhea says, placing her hand on his shoulder in sympathy.

"I don't judge you," Amrit reassures him.

"No," I say, "neither do I."

"Thank you," Mark replies gratefully, smiling slightly.

We all look at one another in deep silence. It's one of those moments where if you say something you are only going to be seen as a twat, so it is probably best to stay silent.

I decide after a while that the silence has gone on too long, though, so I open my mouth to speak. Suddenly we hear a noise that we find very familiar. It is a groaning sound with heavy footsteps. We look around to see where the noise is coming from.

"Oh, shit," Amrit says.

"Is that what I think it is?" Ryan calls out.

"It's fucking infected!" I shout, jumping to my feet. Mark follows suit.

"Quick, everyone, back in the van," he orders.

We all pile into the back as in the background, a group of infected start to take shape through the smog. Mark and Amrit climb through into the front. Mark is in the driving seat and quickly turns the engine on, slamming his foot down. He spins the van around and we dart off into the distance. Sitting in the back is not that comfortable. We are shaking around everywhere like a rattle.

"Hold on, everyone," Mark calls out as his reckless driving reaches a whole new level.

"Amrit?" I yell.

"Yeah?" he responds.

"I think I'm going to be sick again."

"Me first," he replies.

We continue making our way through, well, I don't really know what we are making our way through. I am sitting at the back of a van with no windows; how am I supposed to know what I am going past? I try to lean forward to see out the front, but all I can see is burnt-out cars and piles upon piles of rubbish.

"Look," I shout. I can see in the distance what looks like an abandoned shopping centre. It looks like nobody has visited this place in years. "We should head there."

"I don't know," Mark says.

"We have no other choice," I call out to him.

"Fine," he responds. We then take a very sharp turn to the left and blast our way through what looks like a car park, heading straight towards a building. Mark really does not give a shit about the people in the back, especially me.

He slams on the brakes right in front of what might be an old department store. We all get out as fast as we can, looking around to see if there are any infected that followed us here. I quickly pace away to make sure the coast is clear, while Mark leads everybody else towards the department store. He gets his hands in between the door and opens it wide. I can vaguely see the infected in the distance, too far away for them to see us or cause any real trouble.

"Quick, Layton, let's get in," Ryan says. I quickly turn and run towards them, making sure I am not the last one in there. Inside, Rhea is sitting on the floor; she still hasn't fully recovered from what the Union put her through.

"OK, is everybody here?" Mark says as I walk inside.

"Mark!" Amrit calls as he brings what looks like shelves to help barricade the door. They get some old units to put in front of it to stop anybody getting in.

"I think we'll be safe here," Mark says.

"What do we do now?" I ask him.

"Well, there's nothing else we can do right now," Becky says. "all we can do at the moment is get warm and make sure we are safe. We will need to go for food."

"How are we going to do that?" I ask her. She turns and looks outside, and I can tell straight away that she has no idea what the next plan is.

"There's nothing we can do," Amrit says. "We may have to go hungry today."

"We can't do that," Jane says, "what about Rhea? She needs food, she is not strong enough to last through the night without it."

"I'll be fine," Rhea states. "Don't worry about me." She pants as she speaks. I look over at her and know she is trying to save face; really, she does need something. She looks as if she is getting weaker every moment.

"Are you sure?" I ask her.

She looks up at me, not saying a word, but gently nods to reassure me.

"Very well," I say. "We have had a long day; all we can do is rest for the time being and not get ourselves hurt."

"OK, leader," Amrit jokes. "We should get away from the doors. There is a place in the back where we can stay."

"OK," I say, and we all move to the back of the store.

A few hours pass and all I can feel is hunger. I can feel my stomach turning upside down, asking for some food just to hold it down. It's not a pleasant feeling. It is even coming to the point where I cannot feel anything else. I actually feel my body eating away at itself, as if I am a self-destructive cannibal. Mark has started a fire in the middle of the room to keep out the cold, because it is fucking freezing in here. My nipples are actually fully erect right now.

I look over and see Rhea sitting in silence next to a unit. I walk over to her to see if she is OK. She looks up at me, and I look back at her.

"Hi," she says.

"You OK?" I ask her

"Yeah, I'm fine," she tells me, the corner of her mouth turned up in a weak smile.

"Good." I sit down next to her to keep her company. "Do you want me to tell you a joke?" I ask her.

"No," she replies. It was actually a good joke I had in mind; why would she not want to hear it?

"What do you mean, no?"

"I just want you to sit here," she says, her eyes pleading.

"OK. Why?"

"I just do," she says. "I just want you near me."

She then leans her head on my shoulder. There is nothing I can say. I admit, I do feel a tingle in my stomach. I actually feel too nervous to speak right now. I look down at her and see that she has closed her eyes. I quickly take off my jacket and put it around her to keep her warm, then place my arm around her as if I am here to keep her safe. I know she knows there is nothing I can do in order to keep her safe, but I can try.

To be fair, all I have been doing is trying to understand the full meaning of what Amrit told me earlier when we were surrounded by the dead bodies. I sort of know what he meant, but I don't know if I fully understand. I hope I will one day.

I'm starting to feel drowsy now. I look out of the window and the sun is still out. Well, I can hardly tell; in England a lot of the time we don't have blue skies, just a sheet of white covering us. Before I know it, my eyes close and my mind takes me into a dream. I dream of a field, a field where I can run free and not have any worries. I see a river, trees and many little animals running around me. I try to be a part of this little dream world that has surrounded me.

Then I see him again.

"Why, Layton, why?" Adam calls out to me.

"Adam!" I say, then suddenly I am awake again. I look around and see that everyone is fast asleep. I then realise that this is a memory that I will not forget any time soon. I do not know when I will be able to let it go.

20

Waking up the following morning, I do not feel as comfortable as I felt when we were in Leicester. As scary as the Union were, and even after all the things I saw, at least we had warm beds to sleep in. Instead, I am now waking up on a hard floor which is really hurting my arse, and a shelving unit which is really hurting my back.

I look up and see that Becky is up, pacing around the room. I can just about make out what it is she is doing. I think she is trying to find more stuff to put on the fire; it is beginning to get really cold. Why couldn't we have chosen to escape in the summer? Why did we think winter was the best time to go?

I haul myself up onto my feet, pacing through the room. Jane, Rhea and Ryan are all still asleep, and Amrit and Mark are talking on the other side of the room. I think I better go see what they are talking about. I suppose it would pass the time.

I manage to get a better view of the campsite we have created. In the centre is the fire which Mark started last night; looks like it's starting to die down a little. Shelves upon shelves of emptied boxes surround the room. I can see broken pictures, posters and even a few wrecked televisions. I look at the barricade we made to block the door: a lot of empty shelves lined up to hold the door in place, supported by a few chairs and even some of those broken televisions.

I walk over and can see an oddly shaped box on a desk at the side. There's a sign at the side of it saying Till. I have no idea what that is, although it might have something useful in it. I wonder what is inside; if there is anything inside? I look around, trying to find a way to open it, but I just can't seem to find anything.

I hit it and it comes flying open. I look down and see what looks like paper, but a lot smaller than any paper I have seen before. I place my hand on it, and it doesn't look like anything I know of. There are a lot of them, all with different numbers in the right-hand corner. Some say twenty, a lot of them have a number five or a number ten, and there are a few that say fifty. I can see some little round things as well; not sure what they are. I pick them all up, just about managing to hold them all in my hands. They feel crinkly and slippery.

I look over at the fire Mark made and back down at the paper in my hands. I walk over towards the fire, looking at the rest of the group who are still sleeping, and gently place some of the papers into the fire. One catches my eye as I hold it in my hand; it has a woman's face on it. Who is she? I ask myself. Looking closer, that woman's face appears to be on all of them. Rather than dither with them any more, I just place the remaining papers into the fire and watch it grow as the woman's face turns to cinders. I then turn and look over at Amrit and Mark standing next to the door, and decide to head towards them.

"Morning," I call out as I step over the numerous objects on the floor.

"Morning, Layton." Amrit smiles as I reach them. Mark just looks at me and then turns to look outside the window once more.

"What's up?" I ask.

"We need to get food," Amrit says, and my stomach rumbles. "Mark and I were discussing the best course of action."

"We need to send a scout party," Mark says. "At least two of us to go out and look for some food."

"How are we going to scout? We have no weapons, nothing to defend ourselves. What if we find something, then somebody attacks us?" I ask, touching my sides to demonstrate my defencelessness.

"That's the problem. We've been looking around here and there's nothing but broken pieces of plastic and maybe the odd piece of wood. That's it," Amrit explains as I look around at the broken debris in the room.

"That's all we need," Becky says out of nowhere. "Amrit, you need to stay because Rhea needs you; Mark, you need to stay because the group needs you; Layton and I will go out and scout."

"Wait, what am I needed for?" I ask, questioning my position in the group.

"You can't," Amrit interrupts. "It's too dangerous."

"We'll be fine. I know how to defend myself," she tells them with an air of confidence.

"OK," Mark says, "you and Layton will go out and find what we need—"

"Wait," I try to interrupt.

"Are you sure you want to take Layton?" Amrit asks.

"Yes, I am," Becky replies. "Let the others know we will be as quick as we can."

I still don't have much of an idea of what it is I am actually doing right now. I feel like I am being kept in the dark.

"Hold on," I say, once again trying to interrupt. I then see Mark beginning to move the barrier; I haven't even agreed to this and I'm being pushed out the door.

"Good luck," Amrit encourages us, even though I still haven't agreed to this.

"Here, take these," Mark says, handing us a long piece of wood each.

"Thank you," Becky says. "We will bring something back, I promise." She then nods at me and heads out. I look back and can see Mark and Amrit return to their discussion. I know I have no choice in the matter so I just head out, with a lack of passion for what I am doing. I grip my piece of wood tighter and follow Becky through the door and outside the shopping complex.

We stroll through the car park, looking through the windows of the abandoned cars to see if there is anything there that can be of any use to us. Becky looks through one and I look through another. I try to make sure she is in my sights just so I do not lose her, partly because I do not want her to get in any trouble. The main reason, though, is because she said she can take care of herself, and frankly I am not the best person when it comes to confronting evil.

"Let's check down there," Becky says to me. She points her piece of wood towards the other side of the shopping complex. I look ahead and can see that it is completely barricaded, much like ours, albeit with a little more effort put into it.

"How are we going to get in?" I ask, scoping the place. It's barricaded like a mini fortress.

"We have to go and see what we can do. What do we have to lose?" she asks as she heads for the complex.

"Our lives," I mutter under my breath.

We head towards the other side of the complex and can see it goes around to another side where there is a door which has not been barricaded. We decide to manoeuvre around, just to make sure neither of us causes more hassle than we need to when getting into the building.

To my surprise, as we make our way forward we can see the door slowly open. We quickly hide behind some bins as a man comes strolling outside, holding a cigarette in his hand, about to light it.

"What do we do now?" I whisper to Becky as we watch the man puffing out smoke. She looks at me, as clueless as I am.

"I think we have to take him out," she tells me, getting her stick ready.

"OK, leave it with me," I state, the embodiment of heroism.

"Are you sure?" she asks, looking at me as if she is worried about my well-being; as if she does not think I have the stones for it.

"Yeah, of course," I say. I have no idea where this new-found heroism has come from, but I like it. I feel stronger this way; I feel like I can take anyone on. "Leave it with me, he won't know what hit him," I explain, trying to encourage myself more than anything as I slowly creep around.

"Layton…" she whispers, concerned, but I am gone before she can stop me. I am on my way to take this son of a bitch out so my group can eat. I head towards him, making sure not to make too much noise. I am using nothing more than stealth as I manoeuvre my way. He is standing there, puffing away on his cigarette, completely clueless that he is going to meet his doom.

"Right then," I whisper to myself as I slowly get closer to him. To be honest, the closer I get, the bigger he looks; about six foot five at least, with massive shoulders. No big deal, I'll take him down.

I creep up behind him and he is still too preoccupied with his cigarette to notice me. "OK, prick, time to die," I whisper as I pull back the plank of wood in my hand. I raise it over my head and take a huge swing at the guy, landing it on the back of his head.

Now, in my mind this was going to go down perfectly. I was going to land this wood on the back of his head and he would be knocked out cold. Yet like all things I seem to try to attempt, the reality is very different. I swing the plank of wood at his head and it breaks on top of his thick skull. The man turns around and looks at me and I can see that he looks about fifty, yet he was still tough enough to take a plank of wood to the head.

"What are you doing?" he asks me. I look down at my broken piece of wood and throw it to one side

"You're going to die," I shout at him, trying to be as menacing as I can, even feeling my teeth grind as I glare at him.

"Am I now?" he responds sarcastically. I then run at him and soon find that for an old man, he moves very fast. He throws a punch and hits me square on the jaw, causing me to fall flat on my arse.

"Ah!" I shrug, rubbing my face. "OK," I say, rising to my feet, "you got lucky there. Now watch this." I do some foot movements to distract him, then move around him, sling my left arm around his neck, jump on his back and try to strangle him. I didn't realise, though, that this guy has the thickest neck in the world.

"Ha," he laughs, "what are you doing? Don't, please, that tickles – ha!"

"Don't laugh," I demand, frustrated.

"OK, get off now," he says as he wiggles me around, but I stay gripped to him.

"What are you doing?" Becky asks as she approaches.

"I got this," I tell her.

"You sure?" Becky asks.

"No, he hasn't," the man tells her as he continues to laugh.

"Everything is under control," I say.

"It's not," the man says.

"Can you shut up?" I ask. "You're not helping." Holding on to his neck is making me tired; this guy might look fifty, but he has the energy of a young rhino.

"Do you want some help?" Becky asks me.

"No, it's all good," I say.

"OK, you've had your fun," the man says. He then puts his

hands on my arms and flings me over him. I land flat on my back right in front of Becky.

"OK, maybe I could do with a little help," I admit.

"Right," she sternly remarks.

"Oh, what are you going to do now?" the man asks sarcastically.

"Just try to keep up," Becky says to him. She then lunges up at him and wraps her legs around the guy's head and neck. He falls forward and she holds him in that position. He tries to struggle to get out, however he can't budge. He keeps struggling until out of nowhere, he just stops. Becky then lets go of him and he lies there, motionless. I get up.

"Did you kill him?" I ask.

"No, I just knocked him out," she explains, struggling to wipe the dirt off her back from holding the man in her knockout grip.

"OK. Well, that's probably because I tenderised him for you." I try to give myself some credit, while also trying to sound modest in some way.

"Sure. OK, let's look inside," she suggests as we enter the building

"Hold on," I interrupt as she walks through the door. "Where did you learn to do that?"

"Well, working for the Union as long as I did, you get taught a few things. I suppose the one good thing about them is they do teach you to defend yourself. Anyway, if he's here, then there must be more of them, so don't do anything stupid," she tells me as we walk inside.

"OK," I say.

We walk inside and can definitely tell that somebody has lived here. There are mattresses all over the place, and a lot of tins.

"Where are they?" Becky asks as we patrol the room.

"I have no idea," I say. We walk through the rubbish and mattresses, trying not to get our shoes caught on anything.

Then something catches my eye. "Hold on," I call out to her, and I run to the other side of the room where there's a table with what looks like tools and other items for defending ourselves. A machete, screwdrivers, a baseball bat, a few knives, hammers and other tools.

"Nice one," Becky says. "We should take these before anyone comes back."

I grab a rucksack that I can see lying around and start to put the items in there. I take the machete for myself and Becky takes the baseball bat. Then we hear a noise behind us, and we turn and see the man Becky just knocked out standing on the other side of the room.

"Shit," I say.

"What are you doing?" he asks us.

"We have a group of people that need feeding," Becky tries to explain. "It's nothing personal."

"Why are you taking my weapons?" he asks.

"To defend ourselves," I say, trying not to provoke him in any way.

"You know what?" he begins to say, rubbing his neck. "Take the weapons; it's not like they're any use now."

"What do you mean?" Becky asks.

"Everybody else who lived here is dead," he tells us. "I am the last one. If you want food there's tinned food over there," he says, pointing at the side of the room.

I quickly turn and run straight there. There is a trolley full of tinned beans, fruit, peas and something in a bag.

"Is this meat?" I ask him.

"Yeah, it's rat," he responds.

"Oh, delightful," I say sarcastically.

"Why are you letting us take this?" Becky asks him.

"Because I was planning on leaving here. All I need is my knife," he tells us while pulling it out, "and now I can be on my way."

216

"Thanks," I say.

"Oh, one last thing, though, before I go," he says as he walks towards a wardrobe. "Here's a few friends for you."

He slams the door open and about ten infected come storming out. He quickly runs outside, out of the way.

"Shit!" I shout as I see the infected walking around, blocking the exit.

"Quick, we need to find a way out," Becky calls as my head darts back and forth.

The infected are making their way towards us. Becky then looks over and spots what looks like a storeroom.

"Quick, in there – grab the food!" she shouts. I run in after her and we try to slam the door shut, but the infected just keep blocking it.

"Shit, they're strong," I say.

Becky then slams the trolley full of food against the door, stopping the infected from getting in.

"What a dick!" she shouts.

"I guess we're here for the night," I say to her.

We sit down as we know the infected will not stop trying to get in for at least an hour. We can hear them groaning and scratching at the door. I take a quick look around and can see no way out. I walk back to Becky, who is sitting on the floor, and hunker down next to her. We both just sit there, staring at the door, trying to think of another way to get out.

21

The door is barricaded closed. Becky is pacing up and down. I am starving; however I fear that if I take one tin from the trolley it might make it too light to hold the door. To top it all off, I can hear the infected outside, groaning like a pack of hungry wolves. Could this day get any worse? Yes, it could: I am dying for a piss.

"I need the toilet," I declare to Becky. She looks at me with her mouth open, looking around as if I have said the worst thing in the world to her.

"You have to be joking," she responds.

"I'm not, I really need to go," I state.

"OK," she says, "just go in that corner, I think there's a bucket over there."

I walk over towards the bucket and look down at it. It's nothing special, just an empty plastic bucket. I unzip myself and get going. It's amazing; feels like all the world's problems are just flowing out of me.

"Oh," I say out loud, "that's better", as I feel it all streaming out of me, feeling euphoric.

"Does it have to be so loud?" Becky asks, disgusted, covering her ears. "Stinks as well," she adds, covering her nose.

"Sorry," I say, hurrying up. As soon as I'm done, I turn around and sit next to Becky.

"Well, I guess now we have to sit here with a bucket of your piss in the corner," she informs me, gazing over at the bucket.

"I guess so," I sigh. I look around the room and can't see any way of getting out. It's just a standard grey room. There is an empty freezer at the side, and a wall. There are windows at the top, but they look far too small for either of us to get through.

"We'll just have to wait it out," Becky says as she looks up at the ceiling and sighs to herself.

"I guess so, but what about the others? They'll be worried sick, wondering where we are."

"I'm sure Mark will be fine," she tells me. "He'll probably come after us if we're here for too long."

I look at her and start pondering. My mind does that sometimes when I just have to ask a question.

"So, what's the deal with you two?" I ask her.

"What do you mean?"

"I mean, you two always back each other up, you always stick together – are you… you know?"

"No, nothing like that," she states.

"OK," I say, "I was just checking." I sit there staring forward, then I think of another question. "I do have one more thing to ask you, though."

"What?"

"Do you think we left the Union too soon?"

"I have no idea," she replies, sighing to herself.

Both of us just sit there looking into the greyness, unable to contemplate what our next move will be.

Minutes pass by, feeling much like hours as the wall I'm staring at starts to play tricks on my eyes, making me believe it is something else. It starts to create shapes that I know are not there. I try to look around for an escape route, but in the end I come to the conclusion that there is none. We just have to sit here and wait for the infected to get out of here.

"What are you thinking about?" Becky asks me.

"Nothing," I say. "What about yourself?"

"Same."

"Good talk," I say.

"Sorry for trying to make the time pass," she snaps.

"Well, I don't know what to talk about," I say.

"OK."

We sit there for a moment and I think of something in order to pass the time.

"You want to do it?" I ask, trying to be as smooth as possible.

"What?" she snaps. I don't think that was the best idea in the world.

"You know, do it?" I ask her again.

"Um, no thanks," she responds sarcastically, sounding furious at the suggestion.

"OK, just thought it would help pass the time," I state.

"Sitting silently will be fine," she answers.

"OK. Well," I begin, "how are you today?"

"Seriously?" she asks.

"OK," I start again, "so, where do you come from?"

"Huh?"

"Where did you come from before you ended up in Leicester?" I ask her, interested in her backstory.

"Well, that's the first sensible question," she states. "I'm from Warrington originally, then I travelled down south and ended up here."

"Fair enough," I say. "Where's your family?"

"Same place as everyone else's: probably missing or dead. Truth is, I have no idea," she announces, looking as if she is pondering to herself.

"Sorry," I say.

"Don't be," she says, "everyone is in the same position." She

220

sits for a few seconds before speaking again. "So, what about you, where are you from?"

I have to pause for a moment, before I finally decide to answer her.

"Leicester," I admit.

"Really?" she responds, stunned.

"Yeah, I'm from Leicester. I left before the Union came into town; haven't been back here for about two or three years now – well, the city centre at least," I tell her, feeling slightly guilty about coming from the same place where a tyrant now resides.

"What were you doing beforehand?" she asks me.

"Well," I say, "I was selling stones around the Midlands. I was in Northampton, Derby and Nottingham; even ended up in Birmingham at one point."

"Stones?" she asks.

"Yeah, stones," I explain. "People really go crazy over them."

She looks at me, confused.

"It's better than it sounds."

"OK," she says, surprised. "Well, do you have any family?"

I pause for a moment before answering.

"Well, I did have a mum, a Dad and a brother. Never really knew my Dad, he died when I was about two. My mum kept me and my brother safe; Adam was his name. We used to live with this group in Leicester…" I begin to tell her.

"What happened to them?" she asks.

"Well, my brother was always seen as somebody special, a true hero. I was always the little trickster, the joker. I sometimes did performances for people in the camp. I was quite popular. Then when I was about ten, it all changed," I explain, beginning to feel my memories come back to me.

"What happened?" Becky asks. "If you don't mind me asking?"

I just smile at her and continue.

"Um… our camp was raided, attacked by the border monkeys," I explain, starting to reminisce about my past.

"Oh," Becky gasps.

"Yeah," I say. "My mum was killed, but Adam and I got out. We got pretty far, to be fair. I was about ten at the time and Adam was twelve. We were walking down the street and these bandits came towards us. I remember the ringleader, big guy with a scar through his right eye. They cornered us and tried to attack us. We tried to fight them off, but they held on to Adam and told me to run or I would have the same done to me. Adam looked at me and I knew he wanted to say something, but I didn't wait to hear it, I just ran, without even thinking about it. I just turned and started running. I could hear my brother screaming behind me, I could hear that he was suffering, but I didn't turn back. I just kept going, just kept running.

"After that I wandered around, going from group to group, until I decided to stay on my own. I didn't want to be around other people, seeing as how from the age of ten I was a coward. I let my brother die and didn't help him. I have to live with that for the rest of my life." I feel my throat begin to swell up, so I stop talking. I look over at Becky, hoping she won't judge me.

"Shit," Becky says.

"Yeah."

"Does anyone else in the group know?" she asks me.

"No," I say. "I don't mind if you tell them; I suppose I am going to be with you guys for a while. It only makes sense that you tell them."

"OK," she says, "so how did you meet Amrit and Rhea?"

"Oh, Amrit tried to rob me once, I fought him off and then somehow we became friends."

"Seriously?" she responds, stunned.

"Yeah. As for Rhea, she was in a camp with Amrit and from there we became companions," I tell her, smiling to myself.

"Oh, OK," she says.

Suddenly we can't hear anything outside. The groaning from the infected is gone and there is silence.

"Can you hear that?" I ask her.

"What? I don't hear anything," she says, listening.

"Exactly. There's nothing outside," I say, feeling excited.

"Layton, Becky – you in here?" I hear Amrit calling from the other side.

"Shit," I say, "It's Amrit." I quickly run over, moving the trolley out of the way so we can get through the door.

"Finally," Becky exclaims, as I open the door so we can both get out.

"You guys in here?" Amrit calls out.

"Yeah, we're here," I say as we walk out. I look around and can see that the infected that were after us are all dead.

"You guys OK?" Amrit asks.

"Yeah, we're fine," Becky answers.

"Yeah, we're good," I add.

"Guys?" I hear someone call out.

"Who else is there?" I ask. I then see Ryan come running into the room.

"Oh, hello," Becky says to him.

"Oh, thank God," Ryan says. "Did you get anything?"

"As a matter of fact, we did," I say. I then push forward the trolley of food and show him the rucksack with all of the weapons.

"Nice. Come on, let's get out of here," he urges.

"Yeah, let's go," I say.

We all begin walking towards the door, me carrying the rucksack and Amrit pushing the trolley. We head outside and it is just as cold as it was when we entered the building.

"Layton and I had a good chat," Becky says to Amrit as we stroll across the car park.

"Oh yeah?"

"Yeah," Becky says. "He told me that you two met because you tried to steal from him."

"What?" Amrit shouts. "That's what he said?"

"Yeah," Becky replies.

"Layton, did you tell Becky I robbed you?" he asks me aggressively.

"Maybe." I smirk.

"Tell her the truth," he says.

"Well…" I begin hesitantly.

"This fucker tried to rob me," Amrit shouts, "not the other way round."

"What?" Becky asks.

"That's not exactly true," I say.

"Yes, it is," he responds.

"Well, yes, I tried to rob you, because five minutes earlier you tried to rob me," I tell him, feeling he has missed the point.

"What?" he says, bemused.

"Yes, you did," I state as we stop walking just outside the camp.

"When?" he asks.

"OK, how many people did you try to rob that day?" I ask him.

"Well, I did try to rob a guy before you tried to rob me," he explains.

"Yes," I say. "Was it a guy with a black hoodie, with the hood over his head?"

"Yeah," he hesitantly responds.

"Yeah," I state.

"Shit, was that you?" he asks.

"Yes," I answer.

"So you both tried to rob each other?" Becky asks.

"Yeah, I guess we did," Amrit says.

"Yeah," I say.

"I'm sorry, bro," he says.

"That's OK, bro," I respond.

"I feel bad, bro," he says.

"Don't, bro."

"I won't doubt you again, bro."

"That's OK, bro," I say. We then move in for a hug.

"Sorry, bro," Amrit says.

"No, I'm sorry, bro."

"No, I'm sorry, bro."

"No, I'm sorry, bro."

"No, I'm sorry—"

"If one of you says, 'bro' again, I am going to kick off," Becky shouts.

"Sorry," we both respond, stepping back from our embrace.

"OK," Ryan says, "let's get in." He opens the door to the camp and we all walk inside and can see everybody sitting there waiting for us.

"Layton!" Rhea calls out. She comes running towards me and gives me a massive hug.

"Hi," I say.

"We have food," Becky announces as Rhea lets go of me. "Now we all need to eat so we can get our strength back."

"Sounds good to me," Mark responds. "Let's see what you got."

Everybody gathers around the trolley, getting the food out of there.

"I was really worried about you," Rhea admits to me.

"You were worried about me?" I ask, surprised to learn that she was thinking about me while we were gone.

"Yeah. I don't know why, but when I noticed you were gone I began to fear you wouldn't come back. I know that sounds cheesy," she announces, looking a little shy.

"You have no reason to worry," I explain. "I will always come back."

We look at one another and hug. I feel very comfortable right now; as if I could hold her forever. I do have to let go at some point, but I'm going to enjoy it while it lasts.

22

I know this is going to sound weird, but barbecued rat is actually not that bad. I don't know if it's how Mark cooked it but it's actually really tender. Everyone else is tucking into their food and enjoying it too. Rhea and Jane were a little squeamish with regards to the rat, so they settled for tinned beans instead. I look down and see my piece of rat begin to slowly fall from the bone, the juices surrounding the remainder of the meat that is gripped to it. I take another bite and feel the soft, smoky flavour enter my taste buds, opening up a world of sensual release.

"This is pretty good," I say out loud with chunks of meat in my mouth.

"Yeah, it's not bad," Amrit replies, his mouth full also.

"Well, I guess you're used to a piece of meat in your mouth," I state, chuckling to myself.

"Gay joke, wow," Amrit says sarcastically. "You're used to a piece of meat in your arse."

"Brilliant," I say.

We look at each other and chuckle. Then I look over and see Rhea eating her beans, slowly putting the spoon in her mouth to avoid the heat. "Is that good?" I ask as she blows on the spoon before eating more.

"Yeah," she responds.

"You want to try some of this?" I ask, holding my piece of rat out to her.

"I'm good, thanks," she states.

"Fair enough," I say. I didn't really want to give her any; I was only offering out of politeness. It's one of those times when you offer somebody something and you really want them to say no, but you still offer just for the sake of it.

"OK," Mark says, "we need to get thinking." He finishes his mouthful. "We need to think about our next course of action."

"What do you mean?" Becky asks him.

"We need to think about what we do next," he replies. "We can't stay here forever; we need to think about where we go from this point forward."

We all look at him, knowing that he is right. None of us really wanted to think about it, though – well, I know I didn't.

"I think we should head south," Becky suggests, "probably towards London."

"Why London?" Jane asks.

"Because it's probably better there," Becky says. "It's a larger city, the capital; there are probably real homes there, even a civilisation or something."

"I don't know, I think we should go north," Ryan suggests while wiping his hands. "Probably Scotland. I know that Scotland is a wasteland now, but we should head to where there are fewer people, and we will be safer than, well, and safer than staying here," he explains, looking around.

"Either way, we can't stay here," Mark says.

"Why not?" Jane asks.

"Well, we have the Union not too far away," Mark states, "and there are border monkeys everywhere. Also, I think the reason Scotland is a wasteland is because it was badly hit by the infection, so there are probably a lot of infected up there," he says, dampening the idea of a Scottish retreat.

"I suppose you're right," Amrit admits. "Where do we go from here then – what do you propose?"

"I think we should go to Birmingham," I say to them.

"Why?" Becky asks.

"It's like you said: we should go to where there are more people, right, so why don't we go to Birmingham? There are more people there and it's not too far from here," I suggest.

"I think wherever we go, we should aim for fewer people," Amrit states.

"Warwickshire," Mark suggests.

"Warwickshire?" I ask, confused at such a random suggestion.

"Yes. My family owned property there, back before all this happened. My Dad kept one of the farms he had, kept it secure. It's been years since I've been there, but it's a chance," he suggests, sounding hopeful.

"Sorry, Mark," Ryan says, "but how do you know it's still there? You stayed there years ago; how you can be certain it will still be there?"

"What do you propose?" Mark responds defensively. "We go to Scotland where there's infection everywhere?"

"Well, at least it's realistic," Ryan states. "You're holding on to a pipe dream."

"Pipe dream?" Mark responds abruptly.

They both get to their feet as if they are about to square off, glaring at each other with aggression.

"Look," Amrit points out, getting to his feet too, "we have to agree on one plan."

I look over and can see Rhea beginning to get agitated.

"Yes, we do," Becky says. "We need to decide." She gets to her feet and I do the same, just in case it all kicks off.

"This is stupid," Mark shouts, clenching his fist. "I know Warwickshire is where we should go."

"How?" Ryan retorts. "You're basing this on what exactly?"

Rhea is getting more agitated.

"What about Wales?" Becky suggests. "There are mountains there and nobody around."

"I thought you wanted more people," I point out.

"Don't argue with me, Layton," she shouts, glaring right at me.

"I'm not arguing, you just contradicted yourself," I point out. I don't know why she is getting angry.

"I don't care what you all think," Mark says. "We're going to Warwickshire."

"Since when were you the boss?" Amrit asks, looking very confrontational.

"We're not going there," Ryan says.

"Stop it!" Rhea shouts. "Just fucking stop it, all of you."

We turn and face her, stunned into silence.

"Rhea—" I say.

"I am sick of this," Rhea says. "All my life, and I'm sure it's the same for you, all we do is go from one place to another. We're always on the move and never able to find a home. For once, can we not talk about where we have to go next? Can we just stay here for the time being and not be in such a rush to run off? Can we for once just stay here and enjoy it for a while? We even had to leave the city centre because of the Union. Can we just enjoy this moment here and not have to always think of what will happen tomorrow? I just want to enjoy today."

We all stand there looking at each other, and down at Rhea. I know how she feels.

"You're right," I admit, agreeing with every word.

"Yeah, I agree," says Amrit, beginning to calm his voice.

"Me too," Becky and Ryan add. They look and smile at each other as they realise they said the same thing at the same time.

"Same here," utters Mark reluctantly.

"Yeah," says Jane.

We all sit back down and look at each other with silent forgiveness.

"Thank you," Rhea says.

"What shall we talk about?" Amrit asks as he looks around at us all.

"Let's play a quiz," I suggest as a way of increasing our camaraderie.

"OK," everyone responds.

"What are the rules?" Becky asks.

"Well, we have to ask any question, then whoever gets an answer wrong has to take an item of clothing off," I explain, looking at Jane, who begins to chuckle to herself.

"I like the sound of that," Ryan says.

"Pervert," Becky says.

"Could be fun," Jane declares with enthusiasm.

"Of course," Becky sighs sarcastically.

"Let's play," Mark says, swallowing his pride.

"Right then," I say. "First question for Becky: what is the capital of Russia?"

"Moscow," she replies. "OK, my question for you: how do you spell 'condescend'?"

I know that she knows I don't know the answer.

"Oh. Um…" I begin, feeling my brain begin to turn, trying to find the answer.

"You have to answer," Mark demands, excited.

"C… um… O… N… um… D… um… A," I say, confused. I've never been a good speller.

"Wrong," Mark shouts, and laughs.

"Take it off!" Jane declares.

"Fine," I say, so I take my jacket off. I already know this game is going to turn out to be a bad idea.

A couple of hours pass and we are still quizzing each other. I am now down to my trousers, whereas Jane is down to her bra and pants. Everyone else seems to be getting their questions right; nobody else is getting anything wrong. This is insane – why did I think of playing this stupid game? I know that it has come to a point where if I was to turn around and suggest something else, I would be seen as nothing more than a sore loser.

"OK," Mark says, "next question for Jane. Who was the Queen of England during the Victorian era?" he asks, smiling.

"Um…" Jane says, "Anne?"

"Seriously?" I state, shocked, and the rest of the group giggle at such a ridiculous answer.

"Take it off!" Mark excitedly demands.

"What who was it?" she asks, confused at all of our reactions.

"Queen Victoria," he responds.

"Oh," she says, taking her bra off. We all laugh at the response.

"Wow," I say. I look around and I do feel a bit of pride knowing that everyone is enjoying themselves. It feels like ages since we all sat together and had a laugh.

"Thank you," Rhea says to me. I look at her and smile, feeling good that I made her happy.

Then out of nowhere, we hear banging on the door.

"Shit, what was that?" Ryan asks as we all look round, stunned into a momentary silence.

"Layton, get your clothes on," Becky shouts. I quickly put my clothes back on and we turn and look at the front of the room.

"Ryan, Layton, Amrit, come with me," Mark says.

We all grab our weapons and head to the front of the room. We can still hear the banging. We look through and can see a family standing there: a mum, a dad and a little boy, probably no older than ten. They are very shabbily dressed, with scruffy hair and tatty shoes. Mark leans over and opens the door to talk to them.

"Can we help you?" Amrit asks, concerned.

"Please," the dad asks, "do you have any room for us?"

I look over and can see Rhea, Becky and Jane approach us.

"Why?" Ryan asks, aggravated.

"We are cold and hungry," the mum says.

"Please, our son is sick," the dad states, worried and frustrated.

"How do you mean?" Mark asks. But then we look down at the boy and can tell what has happened to him.

"You're fucking kidding me," Ryan shouts. "He's been bitten!"

"Yes," the dad agrees, "but please, we won't be any trouble."

"We have to let them in," Rhea states.

"I agree," I declare.

"No," Mark says. "If he comes in here, overnight he will turn and infect all of us."

"We cannot let them in," Ryan begins to say. "If we let them in, he could infect all of us; it's just not worth the risk."

"But he's only a child," Rhea pleads.

"Please don't leave us out here," the mum begs.

"Just let us in," the dad cries, "we have a child."

"Sorry, we can't," Becky says.

"Sorry," Mark repeats, and slams the door on them.

I look outside and can see the family standing there, lost and afraid. The parents look just as terrified as the young boy does. They turn and walk away, knowing that there is no hope.

The rest of our group then walk away too, leaving Rhea and me standing there, stunned. Rhea is beginning to get upset, and I try to say something but she walks away before I can. I know that we have sentenced a family to death. I look over and can see Amrit looking just as shocked as Rhea and me at the fact that Ryan and Becky could let them go so easily; they did it and didn't even think about it. It leaves us questioning our decision to stay with them. I know they had their reasons, but there was a child with them, a child – if we can't go out of our way to help a child, then who can we help?

I struggle to fall asleep that night, tossing and turning, unable to close my eyes. I try to think of a way I can relax, but I just don't manage to. I decide to get up instead; maybe a smoke could help me. I look around and find some tobacco in the corner, get some paper and roll a cigarette. I lean over the fire and light it, then sit there in the corner of the room, smoking away. I feel the smoke cover me, even beginning to hurt my eyes. I then look over and see Rhea walking towards me.

"Can I have a drag?" she asks as she takes a seat next to me.

"Sure," I say, handing it over to her. She takes a large drag, then hands it back to me.

"Can't sleep either?" I ask her.

"Nah," she responds, looking as exhausted as I am.

"That was shit earlier," I say.

"I don't want to talk about it," she demands.

I look down and try to think of something else to say. "Sorry."

"It's just," she begins, "if we can't help others, then how can we help ourselves? If we can't help others then what is the point in helping ourselves?"

"General Singh kept reciting Rousseau to me," I tell her, thinking she'll understand.

"Oh, who's that?" she asks.

"Oh, nobody, carry on," I say.

"Right," she says. "If somebody needs help then we have to help them. If somebody gives us trouble then we have to defeat them."

"Like you did with Scarlett," I remind her.

"Yeah," she says, chuckling. "What happened to her?"

I look at her and I know she has no idea.

"She's dead," I tell her.

"What?" she asks, with a very uncomfortable look on her face.

"Rob shot her," I say as she starts to look concerned.

"Shit," she breathes.

"Then General Singh showed me her body, and a lot of

people who he'd been experimenting on. He was telling me how he wants to try and fix the world," I tell her.

"Wow," she says. She pauses for a moment and looks off into the distance. She then turns to me and I can tell she wants to tell me something. I continue to smoke my cigarette.

"Well, why can't we fix the world?"

I look at her, a little perplexed.

"What do you mean?" I ask her.

"I mean," she begins to say, "the world is pretty shit now. So, what if we formed our own society? Obviously not like the Union, but where we can actually help people. We could have our own committee, we can build our own houses…" She continues to talk, and I get lost in her enthusiasm. "I mean, we could even build a school. Wouldn't that be great? Just to have a community, a home, and a place where we can start again?"

"What about the infected?" I ask her.

She pauses for a moment and looks back at me. "Well, we would have to deal with them. They're still people, still human beings who need us to help them."

Somehow, without even trying, I can already see the flaws in her plan.

"But there's no cure," I tell her.

"I know that," she says reluctantly, repositioning herself. She then leans over, takes my cigarette without asking and starts to smoke it.

"Um…" I say, looking at her.

"We have to have faith that there can be a cure out there somewhere," she declares.

"Faith?" I say. "Do you believe in God?"

She looks at me and smiles in that way she does, then looks down at her feet. I look at her feet as well and realise how small and dainty they are.

"No," she tells me. "Sometimes I want to, but I don't. There's no real point, is there?"

I know exactly what she means. She then finishes the cigarette and throws it on the ground.

"So where did you learn to fight?" I ask, remembering her beating up Scarlett.

She laughs. "My Dad," she tells me. "He always wanted me to be able to take care of myself. Before the crash he was a boxer, so he taught me how to fight. Taught me everything I know. How to throw a jab, a straight. I even learned how to turn my back foot and my front foot. He made sure I was prepared."

"Bloody hell," I respond.

"Yeah," she says. "Anyway," she jumps up and stands in front of me, "I'm going to bed. Thanks for the cigarette. You coming?"

"I'll be there in a bit," I tell her.

"OK," she says. "Goodnight." She smiles as she turns and walks away.

I gaze at her as she walks off, and once again, I can't take my eyes off her. I look at her in her T-shirt and three-quarter-lengths and I just want to hold her. Shit, what is happening to me? I need to stop thinking like this, it just isn't healthy. Right, time to think of something else, something to take my mind off her.

Nothing; I can't think of anything else. Thank you, brain.

23

Why did we do that? I keep thinking about it over and over. I look outside and can that it is daylight now. I've not slept a wink just thinking about it.

I can see that Rhea has struggled to sleep as well. It was nice talking to her last night. I look over and can see her just lying there with her eyes closed. How about if I get up and walk around for a bit? I stagger at first, but eventually I manage to get up onto my feet, feeling those morning kinks in my joints clicking into place.

I walk across the room and stare out of the window into the distance. I can't help thinking – did the family manage to find help in the end? Did they get to safety? Are they dead? I then start to think about those kids I saw when we were in Leicester. I wonder what has happened to them? Are they safe, have they got shelter? I don't know. I feel guilty as I'm starting to forget their faces. I know I only met them once, but I still feel guilty. I guess in this shit-stain of a world, being welcoming to somebody is just not on the cards. I don't know, maybe I'm just too soft. Maybe I'm not strong enough to see the errors of what people do. Why didn't I speak up? Why didn't I say no, we are going to help you, come in, we have food and water? Instead I just stayed quiet like a coward. I guess it's not the first time.

"What is that?" I say to myself as I look outside. I can see a fox running across the car park. Its orange fur really does shine in the morning light. I think it's probably looking for food, just roaming around from place to place, not really having a place to call home. Eating as a means to survive, not for enjoyment. I guess we're no different.

I walk towards another part of the room I have yet to explore. I can see that this shop used to sell televisions and radios; I can tell by the old, tattered posters all around the place. I've never watched a television before; I wonder what they were like? One of the posters advertises a fifty-two-inch television for £799. Why not just round it up to £800? I guess people back then were fooled by the saving of one pound. Well, I suppose every little adds up.

Why is it so cold in here? Why does England have to be so cold? Why can't we have a tropical climate or at least a little bit of heat, like Spain or Morocco or Egypt? Well, I guess if we were somewhere like that, we would moan about it being so hot all the time. I guess you can't win either way.

I turn around to look for some food. I'm hungry, so I guess it is time to eat. Everyone else has decided to have a lie-in, but I'm not really in the mood; I fancy walking around for a bit. I can see the rest of the beans that Rhea left last night. She didn't really want to eat any more after we turned those people away. I guess I should finish them off. I grab the spoon and scrape up the beans. They're cold now, but not as bad as I thought they would be. The sauce is very slimy, and the chunks of bean have a dry feel to them. Well, I guess it will fill me up, so no point in complaining.

What would be really nice is to go to a pub. I wonder if there is one around here somewhere? At least there you can get a drink. Feels like ages since I sat down in a pub and had a drink. The last time I did that, Bal and his crew came after me. I wonder what happened to them? I wonder if they're still going around kicking the shit out of people for ripping them off over precious stones? Oh, Bal, that twat.

I look over and see Amrit getting up. I decide to go towards him; I think he is the only person I really feel comfortable talking to right now. He rubs his eyes as he slowly gets to his feet.

"Hey," I say as he turns to face me.

"You all right?" he asks me, yawning.

"Ah, you know me, average at best. How about yourself?" I ask, trying to be cheerful.

"I'm good," he says.

"You hungry?" I ask him.

"I could eat." He smiles.

I walk over to the trolley to see if we have any tins he might like. I rummage through the food and can see we have about fifty tins. That's enough for now, if we ration it. I know I can try my hardest to humour myself. But I know there is only a matter of time until it runs out.

"What we got?" Amrit asks me as I rummage through.

"Well," I say, "we have tinned sweetcorn, tinned tuna, and beans."

"Just some corn would be good," he says as I feel the tin in my hand, rolling it around.

"You sure?" I ask, thinking he would want something else in the morning besides a can of corn; maybe something with a bit of protein.

"Yeah," he says, "can't be arsed cooking."

I bring the tin over to him and he pulls out a knife to open it after thanking me. He dips his fingers into the corn and slides it into his mouth.

"How is it?" I ask.

"It's all right," he replies, crunching his way through a mouthful of corn.

He takes a seat on a table, and I sit there next to him. I don't want to look at him because that could get awkward, so I just stare forwards.

"What's up?" he asks me.

"Nothing," I say.

He puts the tin down and turns to face me. "I know what's up," he says. "The family we turned away yesterday."

I guess that's what makes a good friend: somebody who always knows what you're thinking, without you having to tell them.

"They turned them away," I state, uncomfortable with what I am saying.

"We did," Amrit corrects. "Just because you weren't the one to tell them to go, does not mean you ran out and saved them."

I stare at him, feeling angry at what he said; not because I disagree with him, but because I know I should have done more.

"The worst thing you can do is beat yourself up over it. You have to realise that this world is not meant for the weak. As hard as it is to come to terms with that, we have to save ourselves," he tells me, making me feel far worse.

"I guess," I say.

I then notice the rest of the group waking up, tossing and turning. I look at them and know they were probably doing what they thought was right, even though it makes me hate them a little for doing it.

"Morning," Becky yawns.

"Morning," Amrit responds.

"Hey," Rhea says, walking towards us.

"How you feeling?" I ask her.

"I feel good. I feel like my old self again," she announces with a hint of confidence in her voice. I look at her and wonder if she actually believes in what she was saying yesterday about wanting to build her own society.

"Oh dear," I say sarcastically.

"Shut up," she retorts, hitting me on the arm.

"Um, ouch." I look over and see Mark rummaging through the tins to see what food we have left.

"We need to get more," he declares.

"We have enough," Rhea states.

"Not really. We need to go out and get more," he says, as if we are living on nothing but crumbs.

Rhea begins to look very aggressive.

"Yeah, we do," Ryan says, walking forward. "It's early so not many people will be out; I'll go with one other person," he states, looking for someone to volunteer for the cause.

"I'll go," I say, knowing it will meet with objection.

"No, you won't," Rhea quickly shouts, staring me down to try and get me to budge.

"I have to," I say. I can't look away from her eyes. She looks at me and I don't want her to feel scared about me leaving.

"I'll bring him back, don't worry," Ryan says.

"I'll be fine," I promise, and turn to grab my machete. "Let's go, no time like the present."

I turn and see Amrit and Rhea staring back at me as I walk towards the door. I want to give them one quick look back, but I don't; instead all I do is move away, hiding my face from them like a vale of misunderstanding, entering a cold haven, frosted in a blanket lacking the warmth that will bring comfort.

We walk through the car park towards the motorway. I can imagine that once upon a time there were nothing but cars going up and down these roads, however all that remains now are the empty carcasses of vehicles. We walk towards a group of trees, near what looks like a park.

"We should try and get meat," Ryan says.

"That won't last," I reply. "We need tinned stuff."

"I know," he says. "We'll get meat now, then go for tinned stuff after."

"Ok," I say as we continue to walk down through the park to the other side.

"Hold on," Ryan says.

We halt, look forward and can see a fox snooping around. I think it might be the same fox I saw earlier, I don't know; maybe it's a different one. All I know is that we are going to try and kill this fox so we can eat it for lunch.

"Quietly now," Ryan whispers as he slowly sneaks towards the fox.

I follow closely behind as the fox just stands there, sniffing an old box. We get closer and closer, and Ryan sees his opportunity to attack. He pulls out a knife. Suddenly we hear a giant bang like a gunshot that startles the fox, and it runs away.

"What the fuck was that?" I say out loud.

"I don't know," Ryan responds, "but it doesn't sound good."

We quickly turn and can hear motorbikes in the background.

"Shit," I say.

"What?" he shouts.

"Quickly, we need to hide."

We run and find an old bin that looks like it hasn't been used in years. We quickly jump inside and peer out so we know what is going on. I know the noise that we are hearing.

I see the motorbikes coming down, and a group of people appear.

"Who are they?" Ryan asks.

"Border monkeys," I say to him.

The border monkeys have another person with them who doesn't seem to be wearing the same clothing as them. He hasn't got the boots, the Mohican hairstyle or the numerous items of leather clothing with chains.

"Right then," one of the border monkeys says, bringing the man to the front. It looks like there are about four of them gathered around. The man they bring forward looks like he's in his mid-forties, and wears nothing more than a T-shirt and jeans.

"Yeah, get him," the other border monkeys call out.

"No, please!" the man begs, panicking as the border monkeys stand over him.

"Come here, my little friend," the border monkey holding him says. This border monkey looks like he's seen a few fights. He has a massive scar on the back of his head, and he's bold, with a moustache. "This little man thinks he can just not pay us what he owes. We deserve to have a go on his daughters, and he wants to stop us from doing so."

"Please," he says, "they're my girls."

"We don't give a fuck," the skinhead monkey says. "Also, when we say you have to give us food, you have to give us food," he demands of the man, who is now on his knees.

"But we will starve," the man says.

"Shall we let him go, lads, or make him suffer?" the skinhead monkey shouts.

"Kill, kill, kill," the group chants.

"Very well," the skinhead monkey says, and pulls out a small axe from his back pocket.

"No, please, no!" the man shouts.

"Fuck you," the skinhead monkey says, and slams the axe into the man's neck.

I can hear the man try to scream, but no sound comes from him. It sounds like he is choking on his own blood.

"Come on, lads," the skinhead monkey says, "let's leave this piece of shit to die."

They all ride off, cheering, and as soon as the coast is clear, Ryan and I get out of the bin. We run over to the man who was attacked, and he's dead.

"Poor guy," I say.

"Yeah," Ryan responds. "We better go."

We run back towards what looks like an old supermarket; then see something we did not want to see.

"Fuck off," I shout as we see about seven infected coming towards us. I turn, and find three more behind us. "Shit, they're organised!"

"No, they're not," Ryan says, pulling out a knife. "Just get on with it."

We start slashing at the infected, cutting through them and hitting their heads. One grabs Ryan and he is almost pinned, but manages to break free and kill it. I kill the three behind us and we are safe.

"I thought you said there would be nobody out here," I shout, frustrated and furious.

"I know," he responds, lowering his voice.

"So all this 'we need to find food' business was just a plan to make yourself look like a hero?" I accuse.

Ryan remains silent and keeps looking down, as if he is feeling guilty.

"How about next time we all decide, rather than you and Mark barking orders?" I yell.

"All right," he shouts, "all right, I know I fucked up. I'm sorry."

I look at him and I know he is being genuine, so I decide to stop.

"Come on, let's get back," I say, with greater urgency in my voice.

"Yeah," Ryan says, panting, holding himself and staggering slightly, "let's go."

"You OK?" I ask him, concerned.

"Yeah, I'm good," he says. "Let's just get moving, we can come back later."

"Sure."

We begin to run back, making sure nobody else is in our way, and that we do not get attacked by anyone. We run through the streets, across the park and away, until we can't even see the park any more. Just keep moving forward, that's the secret. Finally we're just outside the building we are staying in.

"Layton?" Ryan says.

"Yeah?"

"I know you're not happy with what we had to do yesterday."

"OK," I respond.

"You know we had to do it for the good of the group, yeah?" he tells me, licking his lips as if they are dry.

"Yeah," I say.

"Good. We have to make sure we are all safe – one slip-up and we could all die, OK?" he says with concern and worry in his voice, panting as he tries to get the words out.

"Why are you telling me this?" I ask, confused.

"Just so you know," he says. "Just so you know that if it comes to it, you may have to kill someone here; you may have to do what you have to do to survive."

I look at him, baffled at what he is telling me.

"OK," I say.

I don't know why he is telling me this. I think it's for my own good; I think he is trying to help. I mean, he could wait till we get in, but I guess this is as good a time as any.

Well, now it's time to tell everyone we didn't get anything to eat; this will be fun. I can't wait to be the bearer of bad news.

24

As we are welcomed back by the rest of the group, Ryan and I can't help but feel disappointed with ourselves. I know what the mission was: we needed to get food so that we could all survive another night.

Nonetheless, all that has happened is we have failed. We were scared off by a group of infected and the thought of what would happen if the border monkeys got hold of us.

"What happened?" Mark asks as we collapse to the ground in a heap of exhaustion. He looks at us and I can see that he has noticed we have brought nothing with us.

"We were attacked," Ryan announces before I have a chance to say anything.

"Attacked?" Becky asks, sounding concerned.

"Yeah," I say, trying to catch my breath, "we were attacked by a group of infected and we saw some border monkeys attacking another man."

"Shit," Amrit says.

"Well, at least you're OK," Rhea says sympathetically.

"Yeah, and we have enough food to last for the next few days, anyway," Jane reassures us.

"Then what?" Ryan asks. "Then all we do is suffer and die."

We all look at him, stunned by how dramatic he can be.

"We'll be fine," I say, trying to calm his temper.

"No we won't, and you know it," he huffs, storming off.

We all stand there staring at him stomp away.

"What's up with him?" Amrit asks.

"I don't know," I respond.

I decide to go after Ryan, moving past the used-up tins that the group have been emptying while we were gone. I can see Ryan sitting under a shelving unit with his head down. He looks up at me as I head towards him. I look behind myself quickly and see that everyone else is out of earshot.

"Hi," Ryan says as I sit near him.

"Hey," I say to him. "OK, what was all that about?"

"Sorry about that. I thought I would be realistic for a moment," he says, with a gulf of certainty in his voice.

"What we did was not a total disaster," I state, trying to bring some optimism to the table.

"I need to go out again tonight," he says, sounding very determined.

I immediately feel that this is a bad idea. "Why?" I ask.

"We need to make sure we have enough food for at least the next couple of weeks," he states.

I look at him, confused. I know today didn't go to plan, but there is no reason for us to do another run just yet.

"There's no need," I say, trying to make sure he doesn't go out for the sake of some heroic journey.

"Yes, there is. We're not all going to get out of here alive," he tells me, his tone dampened slightly.

"Yeah, we are. We just need to devise a plan so that we can survive here as long as possible," I try to explain.

"There's not going to be an 'us'. Just you guys," he tells me dejectedly.

"What do you mean?" I ask him.

He looks me in the eye, hesitating, then looks down. He

struggles to talk, and just looks at me some more. He then resorts to blinking. He blinks continuously for at least five minutes before offering an answer. He first attempts by opening his mouth, taking a breath, then closing it again.

I also want to speak, but don't know the correct words to say. Instead of talking, I just notice Ryan begin to use actions to answer my question. He lifts his top and shows me the side of his torso. There are deep bite marks embedded in the flesh, and blood trickling down, already beginning to look stale.

"Shit," I say to him.

"It was my idea for us to go out," he declares, "then I went and got bit. Now I need to get enough food for you guys."

"OK," I say, "and you want to go tonight before the infection takes hold?" I decide not to argue, just to accept his decision.

"Yeah."

"OK, what time shall we go?" I say, peering over at the group, making sure they are not in earshot.

"No," he says, "I can't put your life in danger again."

"I'm coming with you," I say to him. "There's no compromise on this. When are you going to tell the others?" I ask.

He pauses for a moment and I can tell he is thinking about it. Then I realise what he is planning.

"You're not going to tell them," I state, knowing his decision before he tells me.

"Let's get the food first, then I will tell them," he says, already organised with a plan in his mind.

"OK," I respond.

We both then look at each other, lost for words. I can see that he has something he wants to say. I can tell he is struggling, not able to find the words. I feel as if he is going through one of those moments where you have a thousand words going through your mind, yet nothing seems to be able to break out into your mouth.

"It's funny…" he begins.

"What is?" I ask, wondering if he is going to tell me an actual joke.

"We once lived in a world of possession," he states. "Now we have nothing and yet we still want something. I guess the only possession we all really want is life. That is the only thing that we look for now. I'm done with trying to gain things and having to run. Now I have to do what I can so that you guys have a future, however long it might be."

"OK," I say to him.

We both sit there, waiting for the sun to go down. The hours go past and we can see everybody making the day go by. I look at everybody else and want to tell them what I know, but I can't. It is not my place to tell them what has happened to Ryan; it is up to him. All I see is everybody joking and laughing. It becomes a blur after a while, with them cheering and feasting on the food we have left. They are completely unaware of the task Ryan and I have to undertake; that one of their friends may not be with them for much longer.

A few hours have passed, and as it is winter, the sun comes down at about five o'clock. Ryan comes up to me, nods his head, and I know it is a signal that we have to get moving. We head outside and straight for the opposite building.

"Come on," he says as we head through the door.

I look back and can see Rhea staring back at me. I do not want to tell her anything, however I know she wants to ask. Instead I just turn and face the door, knowing I will have to open it and leave without giving answers to any questions.

"OK, let's get in," I say to Ryan as we approach the other building, looking at the barricade.

"Come on," he says, and we bash our way through.

We head inside, making sure we don't cause too much noise, just in case there are infected or people living inside. We walk through and into a back room. There are huge amounts of tinned goods, meats, fruits and vegetables all over the place. There are even large bottles of water.

"OK," I say, "we need something to carry it all in."

We look around and see a giant trolley, probably used to push heavy goods around. We put everything inside it and begin pushing. We shove it right outside and make our way back to the rest of the group.

"Layton?" Ryan says.

"Yeah?"

"Thanks," he says, with a hint of cheer in his voice.

"What for?" I ask him.

"Just… I know I couldn't have done this without you," Ryan states with a slight smile on his face.

"It's OK," I tell him.

"It's just that…" he begins, then stops. He starts to cough, bending over as if he is about to throw up.

I look at him, worried, patting his back in an attempt to make him feel better.

"You OK, mate?" I ask softly.

He bends over, and next thing I know, he throws up. I quickly jump back to avoid the vomit, making sure my boots are not dirtied. I looked down and can even see some blood in the vomit. He stands up, sweating and beginning to look pale. I can tell that he has hit the fever stage of the infection.

"It's so annoying," he says to me. "If those fucking governments had taken care of everything, we would have had the money to deal with this bloody infection."

"Yeah," I agree.

"They managed to take care of rabies," he states, bitterness in his voice. "This is just a more aggressive form of it. Yet there is nothing that can help me."

"You'll be OK," I say to him.

"Bullshit," he cries, then turns and throws up again. He wipes his mouth, now struggling to open his eyes.

"Come on, we have to keep moving," I state, patting him on the back.

"Hold on," he says to me. He then pulls out a note from his back pocket and shows it to me.

"What's that?" I ask him.

"It's a letter," he begins to explain. "It's from my mum. She was bitten as well, and she wrote this letter to me before she died," he tells me while opening a piece of crumpled paper in his hand.

"Yeah?"

"Do you want me to read it to you?" he asks.

"You don't have to," I state.

"No," he says, "I do." He begins to read.

Dear Ryan,

I know I will not be able to be with you anymore. I know you will be strong. I want you to take care of yourself because you're my big man now.

You have to be strong when I am not around. I want you to be happy; I want you to have a life. Whenever you get scared, whenever you feel alone, just remember I will be there with you. Just close your eyes and imagine my arms around you, and that I'm kissing you to tell you that everything is all right. I will always be in your heart, so whenever you place your hand upon your chest and feel it beat, just remember it is me telling you I love you.

Be happy, my Ryan, because you will always be my beautiful baby boy.

Love from Mum.

I look at him and struggle to find the words that could be meaningful now.

"Wow," I say, feeling my throat tighten and my eyes begin to water.

"I just wanted to read it once more, before I stop being able to even look at it," he tells me.

"OK," I say to him.

We both then begin to walk forward, and I feel nothing but numbness. All he wanted was to be happy, he wanted to survive, not for himself; he wanted it for his mum. Maybe all we can do in this world is just please ourselves. There is nothing else we can do now.

As we walk inside, everybody is staring at us. It feels like we have been brought into a meeting and are about to face the biggest telling-off of our lives. I see the worry on Amrit and Rhea's faces as I walk in with Ryan by my side. It's very late, so late that the sun is beginning to rise. I look over at Ryan and can see that the fever has taken a turn for the worse. As soon as we get in he just collapses on a stool in front of the group. Mark comes storming towards us with purpose.

"Show me," he shouts, staring at Ryan, eyes piercing him as he sadly looks back.

"Mark," Becky says.

"Show me now," Mark shouts again, interrupting Becky. Ryan looks at him and then down at his side.

"What's up?" Jane asks, looking as confused as ever.

"I know what's up," Mark says, looking upset and disappointed. "I can tell by how you're sweating and struggling to walk."

"It's OK," Ryan says to him.

"Just show me," Mark pleads once more.

I look at Ryan and can see that he is struggling to face Mark. Ryan then leans down and raises his top to show the bite on the side of his torso. Mark collapses to his knees, and tears begin to fall from his eyes.

"It's OK," Ryan says to him.

"No, it's not," Mark replies.

"Yes, it is," Ryan pants. "I'm happy."

"What?" Jane asks out of nowhere. She comes walking towards us and looks at Ryan struggling to stand up, sweat streaming from his face, covering his lips.

"When did that happen?" Becky asks, concerned.

"When Layton and I went out for supplies yesterday," Ryan says, trying to be calm.

"But I thought you were fine," Rhea says, panicking.

"Why didn't you tell me?" Mark shouts, as if he is pleading for an answer.

"Layton, did you know?" Becky asks me abruptly.

"Yes, I did," I respond begrudgingly, feeling terrible. A part of me feels as if I should have just announced it to everyone before we left. I feel that I have kept information to myself that should've been shared.

"And you never told us?" Becky shouts furiously.

"Why?" Jane asks.

"He told me not to," I say, pointing at Ryan sitting on the stool.

"Shit," Mark shouts. "Fuck, fuck, and fuck!" he shouts over and over again.

"How did it happen?" Amrit asks.

"It was when we were out," I begin to tell them. "We were attacked by a bunch of infected and he got bitten. I didn't know till we got back."

"I knew it was a bad idea," Rhea says. "Now one of us is hurt."

"We need to get help," Becky says.

"What help?" I ask her.

She turns and faces me. I see the pain in her face and know that she is suffering from her friend being hurt. I want to help her and let her know everything will be OK, however I feel as if it would be foolish of me to do so.

We continue to bicker for another five minutes, one person

blaming the other, and end up just going around in circles, not really coming to any genuine conclusion. Mark begins pacing up and down the room, lost in thought, while Becky and Amrit are arguing, coming close to blows.

"Shut the fuck up, all of you!" Ryan shouts.

"Ryan," Mark cries, lowering his tone.

"Just shut up," he repeats. "This is my last day before I forget who I am. I don't want to spend it watching you guys trying to rip each other's throats out."

"Sorry," Mark stutters.

"Yeah, sorry," Amrit adds.

Ryan then looks at us individually to make sure we have his full attention.

"Knowing you guys has made me what I am," he tells us. "Now I know that I will be happy when I leave you."

"No," Rhea says to herself.

"Funny, really," Ryan begins to say. "We turned away a family because the child was bitten, and then I went and got myself bitten. Strange how life can kick you in the balls."

"What do we do?" Amrit asks.

"Nothing," Mark says, "there's nothing we can do." He looks at Ryan with a hint of anger.

"Mark," Ryan says to him.

"Why didn't you tell me? Why did you wait till now to let us all know about it?" Mark asks, pain fighting its way through his voice.

"I just want to die in peace," Ryan says. "I made sure you guys have enough supplies so that you will be secure." He pants as he talks, as if he has just run a marathon.

"I could have helped you," Mark pleads.

"No," Ryan states. "I wanted you to all be oblivious to it, so your emotions would not get in the way."

"I wish I had been there," Mark states, sobbing. "I wish I had been there, just so I could have saved you."

"You did," Ryan says. "You saved me by knowing me. I was wandering alone until I came to the Union. I met some wonderful people and now I can say that I will die knowing I really made friends."

"I can't do this," Mark says, collapsing in on himself.

"Don't think that way," Ryan cries. "You're the toughest guy I know. You will get through this."

Mark looks at him and I can tell he is trying to believe what Ryan is saying.

"I really love you all, and I want you all to survive and be happy," he explains, looking at us.

"Thank you," Rhea cries.

"I wish I had done something," I say guiltily.

"Don't ever think that," Ryan says. "You did more than enough." He looks at me, and I look back at him.

"So, is there anything we can do for you?" Mark asks, looking like he really wants to help his friend. He looks even guiltier than the rest of us, much as any person would feel if their friend was in danger.

"Survive," Ryan states.

"Yeah," Jane says.

"That is all I ask," Ryan continues. "All I want is for you guys to go forward with your lives and live. I can't have done this for nothing. I want you to be happy, I want you to be free of the shit that this world brings."

"We will," Becky says to him. Ryan then staggers to his feet, and Amrit and Mark run to help him up, making sure he doesn't fall over.

"OK," he says, "I just want to say my goodbyes to you now." He walks to Jane first.

"Goodbye," she says with tears running down her face.

"Don't ever let anyone take advantage of you," Ryan says to her. He gives her a hug and kisses her on the cheek. He then walks towards Becky, and straight away hugs her.

"I'm so sorry," Becky says to him.

"Be strong," he says. "It's your strength that we need now."
He kisses her on the cheek as well. He then turns to Amrit.

"Goodbye," Amrit says.

"I'm sorry we didn't get to know each other more," Ryan says
to him. They hug and Ryan gives Amrit a kiss on the cheek. He
then turns and walks towards Rhea.

"Goodbye, Ryan," she cries as she hugs him.

"Find your strength once more," Ryan tells her, gazing into
her eyes. "You're better than this world."

"Thank you," she sobs.

He then approaches me.

"Layton, don't ever feel guilty about anything," he orders,
and I feel nothing but heartbreak for him.

"OK," I say.

"You're still a twat," he chuckles.

I chuckle back through the sobs. We hug each other and
he kisses me on the cheek. He then turns to Mark, and they
embrace.

"Thank you," Mark says.

"No," Ryan says, "thank you."

Mark then leans over and kisses Ryan on the forehead before
Ryan lets go.

"Right then," he says, and turns for the door.

"What are you doing?" Becky asks.

Ryan stops. "Well," he says, "I'm going to walk through this
door. I'm going to walk away now. I won't turn back, but that's
not because I don't want to. It's because I want to remember you
all for who you are."

"Goodbye, Ryan," Becky cries out.

"Goodbye, mate," I add.

"Goodbye, my friends," he says.

He then opens the door and begins to walk forward. He
does not turn back, just walks forward. He stops for a moment,

puts his hand in his back pocket and pulls out the letter he read to me earlier. He smiles slightly to himself and keeps moving forward until he is far away in the distance.

The rest of us just stand there, staring at him. We know that he is going to find a place to rest. I think this is his moment of escape, and I wonder what this means for the rest of us.

25

The hours which follow Ryan leaving are long and unbearable. We just sit in a circle, none of us able to conjure up a conversation.

I sit there wanting to say something to break the ice. The problem is, it's one of those moments where you don't want to say something that is going to be inappropriate. I can't do anything but play with my hands, forming circles, just making shapes around a pattern in my mind. I can't help but feel that anything that pops into my head is a ridiculous idea. It feels too soon to crack a joke. I look over and see Rhea just sitting in the corner with her head leaning to one side. To my other side, Mark leans back, staring at the ceiling, trying to make sense of it all. It's always hard when somebody you know and have become close to suddenly departs from your life.

Amrit gets up and heads for the back of the room, taking himself away from the rest of us. I look at him and wonder if I should go and talk to him, just so I can speak to a familiar voice. He looks back and sees me, then turns away and keeps walking and sits by himself. If I was to go to him and make jokes, the rest of the group will probably think I am just being a dick, trying to make light of the situation.

It's strange how life brings hope, only to take it away from you. I don't know why but I begin to think about God. I never did see a reason to believe in God. My mum told me that years ago, my family was Sikh. I don't know much about it, just that they are people who defend others from tyranny. I was never taught enough to be able to call myself an expert. I do feel that I could have the traits or stereotypes of a Sikh. My mum told me that one of the main traits Sikhs were known for was that they loved a drink. This was a stereotype, she said, of what Sikhs were like before the crash, usually created by others. She said that her dad told her that before the crash the family used to go to weddings, and they were always a fun experience.

Then the other side of Sikhism is the actual philosophy. It's about equality, about treating anybody, prince or pauper, as an equal. The main thing is to defend their right to survive. I guess this is the way of life, a hero or a warrior. The sad thing is, I'm no warrior, and I'm certainly no hero. I'm just a guy who roamed the world trying to get his end away. I've never really felt the need to care about anybody except for myself. I look at this group and can't help but feel that if they were in danger, I wouldn't attempt to save them. Even when we left the Union, deep down, the reason I wanted them to come with me was so they could help me.

You know what, I'm going to walk over and talk to Amrit. Maybe we can console each other. Maybe one of us can make the other see sense; make them believe it is going to be all right in the end. I hope we can, I really do. I get up and walk over to him. He looks at me as I walk towards him and I can tell that he was waiting for me to come to him.

"All right?" I say to him.

"All right, mate?" he responds. We stand there for a moment before deciding to speak once again.

"Terrible weather we're having," I say, trying to make conversation.

"Seriously? You're going to give me awkward guy small talk?" he says sarcastically.

I look at him, unaware of what I was doing, and chuckle a little.

"Well, I didn't know what to say," I reply.

"OK," he says, chuckling to himself. We look at each other once again, and I ask him a question I have been wondering about.

"So, the infected..." I say.

"Yeah?" Amrit responds.

"General Singh told me about them," I say. "He said that they were the product of a nuclear explosion."

Amrit smiles to himself. Truth be told, I actually have no idea how the infected managed to spread so far across Europe.

"Yeah," he says.

"But how did they spread?" I ask.

"Seriously?" he says sternly, concerned.

"Yeah," I say.

"Has nobody told you?" he asks me, looking at me like a disappointed parent who's just found out their child has tried to eat a spider or something.

"No. Feel free to tell me," I say, slightly embarrassed at my lack of knowledge.

"Well, I guess somebody has to," Amrit says. "It all started before the crash; I think it was in Central Europe or somewhere. There was a hybrid infection which was created from rabies and radiation or something. It was the result of a nuclear explosion, meltdown at a nuclear plant. The meltdown was contained but some of the people who were trapped started to show symptoms like the infected have today. The thing is, the governments, and especially the European Union, could afford to contain the patients so nothing got out.

"Then when the crash happened and money became worthless, the EU collapsed and the programmes to help the infected were abandoned. As a result, the hospitals and labs they were being kept in were abandoned as it became every man for himself. The patients got out and began to spread across all of Europe. This led to governments in India and China wanting to maintain their borders and make sure nothing got through, so they expanded aggressively, knowing that their surrounding enemies were depleted."

I look at him and it all begins to make sense. Yet I still have questions which I believe need answering.

"How did their governments stay intact?" I ask.

"I have no idea," Amrit responds. "All I know is that as a result, Asia is now Indian to the west and—"

"China to the east," I interrupt.

"Exactly," he says. "The infected are still alive, you know."

"They are?" I ask, confused. I thought they were like zombies; dead people who roamed the earth.

"Yeah," Amrit explains. "They are still conscious, just trying to find a cure for their infection," he tells me with sympathy in his voice.

"Shit," I say. "So Ryan is still alive?"

"Yes, he is," Amrit tells me. "He will know where he is and have all his consciousness intact."

"Oh," I say, surprised. "Can I ask you something?"

"Go on," he responds.

"Would you ever go back to the Union?"

He looks at me and pauses for a moment. He looks like he is going to speak, then stops himself. Then he looks at me once again.

"Probably not," he states. "Would you?"

I can't help but feel we did have something comfortable there, and now we are roughing it. Is it better to be comfortable and ruled over by somebody who gives you no freedom, or to be free and uncomfortable for the rest of your life? That is the question, I guess.

"No," I reply. "Rhea said she was thinking of starting her own society," I tell him.

Amrit chuckles to himself and looks at me, trying to prevent himself from bursting into fits of laughter.

"What?" I ask him, confused.

"Nothing," he says. "It's just, a society, commune, republic – they all go to hell in some way or another. People will always want to rule over others. Too weak to create a society; not strong enough to stop themselves killing each other."

I look at him and can't help but feel slightly sorry for him, yet I understand his words. It is a shame to see somebody lose all hope for humanity.

"You know what?" Mark shouts out all of a sudden, drawing everyone's attention. "I was saving this for a while, but I think now is as good a time as any."

Everyone looks at him.

"What?" Jane asks.

Mark then pulls out a giant bottle from his bag, filled with a golden liquid.

"Hooch!" Rhea says, excited.

"You're damn right," Mark states. "I don't think we should sit here moping around. We need to celebrate the life we knew, not the life we miss." He then lifts the bottle and takes a giant swig from it. "So, who wants some?" he asks, looking at the rest of us.

We all look at one another and I can feel my stomach beginning to hurt. However, it is a special occasion, so one little drink couldn't possibly hurt.

Mark pulls out a load of glasses, showing off the bottle to us all. I can't help but think back to the time in the dorm when we arrived at the Union. I remember the sharp, bitter taste, so I'm assuming this won't be much different. I highly doubt it is the type of drink that gets better with age.

"Yes please," I say, and we all gather around. We grab a glass each and pour ourselves some of the liquid escapism.

"Everyone got a glass?" Mark asks as we stand around the

burnt-out fire in the middle of the room. "OK, here's to Ryan, my friend, my brother. Here's to you," he cheers.

"Here's to us," Becky calls out.

"Here's to our journey," I say, raising my glass, almost spilling my drink in my enthusiasm.

"That's very deep of you," Rhea jokes.

"Well, you know me," I respond.

"Yes, I do," she says, smiling. I smile back at her, feeling shy.

"OK," Mark says, "down in one."

We all down our drinks. It's sharp and sour, yet soothing at the same time. The glasses that follow really do lighten the mood. We are all singing and dancing with one another; it feels like we are back at the dorm when we first met, all having a laugh like we did then. We will never forget Ryan; if anything, we will try to live on for him.

"Fuck me," I mumble to myself after a few drinks. To be fair, I have had a few, so I might not be saying things in the best way. My God, that has gone straight to my head; I need to pee, and I'm hungry, maybe a little sick, yet I really want to spin around. I think I might be pissed.

I stagger over to Rhea, who is sitting on the table. I sit next to her and do nothing but stare at her. I know it's quite intense, how I am staring at her. Shit, I don't know; I guess this is me trying to make conversation.

"Hi, Layton," she says tipsily.

"Hello," I say.

"You having fun?" she asks me.

"Yeah, you?"

"Yeah," she says.

We look at each other and start laughing. In the corner, Amrit is dancing with Becky, while Jane and Mark are playing slaps.

"Let's have a song," Becky suddenly calls out.

"Yeah, let's have a sing-song," Amrit agrees.

We gather around.

"OK," Mark slurs, "I have a song for you all."

"Come on, Mark, serenade us," I joyfully cry.

He looks at us all and begins to gulp, and I sense an element of nerves within him.

"Right, this is a song I heard on an old radio once," he explains. "OK, are you ready?"

"Go on," Becky says.

"Right," Mark says. "Where in the world? PC World," he sings.

We all look at him silently.

"Well…" I say.

"OK," Rhea says. "Mark, move aside," she calls out, walking towards the centre of the room as we all sit in a circle. Mark just shrugs away and sits next to Becky.

"Rhea!" I say, a little shocked.

"OK," she says, "I have a song for you all." She looks at us and smiles, staggering a little.

"Go on, Rhea," Amrit yells enthusiastically.

"OK, everyone," Rhea begins, "this is a song my Dad used to sing. He said he heard it from his dad, my grandad."

We all sit there in silence as she takes a breath before her performance. She clears her throat, then opens her mouth to sing.

I was a miner,
I was a docker,
I was a railway man
Between the wars.
I raised a family
In times of austerity
With sweat at the foundry
Between the wars.

I paid the union, and as times got harder,
I looked to the government to help the working man.
And they brought prosperity down at the armoury,
We're arming for peace, me boys,
Between the wars.

I kept the faith, and I kept voting,
Not for the iron fist, but for the helping hand.
For theirs is a land with a wall around it,
And mine is a faith in my fellow man.
Theirs is a land of hope and glory,
Mine is the green field and the factory floor.
Theirs are the skies, all dark with bombers,
And mine is the peace we knew
Between the wars.

Call up the craftsmen,
Bring me the draughtsmen.
Build me a path from cradle to grave.
And I'll give my consent
To any government
That does not deny a man a living wage.

Go find the young men, never to fight again,
Bring up the banners from the days gone by.
Sweet moderation,
Heart of this nation,
Desert us not, we are
Between the wars.

She looks at us all as we stare at her. Becky wipes her eyes, and
Jane and Amrit do so as well.

"Thank you," Rhea says as we all look at her, blown away by
her voice and the song she sang.

"That was brilliant," Amrit says, beginning to clap.

"That was great," I agree, also clapping.

We all applaud her and she begins to smile, takes a quick bow, then walks back over to me.

"Amazing," I hear Becky say. "I never knew she had a voice like that."

"Yeah, I know," Jane agrees.

Rhea picks up her drink, looking at me, and takes a large gulp.

"That was amazing," I say as she downs her drink.

She then runs over to the bottle, picks it up and pours herself another drink. She downs it, then pours another and comes rushing back to me.

"Thanks," she says.

"So your Dad sang that?" I ask, wishing I had known Dillon better.

"Yeah. His Dad taught him it, then he taught me," she tells me.

"Amazing," I say. I down another drink and suddenly feel the alcohol beginning to play with my brain.

"Layton, guess what?" Rhea says as my vision begins to blur.

"What?"

She then looks at me and makes a fart noise with her mouth, sticking her tongue out at me. We both laugh and I grab her and shake her.

"That's not ladylike," I shout jokingly.

"You're a lady," she retorts.

"Hold on, hold on," I say as I stand and face her. "I think you will find I am a gentleman of the century. I am nothing but a loving man of the hour," I state, staggering.

"A drunken man of the hour," Rhea says.

"Look here, you..."

"What?" she asks, grabbing my finger and clenching it tight. I seize her hand and we laugh, tussling back and forth. We fall to the ground, both flat on our backs.

"Oops," I say, chuckling.

"Oh no," she laughs.

I then turn and look at her. She looks back at me. I don't know why I am about to do what I am about to do, but I know it feels right; like the right thing to do.

"Layton..." she says, and I lean in and kiss her on the lips. I pull back for a second and look into her eyes. She kisses me back. This is definitely going to change things.

After a few more drinks, everyone is passed out on the floor, completely shit-faced. I'm trying to sleep; however I just can't seem to convince my body to shut down. I lie there, thinking about the kiss.

It felt nice, it felt so good to kiss her, but I can't stop thinking. Was it the right thing to do? Is it right that I did this? Where do we go from here?

26

I feel as if I am dreaming. I am floating, floating and not seeing anything around me. I look around and I am nowhere near any type of ground, drifting through the air. I can see nothing but bright blue, as if I am in the sky. I clench my throat, struggling to breathe; I can't seem to get air into my lungs.

Why can't I breathe? I then realise I am actually as far from the sky as I can imagine; I am in fact surrounded by water. I am deep down in the sea, feeling the moisture run through my clothes, covering my skin, soaking me from head to toe. I need to get out; I can't keep finding myself in this place, always stuck in the sea. I decide to swim, and I keep swimming, keep moving; I've got to get to the surface. The water isn't helping; it is holding me back, more like mud than liquid. I keep slashing my way through until I begin to make some progress.

I eventually get to the surface and try to put my hand through, but I'm trapped by a layer of ice. I hit the ice, trying to break through as if my hands are flesh-covered hammers, hammering into the solid structure over and over, but nothing comes of it. It stays as strong as ever. There is nothing I can do now but give up.

I decide to let go and begin to float away. I feel myself sinking further and further from the surface, seeing it disappear into the distance. I am halfway down when I feel I need to have one last attempt. I try to swim, but my legs are stuck, attached to invisible chains holding me down. I try again, but I'm trapped. I panic, still unable to breathe. I feel the water going down my throat, through my mouth and nose. I fidget around, trying to find a way out and failing.

Then all of a sudden, I wake, covered in sweat as cold as the icy sea I was dreaming of.

My head is spinning in circles. My stomach feels like… well, the more I think about it, the more I want to just lean over and throw up. Fuck me, I see why some people decide not to drink. That's it, I'm never drinking again. I know I tell myself that all the time and never stick to it, but as of this moment I'm quitting… maybe just for today.

Shit, I wonder what happened last night? I guess it was a good little memorial we gave for Ryan. Oh wait, Rhea. Well, that's awkward. I'm not going to lie, I did always want to have something with her – well, since I saw her in that towel – but not when I'm drunk, though, not like this. She must be so embarrassed; she must feel like shit about last night.

I look around, and I can't seem to see her anywhere. Maybe she's trying to avoid me. I don't know whether I did the right thing or not. I did make the first move, after all.

As soon as I sit up, the room surges around me like a vortex of discomfort. I try to get to my feet, staggering as I do so. I haven't felt like this since the dorm. I decide to try to move my feet around, just so I can get myself going. I move up and down, lifting my legs, trying to get the blood going. There's nothing worse than pins and needles when you're hung-over. I can see Amrit standing at the other side of the room, drinking a hot drink, looking at me and laughing.

"What's so funny?" I ask him.

"You know," he says.

I look around hesitantly. "What? What do you mean, 'you know'?" I ask, walking over to him.

"You and Rhea."

I look at him, shocked and a little embarrassed.

"Yeah, we all know."

I stand there, stunned. "Shit, where's Rhea now?" I ask him, panicking.

"She went out for a patrol with Becky," Amrit explains.

"OK."

Then I smell what he is drinking: coffee; my God, that smells good.

"Any more of that?" I ask him.

He chuckles as he pours me a mug.

"It's not funny, yeah?"

"It is," he says to me.

"How?" I ask.

"Because it's you. Because you're such a silly goose." He speaks in a childlike manner.

"How does she feel about it all?" I ask, trying to not show that I am uncomfortable.

"She's fine with it. I think you might be in there, somehow," Amrit states sarcastically.

"Oh," I mutter to myself, "fair play."

I look over and see Mark leaning against the table, resting his head on it.

"I take it he had quite a few more?" I say, feeling the effects of a full-on hangover.

"Yeah," Amrit says, sipping his coffee. "He's been throwing up all morning."

I can't help but feel sorry for him.

"Shit," I say.

"Ouch," Mark reacts as he places his hand on his head. "Ouch, my brain feels like it's been trampled on."

I can't really judge him; I've lost count of how many times I've had to suffer the morning after a night of drinking. Come to think of it, before I ended up with this lot, I used to wake up every morning with a hangover.

"You look like it," Amrit says.

Jane walks over to us, looking a little concerned. She is wearing a lot of clothing – well, we all seem to these days.

"Layton?" she says, concerned.

"Yeah?" I respond, still slurring my words slightly. I take a sip of my coffee and feel it burn my fragile lips.

"Can I talk to you?" she asks.

"Sure," I say.

She then grabs me by the hand and whisks me away to the other side of the room, out of earshot. I can see that she really wants to talk about something, but I'm not sure what.

"OK, this is good," she says, looking around as if she's trying to make sure the coast is clear.

"Yeah, what's up?" I ask her.

She then looks down at her shoes and closes her eyes slightly before talking.

"OK, I need to show you something," she says to me. She then undoes her jacket, revealing her T-shirt underneath.

"Woah, wait, what are you doing?" I ask, embarrassed.

"Just look," she says, and lifts up her T-shirt. There is a bulge where her stomach should be.

"What the fuck is that?" I ask her.

She places her hand on her stomach, then looks up at me.

"I tried to hide it, but now it is starting to show. I'm three months gone," she explains.

I realise that this is the reason why she was sick all those times when we were living in the dorm. "Gone where?" I ask her bluntly.

"Pregnant," she says abruptly.

I stare at her belly. Hold on, why is she telling me?

271

"Why are you telling me?" I ask her. Surely Mark or Becky would be more appropriate people to tell about this; I mean, they have known her far longer than I have.

"Because I want you to tell everyone else," she says.

"Why can't you?" I ask her.

"Because the father is Ryan," she says.

"Fuck. Did he know?" I ask, as she looks at me with her hand planted firmly on her stomach.

"No. I wish I'd told him, but I just couldn't," she admits, sobbing softly.

"How do you know?" I ask.

"Because I just do," she snaps. "He came to my room once and, well, it was the one time I didn't use the pill."

"They still have those?" I ask, a little confused.

"Yes," she says. "The Union made them."

It's amazing how contraception has managed to stick around.

"Fuck," I say. "Are you sure you're pregnant?"

"Yes."

"Are you sure, you know...?"

"Know what?" she asks sternly.

"You know, are you're sure you've not just got a bit, you know, fat?" I ask her. As soon as I say it, I know it's a dumb thing to ask.

"No, you idiot," she says, "I'm pregnant."

I look over and see Becky and Rhea walking back into the room. Rhea looks at me and I look back. As soon as they walk in, Jane covers her stomach. I look around and feel nervous all of a sudden.

"OK," I say to her. I then take her by the hand and lead her to the centre of the room. "Oi," I shout out, "listen everyone!"

They all gather round and stare at me.

"I have something to say," I state. I look around and can see that this is really happening. "OK, well, Jane here, she is, um..."

"What is it?" Mark asks, still suffering from his hangover.

"Well, Jane is… kind of… pregnant," I try to explain.

"Kind of pregnant?" Becky asks abruptly.

"Well, no; she is pregnant."

"Fuck," Amrit says.

"Since when?" Mark asks in a matter-of-fact tone.

"Three months," Jane explains.

"How are we going to look after a baby?" Rhea asks, a question which we are all thinking at this very moment.

"We have to get rid of it," Mark says, to a few groans from certain members of the group.

Rhea turns and glares at him. "No, we don't," she states, looking as if she is going to lunge at him and attack him.

"I know it sounds harsh," Mark says, "I know it's a baby, but we have to think practically. We can barely look after ourselves; how we are going to look after a baby as well?"

"We can try," I reassure him, trying to think of the child.

"We can," he says, "but we could end up jeopardising all of us."

"Yes, I see what you mean," Amrit suddenly states.

"Fuck off," I say, stunned.

Rhea turns and looks at him, her disappointment clear on her face.

"I don't want to think this way, but we have to be practical about it," he says.

"You're both heartless!" Rhea shouts.

"Hold on," Becky says, "it's not our decision. It's up to Jane." She turns and faces Jane as she stands there quietly, looking at us all. "What do you want to do?" she asks her.

Jane looks down at her stomach and rubs it slightly. She then looks up at the rest of the group.

"Well, I've thought about it, and I want to keep it," she admits.

We all look at her and know that she is not going to budge from this decision, so we have no choice but to live with it, even if some of us don't agree with it.

"Very well," Mark says, sounding defeated.

"Oh yeah, and by the way," I say, "Ryan's the father."

All of them take a step back. Amrit looks as if he is about to collapse, Mark just staggers, and Becky stands frozen.

"What?" they shout at the same time.

They begin to discuss how and why she thinks it is Ryan. Much of it I have heard before, so I decide to step outside for a cheeky cigarette. I light up, feeling that wonderful smoky flavour hitting my throat. That's what I really want from a cigarette: not so much the tobacco, just the smoke flavour on the back of my throat.

"That feels good," I say to myself with satisfaction. I then turn and see Rhea walking out to join me.

"Hi," she says.

"Hello," I reply awkwardly.

"There's no need to be weird," Rhea explains. "I wanted you to kiss me."

"Really?"

"You can do it again if you like," she suggests.

I turn, throwing my cigarette on the floor, and put my hands on her waist. She looks up at me, and I look down into her eyes.

"Kiss me," she says, and I lean in and kiss her on the lips. Then as I am kissing her, this horrible feeling comes over me, and I can't kiss her any more.

"Sorry." I stop abruptly, pulling away.

"What is it?" she asks.

"I can't do this," I say.

"Why not?"

I look at her and I can't help but feel guilty for what I am about to say. I know that I am going to regret this for the rest of my life.

"Because I don't want to start something that could be more than it needs to be," I explain to her.

"Yeah," she says. "Well, it's not as if we are going to fall head over heels in love with each other."

"I know," I say. "What I mean is, it's because of our friendship and how we take care of each other; I can't bear the thought of losing you. Because of how I feel about you, I can't help but look at the world we are living in, and how we might not survive till tomorrow. I can't bear the thought of being with you and losing you, and I don't want the same for you either; I don't want to put you through losing me. So, it's because of my love for you that I can't be with you," I say, feeling like daggers are hitting my stomach with every word.

"OK," she says. She then looks at me, seeming very bemused. "Layton, I don't fancy you."

"Don't you?" I ask, surprised.

"No," she replies, chuckling. "I just kissed you, and I wouldn't mind having a bit of human contact for the first time in ages. Just because I feel like some human contact, doesn't mean I want to be in a relationship with you. I don't need a man in my life to feel good about myself."

"OK, same here. I don't need a woman, I just wanted to make sure I didn't mislead you," I say, trying to hide how I actually feel.

"Sure," Rhea says. "Look, I don't want it to be awkward between us."

"No, it won't be awkward," I say, laughing awkwardly.

"Good," she says. "I thought for a second then that it was going to be weird between us."

"No, no," I say, forcing a laugh. "I'm just going to pop inside for a bit; are you going to stay out here?" I ask, hoping she won't come in with me.

"No, I'll stay out here for a bit," she says, smiling at me.

I nod and quickly turn, storming inside to try and save some scraps of the dignity I have just let go of. I walk through the door and take a huge breath.

"Fuck," I mutter to myself as I look around the room, trying to ignore everybody's happiness. I look around for a place to be by myself, but everywhere seems too exposed, not allowing me any chance to hide away.

I walk over to a corner and sit on an old grey desk, looking blankly at the wall. I have no reason to be doing this; I just am. I glare at it, stare at it; whatever the word is that best describes looking at something for a long period of time, I am doing that. Perhaps another cigarette would be helpful. I pull out a piece of paper and a chunk of tobacco, roll it up and lick the end, ready to be smoked. I then find a piece of old flint in my pocket and spark it up, breathing the horrible stuff into my lungs.

"There you are," Amrit calls out to me. I turn and see him walking towards me. He jumps up and sits next to me, looking a lot happier than I would like him to be.

"Oh, it's you," I say.

He sits there and politely smiles at me. "I saw you talking to her," he explains.

"I told her it wouldn't work, no need for a relationship," I tell him, knowing what I mean. I explain it to him so he knows it was all my idea, just so he doesn't get the wrong idea.

"I see," Amrit responds. "Well, I suppose it's for the best." He looks at me, trying to show some kind of sympathy.

"Yeah," I say.

"Yeah," he agrees as I start to think about what life could have been like.

"Love, hey?" I say.

He sighs, then looks at me inquisitively.

"Let me tell you something…" he says, trying to sound like some kind of old, wise man.

"More words of wisdom?" I say sarcastically.

"Just shut up and listen," he demands. "Life is a dance. We all dance our own routine throughout our lives. Love is another dance that some of us get to do. The best way two people can show their love for each other is to dance together." He looks at me and smiles. I look back at him, feeling a little disgusted.

"That is so gay," I say.

"Yes," he says, chuckling to himself.

We laugh together, seeing out the day. There is nothing better than having people there to care for you. I guess I am feeling some kind of change within me; as if I am changing the world around me to benefit not only myself, but others as well. Change can be good, I guess. What am I going on about?

27

The following day, I find myself in a park around the corner with Amrit. We are doing what Ryan and I were doing when it all went to shit: hunting a fox. We are crouched behind a bin, staring at the fox foraging for food. Amrit has created a makeshift bow and arrow; not a bad product. He has actually created a functional weapon for hunting, or even protection.

"OK," he whispers as he pulls back the arrow.

"I spoke to Rhea yesterday," I mention to him.

"That's good to know," he says, trying to concentrate.

"I mean, I had to tell her the truth about how I feel."

"Uh-huh?" he murmurs. He then pulls the arrow back to line up with his eye, about to let go.

"I mean, it's not that I don't like her—" I say.

"For fuck's sake," he whispers, holding back the arrow.

"It's just, I don't want to lead her on or anything—" I continue, oblivious to him.

"Layton," Amrit interrupts.

"Yeah?" I respond carelessly.

"Shut the fuck up," he says, making it clear what he is doing. I look over and realise I am distracting him.

"Oh, sorry, mate."

He pulls back the arrow and points it right at the fox. The fox doesn't even notice us. Amrit pulls back a little further.

"OK," he whispers to himself.

"Are you sure it can't hear us?" I ask.

"If you say one more word..." Amrit threatens. He stares at the fox, takes a deep breath and releases the arrow. It soars through the air, striking the fox right between its eyes. "Get in there," Amrit shouts, celebrating.

"Well done, mate," I congratulate him. "Let's go get it."

We walk towards the fox, each pulling out a knife. We look at it; it kind of has a sadness to it. It's just lying there, as if it is sleeping. Well, not exactly like it's sleeping; it's got its eyes slightly open, and there is a giant arrow in its forehead. OK, so it doesn't look like it's sleeping, or even peaceful. Just dead, I guess.

"Well, I guess we got to do this," Amrit says to me as he bends down and starts to cut into the fox.

"Yeah, I guess so," I say.

We both start cutting into it, releasing what seems like gallons upon gallons of blood.

"This is nasty," Amrit says.

"Ugh, ugh, ugh," I repeat, looking down at my hands.

"What?" he asks, concerned.

"I just touched the liver," I tell him.

Amrit starts to laugh at me.

"It's not funny, you dick," I shout.

"We're cutting up a fox; I think you can expect to touch one of its organs," he states sarcastically.

"Fuck you," I remark.

We continue cutting the fox up and begin to put it into bags.

"So, what do you think about Jane having a baby?" I ask, as if it is the elephant in the room.

"Personally," he says, "I don't know if it is the right idea. I mean, we have hardly enough food to take care of ourselves, let alone something that needs food to grow."

"Ryan left us a lot of food," I say to him.

"Yes, but a baby isn't just going to be around for a few months; it's going to be around for years. It'll grow, and the more it grows, the more food it will want," he states.

"I see what you mean," I say, "but we will have to teach the baby how to read and write. It might be fun," I suggest optimistically.

"Might be," Amrit says.

"Well, I'll tell you one thing that is going to be weird," I say, thinking I have a very good joke for him.

"What?" he asks.

"This is the first time I can look at a child and say, 'I almost fucked your mum,'" I say, chuckling to myself.

Instead of laughing, Amrit just looks at me, disappointed.

"Sometimes, Layton…" he says, sounding very upset with me.

"What?" I ask, still chuckling.

"Sometimes I wonder why we ever became friends."

I continue to laugh to myself. "Oh, you," I remark to him jokingly. I then notice that he still isn't joining me in the laughter, and looks a lot more serious than I do. "Wait, really?" I ask, concerned.

We continue to hack away at the fox, putting it into little bags that we found in the store. We try to take every part except for the fur, because that would be of no use to us. The innards, the shit parts like the heart, liver, stomach, and even the brain go in the bags. It's not the most attractive of sights, and we look like a couple of butchers by the time we get the job done. We both have blood over our forearms, dripping down.

I am just wrangling my hands around some intestines when I suddenly hear a noise in the distance. I try to ignore it; probably just the wind, nothing to be alarmed by. Then I hear it again; sounds like a rustling noise. As Amrit continues to pack the meat away, I look into the distance to see if I can find out where the noise is coming from, and notice a bush moving slightly.

"Shit, did you hear that?" I ask Amrit, panicking a little.

"What?" he asks as he pushes the remaining parts of the fox into the bag.

"Look," I say, pointing at the bush.

Amrit looks and can see the bush moving.

"Wait here," I say to him as I start to make my way towards the bush.

"OK," Amrit responds, clutching his bow and arrow.

I walk forward, holding my machete, peering at the bush. I pace slowly but surely, making sure not to startle whatever is in the bush. Could be another fox for all we know; maybe even a sheep. I don't actually know why a sheep would be out here, but I do like the sound of lamb or mutton. It doesn't look a fox; looks more like... oh shit.

"Ah!" A man jumps over the bush and lunges at me. He is covered in tattoos, and wears giant boots, jeans and a vest top. He is trying to stab me with a knife, but I just about manage to keep him at bay, although when he jumped up at me, I dropped my machete.

"Get off me, you dick," I shout as the man keeps trying to stab me.

"Get away from him," Amrit shouts, and the man stops.

I look over and see Amrit holding his bow and arrow, pointed right at the man's head. The man holds his hands up as if to beg Amrit not to shoot.

"Who are you?" Amrit says.

"Answer him," I order.

The man then begins to laugh in a really spine-tingling manner.

"Why are you laughing?"

"Ah," he finally says, "you will find out soon enough." He takes another lunge at me, and Amrit shoots him in the arm, causing the man to whimper.

"I will ask you again," Amrit asks as the man cowers on the floor, "who are you?"

The man begins to laugh again as he holds his hand over his arm where the arrow hit. Amrit pulls out another arrow and puts it in his bow, pulling it back.

"Don't answer me one more time, and this will go straight in your eye," he snarls.

"OK," the man says calmly. "I am here to give you a message. You will get a visit soon, and then you will find out why I am here. I am here to tell you about your doom." He speaks in a put-on mystical voice, like he is a magician of some sort.

"Who sent you?" I ask him.

He lifts his finger and puts it to his lips as if to silence me.

"Speak!" Amrit shouts.

The man continues to laugh, and does not answer him.

"That's it," Amrit says, and he aims and shoots the man. I think he was aiming for the leg, but he kind of missed. OK, he hit him in the dick. The man falls backwards, clutching the arrow as it is lodged... well, lodged in there.

"Mate," I shout.

"Shit," Amrit says, stunned.

"You shot him in the dick," I say, shocked, looking at the arrow sticking out between the man's legs.

"I know," Amrit remarks, stunned. "I didn't mean to," he claims, fishing around for excuses.

"Well, that's certainly warned him," I say.

"Ouch, my God, it hurts!" the man screams.

"Shall we pull it out?" I ask Amrit, trying to think of an idea.

"Are you insane?" Amrit responds.

"No, no, ah!" the man shouts as we can see blood start to seep out.

"Well, I guess we have to kill him," Amrit says.

"Yes, you do," I respond, looking at him to make sure he knows that it is his fault this man is hurt.

"Me?" Amrit asks sternly.

"Yes, you," I say as the man continues to roll around on the floor, shouting and whimpering. I can see tears and sweat on his face; the pain is something I just can't imagine. "You're the one who shot him in the dick."

"Yeah," Amrit says, "but if you hadn't gone towards the bush everything would've been fine."

"Oh, so it's my fault, is it?" I bark.

"Well, it was your idea to come out here," he hollers, still trying to pass the buck.

"No, it was yours. You said, 'Layton, let's go hunt,'" I state.

"After you moaned that we didn't have enough meat," Amrit reminds me.

"Oh, you're just pettifogging now," I snap.

"How am I?"

"I can't even see you because of the fog," I say. "Your pettiness is getting the better of you."

"All you've done is moan," Amrit retorts. "All you ever do, all day, is moan and moan and moan – 'Oh, I wish I could have some meat; oh, I wish I had some real food' – every day!"

"I can't believe you," I say. "Why don't you just accept responsibility for shooting an innocent man in the dick?"

"Innocent?" Amrit shouts. "He tried to kill you. How about, 'Gee, Amrit, thanks for saving me', you ungrateful shit?"

"I would've thanked you," I explain, "if you hadn't shot the man in the dick and tried to blame it on me."

"Hold on," Amrit says, "where did he go?"

I look down and can see that the man has moved; a trail of blood leading away. In the distance we can see the man hobbling away, trying not to run too fast because of the arrow lodged in him.

"Shall we stop him?" I ask.

"If we do," Amrit says, "we'll have to kill him."

"Why?" I ask, confused.

"Weren't you listening to what he said?" Amrit barks. "He said we will get a visit soon; what if he goes and reports back?"

I realise what he is saying and agree with him.

"You're right. At the very least, we should keep him prisoner," I say, "get some information out of the guy first."

"I agree," Amrit says.

We both run towards the man as he hobbles away.

"No, go away!" the man shouts as he turns and looks at us. Suddenly he trips and falls face first, cracking his head on the kerb.

"Oh," Amrit and I say as we see the man fly forward, smashing his skull.

"Shit," Amrit says. "Well, I guess we don't have to kill him," he adds, making me feel rather relieved.

"Well, technically, you kind of—" I begin.

"Shut up," Amrit interrupts, and storms off to pick up the fox meat.

"Just saying," I call, out of earshot.

We get back to the camp and the outside is as bare as always. Amrit wouldn't talk to me the whole way back; I think he is still feeling the heat from what happened. We get inside the building and everyone is gathered around, awaiting our return.

"How was it?" Becky asks, looking at us, both with frozen faces, looking back at the group, still feeling moderately stunned.

"It went well," Amrit tells her.

"Yeah," I say, "Amrit shot a guy in the dick."

Amrit turns and glares at me.

"What?" Rhea asks.

"I didn't intentionally shoot him in the dick," Amrit yells.

"So what happened, then?" Rhea asks.

"He attacked us," I tell them. "We managed to fight him off, then after Amrit shot him in the dick, the guy tried to run away and slipped and smacked his head on the kerb."

Becky and Rhea wince a little at the thought.

"So, I take it he's dead?" Rhea asks.

"Yeah," I admit. "He's probably just some crazy person, a weirdo who doesn't know much," I say, hoping that will make everybody feel a little better.

"Well, that's good," Mark replies.

"Yeah," Amrit says, "but the guy said that we will get a visit soon or something."

"What did he mean by that?" Becky asks.

"Not sure," I tell them. "Do you think somebody is coming?"

"I don't know," Rhea says. "I hope not, we're not ready for an attack."

"Yeah," I say.

We all stand around silently, looking at one another.

"Well, we got this." I show them the fox, holding it up and showing it off as if it is a trophy. They all smile and cheer.

Later, we feast on the fox, but the thought of what that man said never really leaves us. That is something we will remember, not something that is easily forgotten.

I can't help but feel that we may be in some kind of danger. We are stuck in this place, and it's not as if we can just escape. I know we are in no position to fight or defend ourselves. We are still quite tired, Jane is pregnant and we do not have the defences. What did that man mean when he said that we would have a visit? I hope it isn't the Union. What if they've found us? What if they know where we are and they are going to come and attack us, or even take us away? This could be a problem.

28

By the time evening arrives, we are all sitting and eating the fox. It has started raining outside, and not just rain; I can hear thunder as well. It is a very wet evening, we can hear it from inside the building. I have to tell the truth: fox really does taste horrible. It's not something I would go out of my way to eat again; it's more like fuel as opposed to something you eat for its taste. I keep biting into it and tastes like grit. Everyone else is chowing down on their piece, some enjoying it more than others. We gave Jane the larger pieces after Mark cooked it up, because of her condition.

The room is getting warmer from the amount of heat that is coming off the barbecued fox. It doesn't even smell that great, but what can you do? We have a lot of tinned food as well, but we needed some real meat to get our strength up. I can't help but start thinking about my favourite foods. I like bacon – I mean, it's hard to come by it, but it always tastes good. To be fair, though, my favourite meat is chicken. I do love some chicken.

"What's your favourite food?" I ask Rhea sitting next to me.

"Probably spaghetti hoops. My Dad once made some from a tin; it was amazing," she says, licking her lips.

"Just plain old toast for me," Becky declares.

"Toast?" Amrit asks, bemused.

"Yeah," she says, "simple food, just hits the spot."

We all begin to imagine a luxurious meal.

"I like a good sausage," Jane says.

"I'm sure you do," I say sarcastically.

Everyone starts laughing and I feel good about myself for getting some humour going.

"You're such a dick," Jane retorts.

"I like a bit of lamb," Mark announces. "Good meat that makes you strong," he states while flexing his arms.

"Strong like bull," I say.

"That's why I have these strong arms," Mark says to us, showing us his biceps like they are a display of male superiority.

"I bet you I could beat you in an arm-wrestle," Rhea says to him, looking like she is willing to step up to the challenge.

"Really?" Mark says to her in a challenging way, chuckling to himself.

"Yeah," Rhea says.

"Well, there's only one way to find out," Amrit says. "Arm-wrestle!"

"Arm-wrestle!" I repeat.

Mark makes his way to a table and takes a seat.

"Come on then," he says to Rhea, holding his arm out.

"Let's go," she says, walking over and sitting opposite him. I look at her and I can see the determination in her eyes.

"I'll take it easy on you, sweetheart," he says patronisingly.

"Sweetheart?" Rhea says, stunned. "You've asked for it now."

They both lock hands and start pushing one another as the rest of us cheer them on.

"Come on, Rhea," Becky shouts.

"Yeah, come on, Rhea," Jane echoes.

They push each other as hard as they can, and I can see Rhea beginning to wince, however Mark is not faring much better.

With a massive surge of strength, Rhea manages to push his arm down and wins.

"Get in, I win!" Rhea jumps up.

"Shit," Mark says, sounding very surprised and devastated at losing to her. He looks at his hand and I can tell he feels slightly upset.

"Yeah," Rhea gloats, "I win; you lose."

"Bloody hell," I say.

Amrit just laughs.

We are all cheering for Rhea when I look over and see Jane sitting there. Her face has gone very pale.

"Ah!" she screams, pointing at the door.

"Jane, what's the matter?" Becky asks, concerned.

"The door," Jane shouts, "the door."

We all turn and look.

"What is that?" I ask.

Through the rain, it does not look as clear, but then I see a figure standing at the door. Amrit, Rhea and I creep forward to get a better look. The figure has a bright white face, probably a mask, and red hair. The rain is pouring over its head, yet somehow the figure does not seem bothered. The figure is wearing a long coat which seems to go down to its knees. It knocks on the window and gives us a very creepy wave, wiggling its fingers.

Amrit, Mark, Rhea and I slowly scrape our feet towards the door, trying not to startle anybody. The figure tilts his head to the left. I can't tell whether it is a man or a woman; it's just some really creepy thing that is glaring at us. I lean over to a nearby table and grab my machete. Amrit glances at me momentarily, making sure not to lose his focus on the figure ahead of us.

"Who are you?" Mark calls out.

The figure says nothing, just looks back at us.

"What do you want?" Mark asks, but again the figure does not react; just continues staring at us.

"What should we do?" Amrit asks.

"I have no idea," I say.

"Do you need help?" Rhea asks the figure.

The figure looks straight at her, and I can tell she is very uncomfortable under its piercing gaze. She falls silent, and the figure remains unfazed by our presence.

"I'll ask you again," Mark says, getting a knife out of his back pocket. "Who are you, and what do you want?"

The figure looks at Mark, and this time it does do something. It simply waves at him, then raises its left hand and does what looks like a click with its fingers.

We look at one another, unsure what it all means. The thunder outside is not helping with how we are feeling, accompanied by the beating rain. The figure clicks its fingers once again, and suddenly something like a gunshot flies through the air and Mark slumps to the ground.

"Mark," I call out as he collapses.

"Shit," he says, clutching his shoulder where it looks like the bullet has lodged itself.

"Mark!" Becky runs to his side.

"I'm fine," he says, trying to get to his feet with blood pouring out of his shoulder.

I look up and see that the figure has gone. Then in the same instant, a van comes storming towards the door and crashes into it, smashing down the barrier we built, and with it the door and windows.

"Shit, look out!" Rhea screams as five men come marching into the room. They look like border monkeys – well, they are border monkeys – and they are wearing their balaclavas over their faces and gathering around us.

Amrit, Rhea and I try to fight them off, but there are too many of them. I throw a punch at one of them and as soon as I hit him, another hits me across the face. Rhea tries to take another of one them out. Before she can however, she is tackled and pinned to the ground. Mark gives as much as he can, but is quickly defeated and pinned down. Amrit keeps fighting even when they are holding him down, until his spirit eventually gives in. I try to run at one of them, but before I can get to him, another hits me right across the face and I collapse to the ground.

Becky and Jane give in without a fight, trying to talk to the men.

"Please don't hurt us," Jane begs.

"What is it you want?" Becky asks. "We have plenty of food, take what you want and go."

"Sit down and shut up," one of the men says to Jane, grabbing her hands and tying her.

"Please be careful," Becky calls out, "she's pregnant!"

We all look at her, wondering if it was the right thing to say. The invaders pause for a moment, look at each other, then look behind them. They then grab us, take us to the back of the room and tie us up, gathered around in a circle.

"Children are that of the future," a voice calls out. The figure who was at the door then comes walking towards us. "Children are of an innocent nature, really."

One of the border monkeys pulls out a chair, and the figure sits down in front of us. I can tell by its husky voice that it is a man.

"What do you want with us?" I ask him as I try to struggle out of my restraints.

"What do I want?" The man echoes. "Well, first, I believe an introduction must be in order. My name is Shaq – well, my real name is Sheldon Carl Battalion, but you can call me Shaq, everybody does," he explains with a certain swagger.

"Shaq," Rhea says.

"Wait," Amrit says. "Shaq, the last king," he remarks, stunned, reminding himself, Rhea and me of what we once saw.

"A little gesture from one of my helpers," Shaq explains with a hint of pride in his voice. "However, that is my name."

"You bastard, you killed my Dad!" Rhea screams, sounding as if her voice is going to bring the whole building down.

"What?" Mark says, grabbing his shoulder. Blood is still pumping out of it, and he winces from the pain.

"This guy slaughtered mine and Rhea's old group," Amrit tells the rest of them.

"Well, it wasn't me personally," Shaq remarks. "That was the work of my little henchmen; however, I did tell them to do it."

"Why?" Rhea asks. "What did they ever do to you?"

"Nothing, really," Shaq says. "If you don't mind, it is rather hot in here; I might just take my mask and wig off."

He then pulls off his mask and shows his face to us. He has a rugged face, with a scar across his lip. He has grey-black hair, slicked back, and a clean-shaven face.

"That's better. OK, you want to know why we killed your group. It's simple really: we needed help," he states.

"Help?" Rhea asks, confused.

"We run a little farm not far from here," Shaq says. "We needed help with the cattle, so we wanted you to help us." He gets up from his seat and walks towards us. "I wanted you to work for me, but your little group said no. So we killed each and every one of them," he tells us with no remorse.

"You're a monster," Rhea shrieks, breathing very heavily from the anger that consumes her.

"The truth of the matter is, we have been watching you three for a while now," Shaq says, pointing at Amrit, Rhea and me.

"Us, why?" I ask, looking at Amrit and Rhea. They look back at me, each of us as baffled as the other.

"You look like good workers," he tells us. "We look at all promising apprentices. You three have had quite the journey. Escaped the warehouse, stayed in a house; you even went to Leicester city centre and lived with the Union for a time, and then came away. Now you live here. I believe you met one of my

291

associates and killed him, if I'm not mistaken," he states, glaring at Amrit and me.

"He attacked us," Amrit explains.

"I'm sure he did," Shaq says. He then walks towards Rhea and kneels down in front of her. "You, my dear, are too beautiful to be frowning all the time." He puts his hand on her face, and Rhea looks at him and spits right in his face.

"Fuck you," she shouts, trying to get up to attack him.

"Oh my," Shaq says, wiping the spit from his face, "quite a feisty one we have here." He chuckles to himself and walks around as if nothing had happened.

"What are you planning to do with us?" Mark asks him.

"You will come with me," Shaq says. "You will come and work with me and my family to my farm, and you're going to love it." He then turns and looks directly at Jane. "Yet, you, this is something I did not foresee. You are with child," he says as he walks towards her and kneels down. "We'll have to take special care of you." He smiles, and Jane struggles to look at him. "We can't have the child being killed now, can we?"

I look at Jane and she has nothing but fear in her face. She looks like she is struggling to breathe, gasping if anything.

"What if we refuse to come with you?" Becky asks.

Shaq then stops for a moment, turns and looks directly at her.

"If you choose not to come with me," he says, "then I will cut that girl's child out of her belly and feed it to her. I will make all of you watch, then cut out your eyes so it is the last thing you see. OK?" He looks at us and smiles, looking very proud of himself.

"You're bluffing," Mark says. Shaq storms towards him and stands over him.

"Bluffing?" he says. He then takes his thumb and pushes it right into the bullet wound on Mark's shoulder.

"Ah, fuck!" Mark cries, beginning to sweat from the pain.

Shaq circles his thumb as he makes Mark suffer. We look at him and wince.

"What are you doing?" I call out, trying to get him to stop.

"Please, no!" Jane cries.

"OK, you made your point. Can't you see you're hurting him?" Rhea says as Mark begins to buckle on his knees. "Is that the kind of person you are: you attack somebody when they are tied down?"

"How's that for bluffing?" Shaq says, and we hear the squishing noise of his thumb moving in Mark's wound. He then pulls it out and walks over to Rhea.

"We'll have to keep a very close eye on you too, won't we?" he says. He raises his bloody hand and rubs it on her face.

Rhea cringes and closes her eyes in disgust. He continues to rub until her face is covered with Mark's blood, turning her pale skin a murky red colour.

"Right then." Shaq turns, facing the other border monkeys. "Take them," he demands, and they all charge over and grab us, drag us to our feet and get us marching.

I look around and see all of our weapons and supplies disappearing out of sight as we are escorted out. We are taken to the front door and one of the border monkeys slams it wide open, while the others push us outside. We are led to a van, and the border monkey who opened the door to the store opens the back of it.

"Come on, smile," Shaq urges, walking up to Rhea. "We're going to have fun."

Rhea does nothing but glare in response.

We are all thrown into the back of the van and it sets off. The remaining border monkeys are raiding our food, making sure we are cleared out. I look over at Rhea and see tears in her eyes. I can see she is very upset, probably thinking about Dillon. She raises her hand to wipe Mark's blood from her face, smudging it over her cheek.

"It'll be OK," I say to her, trying to be reassuring.

"It never seems to be," she responds.

I have no words to comfort her, or anyone else for that matter. All we can do now is sit and see where we end up. Hopefully it won't be that bad; hopefully we will enjoy it and be safe. I know it's optimistic to think this way, but this is the time to have this type of thought. All I know is, the Union is looking really good right about now.

29

We are tossed and turned like cans in a trolley as the van continues its journey. We have no idea where we are going. The van is pelted by rain, and we can hear it outside, rattling like pebbles.

The group is silent, just like we were when we would go to work duty for the Union. The only difference is that then we felt we were doing something we wanted to do, and now we're being forced into it.

It feels like this journey will never end. I look around at the others and they all look worried and in a lot of pain. Becky is leaning over and pressing on Mark's shoulder, trying to stop the bleeding. My ears become a blur and I struggle to hear them speaking; all I hear is muffled sounds.

Becky rips off a piece of material from her shirt and wraps it around Mark's shoulder, with help from Amrit, who is pressing down to try and stop the blood. A puddle of blood stains the floor of the van below them. I then turn to Rhea sitting in the corner, making sure Jane is OK. They all seem to be doing something except for me; I'm just aimlessly sitting in the middle, looking blankly at them.

"We'll be OK," I tell the group.

"Shut up back there," the driver shouts as we continue to move forward.

We drive for a few more miles before we come to an immediate halt. We all look at each other, concerned, contemplating what will happen next. The doors to the back of the van come flying open and there is the large border monkey Ryan and I saw the day he got bitten, and Shaq standing behind him.

"Welcome to your new home," Shaq announces. "This is my younger brother, Jake, he will be taking care of you for the time being," he states, pointing at the large gentleman.

"All right, all of you, out," Jake shouts as we struggle out as best as we can with our hands tied in front of us. We get out and Becky falls flat on her face in the mud in front of us. I manage to keep my footing as I look down and see her on the ground. The three border monkeys around us begin to laugh as Jake grabs her and drags her to her feet.

"OK, you," Shaq shouts, walking towards Jane. "You will be coming with me," he says, grabbing her. "The rest of you, Jake will take you to your room. He's made it nice and cosy for you," he snarls, chuckling to himself.

"This way," Jake shouts at us while pointing a gun. Two of the border monkeys come up behind us and shove us in the back.

We are escorted through a field which has a horrible muddy texture. It's just pure mud with bits of stone lodged in different places. As we keep walking, I can't help catching my feet on bits of uncut grass poking out. I try to look forward but the rain obscures my view. All I can think about is how cold and wet I am, and for the first time in years, I actually feel scared for my life. I feel that I am in real danger. I want to turn and make a run for it, but how far will I get, really? I have no idea, and how will I survive with my hands tied?

We are led to a shed which looks worn and broken. We are

taken inside and the smell is horrific. It smells like stale shit, just all different kinds of awful. I feel vomit rising in my throat as soon as we enter, but I manage to keep it down.

We are taken through to what looks like a cage. One by one, Jake cuts off our hand ties and throws us inside, each one hitting the ground face first.

"You can't keep us in here," Mark shouts.

"Try and stop me," Jake snarls as he closes the door on us.

We look back at him once the door is locked, still hearing the rain thunder down above us.

"This is bullshit," Mark shouts as he kicks the wall of the cage. He then raises his hand and places it on his shoulder. I think it's starting to hurt him. A little blood trickles down from his sleeve and over his hand.

"Where did they take Jane?" Rhea asks.

"I have no idea," I say, darting my eyes back and forth, trying to make sense of it all.

"We need to find a way out," Amrit says, also trying to look around.

"How are we going to do that?" Mark shouts.

"By trying to think," Amrit says, "instead of shouting like an idiot."

Mark just turns and glares at him.

"Let's just take our time and think rationally," Becky says. "We are trapped in a cage in the middle of nowhere. What we should do?"

"Sleep?" I suggest, looking around at them all.

"I suppose," Rhea agrees.

"Yeah," Becky says. "Hopefully the rain will be gone in the morning and we will be able to see what it is they want from us. We can think of what to do then," she suggests, trying to reconcile us.

"OK," Amrit says.

"Are you fucking kidding me?" Mark says. "These guys keep

us locked up like a bunch of prisoners and the first thing you think of doing is sleeping?"

"Yes, Mark," Becky says, "because we need to rest."

Mark looks stunned as we all begin to lie down; then goes along with what the rest of us are doing.

Everyone lies down and tries to sleep. I sit at the side and stare at the wall. I look over at Rhea as she turns her back and curls up in the corner, while Mark lies on his back with his eyes open. I look up at the ceiling, out of ideas.

I wake to a bright light slipping through the cracks in the shed roof, hitting me straight in the eyes. I try to open my eyes, but the light is like a giant rock holding them shut. I turn over to avoid it, open my eyes and sit up, rubbing them as I wake. Everyone else is still asleep. I decide to stand up to get some blood flowing in my legs. I move them around, trying to get some feeling back in them. My neck feels crooked, probably because I slipped, leaning my head against the wall.

We are in what looks like a shed. It has tools inside and hay on the floor; the kind of place you keep animals. I walk towards the front of the cage and see that it is one of those old cages that is all aluminium or something, I don't know; it's just one of those cages where it looks like a bunch of squares. I'm really fucking tired from being dragged through the mud and thrown into a dingy little cell.

Suddenly the door to the shed flies open and sunlight floods the room. I raise my hand to shield my eyes, and can just about make out who is standing there. It's Shaq.

"Oh, so you're awake," he says as he walks in. "Time to wake the rest of you."

He starts clapping and the rest wake up, turning over and looking at Shaq. He grabs a chair, sitting right in front of us, and glares into the cage.

"Did you all sleep well?" he asks patronisingly.

"What do you want?" Rhea asks.

"Now, sweetheart, there's no need for all this hostility towards me," he says in a parody of a calm and sensitive voice.

"I'm not your sweetheart," she snaps, frowning. She glares at him and looks as if she is about to lunge at the wall of the cage.

"Of course," Shaq says. "Jane told me all your names. Rhea." We look at one another, then back at him.

"Why are you keeping us here?" Becky asks.

"I told you," Shaq says, "to help me with the work. I need you to look after the cattle. First of all, you need to help fix the field," he says, getting to his feet. "Jake will show you around, once I have taken you to the main premises," he states, as if we are on an educational trip to do some work experience.

Jake then opens the door and two other border monkeys appear, pointing their guns at us. Shaq moves outside and we follow. A large field surrounds us, looking as damp and waterlogged as it felt when we were walking through it last night. I look down and see the mud begin to wrap around my shoes the harder I press down.

"I can't wait to see that guy dead," Rhea says under her breath as we walk towards a bunch of what look like houses. I look over and see Mark is starting to stagger as he walks.

"Mark, are you OK?" I ask him, feeling very concerned.

"Yeah," he croaks, sweating a lot and panting. "My shoulder, it really hurts; it's really starting to sting." He is beginning to sweat, and I can't help but wonder how long it has been hurting him.

"Oi, wait," I call out.

Shaq stops, and so do the rest of the group.

"This better be important," he shouts abruptly.

"My friend – your men shot him, and he hasn't been given any medical attention," I state, pointing to Mark's shoulder to indicate the pain he is in.

"That is true," Shaq tells us. "Jake, take this one away and have him bandaged up. Can't have a damaged workforce now, can we?"

Jake drags Mark away towards a house. I'm already beginning to feel worried about what I have done.

"Shit," I mutter to myself.

"It's OK," Amrit tells me.

"OK," Shaq says, "let's continue."

He leads us to this street, which looks like it has been abandoned for years. There is a long row of houses with a large building at the end. It looks like a giant cube with about fifteen windows going across in rows of three, five windows in each row. I look on the ground and I see tools scattered all over the ground. Everywhere I look, there is a wrench, a hammer, a screwdriver, and many others. It looks like a tip if anything.

"That is where I stay," he explains to us, "me and my family. The rest of the crew, or border monkeys that I have working for me, live in that house over there," he says, pointing at the one house that has not been burnt down. "You are not to come here. While you are working, you will be followed by one of the monkeys. The rest of the time, you will be kept in your little home."

"Like animals," Rhea says.

"You know what, madam?" Shaq says, turning to her. "I'm getting sick of your tongue." He pulls back his right hand, stares right at her and smacks her across the face, causing her to fall on the ground. "You work for me now, so I demand some respect." He then kneels down and helps her up. "I'm sorry I hurt you, it's just how I was raised. Now, time for work."

We walk towards some tools, and there are three border monkeys armed with guns, staring at us. It is outside a barn, which looks dirty from the outside. I can see that Mark has been sweating a lot, even when he's been gone. I don't know what's wrong with him; he's starting to look really pale. I don't know if they even gave him any medical attention. They most likely just

300

made him worse and said they would give him attention just to keep the rest of us quiet.

"I thought you said we will be looking after cattle?" I ask.

"You are," Shaq says. "Here." He opens the door and I can see two cows sitting in the barn. "We would love some fresh milk, so if you could feed this cow and milk her, that would be excellent. Oh, look." He points, and we look over and see Jake bringing Mark over to us, with a fresh bandage around his shoulder.

"He's good as new," Jake calls out as he hands him over.

"Oh, good," Shaq says. "So we can put him to work, then after that we will feed you. See how nice we are?"

"OK?" I ask Mark, as I can see he is still in pain. Mark looks at me and decides not to speak.

"OK," Shaq says, "now all of you get in, no time to waste, we have to get you all in there."

We all begin to walk into the barn.

"Hold on a second, not you," Shaq says to Rhea. "You're coming with me."

"Fuck off!" Rhea shouts, still rubbing her face. A red glow is beginning to push through her pale complexion.

"I have a better job for you, darling," he says, grinning.

"Fuck off right now, I'm not going anywhere with you," she says.

"Jake," Shaq says.

Jake walks over to Rhea and stands in front of her, towering over her. He then pulls back his fist and punches her square in the face, causing her to fall flat on the ground. I try to walk forward to help her, but one of the border monkeys pushes me back. Rhea staggers to her feet and looks at Jake, then lunges, punching him right in the jaw. However, he does not move. She throws another punch, and Jake grabs her hand and grips it hard. He then punches her twice in the stomach with so much force that I feel it myself. She drops to the ground, wheezing as she catches her breath.

"Leave her alone," Becky calls out.

"Stop," I shout.

Rhea then gets up once again and stares right at Jake.

"Come on," she says, blood trickling from her mouth.

Jake looks surprised to see her back on her feet. He then looks at Shaq, as if he is confused about what to do next.

"Go on then," Shaq orders, egging him on.

Jake turns back to Rhea in front of him and pulls his fist back, but before he can throw it, she punches him right in the nose, causing him to stagger backwards. He raises his hand and places it on his nose, feeling it; looks down and can see blood on his hand, trickling from his nose and over his lip. He then looks at Rhea, and she looks right back at him. His face grows fierce, snarling as he storms towards her. Rhea tries to throw another punch, but Jake grabs her arm and holds her in a close embrace.

"Get off, you prick," Rhea struggles to say as Jake lifts her and begins to carry her away. There's a puddle nearby, filled with rain from the night before, and he throws her in, creating a giant splash.

"Rhea!" Mark calls out

The border monkeys behind us begin to laugh. I turn and look at them for a moment, then back at Rhea. She once again gets back up onto her feet, refusing to stay down. Jake, looking frustrated now, grabs her and wrestles her to the ground, and she squeals a little as he forces her back into the puddle. Her ponytail has come out completely, with his pushing causing her head to go into the puddle and cover her face. Jake sits over her and begins to punch her repeatedly in the face.

"Leave her alone," I shout, "you're going to kill her!"

Jake continues to punch her, Rhea's face growing more battered with each blow he lands. She tries to fight back, but now she is starting to struggle. He then grabs her and turns her over, sticking her face deep into the puddle.

"Stop!" Amrit cries, trying to move forward, but he's held back.

Jake puts his hand on the back of Rhea's head and pushes her face into the water. She struggles and tries to fight, but he just keeps forcing her down. Then she starts to slow down.

"Rhea!" I shout, beginning to panic.

"Alright, Jake, that's enough," Shaq says.

As soon as he does, Jake pulls Rhea's head up and out of the puddle, tossing her aside. Rhea coughs and struggles to breathe, trying to get the water out of her lungs. Jake walks around her as she stands on all fours, still coughing out the water. I can see him pulling back his leg. He then kicks her square in the face with his large leather boot, knocking her out cold.

We all look at her, motionless on the floor. Jake then picks her up and throws her over his shoulder, still breathing heavily from the fight.

"Rhea," I shout, but before I can run after her a couple of border monkeys hold me back.

"Where are you taking her?" Amrit asks Shaq as Jake walks towards us, carrying her over his shoulder.

"She's going to be my little servant girl," Shaq tells us. "You never know, play your cards right and I might need another servant girl, or even a servant boy." He places his hand on Rhea's face as Jake stands there with her over his shoulder. She's covered in blood and mud, smudging her pale complexion.

"There is a lot of spirit in this one," Shaq says, stroking her face. "Too much spirit can be dangerous. Now get to work," he says as the border monkeys push us into the barn, and he and Jake walk off with Rhea over Jake's shoulder. The door closes and we can't see them any more.

"Get to work," one of the monkeys barks.

We start moving the hay from the cows, and Becky goes to try to milk the cow Shaq pointed out.

"Do you know what to do?" I ask her, looking at the cow in confusion.

"I don't," she says, "but I have to do something."

We continue working until the afternoon. It is hard work, but we all just keep on at it. I can't help but think about Rhea, and wonder what Shaq has got planned for her. I hope it is nothing that will hurt her. I hope she is safe; I hope she will not get in any trouble.

30

I wake the following morning with my eyes feeling heavier than ever. The floor has played havoc with my back, and my neck is twisted like an umbrella that has been caught in the wind.

I look up and see a man sitting on a chair in front of the cage. It isn't Jake or Shaq, however; it is another man. This one looks very scrawny and skinny, the complete opposite to Jake and Shaq. I can tell by how he is sitting that he is much shorter than them as well. He has these gangly hands, with nails that I feel are a little too long. I've never trusted a man who has long fingernails, and my opinion will not change any time soon. It's just weird; all you have to do is cut them, simple.

"Morning," the man says to me as I sit up.

I look up at him and do not speak, unsure who he is.

"Can I ask you something?" the man asks me.

I look at him without answering.

"Did you know the human body is the most complicated thing on earth? We can live with just one kidney, without our appendix; however, take away a lung and we get in a lot of bother. Also, did you know that fingernails and hair continue to grow after we die? Humans are a lot like any other animal; if you carve them, you can get a lot of meat from them."

I look at him, a little confused.

"Why are you telling me this?" I ask him finally.

He then pulls out a knife and shows it to me. I move back slightly as I watch it shine.

"This is like a tooth," he states, holding the knife and waving it in front of me. "We can use it to bite into something, and even grind something down. These things have really replaced our teeth, so do we even have a need for them now? We might as well just grind up all of our food with this knife and swallow it," he says, waving the knife around enthusiastically.

I'm feeling very freaked out by him; however I can't do anything, I just have to sit back and look at what he is doing.

"OK," I respond awkwardly, looking at his teeth. I notice he doesn't have a lot of them in his mouth, and the ones he does have are covered in yellow and black.

"If you cut a person's wrists," he then says to me, "you can make them bleed to death."

"OK," I say again.

Suddenly the door comes flying open and Shaq walks into the room. I know it's weird but I feel kind of relieved as this means I don't have to listen to this guy any more.

"Oh," Shaq says as he walks in, "I see you've met my younger brother Norman."

"Yes, I have had the pleasure," I reply sarcastically.

Shaq chuckles to himself and stands beside Norman in front of the cage.

"I'm glad to see you haven't lost your sense of humour. I hope that he has made a good first impression?" he asks as he looks down at his brother.

"If you think the human body is a good topic of discussion," I say, "then yeah, it's been a blast."

Norman just sits there, staring at me intensely.

"He means well. He's just a little confused is all," Shaq states, placing his hand on Norman's shoulder.

"OK," I say.

"Right then," Shaq says pacing in front of the cage.

I look over and see Amrit waking up and turning over to look at us. I also notice within the same breath, that Mark and Becky are not in the cage.

"Where's Becky and Mark?" I ask straight away.

"Oh, them," Shaq says. "That's part of the reason why I'm here. They are not here at the moment, because last night I had a thought – a revelation, you could say. We don't really need much work done here. So, what we will do is keep you guys here to relax and chill out, as they say, then we will get you when we need you. No point in having you come to work for the sake of it," he says in his usual calm tone.

"So what will we be doing?" Amrit asks.

"You will be here," Shaq tells us, indicating the cage.

I look around and feel a little confused.

"What, just here?" I say.

"Like prisoners?" Amrit asks.

"No, not like that, more like guests," Shaq explains. "You can't have guests working for you. That would make me nothing more than a bad host."

Amrit and I just look at each other. This man is very indecisive about what he wants from us; just coming up with ideas as if he is making it up as he goes along.

"That's bullshit," I say to him.

"I know it might seem unusual now, but at least I'm not like the Union, demanding that you work so you can stay. All I ask is that you rest," he says, as if he is doing us a favour.

"Until you kill us," Amrit states in a firm tone.

"How many people have you had stay here before?" I ask, curious as to what answer he will come out with.

"I have had many people come and go from this place. They have all lived in this little home you have here," Shaq says, looking around at the shed.

"Cage," I correct.

"Call it what you like," he says, "but you have to admit, it is fun here. Think of it as a holiday camp."

"It'll be fun," Norman chips in excitedly.

"Yes, it'll be fun," Shaq agrees.

"Fun?" I say sternly. "This guy has been talking to me about body parts!"

"Really?" Amrit asks.

"Yeah," I reply, "he's just been going on about it."

"Wow," Amrit says, "what a freak."

Norman's eyes open wide, and he glares at Amrit. He then lunges at the cage and grabs it, rattling it.

"I'm not a freak," he shouts. "Don't call me a freak! You're fucking dead, you are."

Amrit then stands and squares off to Norman.

"Fucking bring it," he says.

"I'm going to kill you," Norman says. "You're going to die!"

"Spoken like a true freak," Amrit says.

"You're dead," Norman shouts, "you're dead, you're dead!"

"Well, step inside," Amrit says. "Let's do it."

"OK," Shaq says, "let's calm it down now." He rises to his feet and puts his hand on his brother's shoulder. Norman's face has gone bright red with anger. "Go see if they need any help outside."

Norman keeps staring at Amrit, who stares right back at him.

"Now, Norman," Shaq scolds.

Norman looks at him, looks back at Amrit, then walks out the room.

"Wow," I say, looking first at Amrit, then at the door Norman exited from.

"Wow indeed," Shaq repeats, sitting down on the chair Norman was using. "I do apologise for him," he says calmly, "he's always been a strange one. I think our mother took care of him a little too much when he was a child."

"The guy's off his rocker," I say.

"Yeah, he is," Shaq agrees. "However, he did have fun with your friend."

I look at him, and so does Amrit.

"Well, that got your attention," Shaq states calmly.

"What did he do?" I ask, wanting an answer.

"Tell us," Amrit demands.

Shaq looks at us, then claps his hands and the door opens again. Two border monkeys come running in, holding Becky in their arms.

"What the fuck?" I say as I look at Becky all beaten up and passed out. I jump to my feet as they carry her in. One of the border monkeys points a gun at us and the other opens the cage and carries Becky inside, throwing her to the ground in front of us.

"What did you do?" Amrit asks once the monkey closes the cage. He rushes to Becky and tries to comfort her.

"That wasn't me. That was Norman at his finest," Shaq explains, with pride in his voice.

"I can't believe it," I say, looking down at her. "What about the others – Mark, Jane and Rhea, where are they?"

"They are all perfectly safe," Shaq says, but I can't believe a word he says.

"Why haven't you taken us?" Amrit asks.

"Well," Shaq begins, "you two are very valuable. I found a job for Rhea; it's just the two of you I'm struggling with. Don't worry, I'll think of something." He waves his hand and the border monkeys leave the shed.

"What do you mean, special?" Amrit asks.

"Yeah, what do you mean?" I ask, wondering if being special is a good or bad thing.

"Well," Shaq takes a breath, "like I told you before, I have been watching you for a while now. This past year, you have really been busy, and I wanted to see if I could find a use for you.

Therefore, I would like you to become a substantial part of my company – my company of people," he says with his hands on his hips in a posture of authority.

"You're insane," Amrit says.

"What is it with you calling people names?" Shaq asks. Amrit just stares at him, then returns his attention to Becky.

"What will happen to us?" I ask, concerned.

"All will be revealed soon," Shaq says. "Now, I must bid you adieu. Take care, my young companions." He turns and walks out of the shed, leaving Amrit and me in the cage with a passed-out Becky.

"Well…" I say, looking down at her.

A mixture of tears and blood covers her face. Amrit begins to wipe it, getting her hair out of her eyes.

"I know," he responds.

We look at each other with nothing but resentment for the situation we are in. Amrit looks back down at Becky as she lies there motionless, breathing ever so slightly. I want to talk, however there is nothing that I can really say at this time that can make the situation any better.

Becky is finally trying to wake up. She struggles to open her eyes, but manages to get there in the end.

"You OK?" Amrit asks as she wakes.

"Yeah," she says.

"What happened?" I ask her.

She looks at me and Amrit and a tear trickles from her eye.

"That Norman," she says, "he just kept beating me. He hurt me," she whispers as the tears begin to flow. "He told me to take… take my clothes off. Then… then he… he just whipped me until I couldn't walk any more." She sobs, and we watch her as if she is deteriorating in front of us.

"It's OK," Amrit soothes, holding her close to give her comfort.

"You'll be fine," I agree in an attempt to console her.

"Just rest now," Amrit says. He lays Becky down in the corner and she curls up, closing her eyes so she can rest peacefully.

"What now?" I ask as we look at her, trying to come to terms with what these people have done to our friend.

"I don't know," Amrit says, and we look at each other, trying to make sure we are OK to keep going.

The day passes as quickly as it started. The whole day Amrit and I remain in the shed, only occasionally coming out to walk around. We know that for the remaining time we are here, we will be staying in this very spot. There is no way that we will be moving from this place, or that we will be free any time soon.

This is our life for the time being. It is up to us how long our life will be in this position. This place feels as if it is riddled with evil. I know that evil could be argued to be just a point of view, however to keep people imprisoned just because you feel like it is evil in my book. I have no idea why they have brought us here; they just keep giving us bogus excuses. I personally don't think they know why they have brought us here; they just brought us for the sake of bringing us. We are nothing like guests, not even workers. We are here for the simple reason that they want to have power over us, as if we are nothing more than possessions to them. At least with the Union we would get food and payment, and above all a sense of purpose. I don't see the purpose of us being here. This is just some sick game to them. I don't understand. I really want to; however words are just leaving me to form some kind of idea that can be used to negate a reason for all of this.

I want to improve my life; we all want to improve the situation we are in. The problem is that sometimes we are dropped into situations which we have no control over. We have no issues which can be relied on others that can be changed. I just want to feel free once more.

For the first time since we left, I actually miss the Union. I miss the life we had there. I know we wanted to leave and not be a part of that world any more, but we thought we knew better. Now we are stuck here, trapped in this world which we have no idea how to escape from. What has become of me?

I know I am rambling right now, but that is because I am trying to come to terms with the situation I am in. I have no idea how to make sense of anything, or of who I am right now.

31

Darkness covers the room like a blanket. I feel my eyes begin to get accustomed to the dark, even as they grow tired. I look over and see Amrit, Mark and Becky all fast asleep. I smile to myself as I see them there, all at peace.

I decide it's time that I got some rest. My eyes grow heavy, but I fight it for some reason, trying to see if I can stay up all night. In the end, I decide there is no need to try and stay awake for the sake of it; it's better to just fall asleep and go to that better place. I close my eyes and begin to feel myself drifting off.

As soon as my dream begins, I start to grow disgruntled. Trees surround me, and I look down at my feet and see the shoes I wore when I was very young. I am running away, hearing screams in the background; Adam calling out to me as I keep running away from him. I feel the tears running down my face as I look at my child self, running and not wanting to look behind, not even for a second. I keep going through the trees, feeling the ground crumble under me.

"Layton!" I hear Adam call as I keep running away, trying to make ground.

"Don't look back, don't look back," I repeat to myself.

I blink, and I am in another place. I am much older now, and this is a place I have seen recently. I am standing in a stream. I gaze around and see Amrit walking across it in the distance, going from one side to the other. I stare at him as he lifts his shoes out of the water, drops trickling down from them. He doesn't look back at me, he just keeps walking and heads off into the distance. I see him walk into the woods, then he disappears.

I look down and see somebody in the stream, bathing. It's Rhea, washing her skin with the water, pouring it over her. She keeps cleaning herself as I look at her. I begin to walk towards her, and hold my hand out to her. I blink, then she is gone.

"What?" I say, looking around. I search for her, looking left, then right. I look forward, then behind.

I then turn, and I see somebody new standing in the middle of the stream. I see who it is and take a step back. It's General Singh standing there, glaring right back at me. I breathe for a moment, trying to gather my thoughts, trying not to panic. He lifts his right arm and I see a gun in his hand. He points it at me and pulls the trigger, and I fall backwards into the water.

I fall through the water, sinking lower and lower into the depths. I see the surface disappear as I keep falling further down, unable to swim back up. I thrash my arms, but nothing seems to happen. I thrash them more and more, yet I remain in the same place. The water floods into my mouth, and I sink further down. The more water I take in, the heavier I get, and the further I sink. I close my eyes for a moment to try and think of a way out. Nothing comes to my mind, so I open them again.

"Wakey-wakey!" I hear Jake's voice calling out.

I suddenly open my eyes and look up. They are banging on the door repeatedly. Amrit, Mark and Becky all wake up too and look at the door.

"What's going on?" Becky asks as the door come flying open.

It's still dark outside; I don't know why they are here. They come storming in: Shaq, Jake and Norman, and two border monkeys following close behind. We all sit up and look at them.

"I think it's time we had a little fun," Shaq says as he looks down at us all. He clicks his fingers and one of the border monkeys comes forward, pulls out a violin and starts to play it.

"Come on, dance," Jake says, clapping his hands.

"Dancing, dancing," Norman yells, clapping away as we all look at each other.

The other border monkey opens the cage door and grabs each of us in turn, escorting us out. He then grabs Becky by the hand and brings her forwards.

"Come on, Becky," Shaq says, "dance for us."

Becky looks at us as the violin starts to play over and over. She reluctantly lifts her feet and starts to move.

"Yes, yes," Norman cries, clapping his hands repeatedly.

"Now you, Mark," Shaq shouts.

Mark just moves his shoulders a little, making sure not to use too much energy. He grabs his injured shoulder, showing he is still in pain.

"Nice," Jake says as he keeps dancing.

"What the fuck is going on?" I ask Amrit, who just looks at me and shrugs his shoulders.

"Very good, Mark," Shaq says. He then nods at somebody; I don't catch who it is. Suddenly, Mark goes flying backwards, pulled by Norman from what appears to be a giant hook in his shoulder.

"Ah!" Mark screams as Norman pulls him to the ground.

Jake then comes up to me and Amrit and pushes us back in the cage, shutting and locking it as soon as we hit the ground.

"What are you doing?" Amrit shouts as we get to our feet.

"Let us out," I say, grabbing the cage and rattling it.

"Get off him!" Becky shouts, running at Norman. She punches him in the face, causing him to fall down, letting go of the hook.

The border monkey who caged us goes up behind her, grabs her by the hair and drags her back. She squeals as he pulls her to the end of the room. Jake then walks over to Mark and grabs the hook, keeping hold of him. He lifts him to his knees, then places his leg behind Mark's back.

"Now, let's calm it down," Shaq says, holding his hands out in a peaceful manner.

"Let him go," I call out as I look at Mark trapped on the hook. I then look over and see Becky trying to get away, however the border monkey has her hair gripped in his hand. She is also on her knees.

"Norman, go fetch the surprise," Shaq says, waving his hand.

"Gladly," Norman says, rubbing his face. He opens the door to the shed and walks out.

"What are you doing here?" I ask Shaq. "It's the middle of the night, why can't you just let us rest?"

"I could let you rest," Shaq says, chuckling to himself, "but I just wanted my boys to have a little fun." He walks over to Becky. "We're going to have fun," he repeats while stroking her face.

"Don't you touch her," Mark yells as he tries to break free.

"Yeah?" Jake retorts, pulling the hook in Mark's shoulder. "What you going to do about it?"

"Fuck you – ah!" Mark screams as a lot of blood leaks from his wound. I can see where they aimed the hook. They went straight for his bullet wound to stop it healing.

"Stop it," Becky calls out.

The door to the shed swings wide open and Norman walks in.

"Ah, Norman's here," Shaq says as Norman comes walking in holding something in his hand. It looks like a plate covering something. There is an awful smell coming from it. "Put it here," Shaq commands.

Norman puts the plate right in front of Becky, showing it off to us all. "Right, fancy a midnight feast?" he offers, pulling the sheet off the plate.

I look down and start to feel sick.

"What is that?" I ask, already thinking I have an idea. I gag as I take a better look at it, feeling the vomit begin to creep its way up my throat.

"That fucking stinks," Amrit says, covering his mouth and nose.

"It's faeces," Shaq says, presenting it to Becky. "I would like you to eat some."

"Fuck off," I shout.

"No, I won't," Becky says, looking up at him angrily.

Jake then pulls Mark's shoulder with the hook, causing more bleeding.

"Ah!" Mark winces as he raises his other hand to his shoulder in pain.

"We will keep hurting him if you don't eat," Shaq says to Becky, looking down at her.

"Why are you doing this?" Becky asks, pleading with him.

Shaq crouches down and looks her square in the eyes. "Because I can. Now eat, or your friend will suffer more," he demands, pointing at the plate and glaring at her.

"This is insane," I shout.

"Layton," Shaq says, "you are a very confrontational person. Your friend Rhea was very confrontational. She's now been put in her place."

"What did you do to her?" I ask him. I walk towards the cage bars and glare at him, grabbing hold of the bars, ready to try and rip them off.

"Nothing you need to know," Shaq states.

"Please, just go," Amrit pants.

"Not until Becky here does what I ask of her," Shaq says, walking around with his hands behind his back.

"Eat, you stupid bitch!" Norman shouts at her. Jake then pulls at Mark's shoulder once again. He is beginning to sweat from the pain, more blood coming out of him.

"Mark…" Becky says to him.

Mark just shakes his head at her, trying to tell her not to eat. She looks at him and I can see her beginning to well up, and a tear trickles down her face. She blinks, causing more tears to fall. She turns away, looks down at the plate and closes her eyes. She leans towards it and begins to eat the shit Shaq put in front of her.

"That's a good girl," Shaq says as she continues to eat.

"Becky, no," I whisper to myself.

"Oh my God, she's doing it," Norman cries, laughing out loud and pointing at her. The two border monkeys begin to laugh too, and so does Jake.

"Keep going," Shaq says as she continues to eat from the plate, struggling to get through each nibble.

"Look at her go," Norman says, bending down. He slaps her on her behind as she continues to eat. "Keep going, keep going," he shouts. Becky jolts forward slightly from the slaps. Norman then gets up and does a little dance as Becky continues to eat.

"Please stop," Amrit mutters.

"OK, that's enough," Shaq says, kicking the plate away. Becky leans over sobs uncontrollably, wiping the shit from her face.

"Oh, Becky," I say. I feel terrible for her. She tries to wipe her face, but covers her hands with tears.

"All right then," Jake says, pulling the hook out of Mark's shoulder. Mark clutches his wound, gasping as blood flows from it.

"Oh, good," Shaq says. "See, was that so difficult?" he asks Becky patronisingly.

One of the border monkeys then points a gun at Amrit and me as the other opens the cage. Jake drags Mark and throws him into the cage, then goes back for Becky. As soon as she is inside, the cage door closes. Becky continues to cry. Amrit runs straight to her and embraces her, holding her close. I walk over to Mark and kneel down to make sure he is OK.

"Time for bed?" Norman asks Shaq.

"Yes, time for bed," Shaq responds. "Get plenty of rest, you lot, I will see you in the morning."

They leave the room and slam the door, and we sit there feeling very used. I look at Mark and Becky, and they look devastated. I don't know why they did this to them. Why did they feel the need to humiliate them? I never believed in the Devil, however if he does exist I think we're staying in his house. I can't help but feel this is going to be a regular occurrence throughout the time we are here.

32

Days become weeks and weeks become months. The majority of the time I am cooped up in this cage, wanting to break free. It's been three, four, five, maybe six months since we came here. Well, I think it has been. It's hard to keep track of time when you only see the sun every now and then. I don't know what time it is right now, it's hard to say.

One thing I do wish for is another one of those pills Amrit gave me a while ago. I could really do with a mental journey to my own paradise. Well, I call it Paradise; it's just an illusion of a fantastical world that does not exist, escapism from the world I know so well. So not a bad experience, really.

Every day, Mark and Becky are taken out of the cage and we sometimes don't see them for days. The other day I was taken outside to stand in the cold, and I could see Norman dragging Mark by the hook in his shoulder. Mark's shoulder has really gotten worse. It is turning a strange green colour around where the bullet was lodged. They haven't done anything to help him; he has just been getting worse every day. A weaker person probably would've died by now, but Mark is one of the toughest guys I've met, he can handle it – I hope. He throws up every night, and he looks like he's had a fever for the past few months.

I can hear him at night, coughing right through until morning, struggling to sleep.

Becky is regularly taken out, and when she comes back, there are always new bruises and cuts on her body. All the time, Amrit and I are just brought out for odd jobs here and there; nothing that involves too much energy. I don't know what we have done to deserve this treatment, while Mark and Becky have to suffer every day. I can't remember the last time I saw Rhea, and as for Jane, I haven't seen her since we got here.

It's winter now, I can tell by how cold it is, and by the amount of snow everywhere. It's not like they're doing anything to keep us warm here. My clothes feel dirty, and so do my face and teeth. I feel slimy all over after wearing the same clothes for the past few months. I feel disgusting, just pure disgust at how I feel right now. I sit there looking at the walls in the shed, row after row of grey bricks, looking as if the cold is beginning to turn them to ice.

I suddenly hear a noise and can't help but feel disappointed at having my peace disrupted. I look over and see where the noise is coming from. The door flies open and Shaq comes walking inside. I look around and see that I am the only one in the cage this morning. God knows what has happened to the rest of us.

"Good morning," Shaq calls out as he enters the room. "Rise and shine, my little buddy, old pal!"

I slowly lift my weakened body from the floor. "What do you want?" I ask, straining my voice as I speak.

"It's a working day," he announces. "I have a fence that has fallen down and would love it if you would be so kind as to pick it up for me. Will you be a dear and do this for me?" he asks me in a patronising manner.

"Do I have a choice?" I ask him, already knowing the answer. He opens the cage and looks down at me and smiles as I look up at him, feeling my neck crack.

"No, not really," he responds once the cage is open.

I stagger to my feet, feeling a little light-headed, and start walking with him outside. All I see as soon as we walk out is a bright light. It feels like a while since I've been outside; my legs are just coming to terms with themselves. I look around and can see nothing more than a sea of white. There is snow covering the field and the house in a blanket of frozen flakes.

"Can I have a coat?" I ask Shaq.

He just laughs at me as if I'm joking. The thing is, I was actually being kind of serious. It's fucking freezing out here, and I want to be warm.

"OK," Shaq says. "The fence is over here." He points at this crooked old fence that looks like the wood has been decaying for the past century.

"Here?" I ask him, pointing at it as he walks me towards it.

"Yes, here," he says. "I want you to fix this fence so it's standing once again."

"Do I have any tools?" I ask him, looking around.

"Yes," he says, "the tools are down here. Just fix it and make it look good again."

I look at the fence and can see that it has collapsed in the middle. The snow is covering it. I pick up a hammer and look up at Shaq, staring at me holding the hammer. I stare back at him, holding the tool in my hand. The longer I look at Shaq, the tighter my grip on the hammer gets. He glances down at the hammer, smirking to himself.

"Do it," he says.

"You think I won't?" I respond.

He then steps closer to me and stares down at me.

"Do it, I know you want to," he tempts me.

I look at him and a smile begins to break its way through his lips.

"You would like that, wouldn't you?" I say to him.

He chuckles at me and turns away. I really want to just go up to him and smash the back of his head with this hammer. I want to crack his head wide open and watch him suffer on the ground, bleeding as I watch him die.

"Nothing personal, hey," he says and walks away, leaving me with the fence.

I look at him as he disappears into the distance and can't help but feel some kind of regret. Why didn't I just kill him? Why did I let him go? Why didn't I just hit him and kill him?

I work on the fence for a good few hours. The fucking cold is causing my fingers to freeze up and go stiff, stopping me from moving them properly. I try to stick the different planks of wood into the ground, however I can't seem to make them stable. I hammer the planks into the ground and they are stable for a moment, then fall out again. These things are so annoying, I feel like just smashing the whole fence apart so it isn't a problem.

I look up and see the woods in front of me. Maybe, just maybe… No, it'll never work. I look around. Nobody is around – no Shaq, no Jake, no Norman, no border monkeys; just me and the woods in front of me. I could just… no, I can't. What about everybody else?

Well, it was being with everybody else that got me in this mess. I was never in this kind of danger when I was on my own. It's other people who bring the hardships upon you. I would never have had to go to Leicester, would never have ended up here – I would have been fine. I would have been doing OK, just ripping people off with fancy stones and seeing how I can make them fall for my bullshit. I could go back to that life so easily. I just need to… just… all I need is…

Wait, now is not the time. I need to scope the area first before making a decision like this. I need more time to think, and to formulate an appropriate plan of attack.

What is that I see? A rabbit. I see it hopping around, its brown fur standing out against the snow. It just hops around, leaving its footprints. It stands there and looks forward. I look back at it, and it doesn't seem to want to leave. Or maybe it's planning the best time to leave. It turns around and hops away into the distance, free to go wherever it wants to go. I just need to sort everything out here; make sure we're all safe first. Once I have done that, then I will be able to… Shit, somebody's coming.

"How's it going?" Shaq asks me as he approaches. I look up at him and can see him looking up and down at the fence.

"As well as it can, I suppose," I respond begrudgingly. I shiver as soon as I stop working. I am feeling the cold a lot more since I have been here.

"Well, I guess you've done as well as you can," he says, pacing up and down the fence, looking at all the holes I have made. "I guess I've worked you enough for one day; I think it's time you had a break."

I look at him, confused as to why he is offering me this.

"OK," I say. I am a little troubled – he never lets people have breaks, and I can't help but feel there is a catch.

"Come with me, I want you to meet someone," he says, placing his hand on my shoulder.

I drop the hammer and follow him. As I hear the hammer hit the ground, I realise I have just passed up another opportunity.

We head towards the large house in the middle of the road and Shaq opens the large brown door, leading me into a giant hallway.

"Wow," I say, looking around as if I have entered a fairy tale. He walks me down the hallway towards some stairs. This hall looks like something from the Victorian era or something. There are pictures all over the walls, paintings of people who look like they lived hundreds of years ago.

"What are these?" I ask him in amazement.

"These are pictures of my ancestors. You see, I come from a long line of aristocrats," he explains as we walk through, taking in the history of the building.

"Yeah?" I say.

"Yeah," he repeats. "My family, the Battalions, have lived here for many years. This is my family home, as you might call it."

"So you're related to all of these people?" I ask him, pointing at the paintings on the wall. Each of them is a portrait of a different person striking a pose in period clothing. Some of them must be really old, because I can see some portraits of men in wigs.

"Most definitely," he says. "We were there at the time of the Empire, and have ruled our own little kingdom for many years."

I stop walking and look around, confused.

"What's the matter?" he asks me.

"That doesn't mean anything," I say to him.

He turns and faces me, looking fierce as he walks towards me.

"What do you mean?" he asks sternly. He looks very defensive.

"I mean," I say, "having a title or a family home means nothing in this day and age."

He places his hand on my shoulder and takes a deep breath.

"Those who have no title will say that," he explains. "Those who have had titles and are of a certain… grandeur… we would like to preserve this. We are preserving our history, my history, do you understand?" he says to me, hammering the idea home.

"OK," I respond. I think this is a lot of trouble to go to just to keep alive a past that doesn't mean anything any more, but each to their own, I guess.

I then hear a loud cry, like a woman's scream. I look around, trying to see where it is coming from, and realise it's coming from the door in front of us.

"Oh, it's time," Shaq says, grabbing my arm and opening the door.

We walk inside and I can see a giant bed at the end of the room. Norman and this other man are standing there, and there is an old woman sitting in the corner wearing what looks like a wedding dress. She is very pale, and so old that you can actually begin to see her bones poking through her skin. I look over at the bed and see Jane lying there, screaming in pain.

"It's time," the man says to Shaq.

"Jane," I shout out, running towards her to see if she is OK.

"Not too close," I hear a voice say.

Jake stands behind me with Rhea. My heart breaks as soon as I see her. She has a rope tied around her neck and her hands are bound. She looks like she has bruises all over her and is in a lot of pain.

"Rhea!" I say. She looks at me, too afraid to say a word.

"Don't look at her," Shaq says. "The real show is over here." He points at Jane.

"She's ready," the man who ran up to Shaq says. "OK, we need you to push." He hovers over Jane, and she looks up at him and begins to breathe, sounding as if each breath is suffocating her.

"I can't," she cries, breathing heavily.

"You have to, darling," Shaq explains to her. "How else you are going to give birth to our heir?"

"Your heir?" I ask, taken aback slightly. I look at Jane for a moment, then back at him, feeling a frown crease my face.

"Yes. Why else do you think she is here?" he asks, presenting his hands and showing off Jane to me. I can't help but think that this has all been part of his own twisted little plan.

"OK, push," the man says to Jane, and she pushes. She screams as she pushes and I want to go over to her and help her, but every time I move towards her Jake pushes me away.

"Here it comes," Norman shouts, excited.

"Is that my baby coming?" the old woman in the corner says in a croaky voice.

"Come on," the man calls, "one more push!"

Jane gives a giant heave and pushes out the baby. It begins to cry.

"Oh God," Rhea cries under her breath.

"The baby!" I shout as I see it appearing. I can't think of anything else to say, so all I can say is that, really.

"Oh, good!" Shaq applauds. "Congratulations, all of us."

"Yes," Norman shouts as Jane pants and closes her eyes, covered in sweat.

"It's a girl," the man standing over Jane says.

Shaq then stops and looks down at the baby. I can feel the mood in the room suddenly change from one of celebration to one of disgust.

"What?" Norman shouts.

"What a piece of shit. We should get rid of it," Jake says, pointing at the baby.

"No!" Rhea shouts, trying to move forward to grab the baby.

"Shut up," Jake snaps and yanks the rope around her neck, causing her to fall to the ground.

"Oi," I say, standing up and trying to confront him.

"It's still my baby," the old woman cheers. "Bring me my baby."

Shaq then grabs the baby and brings her over to the old woman.

"Hello, little baby, hello," she says to her as the baby begins to calm down.

I look at the baby and feel tears run from my eyes as I watch her being caressed by this old woman.

"When she is of age," the old woman says, "one of you will mate with her, creating an heir. Then we will have an heir of our blood, not tainted blood. She will be raised in our family, be a member of our household; the house of Battalion."

The others nod.

"Yeah," Shaq says.

Rhea looks at Jane and can see that she is in a lot of pain.

"Oh my God, Jane!" she cries. She has passed out from the pain, and there is blood all over the sheets, surrounding her in a sea of red.

"That's not good," the man at her bedside says. He looks at Jane, seeming as if he is confused about what to do.

"Oh well, she's of no use to us now," Shaq says, dismissing Jane as he walks over to the baby.

"But she will die if we don't help her!" the man shouts, grabbing little bits from around the room. He tries to get some towels and sheets out to help her.

"So what?" Shaq says. He pulls out a gun and points it at the man. "You're also of no use to us now," he adds, and without hesitation, shoots the man square in the forehead. He dies right there on the floor, blood squirting everywhere.

Rhea gasps, and I look down at the man. He still has his eyes open in the shock of seeing the gun. I decide I need to get to Jane as all of this commotion is going on. I manage to run past Jake and get to her side.

"We need to help her," I shout as I see that Jane is struggling to breathe.

"Why?" Norman asks, confused.

"Because she's a person," Rhea says, trying to awaken some kind of sympathy in them.

"Who cares?" Shaq says.

"Layton..." Jane stirs, panting as she speaks.

"Jane!" I say.

She struggles to open her eyes. I kneel down, looking into her eyes. She holds out her hand and I take it straight away. I expect it to be hot, but it's like an ice cube.

"My baby. What is it?" she mutters.

"It's a girl," I tell her. "It's a baby girl."

A little smile appears on her lips as she looks at me.

"Good," she says. "Let me hold her?" she asks, struggling to hold her arms out.

"Let her hold her child," I demand, looking at the old woman.

"No, she can't," the old woman shouts, turning away. "She's my baby now, she belongs to me."

"My mother is right," Shaq says.

Fuck me, is that his mum? My God, she's still around. Why won't they just let Jane hold the baby?

"I don't care," I shout at them, "just give her the baby, please."

"Please," Jane says.

Shaq walks over to Jane and gets right in her face and stares at her as she breathes over and over again, looking back at him.

"No," he replies smugly and turns, waving off Jake and his mother. Jake drags Rhea, and his mother gets up holding the baby and begins to walk away.

"No, you can't!" Rhea calls out as Jake yanks her away.

"No!" Jane strains on the bed. "Please, my baby, give me my baby!"

I turn and try to run after them, but Shaq grabs me. The door shuts and they are gone, and Jane breaks down into tears.

When she next speaks, she sounds very drowsy. "Layton," she calls out to me.

"Yes, Jane?" I say, crawling over the bed towards her.

"My baby's name," she begins to explain. "I want to name her after my mum, Louise."

I look at her and know that this might be her last wish. I know what she has had to go through, and so I will honour this request.

"Louise," I repeat. "That is her name. That will be her name and she will always be called Louise, you have my word."

She smiles at me, and I smile back to make her feel better.

"Pretty name," Shaq says, "but we will give her a more appropriate one."

I look back at Jane, and she passes out.

"Jane," I call out to her. She does not respond. "Jane!" Still, she is motionless. "Jane," I repeat, holding her shoulders, shaking her to try to get her to wake up.

"Oh, what a shame," Shaq remarks sarcastically.

I break down into tears and rub my face on Jane as she begins to turn very cold.

"Jane, please wake up. Wake up, Jane, wake up. Please don't go," I cry as I feel the life leave her.

"She's gone, little buddy," Shaq says to me, sounding very patronising.

"She's long gone," Norman says. "Maybe I can have her as my toy now."

I can't help it; I just get up, walk over to him and punch him right in the face. He falls flat on the floor, motionless. What a prick.

"Now, that's not very nice, is it?" Shaq says as I turn around, and he hits me with the butt of his gun, causing me to fall back.

I lie there on the floor, staring up at the ceiling, feeling my eyes slowly close as he stands above me. I know I am going to wake up in the shed; I know I will still be in this shithole. I should've just taken my chances in the woods when I had the opportunity. I won't make that mistake again.

33

Of course, the place I wake up is back in the cage in the shed. My head is spinning; it feels horrible. There's a stinging pain in my head, like a piece of glass scratching my skull. My brain scrapes and hurts when I open my eyes. I finally find the strength to open them fully, looking around to see a place I feel is just like home now.

I sit up and see Mark hunched over in the corner, Amrit on the other side and Becky lying on the ground. They all look shattered. I suppose they've been worked as hard as I have, knocked out more times than they care to remember. I feel weak, unable to stand or walk. I'm constantly hungry, unable to have the strength to move on much longer. I look down at my clothes, and I can feel that my stomach has sunk inwards. There is more room under my top than there used to be.

"You OK?" Amrit asks me as I try to get my head together.

I look at him and start to cry.

"What happened?" he asks me as I try to wipe the tears from my eyes.

"Jane," I say to him. "She had the baby."

"Did she?" Becky asks, sitting up. I look forward at them and can see them all looking at me.

"W-what was it?" Mark stutters. I can see that his whole left shoulder is completely motionless.

"A girl," I tell him. "Louise, she called her." I look at them all, smiling as soon as I mention the baby's name.

"Louise," Becky says, smiling, "that was her mum's name."

I nod and smile.

"It's a good name," Mark says. He coughs a few times after speaking.

"The thing is…" I begin, knowing what I have to tell them. I can't say this while looking at them. "She was bleeding a lot after the baby was born… she died."

I look up and I can see that their reactions are not the same as when I told them about the baby. Becky's eyes begin to water, and Mark just looks down.

"Died?" Becky mutters, struggling to speak through her tears.

"Yeah," I respond, wishing I had other news for them.

"Oh God," Becky cries, planting her face in her hands.

"Fuck this," Mark says. He grunts to himself, wanting to speak again. "What h-happened to the b-baby?" he asks eventually, still stuttering slightly.

"She was taken by Shaq's mother," I tell them.

"Shaq's mother?" Amrit says, stunned.

"Yeah. Weird shit," I tell them.

"Shit just gets weirder," Amrit says.

"Fuck," Mark calls out as we all look at the ground.

"The weird thing is," I say to them, "yesterday, when I was fixing the fence for Shaq, I couldn't help it. I just wanted to run off into the woods. I could've as well, nobody was around."

They all look at one another; then Amrit looks down as Mark and Becky look straight at me.

"Why did you stay?" Becky asks.

"For you guys," I tell them.

They look at each other again, uncomfortably, and then back at me.

"You should've just run," Amrit says, raising his head to face me.

"What?" I say, stunned.

"Yeah," Mark says. "You should've just gone."

"Why?" I'm actually shocked that this is how they're reacting. "Where would I have gone? What would I have done?" I ask them, bemused.

"Doesn't matter," Mark says. "You had a chance to be free."

"Layton," Becky says, leaning over to me, "if you have the chance to run, then you run."

"Why are you talking like this?" I ask her. "What have they done to you?"

She and Mark look at each other, then back at me.

"We don't feel like running," Becky says. "I can't run any more; they've tortured me every day. They've beaten me, tied me to a post and branded me," she explains, showing me the marks on her stomach.

"They tied me up," Mark says. He raises his hands and shows them to me. I look at his wrists and I can see deep red marks in them, covered in pale bloodstains. "They tied me by my hands and whipped me until I fainted. Then they woke me and whipped me some more," he describes to me, making me wince. "They even made me stand naked in the cold, the snow just stuck to me."

I look at him and feel nothing but regret and guilt, knowing what my friends have suffered.

"I had no idea," I say.

"They've been torturing them every day, Layton," Amrit says. "Every day while we have been sent out to work, they've been tortured."

"I had no idea," I say again, knowing that I am repeating myself.

"That's not the worst," Becky says to me. "The other day,

Shaq and his brothers tied me up. They said they were going to take turns with me, but then they just left me with that fucker Norman. He beat me so hard I couldn't feel anything. Then he drugged me, and I don't know what happened after that." She lies down, turning her back to us as if she doesn't want us to see her face.

"What did he drug you with?" I ask her.

"I have no idea," she responds.

"We have to get out of here!" I say.

"You can," Amrit states. "You need to escape the next time they tell you to go to work."

"I can't," I say. "Why can't you?" I ask him.

"Because…" he says. Then he stops. "You can get away, while I stop them getting to you. Next time you have to go out to work, I will jump Shaq and you make a run for it. I will jump Shaq, Jake or Norman; I don't care, I will take them out. Even if they've hired their precious border monkeys to come in and help them."

"What do the border monkeys do?" I ask him.

"I have no idea," Amrit responds.

"What should I do if I escape?" I ask, confused and wanting an answer.

"Well," Amrit says, "what you do is head straight back to the camp we were in. Get in there and get our weapons."

"But they'll have taken them all," I state.

"Yeah, but I stashed some in the back closet," he explains, trying to convince me.

"You kept weapons there?" I ask, surprised and slightly glad.

"Yeah. If you get them, just bring them here. Or you can try something else," he suggests.

"What?" I ask, wondering what it could be.

"You can head back to Oadby," he says. "Try and get Bal."

"What?" I ask him. "No way will that work." I can't imagine Bal ever trying to help me or Amrit in any way, no matter how much we are suffering.

"Anything's better than this," he says.

I look at him and can see he has no real plan. He's desperate, just clutching at straws, trying to get any idea to work. I know how he feels; I feel like I could do with any idea right now too.

We sit there for a good while until the door opens once again. Shaq stands there, staring at us. I look over at Amrit and he's just staring at Shaq, defeated.

"How are we feeling?" Shaq asks us as he walks inside.

I look back at him, not wanting to talk to him.

"Took a bit of a hit to the head now, didn't we?" he says to me, chuckling to himself. "Well, I'm not going to keep you long," he explains as he stands at the end of the cage. "Layton, you didn't do a great job with that fence earlier, so I thought Amrit can come and help you."

He opens the cage to let us out.

"Come on then," he says.

We both get up, neither of us fighting, neither us deciding to argue, and just walk out of the cage. I look back and see Mark and Becky watching us .

"Finally," Amrit whispers as we walk out. "A bit of luck at last."

I know exactly what he is planning to do as soon as we get to the fence.

We walk with Shaq through the field towards the fence. It is snowing a lot now, feels like a blizzard. The snow strikes my face, making it feel like glass. Shaq is wrapped up warm in a large overcoat, while Amrit and I are still in the clothes we have been wearing for the past few months. He walks with us, leading us towards the fence once again. I can see Jake and Norman standing there.

"OK," Shaq says to us, "these two will watch over you. Your little friend Rhea is busy in the kitchen, helping to prepare our supper; it's going to be delicious. Will you two be OK being left here?" he asks us in a patronising manner.

We both nod at him, not wanting to speak.

"Good," he says. "Norman and Jake, make sure they behave."

"Will do," Jake says, and Norman stands there and smiles at us. Shaq then walks off towards the house while Amrit and I just stand there looking at the fence.

"Well, get on with it then," Norman says.

Amrit gives him a dirty look, and I just look straight at the fence. We pick up the tools and get to work. I look at Amrit and can see what he is planning.

"We want that fence to be good as new," Jake says as they stand there, each with an axe in their hand.

"You know what?" Amrit says to me, beginning to raise his voice.

"Stop talking," Norman tells him.

"We've come too far, Layton—" Amrit explains, making me think of what we have gone through to get here.

"I told you, stop talking," Norman interrupts.

"...to let some freak tell us what to do," Amrit continues, trying to needle Norman into a reaction.

"I will kill you right now," Norman shouts, trying to get to Amrit. Jake holds him back, and out of the corner of my eye I can see him snarling.

"Get back to work," Jake says to us calmly.

We continue working on the fence, hammering in the nails. Norman comes closer, standing behind us, inspecting our work.

"Layton?" Amrit says.

"What?" I respond, trying to whisper.

"I said no talking!" Norman shouts.

Amrit looks behind at Norman, then back at me. He takes a deep breath and backs away from the fence. He looks at me, then down at the hammer in his hand. I can see his grip tighten.

"Run!" he shouts.

Before I have a chance to respond, Amrit turns around and hits Norman square on the forehead, causing him to fall flat on his back.

"What the fuck?" Jake says, rushing towards us.

"Layton, run!" Amrit shouts as he lunges at Jake. Jake jumps on top of him and holds him down.

I do as he says: I turn, jump over the fence and start running. I keep running as fast as my legs can carry me.

"Shit, shit," I keep repeating as I shift my feet through the snow and into the trees. I run through, avoiding the branches, making sure I don't get caught. I feel as if I am going at a hundred miles per hour, as the sound of Amrit and Jake struggling disappears and the only sound I can hear is that of my feet crunching through the snow.

Under the branches, through the bushes I run. I jump over logs that are in the way; nothing is getting near me. I balance over the snow, making sure not to slow down. I can't slow down, I have to keep going. I have to keep going, I have to, I have to get away.

Then the adrenaline rush begins to die down and my hunger reappears. I start to slow down, feeling tired, and collapse to the ground. I lie there for a good while, trying to get myself back up. I just can't move any more; I can't make myself get up. But I have to get up, I have to get away.

I hear footsteps behind me; I can tell by the sound of the snow crunching. I fight to stand up, and turn around to see Jake standing there.

"Oh, Layton," he says, walking slowly towards me, crunching the snow underfoot. "What are you doing? What did you think you were going to do?" he asks me as if I am stupid.

"Please just let me go," I beg.

"Oh, Layton," he says, "if only."

I turn to try and run away, and he pounces on top of me. I struggle to get away, but then I feel a needle poke into my neck.

It feels like the same sting that I felt when I was drugged by the Union. Slowly, I stop struggling. I lie down on the ground, and Jake stands over me. I look up and can only see the bright whiteness of the sky. I can hear the birds chirping, feel the cold on my face. Then m

When I wake, I am inside. I can tell this because I am warm; it feels like there is a fire beside me. I feel drowsy, and my eyes struggle to open. I look around and there is a giant table in front of me, a chandelier, paintings on the walls and a roaring fire in the corner. I can see food all over the table. It looks amazing; there's potatoes, carrots, bread, you name it, it's all there.

Shaq's mother sits at the head of the table, with Shaq on one side and Norman and Jake on the other. I look over and see Amrit with his hands strung up in the corner of the room. He looks like he's breathing, but really beaten up. On the other side is Rhea, standing there tied to a post with a gag around her mouth.

"Ah, you're awake," Shaq says to me as I look forward and see his mother holding Louise. "Nice of you to join us."

"It's supper time," Norman shouts out.

"Yes, it is, little brother," Shaq says. "It's our time to eat." He pulls up a chair next to me, and I look down and see that my hands are tied to the arms of my chair and my legs to its legs.

"Just kill me," I say.

"Now, that's not the attitude to have." Shaq smirks. "I thought you had more fight in you."

"He's a pussy," Jake shouts as he takes a bite out of a piece of bread.

"Now, it is not our place to judge," Shaq tells him as he continues to devour another piece of bread.

"Why won't you let me leave?" I croak.

"Like I said," he begins, "I have a plan for you." He gets up and looks down at me.

"What plan is that?" I ask him. "What can you possibly want from me?"

"I want you to be one of my beloved servants. We have been here for centuries. Once upon a time, we had a large house with servants, maids, you name it. Why can't we still have that life now? My mother remembers that world," he states, looking around the room.

"It was magical," she expresses to me.

"I'm sure it was," I say to Shaq, feeling bitter inside.

"Yes, it was," Shaq says. "But then, the servants knew obedience. Nowadays we have to teach people it. We've had many other servants in the past, but this time, I think we will get it right." He walks over to the other end of the table.

"The meat is really good," Norman says to me.

"Yes, it is," Shaq agrees. "You see, we will always find a use for you – how nice is that? In life and death, you can always have a use to us."

"I thought you brought me here to take care of cattle," I say.

Shaq looks at me and walks over to this plate with a massive silver lid over it. He smiles.

"For a place to have purpose, it needs order," he says, looking around the room, presenting it to me with his arms wide open.

"Hear, hear," Jake says, raising a glass.

"My brothers and I have lived here all our lives," Shaq says.

"Now so does my baby," his mother adds.

"That's right, Mother," Shaq says. "You see, Layton, cattle are involved, and don't get me wrong, they are the reason you are here. However, you're not looking after the cattle." He places his hand on the lid of the plate. "You are the cattle."

He lifts the lid, and I feel faint. I feel sick and drowsy once again. Under that lid, on that plate, is a head. It's Jane, it's her head just lying there. I look around and I can see that they have been eating her. They have been eating my friend. I lean over and

I begin to feel sick, like I could throw up. My forehead begins to sweat and I can feel it running down my face.

"You're sick!" I shout. I glance over and can see Rhea begin to cry. She looks like she is trying to say something, but the gag keeps her from making any noise.

"You see, Layton," Shaq says to me, "you will always be of use to me." He then clicks his fingers and Jake walks through a door at the end of the room.

"Why?" I ask him. "She was a human being. You're a monster!"

"The world is about survival," he responds. "The fittest will always survive."

Jake comes back in, carrying Becky. He kneels her down at the end of the table and I look forward at her.

"Let her go," I demand as they force her down. I can see panic in her eyes. She is breathing very heavily and I know she wants to say something, however she looks like she just doesn't have the strength.

"You see," Shaq says, pulling out a knife and waving it in front of himself, "this one is of no use to me now, so there is only one thing to do."

Becky looks up at me and closes her eyes.

"No!" I cry, and without hesitating, Shaq cuts her throat.

I sit there stunned, watching the blood pour out of Becky. Rhea is screaming, trying to speak, but can't because of the gag around her mouth. Becky coughs a few times, choking on her blood, as if she is trying to say something; then stops and just collapses into herself.

"Oh, fun," Norman shouts, and runs over to Becky and rubs his face in her blood.

Jake then gets up and comes walking towards me. He unties my hands and feet, but I am in too much shock and too upset and sick at what they have done to fight. I just collapse on the end of the table, tears falling from my eyes. I feel light-headed.

I glance once again at Jane's head on the table, then look down at Becky curled up on the ground with blood gushing out of her neck. It all becomes a bit much and I throw up all over the ground, making me feel even more light-headed and faint.

"I expected so much from you, Layton," Shaq says whilst walking towards me. "Now, I guess we will have to think of another use for you."

Jake grabs me and drags me away. I am taken through the door, out through the hallway and into another room. In there is another cage, empty, just big enough for one person. He opens the cage and throws me in, and I collapse as Jake locks the door and leaves me there. I curl up at the bottom of the cage and it feels just as cold as the other one was. The only difference is, now I can't get that vision out of my head. I worry about the others; what is going to happen to them? I still feel sick and faint. I look around and everything is blurred.

Why? I ask myself as I lie there, surrounded by darkness. I am left here, unable to talk, unable to move. I feel numb, I feel sick, and like all I want to do is die. I want to die right now, I can't take being in this world any more. Nobody deserves this. I want rid of them all, and rid of this place. If dying means that I can find a way out, then so be it. Maybe if I die I can finally be free.

34

Moments, seconds, minutes, hours – who cares any more? All I see when I look around is this room. I am still in the cage; the one I can barely stand and walk around in. I am in a tiny room, with nothing but walls and a door. I have come to my own personal cell. I guess this is my new home.

There's literally nothing else in here, it's just some dark, grey, dusty room. It doesn't even smell of anything special. Well, I say that; there is a rotten smell in here. I guess I'm not the first person to be put in here. In the dim light, I look at the walls, and there are some red stains on there. The light on the ceiling lets me see just enough to keep me from going insane. Then the light goes out, the bastards.

I lie here, trapped and shut away from the world outside, and I start to think to myself; there's nothing else I can really do now. Becky, my God, Becky – shit, why did any of this have to happen to a good person like her? I watched her die, I saw the blood pour out of her neck. Then that freak Norman had to go and rub his face in it, like he was cleansing himself. I can't believe it, I can't believe what has happened to her. I can't believe what has happened to all of us. They were eating Jane, like she was a piece of meat. They don't care about anybody, they only care about themselves.

I dragged my friends away from the Union to bring them to a place where they would be so cheaply disposed of. It's all my fault. If I hadn't made everybody leave Leicester, we wouldn't be in this mess; we would all be safe. All I ever do is lead people to their deaths. I try to be this funny, clever guy; cheap price for a non-existent future.

All I can feel now is pain. There is a horrible pain pressing down on my chest, forcing me to keep my eyes open to what I have done. I need to sleep, I need to close my eyes. I close my eyes to try and get the visions out my head, but it doesn't help. Nothing is leaving me. I even try moving my body, tossing and turning, but nothing happens. I still only see Jane's head on that plate and Becky on the floor. What about the others? What are they going to do to Mark, Amrit or even Rhea? What are their plans for Louise? What are they going to do to me? I have to save them, I have to get us all out of here before they hurt any more of us.

"Let me out," I shout, getting to my feet. I walk over – well, as much as I can walk – to the cage wall and wrap my fingers around. "Let me out now, you fuckers," I scream, shaking the cage, trying to break it. "Let me out of here! I'm going to kill all of you."

Nothing happens; all I see is the darkness of the room.

"Fuck them," I say to myself, walking away from the cage wall. "Fuck them all, fuck all of them. What do I do, what do I have to do?"

The problem I have is getting Jane out of my head. I keep seeing Norman eating her flesh, just eating parts of her and smiling like the miserable fuck he is. They waited for her to die; they wanted her dead. They wanted her to have her baby, then they didn't even care if she stayed alive or not; they just wanted to dispose of her. Like Shaq said, she was of no use to them, so they ate her. They fucking ate her, then killed Becky. I feel awful, I feel sick. I lean over and whatever food is left inside me just comes out. It's mostly spit now.

"Fuck," I shout as I look at my puke. It's a poor excuse for puke, just leftover water really.

What if I lie down for a bit? I need to rest; I need to get my strength up. I need to be able to survive all of this. I lie down, avoiding the vomit, and look at the ceiling. I close my eyes, then open them immediately, because I can't seem to get the vision out my head. Oh my God, they're probably going to eat Becky as well. Closing my eyes seems to be my worst enemy at the moment.

I sit up, leaning against the wall and looking at the cage. I scan the bars, searching for a way to break out. What if I unclip the bottom of it, maybe detach the cage from the floor, then just push it over? Perhaps that could be the way out. I guess that could work, I don't know.

"Fuck," I say to myself. "I want to go!" I look around at the ceiling of the cage. "I want my mum," I cry. It is the first time in years that I have called out to her, but now seems like the best time to do so. I want her there to just hold me and tell me that everything is going to be OK. I want her to tell me that I am going to get out of here, that she loves me. I think of her for the first time in years, and for the first time in a long time, I remember her face.

After a while the cage is starting to play with my mind. I know it's playing with my mind, but I can't help but feel it is real. The cage grows wider and looks like I have more room. It expands and the floor looks like I can roll over it. Then within an instant it collapses and closes up, as small as a paper slit. This continues for the next hour as I just sit there in the cage, staring at the wall.

"I could really do with one of Amrit's pills right about now," I say to myself as I look up at the ceiling. "Some rabbit is just what I need." I need something that'll let me escape from here, physically or in my mind, I don't care; I just want some part of me away from this place.

Then I hear a noise. I look up and a light bulb I didn't notice before flares into life. This is brilliant; my eyes hurt a little bit but I don't care, at least I can see things now. I jump to my feet and look around. Maybe they're going to let me out; maybe I'm going to be free. The door to the room opens slightly. I think they've come to their senses; maybe they're going to let me out.

I then see a bowl come sliding into the room and under this slit in the cage; something I had not noticed until now. It looks like porridge. The door shuts and I am left alone with the food. I kneel down and dip my finger in it. It's cold and lumpy. I don't care, I'm starving. I shovel the porridge into my mouth, and the taste of cement comes to mind; cold, stale cement, however it's doing the trick. I keep eating, and by the end, I am even licking the bowl. Then as soon as I am finished, the light goes off and I am plunged back into darkness.

I need to piss; how about I go for a piss? I walk over towards the corner of the cage. I don't want to piss in my cage; I have to sleep here. I make sure to aim outside and just let it all out. It feels amazing, I am just flowing until I suddenly start to feel tired. Finally, I need to get some sleep; this is killing me. As soon as I am done I lie down and rest my eyes.

"Just one more drink," I hear Becky saying.

I walk forward and see myself in the dorm at the Union. I look around at the pasty white walls that I have come to miss.

"Down it, down it," Ryan chants.

I continue to walk forward, guided by the voices in the background.

"Let's do shots," Mark announces.

"Getting smashed now," Amrit says.

I walk into the room and look at them all sitting there, drinking away.

"Come sit down, Layton," Rhea says. "Jane's off her face."

"I'm not that drunk," Jane slurs.

I chuckle to myself and sit down with them.

"OK, I dare Becky to down this glass," Mark says, pouring a glass of hooch. Becky looks at it, then downs it in one and everyone cheers.

"You want a drink, Layton?" Amrit asks, leaning over for a glass.

"OK," I say, holding my hand out.

"If you down that," Jane says, "I'll give you a night of passion."

"Here she goes again," Rhea says, chuckling to herself. I look at her and smile, feeling safe.

"What?" Jane asks.

I look at them all, smiling yet unable to stop the tears forming in my eyes.

"Down the hatch," I say, croaking slightly as I speak. I raise the glass, still smiling, and down it as I look up at the ceiling. I even feel myself smile as I'm downing the drink.

I then look down, and they all look strange; murky somehow.

"You guys all right?" I ask them.

They begin to turn grey, and start sweating a lot. I feel my face crease as they all turn and look at me. Rhea has an eye missing all of a sudden, Amrit and Mark are missing an arm each, and the rest of them just look rotten. They all look like the infected, and they jump at me. I scream.

I open my eyes and look around. I am still here in this shithole. The only difference is that I am becoming accustomed to the darkness. You only have to be in the dark for so long until the darkness becomes your version of light. I don't want to go out like this, lying in a cage, withering away like some useless animal.

The hours pass by – well, it feels like hours, I don't know what time it is at the moment. Is it daytime, is it the evening? I have no idea where I am right now. Well, I do, I don't know. I am just confused; I don't know what I am doing any more. What is the point, really? What is the point of all this right now, after looking back on what I once was and where I had once been?

Why? I ask myself as I lie there on the cage floor, looking around and making sense of the cage once again. I want to go back to that time when we were all together; even when we left the Union and we were all in the shop, our own little campsite. That was my happiest time. I want to go back to that time.

After being alone for so long, it's nice to be with people who actually care about you. The thing is, though, when I was alone, I didn't need to care about others. My main priority was me and me alone. Maybe that was my happiest time.

35

Sitting in this room still, nothing's changed here. Then I see the door has opened again, and a cigarette is thrown in with a lighter. Well, this could come in handy. I look at it for a moment, thinking it could be some kind of trap. They must have dosed it with something; some kind of poison. You know what, fuck it, I'll have it. I lean over and reach through the bottom of the cage, grab it, sit back against the wall and spark up my cigarette. It tastes absolutely amazing, warm and luscious.

As the smoke engulfs me, I see somebody standing outside the cage. I know who it is.

"What do you want?" I ask as Adam stands there looking at me in the cage. I take another drag on the cigarette before speaking to him again. "Can I help you with something?" I ask.

He just stands there staring at me from outside the cage.

"I know you're not real," I say as I take another drag. "Say something, then," I shout.

He begins to walk forward, slowly, towards the cage.

"What are you doing?" I ask.

He slowly creeps forward and moulds into the cage. I move backwards, feeling very uncomfortable.

"Go away," I shout as he keeps coming forward. "No, go away!"

He is now inside the cage, and walks towards me and looks me.

"No, no, go away," I scream. I cover my eyes to try to avoid looking at him. "No, please, no!"

I close my eyes. Then within a moment, as soon as I open them, he is gone.

Smoking seems to keep me going. Adam disappears, but I keep on smoking just to get to the end of it all. I get to the filter of the cigarette, and I feel disappointed. I put it out, feeling like I could do with another smoke. My chest burns and my mouth is dry from the tobacco.

"What a fucking day," I say to myself. "Sleep."

I lie down on the floor, resting my head. Perhaps that's what I need. It wasn't that long ago that I rested; I don't even know if it is morning right now. Could be mid-afternoon for all I know. Only way to find out is to look outside, however there is no way of me getting outside so I can have a look. I am just stuck here in this cage of mine, nowhere to go.

Sitting here, I drift off as I just about manage to close my eyes.

I feel like I am falling, just falling further and further down. It's like a spiral, and I'm starting to feel dizzy. Spinning around, I fall further and further down, through the ground and all of the buildings, past all the earth. I tumble down and finally land in water. I always seem to find myself in water.

The water is cold, yet warm at the same time. However, the falling does not stop. I keep on falling, deeper into the water. I look up and try to swim to the top, but I just keep swimming in the same spot, not getting anywhere. My hands begin to go numb, and my legs follow.

I want to get out, I want to be away from here. I am drowning, suffocating in this place. I am closed in, wanting to break out. I want to be free from this tyranny, free from all this shit that surrounds the people I love. I want to keep my eyes shut, but my dreams are just as awful as the world around me. It is continuous, no way of getting out, no way of being free. I want to hold myself high and leave through the front door to a better tomorrow. However, tomorrow always seems so far away.

My eyes hurt as the light is switched on. I look up and the bulb blinds me. I look down and stare right in front of me to avoid the pain.

Then I hear a noise. The door to the room gradually begins to open, and I see a shoe. Shaq walks in, carrying a chair with him. He wears that wig he had on when he kidnapped us, and the mask as well. He places the chair in front of the cage and sits right in front of me. He pulls off the mask and the wig, throwing them on the floor. He sits back as I lean against the wall, brushing his hair back and glaring right at me.

"Welcome," I say sarcastically. I try to be calm, however I can't help but feel a slight panic as he looks through me. "Tell me," I begin to ask, "why the fucking mask?"

He looks down at the mask and wig, smiles to himself, then looks back at me.

"It's just something to give people that first little scare," he explains. He looks at me and sighs to himself. "What a shame," Shaq says to me. "You could've been a really promising part of our lives here. You could have been my trusted servant, and instead you ran away like a disloyal toad."

"I would never want to be around you," I say to him. "You are a monster who just brings people here to work them to death, then you turn them into meat and eat them like animals."

"What is a monster?" he asks. "You call me a monster; however I can look at you and call you one. You are a person who makes sarcastic comments without caring how they will affect others, which makes you a monster."

"Oh, come off it, Shaq," I shout, hearing the frustration in my voice.

"What?" he asks. "You are the epitome of selfishness."

"Am I now?" I say. "You have the nerve to take issue with me being sarcastic when you are out there, torturing my friends, punishing them for no reason, then killing and eating them? God knows how many people you have done that to throughout the years."

He looks at me as he brushes his hand through his hair.

"Well, I don't put people down for the sake of it," he says.

"Well, I don't eat people," I retort.

He sighs to himself before speaking again.

"Why do I eat people?" he says. "It's not because I want to. I do what I do because the world I am living in asked me to make this trade. The world I live in creates people like me who have to feed on others to ensure we ourselves are not killed. We are now a society of survivors, and to survive, we sometimes have to do things we may not want to do."

I look at him and think that he is talking so much shit right now.

"Like working with border monkeys?" I say, far more frustration simmering in my voice than before.

"Do you even know what a border monkey is?" he asks me.

I look at him blankly.

"I thought as much," he says. "A border monkey is somebody who has no promise, a person who has no idea where they are going, why they are alive. They go through life without that purpose that we all need. Long ago, they were people on the fringes of society; it was a term that was given to people who just went around causing trouble. Around these parts they were stereotyped as people with stupid leather jackets, big boots and motorbikes.

"Some people even try to play on this stupid name. If you go to other parts of the county, they might have a different definition of the term 'border monkey'. I take in your so-called border monkeys and give them food, they give my land security, and it's a perfect match to keep my family alive. They call me the head monkey, fucking head monkey; I have a purpose. You are a person with no purpose, no sense of being. That makes you more of a border monkey than I will ever be."

I look at him and feel pure fury at what he is saying.

"I don't kill people," I state very clearly, feeling the anger inside me build up and brew to what could be like a volcanic explosion.

"You will," he says. "You don't kill because you want to keep that last shred of humanity, but you will lose it. We all do."

He pulls out a necklace from his pocket.

"What's that?" I ask him bluntly.

"This," he tells me, "is my last piece of humanity. Before I became this monster, as you call me, I had a normal life. I had a wife, I had a child, my little boy. I had everything a person could ask for." He wipes his face, planning his next words. "They were killed by my brother."

I look at him, stunned.

"That's right," he says to me, "there used to be four of us. I found my brother Clark in bed with my wife once. I thought she was having an affair, then she told me that he had forced himself on her. I told my brother that I wouldn't let that stand, and that he should leave my family forever. Now, my brother Clark wasn't the kind of person to take kindly to being told what to do, so what did he do? He killed my wife Clara and my son Ralph."

I can see him beginning to well up as he continues to speak. "He strangled them to death. That means he looked into their eyes as the light went out of them." He wraps the necklace around his hand. "Once I found out, I didn't even hesitate; I just got an axe and cut his head off. That was the day I lost my humanity."

"I'm sorry," I say with some scrap of sympathy.

"You have nothing to be sorry for," he responds. "In this

352

world, you have to fight in order to survive. I didn't fight and my family was taken from me by my own brother. Jake and Norman are not the brightest sparks, but they are loyal."

He puts the necklace back in his pocket, and I can see him rummaging around again.

"Look," he says to me as he pulls out his hand. I look at him and can't quite make out what he's holding.

"What's that?" I ask, confused.

"You see this?" he says, showing me the object and rolling it around. It is a small, flat, circular object. "This here is called a coin. The value of this coin was one pound sterling. You couldn't get much for it; probably a packet of sweets and some snacks and that is about it. This woman," he holds out the coin and points to the face imprinted on it, "was the Queen, our head of state. She was pictured on our money at the time of civilisation. Nevertheless, in the paper trade of how things have come to be, this has no value now," he explains while rolling the coin in his hand as I look at its tainted golden brown colour.

"You see, it has a lot more value than it ever did. You might not be able to get things for it, but it means so much more now. It is our history, our heritage. This is one of the last elements of our once great civilisation."

"Fair enough," I say.

He then flicks the coin up, catches it and puts it back in his pocket.

"Here," he says, and pulls out a cigarette. He lights it up and pokes it through the cage bars. I get hold of it and begin to smoke it. He then pulls one out for himself, lights up and begins to smoke.

"Thanks," I say as I puff on the cigarette.

"It's OK," he says as he continues to smoke his cigarette, breathing the smoke into the cage as he does so. "You see," he says between drags, "I have lost too much in this world to have sympathy for others. My family has lost too much. My mother was used to a way of life that she does not want to forget. She wears her fucking wedding dress, for goodness' sake, to remember the good times. I remember the good times from when I was child. We had servants, status, we had a purpose. Then the world took that purpose away from us, and now I want it back. My son could've been my heir, but he is gone now. However, I can't give up on my dream of rebuilding my family's position in the world. You know this country we live in. This grand, wonderful land. We used to be called the United Kingdom. Great Britain. We once had an empire. A quarter of the globe was in the palm of our hands. We held it, moulded it and formed it to how we wanted it. God was supposed to create the world in the image he wanted. However, we did that when we ruled. So that meant we were gods among men."

"Why are you telling me this?" I ask, a little baffled by all of this information.

"Because you are going to die," he says to me. "I wanted to tell you a little about me before I let you go." He looks around at the cage, then back at me. "I have lost count how many people I have seen come and go in here. Now it's you." He gets up and begins to walk out. "It's been nice knowing you, Layton."

Well, I guess that's my sentence: death.

I sit there staring at the wall as the light switches off once again, and then I see the water. I only see the surface; seems as if it is miles away. I try to swim up there, however I just don't seem to be getting anywhere. I am stuck in the same place, unable to move, unable to get any closer to where I want to be. I close my eyes and see only the water, nothing surrounding me but water. I can't breathe, I can't move; I feel like I am suffocating. I'm trapped.

I open my eyes and see somebody in front of me who I did not want to see again for a long time.

"Hello, Layton," the person says to me.

"General Singh," I say as I look at him looking down at me.

He is standing inside the cage with me, and I stand up to try and move away from him.

"How are you today?" he asks me with the usual sarcasm in his voice.

"What are you doing here?" I ask him as he walks towards me.

"I've come to see you," he says, walking ever closer.

"You're not real," I say as he keeps walking towards me.

"Of course I am," he says.

"No, you're not," I state, beginning to panic.

"I am as real as you wish me to be," he says. He walks around the cage and looks back at me. "Quite a little pickle you've got yourself in here, isn't it?"

"I don't need you here," I shout.

"Frustrated, aren't we?" he says. He looks around. "You didn't want to be part of my Union because you wanted a better life. I see you've found that now, haven't you?" he says condescendingly.

"I'll get out," I say.

"How are you going to do that?" he asks. "Will you try and talk your way out? Fight your way out? How exactly are you going to get out? You had a home with us, a place where you could have been somebody. You could have been a powerful man. That's what the world is about now: taking charge. Somebody needs to take charge of the world, somebody needs to be in control. Without control, the world is just plunged into chaos."

"Seems like everybody has an expectation of me," I say.

He looks at me and smirks slightly.

"Well, you are a person who is very likeable, to some." He looks around, then smiles to himself once again. "How are the friends you left with?"

I snarl as I glare at him.

"Don't." I try to shut him down, glaring at him hoping to not do anything I might regret.

He just chuckles to himself as he paces up and down the cell.

"Just remember, they are all going to die," he says.

I look at him, feeling fiercer than before. I pull back my fist and throw a punch at him, however I just fall through him and land on the ground. He turns with his hands behind his back and smiles at me.

"Enjoy that, did you?" he asks me sarcastically.

I get to my feet, walk straight up to him and glare right into his eyes.

"No, they're not," I tell him. "They're not going to die here."

"So you say," he responds, and his smile becomes far more serious. "Come back," he offers. "The world needs people like us, people who can take control."

"I've seen your control, and I didn't like what I saw."

"Oh, this?" he sighs.

I then turn, and there is one of the experiments I saw, the man with no arms. I turn around again, and there's another experiment behind me.

"What are you doing?" I ask General Singh, beginning to panic.

"It was because of this you wished to leave," he says to me. "But I want to bring education back to the world."

"With you at the centre of it," I state.

"I do it for them," he says. "If they praise me for it, that is their choice."

I don't want to see him anymore. I look around and feel agitated. I keep looking up and down, feeling my body begin to panic.

"Get out. Get out, get out, get out!" I shout, closing my eyes with my hands on top of my head.

He laughs at me, just laughing and laughing. I spin around, shouting that I want him to leave, I want him out of here. All he does is stand there and laugh. I continue to spin around in a circle, trying to get him out.

Then the laughter stops. I look up and I am in another dark room; one without cages and or doors, just a room with a spotlight and blackened walls. I look towards the spotlight and see a figure sitting on a chair. I walk towards the figure, wondering who it could be, yet at the same time thinking I should step back and move away. But my curiosity gets the better of me, urging me forward.

I look at the figure sitting in the chair. It is a man, and he is tied up with his hands behind his back and his head pointing downwards.

"Please help me," the man says as he looks up at me. It is the man General Singh experimented on in front of me.

"No, please, no," I shout.

His expression then changes from worry to a very troubling grin, and he begins to laugh. General Singh appears behind him, placing his hands on his shoulders and joining in the laughter. I cover my eyes, trying to block them out. I feel like the room is spinning around me as I breathe heavily, trying not to peer through my fingers.

Then all of a sudden, the laughter stops. I am hesitant to bring my hands away from my face, however with great reluctance I do so, peering over my fingers. I see the cage wall, and decide it is time to look up.

General Singh, the man and all the chaos have gone, and I am once again stuck alone in the cage. I feel a soft tingle down my spine, fully aware that this is not the first non-drug-related acid trip I will have while I'm here. I am struggling to keep my eyes from watering, remembering what that man must have gone through, what all those people General Singh and the Union were put through, and I am frozen by guilt and sadness.

Then I see Adam sitting in the corner of the room, outside the cage. I collapse against the wall and slide down to the floor. I sit there, leaning against the wall, staring at the ceiling. I look forward, I look up, but no matter where I look, I only see Adam sitting in the corner looking back at me. He looks at me, and I look back at him.

I curl up in the corner of the cage and close my eyes. I feel cold. I try to warm myself up, but nothing seems to work. Yet something miraculous happens, as I close my eyes, drift off and finally manage to fall asleep.

36

Water everywhere. I am in the middle of an ocean, an ocean that shackles me to the pits of Hell. I can't even see the bottom. I need to get out of here, I need to keep swimming, keep swimming to the top. I know I can get out of here if I can only swim my way out.

I keep thrusting my arms back and forth, unable to move. Gradually I force myself further and further up. I can see somebody looking at me in the distance. I can't make out who it is. I look once again, and I begin to realise who it is. It's my mum. I don't want to see her right now; I don't want her to see me with gallons of water in my stomach. I swim further, gradually getting there, feeling the waves pass me as I use all of my strength.

"Come on," I say out loud with a mouthful of water. I keep going and going, until I see somebody floating past me. It's Adam floating past, unable to stop.

"Why?" a voice asks behind me. I look back and see Ryan floating past me, unable to stop.

I have to get out of here, I have to survive. I want to survive. Should I survive? Can I survive this?

"Keep going," I say, fighting through the water.

I swim and swim, trying to get there. The light is shining, I have to reach it. I stretch my hands out in front of me, trying to touch the surface. I can see a light up there; I know I am getting to freedom. Not long now, just need to swim a little further and I'll be there.

I eventually touch the surface and it feels cold and hard.

"Where are you going?" a voice says.

It's General Singh hovering nearby. I look up and see nothing but the clear blue sky. Then something tugs at my leg. I look down and it's an infected holding on to my leg, pulling me down. It pulls me further and further down, and I keep trying to shake it off but it just keeps pulling me.

"Shit," I say.

I manage to shake it off and swim a little further to the top. I reach the surface – well, I think I've reached the surface, I place my hands there and all I feel is ice. I feel around more, but it is nothing but ice. I try to hit it, to break through, but I am trapped.

"No escape," a voice says. I look behind me and see Rhea floating away from me.

I then see a group of infected swimming up towards me, grabbing my legs. They start to pull me down again, away from the icy surface. I struggle a little, then stop. I float down, the water engulfing me, crawling around my face. I feel it stroking my hair and seeping into my clothes. What's the point in trying? Nothing is going to come of this; all I am going to do is suffer more. I might just let myself drift away.

I guess this is where my story ends, where I must close the book. Everything I see goes black.

"Layton!" a voice calls out to me.

I move my head around, trying to find some light, yet all I see is darkness.

"Layton!"

I finally open my eyes and look around. I see a place that I vaguely recognise: a large field with a row of brown shacks in front of me, and one in particular that I have not seen in a long time.

"Layton!" the voice calls again.

I turn around and finally see who is calling out my name. I am taken aback by what – or should I say, who – I see.

"Mum!" I say.

"My little Layton," she says as she walks towards me holding her arms out. She has on the long, colourful shawl she always used to wear, her hands look as perfect as ever, and her smile is one I will never forget.

"Mum," I call out, feeling excited and confused. "It's actually you," I state, feeling safe for the first time in years.

I rush over to her and hold my mum in a close embrace. We stand there holding each other for what feels like hours; I don't care, I just don't want to let go. Her jet-black hair smells, as always, of almonds, and her smile is as welcoming as ever when I look into her brown eyes.

"Now," she says as she begins to let go, "come with me." She turns around and takes my hand, heading towards the shack I recognise so well. I know this place. This used to be my home when I was growing up. I haven't thought of this place in many years.

"My God," I say as we walk inside. I look around and see an old room which I spent many happy years in. There is one bed, a couple of chairs and a stove. I look outside briefly to see the other shacks lined up, like our own little neighbourhood. "The commune," I say as I smile at my mum.

She smiles back at me and nods. "Are you hungry?" she asks.

Her famous stew is cooking away on the stove. I can see the lamb melting in the pod with the smoky gravy making it as moist as ever. I know this room. My mum used to sleep on the floor and me and Adam slept in the bed. She would do anything to make sure we were comfortable, even if it meant she had to suffer.

"The food is hot, I'll get you a bowl," she states, turning around and walking towards the stove.

"Wait," I call out.

She turns and looks at me, a little confused. "What is it, my baby?" she asks.

I look at her and can't help but realise how much I miss her right now. "This can't be real," I say.

She smiles and walks towards me, places her hand on my face and strokes my cheek. Her hands feel incredibly soothing as she strokes my face, making me feel safe.

"This is your memory," she states, and suddenly I feel disappointed. "It will always be real."

I look at her and all of a sudden, I feel nothing but sadness within me.

"I just wish that I could be there to see you grow up, become a man; tell you to shave, see you have children and be happy," she says.

My throat begins to feel heavy. "All those years lost," I say.

"The years are lost, yes," she begins to explain to me, "but I am always with you. You have never lost me."

"I miss you," I say, feeling my eyes begin to water.

"I miss you too, my baby," she says, stroking my face once again, giving me the comfort only she can bring. "You are my special little guy, my special little boy; I miss every day that we are not together."

Then something catches my eye. I look over and see children playing outside. I walk out of the hut and my mum joins me. Two young boys are running around, chasing one another, laughing and smiling.

"That's me," I say as I see the five-year-old me running around with Adam. We are chasing each other, laughing and looking as if we are as free as the clouds.

"You used to smile so much," Mum says as we look on, smiling to each other.

"I don't know what to do, Mum," I tell her. I look at her and feel ashamed. "I've ruined so much; I just feel nothing inside."

Her face begins to change. "Nothing?" she repeats in an angry voice.

I look away, feeling my face slide and my head drop down.

"Look at me, Layton Rai," she demands.

I look at her and see her glaring right at me.

"I never raised you to just give up. All I want to do is go back to those years and hold you in my arms one last time. But I can't, and you have to be strong. None of this is worth giving up. You have so much that is not worth giving up on. You are a fighter."

I look down, feeling like I am in a lot of trouble. She then places her hand on my chin and raises my head up to look back at her.

"Layton, what do we do when we feel stuck?" she asks me.

I look at her and feel good that I know the answer.

"We find a way," I say.

"Exactly," she says, wiping my eyes. "Find a way, Layton," she demands of me.

"I love you, Mum," I tell her, knowing I will never have a chance to tell her again as I feel myself begin to drift off.

"Your mother will always love you, and I will always be with you," she says as I begin to drift away from her.

I then feel the darkness engulf me, and find myself once again in water. I guess a weaker man would just give up now. No! Not like this, I won't go down like this. I have to save my friends, I have to save my family. I look down at the infected holding on to me and start to fight them off. A sudden strength builds up within me, making me feel invincible.

"Fuck off!" I shout at them through the water, and manage to kick them away. I watch as each one floats away, still trying to grab at me. They groan as they float further and further into the depths below.

I swim for what feels like miles. I keep going, not looking down, not wanting to give up. I swim up towards the surface and come across the ice once again. I scratch the ice a few times to try and escape. It makes no difference. I realise then that there is only one thing I can do. I hit the ice over and over, feeling it push down on my hand. However, instead of wincing from the pain, I just hit it again, using all of my strength to fight though the water to make sure my fist reaches the ice.

I hit it once more and see Ryan looking down at me. "You can save us," he says as I hit the ice.

I hit it again and see Becky looking back at me. "It's not your fault," she says as I hit the ice over and over.

I hit it again and see my younger self, looking around in the woods from when I ran, leaving Adam behind.

"Come on, Layton," Amrit shouts as I hit the ice again, and I see my younger self again looking scared and confused as to how he can get away. I see my scared young face, wanting to be free and safe.

"Do it for us," Mark says as I strike the ice once more, and cracks start to appear.

"Do it for me," Rhea calls.

I hit the ice again and then stop for a moment as I see my mum looking back at me. The cracks start to get larger and larger, and I see my younger self, breathing heavily, looking scared and cold. I just want to hold him, tell him he will be OK, that he will be all right in the end. I want to tell him to never regret anything, never look behind him and feel that he has let everybody down.

"Do it for all of us," Mum says to me as I hit the ice again. The cracks continue to get larger from my repeated blows.

"I'll do it for you," I say, seeing nothing but the surface. The ice cracks a little more. "I'll do it for my friends. I'll do it for my family," I shout, pounding the ice once again. "And I'll do it for me," I shout one last time, and break through, feeling the crunch as my hand smashes the ice.

I grab what I can of the edges and pull the surrounding ice down, forming an exit. I dig more and more to make a hole big enough for me to climb out. I continue to dig until I see a large, gaping hole in the ice. I look at it and realise I have created an exit; just enough room for me to get out of here.

I quickly swim through and feel the cool breeze on my face. I place my hands on the edge and grip with all my strength, feeling my arms strain as I pull myself up. I lift and roar out loud as I raise myself out of the water. The cold air surrounds me, covering me in its frozen blanket. It's comforting somehow, and I welcome it, longing for it to stay a little longer.

I move forward, raising myself out of the hole, kneeling beside the watery pit I was once trapped in. I rise to my feet and stand tall. I see mountains, miles away in the distance, and a blanket of ice surrounding me. I lean back, closing my eyes, and feel my textured freedom. I breathe as new strength rises within me; I feel like I have found a new part of myself. The cold soothes my insides, making me stronger by the second. I feel like a lion amongst the cubs, like a king amongst the people, a god amongst the worlds. I take one more breath and open my eyes.

I sit up and scream with joy. I look around and see that I am still in the cell. Adam is sitting in the corner, looking back at me. I look down and see a cigarette on the floor, probably left here from earlier. I look at Adam, and I look down at my hands. I then get up and walk towards him and he stands and looks back at me.

"I'm sorry for what happened," I say to him. "I have always said I'm sorry, but I never really believed it myself. Now I am coming to know who I am. I know you forgive me, I know you won't hold it against me. Now I have to forgive myself. I have to let you go. Not because I do not love you; it's because I want you to be free of me, just as I want to be free of you. I love you, Adam. You will always be my brother."

Tears drip down my cheeks. Adam places his hand on the cage, and I do the same, touching his hand. I feel his skin on mine, sensing a bond I will never forget. I look at him and he looks back at me. He smiles, then slowly drifts away from my vision. He disappears and I see nothing after but the wall behind him.

"Goodbye," I tell him, and then fall to the ground as soon as he is gone. I look down at the ground, then back up at the ceiling.

I move over towards the wall and sit with my back to it. I look up at the ceiling, as I always seem to. I have become accustomed to the dark now; it just seems normal. I stroke my face, feeling a sense of liberation, of having handcuffs removed from me. A smile creeps across my face.

"I'm ready," I say to myself.

I brush my hair out of my eyes and lean my head back against the wall. I close my eyes for a moment, feeling a peace I have not felt for a long time. Then I open them and feel fierce determination.

37

The light is as bright as ever. My eyes feel a slight prickling, followed by an itching pain as they start to become accustomed to the light. I brush my hair back, feeling how long and ropy it has gotten. I look forward at the door and see it begin to open.

The door swings wide open and two border monkeys come marching in. Norman follows very close behind. They walk in and look in the cage at me. I look back at them and can't help but smile.

"It's time," Norman announces.

"What, no last meal?" I remark sarcastically.

"Shaq sent me," Norman says. "He wanted me to perform the execution. He—"

"I know," I interrupt. "Let's get this over and done with – no point waiting around now, is there?"

They open the door to the cage and walk inside. The two border monkeys grab me by the sides and lift me up. Norman leads us through the cage door and out of the room. I quickly glance back at the cage, knowing that my home of a few days is gone. I honestly am excited to see the daylight, even if it is for the last time.

We walk through the hallway and out to the front of the

house. The breeze hits my face like cold daggers on a piece of warm meat. My feet are dragged across the ground as I try to keep my footing. The border monkeys hold me up by my shoulders, making them feel as if they are going to come out of their sockets.

The outside is blinding. The white snow just crushes my eyes like icebergs crashing into a building. I look down, seeing the footprints I am forming in the snow. The border monkeys don't even look at me as they drag me along.

"Not even a smile?" I ask them sarcastically as they continue to look disgruntled at me.

"Can you shut up, please?" Norman says as we continue to walk through the snow.

For the first time I notice that my shoes have got large holes in them. I don't know why I have only noticed this now; I guess it's because I never really paid attention to them. People don't really wear shoes for style's sake, they just want them to be comfortable. I've had the same pair of shoes for a few years now and haven't had a reason to change them. They're not handy in the snow, though, as the holes keep letting in the cold and wet.

"Why," I ask him. "Can't I have a little fun?"

He's starting to get annoyed, so I decide to ignore my shoes now and just divert all my attention to them instead.

"No," he shouts as we continue to walk through the snow to the other side of the house.

We approach what looks like a felled tree and a tractor, which looks like it hasn't been used in years.

"Now where?" I ask as we continue to walk. "I say we talk about how much we love tits. I love a nice pair of tits. All kinds of tits – round ones, supple ones, and even little perky ones."

"For fuck's sake," one of the border monkeys grunts.

"One thing I love," I say, "is how we can eat so much, feel so fat, then we shit it all out. Don't you think poo is amazing, how it can just slip right out of there?"

"Fuck me," the other border monkey mutters.

"You're very handsome," I tell one of them. "Has anybody told you that you are the most handsome man I have ever seen?"

I look forward to a bloodied circle which we are heading towards. I can see some tools, hammers and screwdrivers, lying around.

"Has anybody ever told you that you look like a mother's dream son-in-law?" I continue, seeing his face grow redder the more I talk to him.

"Does this guy ever shut up?" the border monkey I'm talking to shouts to Norman.

"Layton, shut up," Norman snaps. His face is also turning red as he gets angrier.

"Hey, you," I say to the border monkey. "Oi, you."

"What?" he grunts.

"How about you let me go? I'll make it worth your while, you sexy piece of meat," I say, trying to needle him further.

"Shut up," he shouts.

"Right, here will do," Norman says, pointing at the circle covered in blood.

"Yes, a circle covered in blood which looks like it has seen many killings, such a random choice," I remark sarcastically.

"Shut up," the other border monkey shouts as they stand me in the centre of the circle.

"OK, on your knees," Norman says.

The border monkeys force me to my knees, facing the woods in the distance. I feel the snow seep through my trousers, making my knees even colder.

"Seriously," I say to the border monkey I was propositioning, winking at him, "last chance."

"Shut up!"

I kneel there, staring at the woods in the distance as Norman stands behind me.

"Any last words?" he asks.

"I have a few, if that's OK," I say.

"OK," Norman reluctantly responds.

"I will leave you with a song I was taught," I express gallantly to them as I kneel there staring into the distance. I clear my throat before I start to sing. "This is a song I was taught by somebody when I was just a youngster."

I begin to sing. "Don't go chasing waterfalls, please stick to the rivers and the lakes that you're used to—"

"What the fuck?" the border monkey I was talking to says as I begin to serenade him with what I believe is a great song.

"I know that you're gonna have it your way or nothing at all—"

"What is this he's singing?" Norman asks.

"But I think you're moving too fast," I finish, and quickly roll to the ground, kicking one of the border monkeys in the privates.

"Shit!" one of them shouts as Norman begins to shoot.

I quickly grab the border monkey I kicked, and Norman ends up shooting him in the back. He stares at us as the border monkey falls on top of me, dead, and backs away as the other border monkey edges towards me. I throw the dead border monkey off me, looking at the other goon and Norman peering at me.

"Get him," Norman shouts as he runs away, realising he is out of bullets.

The border monkey jumps on me and I put him in the hold that Becky showed me. I hold him close and he struggles, trying to get free, until he suddenly passes out. I push him to one side, watching Norman run off into the distance.

"OK," I say, getting up and looking at the two bodies. I quickly turn to make my way into the woods, but then the border monkey I thought was unconscious jumps on me.

"Die," he shouts as he holds me down. He hits my head

370

several times, and it feels as if he is pounding it further and further into the ground.

He keeps on going until I punch him in the ribs, causing him to freeze for a moment. He backs off, and I get up and head-butt him in the face. He moves back and I jump on top of him, then look over and see a hammer lying at the side. I try to jump over to get it, but he jumps on top of me, forcing me onto my back.

He tightens his hands around my neck, strangling me. I lean over, trying to reach for the hammer, feeling fainter all the time. I try to hold his hands off, and I can see his face beginning to turn red from the pressure he is putting on me. I can think of nothing else to do but try and blind him.

I poke him in the eyes, causing him to loosen his grip. I then lean over and grab the hammer, hitting him straight in the head. He falls over, and I get on top of him and start hitting him.

"Now you die," I shout as I hit him over and over again until he begins to pass out. I continue to pound him until his head begins to collapse.

The man's face is unrecognisable after I am done hitting him. I look at him and realise I have killed someone. I back away, knowing that I have killed somebody for the first time in my life.

"Shit," I say as I walk backwards, away from him.

I feel tired once again, and collapse to the ground. I feel like there is nothing I want to do right now but rest. I begin to close my eyes, until I see somebody hovering over me. It's Shaq. He grabs me by my shoulder and begins to drag me through the snow.

"Layton, Layton, Layton," he says as he continues to drag me through the snow like a sack of coal. "You couldn't just be a good boy and die, could you?"

I look up and see that he is dragging me further and further into the woods.

"Where are you taking me?" I struggle to speak as I just about manage to find my feet.

"I am going to do what Norman could not," he says as he takes me to the centre of the woods.

I look up and see trees surrounding us. I look down and see the white blanket of snow on the ground.

"It's beginning to snow again," Shaq says as the snow starts to trickle down through the trees to the ground.

He then stands me in the centre of a circle of trees. There is a gap where the snow is coming down, through which I can see the clouds covering the sky and the sun trying to break through. I look up and feel the gentle heat brushing my face.

"You feel that?" Shaq asks me, opening his arms and looking around as the smallest amount of light shines through the little gap between the trees to the ground.

"What?" I ask, a little confused.

"That is God," he says. "If there is any point in believing in a god any more. Do you believe in God, Layton?" he asks me.

"No," I reply, feeling a little surprised that he is talking like this to me. I am too busy thinking, trying to look for a way to escape, and still feeling the pain in my face from earlier.

"Neither do I. However, sometimes I like to come to this place. Feels like if there is a god, this is where he would be. I find this place peaceful, I find it nice," he says, in a far calmer tone than usual.

"I see what you mean," I respond, feeling the snow begin to drip from the trees and land on top of my head, causing my scalp to feel ice-cold, and some of it to trickle down the back of my neck.

"OK," he says, walking towards me with a gun and pointing it in my face.

"Just do it already," I shout.

"No," he responds, throwing the gun to the ground. "I don't want to kill you that quickly. I want to see you suffer." He punches me in the face, and I to fall to the ground. "I know it would make sense to kill you, but that would be too easy. I want you to suffer and I want you to be in pain," he explains as I wiggle around on the ground, feeling the sharp pain in my face.

"That hurt," I say as I look down at the ground, blood coming from my mouth.

"You couldn't just let me have my day, could you?" Shaq shouts, kicking me in the stomach.

I fall to the side, clutching my ribs. He then lifts me up and punches me in the face again.

"Why can't people like you just go, why can't you just die?" he shouts, punching and pushing me to the ground. "You see, I just want my family to be safe. This started when they began letting people in who weren't of this land."

"What?" I ask as he punches me in the face again. The inside of my cheek scrapes against my teeth, leaving a horrible bloody taste in my mouth.

"They say you are a racist if you are against others," he shouts. "But," he begins to speak in a calmer voice, "I just want my people to be safe. I believe that people must stay where they are; that way, civilisation can continue. Too many different cultures led to us all falling apart."

"What are you on about?" I ask.

"You're a brown man," he says. "I am a white man; I don't think we could ever mix." He punches my face again. "My mother taught me this. Maybe she was wrong, maybe she was right. What is right, what is wrong anymore?"

He then grabs me by the collar and punches me in the face again, causing me to black out for a second. I see Rhea lying next to me. He lifts me up and punches me again, and I suddenly see Amrit.

"I just want to be safe. I do it for my family, I say, but no. I do it for me, for me," Shaq shouts, punching me.

I then see us all in the shop, sitting around eating beans and laughing. I can feel the blood running down my face.

Shaq kicks me several times in the side.

"Uh…" I squirm as I feel his boot hit me. I wince when I see the blood trickling from my face to the ground. I cough, and a little more blood splatters from my mouth.

"Why can't I be happy?" he shouts as he kicks me again, and I think about the time in the dorm at the Union. He then grabs me and punches me once more to the ground, and I think of Rhea. I think of when I kissed her and felt the best I have ever felt.

"Uh…" I say again as he suddenly grabs me by my T-shirt. He pulls me up to my feet and stares at me.

"This is where we come to our end," Shaq says as he raises me to my feet.

I look him in the eye, and he looks back at me. I stare at him and feel nothing but hate, yet satisfaction too. I feel that I have a power inside of me, something in me that he can't fight. I can take anything on; I can defeat anyone.

"Goodbye, Layton," he says, reaching behind himself for what looks like a knife, while with the other hand still holding on to my T-shirt.

I stare at him and he brings the knife forward, gently close my eyes, I decide to take a deep breath, and come to a sense of calmness. I then open them, stare right at him and lunge at him. I open my mouth and grip his throat with my teeth, lock my jaw and crunch down, gnashing through the flesh. His body freezes as I bite down harder. I feel his skin break, his blood pour into my mouth, and flesh between my teeth. I feel it crunch as I pull back, ripping his throat out.

Shaq drops the knife, clutches his neck as he staggers backwards, further and further until he falls down. I look down at him, standing over him like I have conquered a country. I then spit his flesh out onto the ground, like a pellet of blood firing from my mouth. He looks up at me, bleeding out, trying to speak. I lean down, take off his boots and put them on, feeling some warmth on my feet. I then take off his jacket and put that on too. Following this, I kneel down, looking at him choking and suffering on the ground.

"Goodbye, Shaq," I say as I get up and begin to walk away from him, knowing he is in pain behind me. I feel accomplished, knowing that he is bleeding, unable to get up, to attack, knowing that I am walking on.

I quickly turn and look away into the distance. Should I go? I could leave and get help, or I could just leave and not come back. I stand there, staring at the wilderness in front of me a moment longer. No, not like this. They need my help; they need me to go and help them. I will save them or die trying.

I turn and face the house in the distance. Time to go help them, to fight for them. Time to save my friends and be free of this place.

38

Knees wet, feet warmish, a jacket on me. I have a choice to make at this point in time. Just forgetting everybody, looking out for myself, is not an option. So all I can do is try and save them, get them out of this shithole and free from it all. I have made the right choice.

I head towards the house, ploughing through the snow with my new boots, trying to get there as fast as possible. Wait – first I should check the shed; Amrit might be there, and he could help me save everybody. I rush over towards it, making sure not to slip. Luckily, Shaq's boots fit me – who would've thought we would be the same size? His long grey coat brings me some warmth. It is definitely not style over comfort.

Jumping over the fence towards the shed, I see the bodies of the two border monkeys still lying there from the fight before. My face is still hurting from all of that, however I can't let a little thing like pain get in my way right now. I've never been a fighter, I could barely throw two punches without falling over myself, but this time I am going to prove all of that wrong. I mean, I've already won another scrap. I am going to get everybody out of here.

There's the shed, I can see it, covered in snow. I run towards it and see a machete on the ground – what's it doing there? Who cares, it's mine now. I pick it up and keep running towards the shed, making sure not to trip over the snow.

Eventually I get to the shed, kick in the door and thunder in. I look to see if anybody is inside, to free them and hopefully get them to help me. There is nobody in the cage, nobody in the shed. Nothing – not a noise, not a sound, nothing to hear and nothing to see. It's empty.

"Shit," I mutter to myself, looking at the empty cage. "That means…"

I look outside at the house and know that everybody is being kept there. The bastards; they are all being kept over there, probably being punished for what I did.

I quickly run out and head towards the house. The snow has become a full-on blizzard and hits me in the face repeatedly, slowing me down. Even when I put my hand up for cover, some of the snow breaks through. I keep running forward as well as I can, making sure the target is met. I rush through the field leading towards the large white house, just making it out through the snow. A light glows from its window.

"The dining room," I say to myself, feeling worried as I start to make the trek towards the front door. I keep running and running, making sure not to look behind me. That will only slow me down.

I rush up to the front door and without hesitation, run straight towards it. Maybe it's unlocked; maybe, I'm not sure. It can't be. I place my hand on the door handle and turn it. It opens – thank God for that.

I run in and hear loud music; sounds like drum and bass I heard years ago. I creep towards the hallway, and can just about hear a voice through the music.

"Take that!" Norman shouts.

I slowly creep forward, trying not to make a sound. Luckily the music masks any sound I do make. I don't want to draw too much attention to myself; I know it sounds bad but if I want to kill these guys, their attention needs to stay on my friends.

"Fuck you!" Rhea cries as I creep a little closer.

"You shut up," I then hear Jake call out.

I walk towards the door leading to the dining room and hear a loud smash and something that sounds like a whip hitting skin.

"Shaq will be here soon. Once he's done with your friend Layton, we can kill the rest of you."

I slowly open the door and creep inside. I crouch down, making sure not to be seen.

"Stop it, you're killing him," Rhea shouts as a whip cracks once more.

I look down and see Amrit lying on the ground in the corner, tied up. I slowly creep towards him and he looks up. I hold my finger to my lips to tell him to be quiet. He turns over and I untie him, making sure the rope around his wrists is completely unwrapped. He gets up and we both hide behind a table, peering over.

"I don't care if he dies," Norman says, cracking the whip again.

I look up and see Rhea kneeling, her hands bound and a leash around her neck being held by Jake. Mark is tied to a chair, blood dripping from him; he looks like he is passing out.

"Is that the best you got?" Mark snarls at Norman, and he hits him again. Mark spits blood from his mouth and glares back at Norman. I look at Amrit and to signal him. He looks back at me and knows what I mean.

"I got Norman," he whispers. I nod to show I understand and we both count down from three, me raising my fingers to signal us in.

"Three, two, one," I whisper, then we both get up and run at them.

"What the fuck?" Jake says as I slash down with my machete.

He blocks it and I jump at him. He grabs me as I try to take him down, and throws me to the ground.

I look over and see Amrit fly at Norman, causing him to hit the radio nearby. The music stops, and Amrit begins to hit him repeatedly. Jake punches me and I manage to block the blows, yet I can't seem to land a punch on him.

Then out of nowhere, he's flung backwards and held back. I stand up and look at him.

"No!" Norman shouts.

Rhea has her bound hands around Jake's neck, pulling harder and harder. Jake tries to break free, but Rhea overpowers him. His face begins to turn blue, and his eyes start to look like tomatoes as they turn a rich red.

"You watch," Amrit shouts at Norman and holds him up, forcing him to watch Jake drifting away.

"Fuck you," Rhea snarls as she pulls harder and harder, sweating from the effort.

Jake's struggling slows down and I can see his grip loosen. Then all of a sudden, he stops moving. Rhea throws him to one side and leans over him. She reaches into his pocket and pulls out a thin, sharp knife. She looks down, and I notice that Jake is still breathing slightly. She then gets on top of him with her hands still bound and starts to stab him in the chest repeatedly.

"Fucking prick," she shouts as she stabs him over and over again, causing blood to gush out of him like a fountain. Covered in his blood, she keeps stabbing until she's made a gaping hole in the centre of his body. Rhea then stops, hair covering her eyes and breathing heavily, coughing slightly with exhaustion.

"Wanker," she shouts as she drops the knife and sits back looking at him.

"You OK?" I ask her.

"Yeah," she responds, getting to her feet.

I take the machete and cut her bonds, setting her free, then look over and see Norman glaring back at us.

"What do we do with him?" I ask as we all look at him whimpering away.

"I think we should do with him what we did with his brother," Amrit says, and Norman begins to squirm.

"No!" he shouts. "Shaq will be here soon, and he's going to kill all of you. Yeah," he says, chuckling, "just you watch when he gets here."

"Shaq's dead," I announce, walking towards him.

"No, you're lying," he says.

"I'm not," I tell him, feeling very proud.

He laughs. "How am I supposed to believe you?"

"Don't you recognise the coat?" I ask him.

He looks at it, then his chuckles become very serious. He looks blankly at me, motionless.

"No," he says. "No, you monster!"

"He's the monster?" Rhea asks, looking at him with an expression of sarcasm mixed with anger.

"I'll kill you all," Norman shouts.

"How?" Amrit asks.

"Um…" Norman hesitates. He looks at us, then pulls out a knife. "Stand back," he says as we edge towards him. He waves the knife around to try and get us to back away from him.

"Come on, Norman," Amrit says calmly, "just give up."

"Never," he responds.

Norman then lunges at Amrit, trying to stab him. Amrit manages to dodge the attack, then grabs him, punching him in the face. Norman staggers, then tries to go for Amrit again. Amrit blocks him and throws him to the ground.

"You prick," he snarls as he climbs on top of him.

"I'm going to kill you," Norman shouts. Amrit then punches him in the face, making his nose bleed.

"You think you can keep us prisoner?" Amrit shouts.

"Torture us, kill us? What you did to Becky, what you did to Jane – who do you think you are?" I have never seen Amrit like this. I have never seen him this angry.

"For my family," Norman says quietly.

Amrit looks down at him and stares right into his eyes, as if he is looking into his soul.

"And this is for mine," he snarls, and puts his hands on Norman's face. I see him moving his hands around, and his thumbs in particular.

"No!"

Norman tries to shout, to move his head and struggle away, but Amrit holds him firmly in place. He places his thumbs on Norman's eyes and begins to press down.

"No, no, please, no," Norman shouts as Amrit applies more pressure.

Eventually his thumbs sink into the eyeballs and Norman screams like a child as blood begins to gush out. Amrit then lifts his head with his thumbs still inside, and bashes it repeatedly until Norman's screams grow fainter and fainter. I look up at Amrit and see him snarling, gritting his teeth with every bash, until Norman finally stops struggling.

Amrit then screams; not like Norman did, this scream is far fiercer. It's more like a roar, animalistic if anything. After he is done, Amrit gets up and wipes the blood off his hands. He turns to me and looks me right in the eyes. I look back at him and feel that he did what he needed to do. It was us or them, I guess.

Rhea runs over to Mark who is sitting, tied up, on the chair, blood gushing out of his face and torso. She unties him and grabs hold of his hands.

"You OK?" I ask Amrit as I walk towards him, looking at him breathing as if the adrenaline is dying down within him.

"Yeah," he says, stunned.

"Come on, Mark," Rhea says, helping him to his feet. She

holds him up, trying to keep him steady. He staggers a bit, but Rhea just about manages to stabilise him.

"Oh," I say, running past Amrit and putting Mark's arm over my shoulder. I help hold him up while Amrit runs over.

"I got him," he says to Rhea, and we start to carry him out.

But Mark doesn't seem to be opening his eyes. He is struggling to walk, breathing very heavily, unable to speak. Rhea stops and stares at him as Amrit and I try to carry him.

"What is it?" I ask her.

She gulps and points to Mark's left side, the side I'm supporting. I take my free hand and put it there. It feels wet, and when I look at my hand, I see blood. I feel his side again and lift his shirt; there's a massive gash there, blood just gushing out.

"Shit," I say. I look up at Mark's eyes and he is struggling to open them, breathing very lightly.

"Here," Amrit says, handing me a cloth. I press it on the wound in Mark's side to try and stem the bleeding, however it just keeps flowing over my hands.

"Come on, we need to be quick," Rhea says.

We move as fast as we can towards the door to the dining room, and Rhea pushes it wide open. We walk out, then she stops again.

"What now?" I ask, frustrated. She has a panicked look on her face.

"Louise," she says.

Amrit and I look at each other, worried.

"You two go," he says to me. "I'll stay with Mark."

"Are you sure?" I ask him. "Don't we need to help Mark too?"

I look over at Rhea and she looks at Amrit as we all try to think of what to do next. I know Amrit by now, and I can see when he is struggling to think of a plan.

"You go," I suddenly hear Mark struggle to say. We all look at him, and I feel a little stuck as to what to do.

"Mark!" Rhea says, surprised.

"I'll keep, don't worry about me. Amrit will keep me safe," Mark states, looking at him.

"OK, you guys go," Amrit says, nodding to us.

"OK," I say. "Let's go."

Rhea and I rush off.

"Where is she?" I ask her.

"In the nursery. They kept her there with their mother," she says as we run up the stairs and towards another brown door.

We look at it, and without hesitating, Rhea pushes the door wide open. Inside, we see all of these old toys, dusty dolls and a cot that looks like it is going to fall apart. Shaq's mother is sitting in the corner, holding Louise in her arms, rocking her. I don't know her name so I guess I will just refer to her as Mother for the time being. A little weird, I know, but it's the only way I can think of to address her.

"Where are my boys?" she asks us innocently, looking around as if she is lost and a little confused.

"We've come to take Louise," Rhea states, not mincing her words.

"You?" Mother says. "You're free, you're not supposed to be free." She then looks at me and becomes hesitant. "What's happening?" she asks, panicking.

"We're taking the child," Rhea demands. "Hand her over now."

"She's my baby," Mother says. "You can't have her!" She stands up, causing the baby to wake.

"Give her over now," I demand.

Louise starts crying, and Mother looks down at her and gasps.

"See what you've done?" she shouts. "She's awake, she's upset; you've upset my baby."

"She's not yours," I say softly.

"Hand her over and nobody gets hurt," Rhea says, edging closer.

"No," Mother says, holding Louise closer to her, shaking her a little.

"Don't hurt her!" Rhea shouts.

Mother then looks down at a nearby table, which has a knife on it. She tries to edge towards it, but does not notice that Rhea has already seen it and grabs the knife, holding it up to her.

"You can't take her," Mother repeats. "My boys will kill you."

"Your sons are dead. All of them are dead," I tell her.

Her face changes.

"What?" she says. "You beasts, you killed my sons, my boys – you beasts!" She cries loudly, shaking Louise in her hands.

"Stop!" Rhea shouts, panicking.

"Fucking hell, stop," I say as she keeps shaking Louise.

"You killed my boys, now you want to take my baby. Who do you think you are? My baby, my baby, my baby," she repeats over and over again. Then she slows down and looks down at Louise, wrapped up in her arms.

"What do we do?" I ask Rhea. She just stares at Mother, clueless.

"You can't look after my baby," Mother says, holding Louise very close to her like she is a rare object.

"We are taking Louise with us," I say to her.

"Louise?" she asks, confused. "Her name is Edna, after my great-grandmother."

"No, it's not," Rhea states. "Her mother wanted her to be called Louise."

"But I'm her mother," Mother says. "I gave birth to her. My Richard got me pregnant again, and now we have the daughter we always wanted. My baby, my Edna."

"What?" I say, looking sharply at her.

"You really think she's yours?" Rhea says, just as confused as me. She looks like she is beginning to feel a little sympathetic towards her.

"Yes," Mother says, "of course she is – she is a Battalion."

"Well, can we play with Edna?" I ask her all of a sudden.

"Hmm…" she responds.

Rhea looks at me, perplexed.

"Yeah," I say. "Can we play with Edna, or just hold her for a little?" I ask, trying to be delicate.

"I guess," she says. "Richard would've wanted it. Isn't she beautiful?" She holds Louise out in front of me.

"Yes, she is," I agree, looking down at Louise, who is wrapped in a white towel.

"She has Richard's eyes," Mother says, showing her to me.

"Yeah," I begrudgingly agree with her. "She sure does." I hold my hands out. "May I?"

"Be careful," she says, handing the baby over to me. "She's my little petal."

Louise stops crying as soon as I lay my hands on her. I take a small step back. Mother looks at me and smiles as I look down at Louise.

"You can't hold her," she says to Rhea. "You can't be trusted."

I back away slightly with Louise and look at Rhea, then at Mother.

"Oh, isn't she precious?" she says. She looks at me holding her and smiles, rubbing her fingers together as I hold Louise close to me.

"Yes, she is," Rhea states.

Mother looks at her and Rhea storms towards her and stabs her straight in the chest. Mother falls backwards, looking down at the knife.

"What? No! Oh, no," she cries.

Rhea then walks over to me, takes Louise off me and walks in front of Mother and stares at her.

"This child is ours. You are not her mother, and your false world is now over," she snarls as she backs away.

"No!" Mother says. "No, no!" She gasps, holding her chest, before drifting off and collapsing, dead on the floor.

"Come on," Rhea says, holding Louise in her arms.

We both turn and walk out of the nursery, leaving Mother on the floor. We head downstairs and see Amrit holding Mark's side.

"Good," Amrit says as we walk towards them.

"Let's go," Rhea suggests, and we walk through the door.

Outside, the snow has stopped falling and has begun to settle.

"There's a van over here," Rhea says.

"How do you know?" I ask her.

"Being somebody's personal slave has its perks," she says as she leads us to a van, similar to the one that brought us here.

We open the doors and jump inside – me in the driving seat, Rhea and Louise next to me, and Mark and Amrit in the back so Mark can lie down. I look down and see the keys in the ignition.

"Where do we go?" I ask.

"Just drive," Rhea says, keeping Louise silent. "We'll get somewhere."

I turn the key, start the engine and get driving. I put my foot down and head straight out. The only route I see is through the woods. We keep going, leaving tracks in the snow. Then I see something in the corner of my eye: in the distance, Shaq on the side.

"Pull over!" Rhea shouts.

I pull over and she hands Louise to me and gets out of the car. I see her walking towards Shaq, lying there on the ground. I can see that he is still alive, unable to speak, unable to get up, however he is panting and for some reason still alive.

"What's she doing?" Amrit asks.

"I think we're about to find out," I say.

Rhea stands over him and looks down at him. She sees the knife that he tried to kill me with, picks it up and looks at him again.

"This is for my Dad," she says, and stabs him in the head.

Shaq stops panting and is still. She leaves the knife in his head and walks back to the van, getting inside. I hand her Louise so I can drive.

I don't say anything to her, I just put my foot down and get driving. I drive through the snow and eventually out of the woods. I try to get as much distance between us and the house as possible. I want that memory as far out of our minds as possible. I want us to find safety, and this time I want it to last.

39

Bumping up and down, thundering through, with the remainders of the leaves from the branches left on the windscreen. I manage to avoid as many of the branches as I can, but some of them do break through and I hear them scratching the side of the van.

The road is bumpy from the snow, which has started to form small mounds. I keep my foot down, looking at the dashboard. Good, we have enough fuel; we aren't going to break down any time soon. I need to get us out of here, I need to keep driving. These trees just don't seem to want to go away; feels like there's millions of them.

"Everybody OK?" I ask, trying to get a dialogue going. I look over at Rhea and down at Louise in her arms. "How is she?"

"She's fine," Rhea says. "We need to get her food, though," she adds worriedly.

"Is she hungry?" I ask, hoping we won't need to stop any time soon.

"Doesn't matter if she's hungry," Rhea says. "We need to find food anyway."

"OK," I say. "How's Mark doing?" I ask Amrit in the back.

Amrit does not answer. I look at him in the mirror and see

him pressing down on Mark's side, getting pieces of material and wrapping them around his torso. "Amrit, how's he looking?" I say, trying to get his attention.

"It's not good," Amrit says. "I've bandaged him up, but he doesn't seem to be responding to anything I'm saying."

I look over at Rhea and she looks back at me, worried. I turn and face the road, putting my foot down, getting through the trees, and then I see something I have been hoping for. There it is: a road, an open road out of the woods. We drive out and onto the road, heading straight out.

"OK, let's go," I say as we drive onto a country road, the van shaking under its burden of snow. I look around and see a lot of other cars, parked, with snow covering them like little buildings.

"Look!" Rhea shouts, pointing at something in the distance. I look over and see that it's a petrol station.

"What if somebody's there?" I ask her, afraid of another confrontation.

"It's a risk we have to take," she makes clear to me, and I head in that direction.

"We need to get to safety now," Amrit says.

"OK," I say.

I drive a few more yards until I hear a sound behind me. It sounds like somebody trying to speak.

"What's that?" I ask, looking around.

"Mark?" Amrit says as he looks at him, seeming very concerned.

"Where... where am I?" he stutters.

"We're away from there now," Amrit tells him. "Rest now."

"OK," Mark responds. In the rear-view mirror, I see him slowly close his eyes, blinking slightly as he does so.

I drive for a few more yards and eventually make it to the petrol station. I look at it, cautiously driving in. I'm still quite nervous about pulling up. I look around first, then gradually edge the van forward. We pull up and look around. The petrol that was once here is now all gone. I glance at the shop doors, then look around again. It looks pretty closed off, need to be careful.

"I'll go check," I say to them. I open the door to get out until I feel a hand on my arm. I look over and see Rhea holding my arm.

"Be careful," she pleads gently.

I nod, then head straight out, carrying my machete. I look at the store and I can see the shelves are packed, filled with lots of goods, lots of different food for us to have.

"This is too good to be true," I say to myself.

I walk over to the door and kick it several times. I have to take a bit of a breather before I attempt again. I try kicking again but my legs are feeling very weak all of a sudden. I think Im just tired. I decide however to take my machete and place it in the corner of the door near the latch. I hope this works. I use the little strength I have left to push down on it. I head the latch break. Success, we can go inside. I open the door and I am amazed by what I see. Inside are shelves of food; mostly tinned goods, but its good enough. I walk around a little to make sure everything is clear, and that nobody is going to suddenly jump out and attack me. I peer behind the counter, and then I see it. There is a man lying there on the floor, motionless. His clothes are ragged, his face pale, and he has a hole in his forehead. I look down at his arm and see bite marks. He looks like he was bitten by an infected, and shot himself in the head. Poor guy; this was his place, and now we've come here to take it.

"Shit," I say to myself as I turn around and walk outside. I can't just leave him. I turn around and walk back to his motionless body. I put my arms around him and pick him up, cradling him. I carry him outside and see Rhea in the van, looking back at me. I walk around the back of the petrol station and place him on the ground. I spend a moment looking down at him, sighing to myself. Then I turn around and run to the van, heading straight for the back. I open the doors so forcefully I almost hit myself in the face.

"Is it good?" Amrit asks, looking behind me.

"Yeah," I say to him, "it's good."

He gets up, bringing Mark with him, slowly keeping him stable as he gets out of the van. Rhea opens the door and stands there with Louise in her arms. I run inside and start rummaging through the shelves as Rhea walks in with Louise and Amrit follows, holding Mark up. Then I find it – baby formula. How the fuck is this here? I don't care how it got here, I don't care why it's here; all that matters is that it's here. I show the formula to Rhea.

"Brilliant," she says, smiling yet sobbing at the same time, looking very relieved as she holds Louise close to her chest as if to make sure she doesn't lose her.

"Yeah, it is," I say as Amrit brings Mark in and sits him down next to the counter.

"OK," Amrit says, "we need water."

"Here," I say, finding a bottle on the ground. I throw it to Amrit and he opens it, running straight to Mark.

"Here, Mark," he says, putting the bottle to his mouth. "Drink this."

Mark opens his mouth slightly and Amrit pours the water into his mouth, some of it dripping down as Mark gulps.

"Feel better?" Rhea asks him as he leans back.

"Yeah," he says, sighing.

"OK, I guess we should find some food," I say to them.

"Can I...?" Mark struggles to ask. He then coughs, clearing his throat. "The baby, where is she?"

"Right here," Rhea says.

Mark slowly holds his hands out. Rhea looks at us and we nod, so she places Louise in his arms.

"Louise," Mark says to her as he looks down at her. "You're going to have a future, you're going to live my dreams."

Louise makes a little noise, that standard baby noise that only a baby makes.

"You're safe now, you'll always be safe."

Tears appear in our eyes as he continues to speak.

"You're our little princess. I will always be here." He kisses his finger and places it over her heart. He then leans over and kisses her on the forehead, eventually sitting back. Tears trickle from his eyes and down his cheeks. He raises Louise and Rhea comes over, taking her from him. She carries her away, still looking at him.

"We're going to be OK," I say, kneeling before him.

"Yes," he says, "you are. Thank you. Thank you for everything."

He then looks down and slowly starts to drift off. His heavy breathing settles and he falls silent, then his eyes begin to close, the last of his tears trickling from his cheek and onto his shoulder. His body stops moving and his shoulders drop, making him look peaceful.

"Mark?" I say. I place my hand on his shoulder and can't help but burst into tears. I sob like a child as I kneel down next to him. I can't hold it in, I feel so much anger inside.

"Come on," Amrit says.

He helps me up, and I wipe away my tears. We walk outside and head towards a patch of grass around the back of the station. There is a shovel. Amrit grabs it, I use my machete and we begin digging. The ground is frozen solid, however we manage to get through. We dig and dig, shovelling the dirt out the way. With every hack at the frozen ground, the machete feels heavier. I then stop, panting and unable to go on. Amrit looks at me and turns me around.

"I... I..." I say.

Amrit doesn't hesitate; he just grabs me and holds me in an embrace, making me feel warm and safe for the first time in what feels like years. We hug for what feels like an hour, and tears cascade down my face. I then look up at him and we let go and get back to digging.

We dig a large hole, big enough for Mark. We then go inside and see him still sitting there next to the counter. He looks so peaceful, like he can finally be at rest. Amrit and I pick him up and carry him out, Rhea following with Louise. We head towards the hole that Amrit and I have dug, placing him gently inside. We all stand there, looking down at him lying there as if he has fallen asleep.

"Goodbye, my friend," Amrit says, taking a bit of soil and throwing it on Mark's chest.

Rhea then walks over to the dirt pile, picks up a bit and holds it in her hand.

"Goodbye, Mark," she says, scattering the soil.

Then it is my turn. I pick up a handful of earth and look down at him.

"Thank you," I say, and throw the dirt on his chest.

Amrit and I then begin to bury him while Rhea watches, still holding Louise. It feels tougher with the cold snow freezing everything, however we get there.

When we're done, we all walk inside and head towards the counter where Mark died. Rhea sits down, leaning against the counter, holding Louise. Amrit stands on her right side and leans towards her. She looks at him and smiles as he sits down next to her. I then sit down on her left side and lean closer to her. She smiles at me, and so does Amrit.

We all just sit there; nobody says a word. We sit in silence, all three of us gazing into the distance, awaiting the next day and knowing that it is going to be another day which we'll have to endure.

"It's just the three of us now," I say.

"Four," Amrit corrects me.

We then look down at Louise lying in Rhea's arms.

"Yeah," Rhea agrees, "four of us."

We look at Louise and smile, knowing that she is our priority now. For so long we were just trying to keep ourselves alive. We have fought different people and had to go through so much. I have seen my friends killed, and am scared that my closest friends will be killed as well. We have lost so much, yet gained a lot.

I look at Louise once again and I feel that we have more to worry about now. Not that this is a bad thing – in many ways, it could be good. Now I can't just think about myself. I hope that with Rhea and Amrit alongside me, we can create what could be some form of family. I haven't had that since I was at the commune, many years ago.

I listen to Louise make that little baby noise once again, and notice, out of the corner of my eye, that Rhea and Amrit are both smiling, knowing that life is never going to be the same again. After all this, it has come to the point now where we have somebody far more important than all of us to take care of.

40

The sound of Louise crying the next morning makes me sit straight up. She is lying with Rhea curled up around her and Amrit on the other side. I walk over and look down at her, smiling. I pick Louise up and gaze at her, shushing her to help keep her calm. I look at her pale skin and see her little eyes flicking towards me.

"Hush now," I whisper. "Hush now, come on." I gently rock her side to side.

She begins to calm down, so I walk over to some formula that Rhea mixed up last night. I heat it up quickly on a portable heater we found and pour it into a baby bottle which we also found. I shake it and put the bottle in Louise's mouth. She sucks and begins to calm down.

"That's it," I say, "that's a good girl." I rock her.

"You're a natural," Rhea says. I turn and see her looking up at me, smiling. She grabs a bobble and starts to tie her hair back.

"I guess so," I say.

She gets up, pulling her trousers up, puts her feet in her boots and walks over to me.

"Aw, look at her," she says, smiling at Louise and stroking her cheek. "She likes you. Are you hungry?" she asks, walking over to the tins and looking through them as if we have a variety of different cuisine stored up for us.

"Starving. What do we have?" I ask as I watch her walking from one aisle to the other, peering at everything.

"Well, we have beans and more beans," she chuckles.

I look at her and can't help but smile. She smiles back, grinning for the first time in ages.

"Sounds great," I say.

"Oh, that's good." She walks over and pulls out a saucepan, gets a knife and opens the beans. She pours the beans into the saucepan, places it on the portable heater and begins to cook them. She gets a spoon and stirs them as she cooks.

"Hey, I've got a question for you," I say.

"Yeah?" she says, looking up and brushing the hair from her eyes.

"I was wondering…" I say, feeling the motor in my brain beginning to turn.

"What?" she asks, tightening her ponytail and placing her headband over the top of her head.

"You know when we were with Shaq and all that lot?" I begin.

"Yeah," she says, and I can tell she is remembering.

"When Jake attacked you…"

She stops what she's doing for a moment and looks down.

"He kept beating you, pummelling you. You didn't give in though, you just kept fighting back," I recall.

"Yeah," she responds, letting go of the spoon and looking away.

"My question is, why?" I ask her. "Why did you keep fighting back, knowing he had twice your strength?"

She looks at me and licks her lips.

"Actually, don't worry about it, it's fine," I say, feeling bad about asking.

"No, it's fine," she replies as I begin to turn away. "Truth is, Layton, I don't know. I didn't want him, or any of them, to think I would just lie down. I feel that if you willingly submit to somebody who is wrong, they will always have power over you. I always believed I'd never bend to somebody's will. If anybody wants to fight me, I will fight them back. Win or lose, doesn't matter, just as long as I can show them I am strong enough to fight."

I look at her and I completely understand what she is talking about. I look down at Louise in my arms and see her looking up at me as I look back at Rhea once again. She gives me a gentle smile as I rock Louise.

"Wow, beans," Amrit calls out, yawning as he looks over to us.

"Hope you enjoy," Rhea says as he rubs his eyes and sits up.

He looks at me and halts, stunned.

"Well, that's a strange sight," he says.

"What?" I ask him

His mouth and eyes open wide. "You and a baby," he says. "I thought the only time I'd see that would be if one of those girls you used to shag turned up and said, 'This is yours, Layton.'" He chuckles.

"What girls?" Rhea asks, grinning.

"Never you mind," I say quickly, turning to her. "You're being a dick again, Amrit."

"Yes, I'm just being a dick," Amrit states sarcastically.

"I mean, who would be more of an expert on dick than Amrit over here?" I ask, chuckling to myself as I await his reaction.

"Brilliant," he says, rolling his eyes. "Oh, I have something," he remembers, getting to his feet in a flash. He runs over to behind the counter and starts rummaging around.

"What is it?" I ask, very interested to see what he has found. Could it be a gun; an array of weapons? This thought has me rather excited.

"Well," he begins, "last night when you guys were sleeping, I started to investigate the place. I managed to find this." He then pulls out what looks like a baby carrier.

"Wow," Rhea says, surprised and excited, as if she is about to jump for joy.

"Yeah, not too bad," he states, showing it off to us.

"Looks brilliant," I say.

Amrit puts the carrier on the floor in front of us, and I walk over and place Louise inside.

"Look at you," Rhea says to Louise, "don't you look all comfy?" She smiles as Louise rocks back and forth.

"Nice one, mate," I say to Amrit, proud that he is a friend of mine.

"Cheers," he responds, patting me on the back.

I look at him, he nods at me and I smile to show my gratitude. He really did do a good job in finding that carrier. It'll come in handy for us all, and it'll be nice to help Louise be comfortable. Fuck me, I just realised she is going to be with us all the time from now on. I think we will do a good job… yeah, I know we will.

"OK," Rhea says, "I have three bowls here. Louise and I don't want any excuses. I worked my hardest to make these beans as good as they can be." She passes Amrit and me a bowl and a spoon each.

"Thanks," I say. I place the spoon in the bowl and swirl it around before taking a nice mouthful. The lumpy tomato sauce is hot; however, once I have a taste of it, I devour the lot and practically scrape the bowl clean. I then set the bowl down and let out a bit of a burp.

"Enjoy that?" Rhea says, chuckling to herself. I look at her smiling, and realise how much I've missed watching her smile. I miss all of us having the chance to sit around and laugh together.

Amrit chuckles, looking at me. I look at them both with my hand in my mouth, putting the rest of the beans into my mouth.

"Yeah," I say to Rhea, putting my bowl down.

I look at them and feel safe being with them. I feel proud of what we have gone through, and that we are still able to stand up tall. However, danger is still out there, waiting to attack at any second, just wanting to make us all suffer.

"Right then," I announce, putting on my coat and picking up my machete, "I better head on out."

"Where?" Amrit asks as I tie my bootlaces.

I lift my weapon up and look at him.

"Patrol," I say. "Also, I just feel like having a walk, being alone for a bit." I can already feel the cold air hitting my face.

"OK," Amrit says, smiling at me as I walk towards the door, open it and begin to walk through.

"Wait," Rhea calls, running after me.

I turn and look at her as the breeze hits me with its cold, soothing cluster. Snow covers the area around us.

"Yeah?" I say.

She is wearing her headband again, wrapping it around her hair, which is tied up in a ponytail.

"Make sure you come back," she says.

I look deep into her eyes and see my own reflection there. I look down at her necklace, remembering what we have been through, then back at her eyes, getting lost for a moment.

"For you," I say, "I will always come back."

She wraps her arms around me. I hold her close and we embrace for a moment. I sigh to myself, feeling her head on my chest. She lets go as soon as I do and looks at me. I smile, turn around and begin walking.

"Well, OK," Amrit says, looking at the two of us pretending to be awkward.

"Shut up," Rhea jokingly responds, and Amrit chuckles.

I walk off smiling to myself, and I can see her in my mind, smiling with Amrit as I walk away from the petrol station. I take one more look back and see Amrit go to lie back down. Rhea picks Louise up and starts rocking her back and forth as if to comfort her. I smile as I watch them, and I have a feeling of safety I have not felt in a while.

I walk off down the road. It is covered in snow, roads blocked by abandoned cars. I continue down the pavement towards what looks like a hill, and head up it, making my way to the centre of the road.

I look forward into the distance. I see it, Leicester; I see the buildings standing tall, derelict and deserted. I know that no matter how far we go, there will be somebody there waiting for me, waiting for us. I know he is sitting there right now, probably plotting his next move to cause more destruction to the world.

I place my hands in the pockets of my new coat and feel around, trying to shield them from the icy air outside. Suddenly, I feel something: a small, hard object in my hand. I lift it out and look at it. It's the coin that Shaq showed me. I rub it with my thumb and look at the little image of the Queen on the front. I guess he might have had a point about our history and the history of civilisation; it's just a shame I don't have a clue what it is. The history of civilisation means nothing to me, as this is the only world I know. My only knowledge is my life. I decide it's best to just put the coin back into my pocket and look forward.

I then remember that there is something else out there: a person who, given the chance, will try to hunt me and my friends down.

"I know you're out there," I say out loud. "I know you will chase us, I know you will try to hunt us down." I pause for a moment, taking a breath. "When you do, I will run until I can run no more," I mutter. "And I when I can't run, I will fight."

I like to think he is sitting there, looking out of his window in my direction, as if we are glaring at one another. I feel him looking at me, his eyes piercing me. I want him to feel me looking at him too. I want him to know that I am here, waiting for him, waiting for his first move.

I once admired all that he had accomplished. I once feared his wrath, thinking it could put me and the others in danger. Now I just loathe him, and pity the way he feels as if he has to try and fix everything. I think he has a complex that makes him the way he is. For as long as I live, I will never admire or fear him again.

I know what he has been through in his life. However, to come out of it and state that you are a born leader is just a way to satisfy your own ego. He even told me that I will leave this world as a king. I do not have any idea why he believes that. It's probably just his way of trying to draw in another person for him to command. He is nothing more than the fallen king of a broken empire.

I wonder if Rhea is serious about starting her own community? I wonder if we can build our own society from the ground up to make it better than the Union? They aren't exactly the blueprint for the best kind of civilisation. We can build a better world. We can make a stronger community, a society that can function for the good of everybody. For everybody to succeed and be successful, we all have to work together. It is only when we are together that we can be stronger.

I guess I am thinking differently from just being a lone individual now. Being an individual on your own is just a sign of loneliness. Being an individual amongst others; that is the sign of a progressive world. Well, that's how I feel on the matter.

It all makes sense now, what Amrit told me. I didn't get it at first, but now I think I do. We go through a lot of moments in our lives. If it wasn't for every situation we went through I wouldn't be standing here looking at a city that once had such promise and is now the ruins of a broken dream. Yet we can't forget it is this moment that will determine what will happen next.

It would be foolish to not look forward to what the world could have install for all of us. I have changed in this past year.

I don't want to be alone any more; I like being in a group, and I like being a part of something.

Well, this has been my story, I guess; how I get on in this world where nothing is worth anything, at least as far as money is concerned. My friends are worth something. Louise is definitely worth something. Amrit is worth something, and Rhea will always be worth something. I'm worth something. People value people, we value each other, and that's all that matters.

Amazing how a lot of jumbled ideas can result in an inquisitive thought. I suppose it depends on who is thinking it. Anything can be a thought, anything can be an idea, or some of it could just be a load of rambling with no real point. I believe I am starting to do that right now.

Well, as fun as this has all been, I guess I better get back. I have even come to a conclusion as to what a border monkey actually is. For many years, I believed it was somebody who roamed around in biker clothing, causing destruction wherever they went. Now I have come to realise it is more than that. A border monkey is somebody who isn't accepted within a community. When I was in the commune, we said border monkeys were outsiders; people who just stole from and killed you. I guess we were only moaning about outsiders.

I suppose now, we're outside of society. What is society now? There is no real, functioning civilisation anymore, so doesn't that make us all border monkeys in some way? Just a thought.

I've been out here for a while now, and thinking about it, I really need to get back to the petrol station to check on the others, as fun as it is to talk about stories and society and all that shit. Oh my God, why has it gone so cold all of a sudden? OK, I really need to get back now; I'm freezing my balls off out here. I better turn and walk back.

Well, after all I have been through and all I have seen, there is only one thing to say. This has been my story. Yet the more I think about it, this is only my story so far. As soon as the book closes, that doesn't mean the story is over; it just means this part of it has come to an end. Who knows where the story will go from here? A story is not over because the book has closed; it will continue until an ending comes. If there has been no ending, then the story is not yet complete.